D0342762

SEED

Ziegler, Rob.
Seed /

2011.
▬▬▬▬▬▬
cu   11/22/11

SEED

ROB ZIEGLER

NIGHT SHADE BOOKS
SAN FRANCISCO

Seed © 2011 by Rob Ziegler
This edition of *Seed* © 2011 by Night Shade Books

Cover art and design by Cody Tilson
Interior layout and design by Amy Popovich

Edited by Ross E. Lockhart

All rights reserved

First Edition

ISBN: 978-1-59780-323-6

Night Shade Books
Please visit us on the web at
http://www.nightshadebooks.com

For Cindy

CHAPTER 1

The prairie saint wore a white lab coat with a black cross fire-branded onto the lapel, blotting out the name of some long dead doctor. He paced, pale and tall, between two burning fifty-gal drums. Spit flew from his lips as he sermonized, his stage the wrecked maw of a department store at the end of the abandoned shopping mall, his audience a captive huddle of migrants clad in paper FEMA refugee suits, sheltering from the sandblasting north Texas wind. Sweat gleamed on his forehead.

He preached the end of days.

Brood yawned. He sat against the wall with Pollo and Hondo Loco, carving grit from beneath his fingernails with a sheet metal blade ground into the shape of a hook. The rhythms of the prairie saint's grind lulled him. When he could no longer keep his eyes open, he tied black hair behind his head with a leather thong and settled deep into the oversized flak jacket he wore hidden beneath the broad spread of a canvas zarape.

Beside him, Pollo'd quietly bent bird-thin shoulders over a clamshell he held in one dirty palm. He seemed fixed on the sewing needle he held in his other hand. With intense concentration, he dipped the needle's point into the tiny black pool of charcoal and water he'd mixed in the shell. Raised the needle, pressed it to sun-browned skin at the tip of his protruding sternum. The tiny glyph of a flightless desert bird slowly took shape there. One animal in a broad spiral that covered the boy's ribs, shoulders, arms. Goners, he called them. Brood laid a hand lightly on the back of Pollo's shaved head. Stubble upbraided his fingertips.

"*Hermano*," Pollo murmured. He didn't look up, didn't break the meditative rhythm of his dip-and-pierce. He stared at an empty spot in front of him. Wind moaned against the building. The prairie saint ground on.

Brood let his eyes close. Found a happy half-waking dream already waiting: Rosa Lee was mere days away.

It had been hard work to make Rosa laugh. A speckle of acne on her cheeks made her shy, and she tried to be hard. Hard like her stone-faced Tewa brothers who spent their days watching the south road into Ojo Caliente, scoped rifles cradled in their arms. Likely to shoot anyone who came along and couldn't show seed, and even some who could. But Rosa's hair shone black as the charcoal in one of Hondo Loco's water filters, and Brood hadn't been able to let her alone. When he'd finally coaxed a laugh out of her it was as though he'd found a secret button in her belly, and every time he pressed it a bell would ring.

His mother had told him, when he was very young, not to fall in love until he was eighteen. The world was a hard place, she'd said, and love just made things harder. But Brood figured he'd never live to be eighteen, so he may as well be in love.

He held the memory of Rosa Lee deep in his chest, a second and secret heart, beating life into him. He could still hear the jingle of what seemed a thousand silver bracelets, fine as spider webs against her brown wrists as she'd taken him by the hand. Led him deep under the Ojo pueblo to a secret cave lit by biolumes. There in the thick sulfur stench of the hot spring got him drunk on myconal brewed from mushrooms. She'd pulled off her stained t-shirt and brought Brood to her breasts, cocooned him within the folds of her black, black hair. She'd smelled like the sweet figs that the Tewa grew in long plastic greenhouses lining the Ojo ridge top.

Brood inhaled deeply. Came awake to the smell of dust, acrid plastic smoke from the barrel fires, the sour shit stench of dysentery.

The prairie saint's grind crescendoed. He paused, stared out at the migrants, waited. The silence stretched. The prairie saint glared. The migrants regarded him with hollow faces. The prairie saint's three acolytes stepped forth from the department store's shadow. Tall boys, thick faces, well fed. They each wore the red scarves over their heads and red-splashed paper FEMAs, signifying *La Chupacabra*. They stepped forward, glaring, until a few weary "amens" rose from the migrants. The prairie saint pulled his shoulders back, smiled approval, preached on.

"Amen," Pollo echoed. He smiled but his eyes remained empty, fixed on his clam shell and needle.

Hondo Loco trembled with silent laughter beneath the greasy foil blanket he'd wrapped around bony shoulders. He pushed grey dreads out of his face and smiled black gums at Brood.

"Blessed are the meek," he whispered, and laughter wheezed out of him. He settled back under his blanket, settled his chin against his chest, let dreads cover his face. A tired old man—he even pretended to snore a little.

One of the *Chupes* stepped forward, tossed a broken hunk of Styrofoam into a barrel fire. He stood over it for a moment, scanned the gathered migrants, then leered at a group huddled nearby.

Brood saw a girl there. A smear of dirt on her cheek, rats' nests in her hair. She shuddered, obviously sick. Tendons protruded from her neck. The Tet, in full rigor. The *Chupe* boy motioned and his two companions stepped up. The girl turned her back, scooted closer into her group, a herd animal sheltering from predators. An older woman wrapped an arm around her. A young boy whispered something and the woman shushed him. The *Chupes* surrounded the group. One grabbed the girl's hair.

"You got bad Tet, don't you, baby bitch?" Brood heard him say. "You going north with us."

The older woman stood. Soiled yellow FEMAs hung loose from her hungry frame as she faced the *Chupes.* The third *Chupe* gave her a kindly smile. Then drove his fist into her face. The old woman dropped. The sick girl cried out.

Anger flared in Brood. The girl had black hair. Black like Rosa Lee's, black like Brood's mother. He started to rise.

Hondo's hand snaked out, gripped Brood's forearm, hard as a hawk's claw. The old man gave his head a tiny shake. As Brood watched, a blade flashed in the barrel fires' sallow glow. A *Chupe* had his knife under the girl's chin. He stood her up, marched her away from the crowd, sat her against the wall.

"You wait right here, girlie. You think about going anywhere, I cut up your momma." He held up the blade for her to see. The girl sobbed, quivering like a snared rabbit. The other two *Chupes* laughed. The prairie saint preached on, never pausing.

Brood clenched his jaw, let out a breath, settled back against the wall. Hondo released his arm.

"Satori pays for Tet, *homito*," he said. "*La Chupes* just getting themselves fed. Same as us." He leveled one milky eye at Brood. "Same as us."

"*Sí.*" Brood spit onto the cracked tile floor. "Don't mean they ain't bitches, every single one of them." A slight smile crossed Hondo's grizzled lips.

"*Sí.*"

The girl's head fell between her knees and she shuddered, whether with sobs or Tet, Brood couldn't tell. He eyed her for a moment, shook his head, and shut her from his mind.

He reached inside his zarape, shifted aside the ancient flak jacket and withdrew a hunk of smoked rabbit meat. Tore a piece off, nudged Pollo's shoulder. Pollo snatched the meat without looking.

"Amen," he said quietly.

"*De nada.*"

"Don't be shy," Hondo said. He extended his hand once more. Brood tore off a second hunk and placed it Hondo's calloused palm. Hondo winked. "Amen."

....

It had been a *Chupe* who'd turned them on to the prairie saint. They'd been rolling north on Hondo's wagon, tailing a caravan up Route 83 a hundred or so miles north of old Laredo when they'd pulled into a hollowed-out gas station to siesta away the day's heat. They'd found the *Chupe* there. A short whiteboy in splashed-red FEMAs, squatting on the remnants of a curb in the shade of a solitary cinderblock wall.

"*Que onda, guero?*" Brood called as Hondo pulled the wagon up short on the broken asphalt.

"Sorry, sir," the whiteboy mumbled. "Don't speak Spic." Indecipherable swirls of tattoos covered his cheeks and forehead. Brood hopped down from the wagon.

"Crazy Tats. Where'd you get those tats, homes?"

The *Chupe* said nothing, just stared out at the empty distance where heat shimmers rose off the desert floor and the hollow west Texas wind whipped phantoms out of the dust.

"*Él está bendecido.*" Hondo tapped a finger against his temple. Brood shrugged. "What's the matter, son?" Hondo asked the kid. The whiteboy blinked, then, and turned his eyes to Brood.

"Got anything to eat?"

"Your boys don't take care of you?" Brood aimed a finger at the splash of red on the whiteboy's paper FEMAs. The whiteboy stuck his tongue behind his lip and shook his head a little.

"Not so much."

"We maybe got something to eat." Brood smiled. "You anything to trade?"

"Maybe."

"Satori?"

"What else? Got wheat."

"Let's see."

The whiteboy hesitated. His eyes narrowed, fixed again on some distant patch of desert. Brood spread his hands wide.

"Don't be scared, homie. S'all good."

"All good," Pollo echoed, distantly.

"You hungry, right?"

The whiteboy's eyes refocused on Brood. He nodded, slid a bony hand inside the open top of his *Chupe*-stained FEMAs and withdrew a square of greasy cloth. Unfolded it, delicately proffered it. A dozen seeds lay there, thin as needles. Brood held his breath and leaned in real close, squinting. Knew instantly the seeds were wrong, too long, too frayed. Hope forced him to reach out anyway. He pinched a single seed between thumb and forefinger, brought it close to his nose, swallowed hard as he saw the tiny Satori barcode running its length. He closed his eyes, ran the barcode against his finger, searching for smooth perfection, genetic inherency.

Felt instead the lazed edge of a counterfeit.

He smiled again at the *Chupe*. Held the seed aloft on the tip of his index finger. It balanced there for a moment, trembling in the dry breeze as though mustering its courage, then sailed away into the Texas wastes.

"Hey!" the whiteboy cried.

"Fucking cheat grass." Brood swatted the cloth away from the boy's hand. Worthless seed drifted up, out, was gone. The whiteboy stood, watching it go. Violence rose in his face. Brood took a short step back—reached beneath his zarape, gripped the leather-wrapped handle of the hooked blade tucked in the waistband of his canvas pants.

The whiteboy hesitated, gradually seemed to chill, to assess the situation for the first time. He took them in, Brood standing before him, hand hidden beneath his zarape. Pollo, sitting cross-legged on a frayed Kevlar vest, scratching his canvas pant leg with a piece of charcoal. The whiteboy's eyes lingered on the old carbon-mold Mossberg propped against the wagon's water tank, within easy reach of where Hondo stood by the tiller. Hondo cocked a grey eyebrow, showed the boy friendly black gums.

"Well." And now the whiteboy smiled, revealing a brown cavity the size of a pea in one front tooth. "Wouldn't trade any Satori even if I had it."

"First thing you said today, *ese*," Brood told him, "makes me think you might be something other than stupid."

"Ya'll do look like capable gentlemen." A swirl of tattoo wrinkled on the whiteboy's cheek as his gaze grew speculative. "Could be I know something worth knowing. Sort of thing capable gentlemen might be able to do something with."

"We're capable," Brood assured him.

Hondo snorted. "We something."

"We're capable," Brood told the whiteboy. "Let's hear it."

They'd set up camp there and the whiteboy'd spoken to them late into the night. They'd fed him pickled Satori radishes and snake meat. In the morning, they'd shaken hands, left the whiteboy with a jar of canned potatoes, and a promise.

....

Hunger gripped Brood, momentarily so powerful he knew nothing else. Then it receded, resuming its normal place in the back of his mind. A raw nerve, like a toothache he could never quite shake, that ran the entire length of his body. He sucked hard on the rabbit meat, trying to trick his body into believing it gave him real sustenance.

A hint of salt. He recalled his mother teaching him how to eat a tomato, before the migrations had begun.

"Like this." She'd opened her wide mouth, pressed tongue to tomato's ripe edge. Brood recalled a greenhouse, clear scrap plastic tacked over a wood frame, attached to a sheet metal shanty where they'd lived. A small windmill had churned overhead. Pollo had been there, a baby sitting naked and silent in an empty metal irrigation tub, his eyes even then registering nothing outside, scanning instead some unfathomable inner topography.

Brood had done as his mother'd showed him. Licked the tomato's smooth skin, dribbled salt from a tin can, marveled as it clung to his saliva. Then bit into it and...heaven. His mother had worn cutoff fatigues and the dark skin of her knees had pressed into the soft earth between two rows of tomato vines. She'd shifted and clumps of dirt had clung to her skin, part of her.

"Yo." Hondo jerked his head at the sermon. One of the *Chupe* acolytes had moved into the crowd and now stepped methodically from one migrant to the next. He was big, over six feet, well-fed enough to be strong. He glared down at them, shook a galvanized steel bucket in front of their faces. The migrants broke under his hard gaze. They reached deep into hidden places—sewn folds in blankets, pockets, orifices. Pulled forth small handfuls of Satori seed. Brood leaned forward, watching. He swallowed hard.

The bucket rattled with seed. Seed the government doled at the Amarillo stadium to migrants with family and plot claims up north. Seed gotten by other means by those, like Brood and Hondo, whom the government deemed ineligible. The ones who had no provable family.

"Look at that," Hondo said. "Straight up robbery right in front of everybody. We should be this good."

"You know anything about preaching?"

"*Dios y yo somos así.*" Hondo held up two crossed fingers, and Brood shook his head.

"Met shit less full of shit than you."

"Don't tell nobody." Hondo smiled wetly and pressed a finger to his bearded lips. Then turned serious. "Heads up."

"Donation." The *Chupe* towered over Brood. He pushed the bucket close to Brood's face and shook it. Brood peered down inside at the small heap of seed. Wheat, corn, cucumber, tomato, barrel squash. All smooth, regular, and every single seed zippered by a tiny Satori barcode. "Donation," the *Chupe* growled. Brood looked up, saw high Indian cheekbones mottled by burn scars.

"You Tewa?" he asked.

"Nah," The *Chupe* said. "Cherokee. Fuck you care?"

"Got some Tewa friends up north. Thought it might be a small world."

"Well any friend of the Tewa…" The *Chupe* gave Brood a humorless smile, burn scars twisting deep lines into his face. He shook the bucket again. "Time to donate," and his free hand curled into a massive fist.

"Relax, homes." Brood held up a hand, placating, and reached inside his zarape. Produced another hunk of rabbit meat. He considered it for a moment, then tore it in half and set one piece in the bucket. The other he placed in his mouth. "*Dios los bendiga.*" Smiling up at the big *Chupe,* chewing.

"Don't want no stringy ass rat meat," the *Chupe* said.

"Not rat, *ese. Conejo.* Much better for a big boy like you."

"No fucking *conejo* neither. Satori. You got your dole yet?"

Brood laughed. "I look like a family man to you?"

"Fucking gutter Spics all got dependents, don't pretend you don't."

"He's my dependent." It was Pollo who spoke. He kept his gaze fixed lapwards, his voice a carefully enunciated monotone. The hand holding the needle rose, weirdly independent, marionette-like, and pointed at Brood. "My dependent," he repeated, emptily. "We under age, so no Satori. No Satori. No Satori." His voice trailed off in hollow repetition, a fading echo. The *Chupe* stared. Scars puckered cruelly as a sneer worked its way across his mouth.

"Donation," he commanded. Pollo didn't respond. His shoulders remained curled over, eyes fixed on the needle, once again dipping rhythmically into the shell of charcoal ink he held. The *Chupe* stuck forth a canvas-wrapped foot and with a toe poked one of Pollo's bandy legs. Pollo began to rock back and forth. He quietly moaned.

"Fuck's wrong with you?" The *Chupe* bent down, peering close. "You Tetted up, boy?" Pollo said nothing, just kept oscillating, eyes empty, the needle dipping, dipping, dipping.

Rage rose in Brood's chest, the eruption of some deep and vicious brotherly instinct. Beneath it, the unspeakable fear, as real and constant as hunger, something he never let his mind touch, but which sometimes infected his dreams: what he would do if he ever lost Pollo. What he would be...nothing but a mouth, wandering the dust of seasonal migration routes, trying to feed itself. *Espiritu enojado,* a hungry ghost. His muscles drew taut, the urge to do serious harm barely checked. He kept his voice real quiet as he spoke.

"Ain't nothing wrong with him, *gordo.*" His hands snuck

under the zarape—gripped the hooked blade, wrapped around the chipped wood handle of the ancient .32 he'd found one summer in old Juarez beside the body of a skinned dog. "He just like that."

The *Chupe* turned. Eyes narrowed as he saw the look on Brood's face. He glanced down at movement beneath the zarape.

"No fucking Satori," Brood told him. They held each other's gaze, a moment of perfect mutual understanding, then the *Chupe* nodded once. He grinned twisted yellow teeth, about-faced and strode away.

"Thought you was about to have some fun," Hondo observed. He unconsciously probed a finger into the scabrous pock of a sun sore on one cheek, and chuckled. "Guess Cherokees ain't stupid."

Pollo kept tilting back and forth, metronomic, unable to stop once in motion. Brood laid a hand on his brother's shoulder, stilling him. Bones, hungry and fragile, protruded against his palm.

"You stupid?" he hissed.

"Helpful," Pollo said.

"Somebody fuck you up, you stick your head out like that."

Pollo turned his head, for an instant met Brood's eye. Defiance there, and pity, and something deeper that reminded Brood of their mother. Then it was gone and Pollo sank once more back into himself, a boy who couldn't stay afloat in this world.

The prairie saint and his three *La Chupes* milled around for an hour after collecting their seed, waiting for the wind to abate. When it did, two *Chupes* gathered the Tet girl under the arms and they all left abruptly, sauntering past the gathered migrants, disappearing into the hot light at the end of the long empty corridor. The bucket of Satori dangled like a taunt from the Cherokee's hand. Brood, Hondo and Pollo waited a few moments, then Hondo scratched the sun sore on his cheek, shed the foil blanket and stretched, all sinew beneath his ancient Kevlar. He wrapped up the foil blanket and then picked up the Mossberg from where it had lain concealed beneath him.

"Gear up."

....

A line of migrant caravans stretched along the scar of I-27, as far south as Brood could see. Aiming for where the stadium rose, gleaming in the late February sunshine, a monolith of old world concrete. It towered, stuffed with Satori seed, over the ruined twen-cen brick of Amarillo's downtown. Three fat government zeps hung there, anchored to its rim.

"Looks like you got a shot," Hondo said, peering over the top rail of the corral they'd chosen as a blind. The prairie saint and his *Chupes* had led them to the far outskirts of Amarillo's ruins, to a district of gutted agri-warehouses. Crumbling concrete domes protruding like the backs of half-buried beasts from farmland gone white with alkali. "You got a shot?"

"*Sí, esta bien*," Brood said, "assuming the wind don't pick up." He laid his blanket gently in the dust and unwrapped it, revealing the broken-down compound bow and seven aluminum arrows. He pieced the bow together and plucked its double-folded string as though it were a harp. It twanged briefly, and he nodded, satisfied. He pulled a tiny spotting scope from the pocket of a quiver he'd fashioned from a vinyl rifle holster, put it to his eye and peered through a gap in the corral's dry-rotted slats.

Across a hardpan lot, four *La Chupes* mingled at the warehouse's arched entrance, close enough in the scope that Brood could make out acne on necks, nascent mustaches, the Cherokee's mottled skin.

"Ninety-four meters. *Muy bien*, definitely. Don't know how fast I can hit all four, though. And who knows how many more inside."

"We'll wait. Just before dawn."

"I like dawn," Pollo said quietly. He intently traced lines on his FEMA'd legs with a piece of charcoal. A bird, a snake, a rabbit and a rat, all linked in a complicated series of arrows. "Everyone's asleep. Except me. I'm the only one in the world."

Brood knelt beside him. He took the boy's chin gently between his fingers and forced his face up until wide, dark eyes met his own. Pollo's pupils dilated as though facing bright light, but he did not look away. Brood smiled.

"Exactly, little bro. Nobody but us." Pollo gave a quick smile, then pulled away and leaned with one shoulder against the fence.

"Pollo." Hondo reached under his Kevlar vest and withdrew an ancient polycarb pistol, it's grip barely large enough to get two fingers around. "Take this, little homes." Pollo glanced furtively at the gun, at Hondo, locked his eyes on the ground. The tats on his chest seemed to grow as he swelled with obvious pride. He reached out and Hondo laid the tiny pistol in his hand.

"Fuck'd you get that?" Brood demanded. Hondo shrugged
"Had it."

"Up your ass? Ain't seen that pistol once in ten years I known you." Brood thought real hard, mentally cataloging every nook and cranny on the wagon where Hondo might've hidden the pistol, and came up with nada. "Well, don't give it to Pollo. He liable to shoot his own dick off with it. Or worse, mine."

"*Entiendo exactamente cómo funciona*," Pollo stated. Without looking, he pointed to his paper pant leg. There, beneath his charcoaled fingertip, Brood saw a tiny diagram of the pistol, pieced out and linked by arrows, so precise it could have come from an instruction manual. Brood leveled a finger at Hondo.

"You cagey, *chamuco*."

"I know exactly how to use it," Pollo said.

"*No te preocupes, ese, no está cargada*." Hondo showed happy gums. "Ain't seen bullets for that thing since before you was born."

"And when to use it," Pollo insisted.

"*Chale*."

"And when not to use it."

"We got a extra gun hand." Hondo's dreads swayed as he jerked his head in Pollo's direction. "Ain't no use without no gun."

Brood turned to Pollo and found the boy sitting in the dirt, leaning back against the fence. He had already secreted away the pistol and begun drawing once more on his FEMAs, apparently considering the matter settled.

"Just 'cause you got a gun doesn't mean you do anything with it," Brood told him. "It's just for emergencies. *Entendido?*"

"*Entiendo.*" A smile split Pollo's face. His eyes remained empty.

. . . .

"Yo," Hondo hissed. "'Bout that time." He sat on his knees, watching through the fence, one hand gripping the Mossberg.

Brood blinked in the cold night air. The wind had died and stars blazed, clear as bullet holes in the Texas sky. A sliver of dawn light edged the horizon, backlighting the stadium. Brood reached out, felt Pollo's knee, solid and real, and realized he had been holding his breath, submerged in some dream he'd already forgotten. He exhaled, rolled over, peered through the corral's slats. The warehouse's entrance flickered with firelight. Two *La Chupes* sat there in the dirt, wrapped in blankets. They were still, hopefully asleep.

"How many inside?" he asked.

"Four. Plus some girls."

"I didn't see no girls."

Hondo glanced sidelong at him. "You sleeping."

"*Mierda.*"

"Like a baby."

"Shit."

"Snoring."

"Fuck you." Brood looked down at Pollo. The boy slept wrapped in a blanket, curled against the fence in a way that reminded Brood of a nested bird, small and fragile. "We do it like usual?"

Hondo nodded. "Just don't put no arrows up my ass."

"Only if that's where they need to be, *ese*. Wait until I get there before you go through the door this time."

Hondo slung the Mossberg over his shoulder, pulled a skinny meat carving blade from somewhere beneath his Kevlar. A puckering sound came from his mouth as he smiled in the darkness, then he disappeared silently around the back side of the corral.

Brood picked up his bow, let its familiar weight settle in his palm. Plucked the string twice with the calloused tips of his fingers, tuning himself to it. He reached for the quiver. Only one of the arrows had a tip, a four-razored broad head. The shaft of this he'd marked with a ring of black electrical tape. The other six arrows were headless, but the bow drew with enough force to punch even their blunt noses through a cinderblock. He pulled out three of these, nocked one, leaned the other two against the fence.

"'Bout that time," Pollo whispered. Brood turned, found his brother watching, eyes bright and alert. Completely there.

"Don't be scared," Brood told him.

"I ain't. But you are."

"*Sí.*" He watched Pollo's face, and marveled at the calm focus the boy possessed when his personality managed to navigate to the surface. "You stay here until I come get you. Keep your head down."

"*Entiendo.*"

Brood touched the top of Pollo's shaved head, a gesture that bordered on the religious, and settled himself against the fence. He forced himself to breathe slowly, inhaling through the nose, exhaling through the mouth, just as Hondo had taught him, letting the fire in his nerves spread through his limbs, bringing his body awake, sharp as a hunger pang. He held a hand out flat: steady as a motherfucker.

Hondo appeared, a dreadlocked shadow moving silently along the warehouse's curved side. He stopped ten paces from the *Chupes*, crouched, raised his hand. Brood saw the thin curve of the carving blade.

He stood. The bow squeaked slightly as he pulled the string back to his cheek. He sighted down the arrow through the crosshair sight at the *Chupe* closest Hondo. A little high at this distance, a hair to the right to compensate for the bow's leftward push. Hondo signaled, a short chopping motion.

Brood exhaled…released.

The bow emitted a whip-snap sound, echoed an instant later by the arrow cracking into its target. Brood reached for a second arrow, nocked it, sighted on the second *Chupe*. Exhaled. Released.

Another crack, and this time the *Chupe* twitched. Brood heard a gurgling sound. Hondo moved now, smooth as a viper.

"*Chale!*" Brood hissed.

He nocked the third arrow, sighted it, released just as Hondo reached the second *Chupe*. The arrow cracked home. The *Chupe* twitched once, and sagged. Hondo turned and held up his hands, like: what the fuck? Brood smiled, grabbed his quiver.

"Wait here," he told Pollo, and vaulted the fence.

Hondo glared as Brood trotted quietly up beside him. "Thought I told you not to put an arrow up my ass." The old man stood over the *Chupe* closest the door, the one he had been about to knife. Two arrows protruded from the overfed boy, one from the throat, a second from his cheek just below the eye. Both had pinned him to the concrete wall. Another arrow protruded from the center of the first *Chupe*'s forehead—no wonder he hadn't made a sound.

"Move a little faster and I won't have to," Brood whispered.

"Shoot a little straighter, motherfucker, and *I* won't have to."

Brood grinned. Pulled the .32 from his back pocket and stuffed it into the waist of his canvas pants beside the hooked blade, then nocked another blunt arrow.

"You ready?"

Hondo unslung the Mossberg. He pistol-gripped it in one hand, held the carving blade in the other. Paused long enough to let out a supernaturally long breath, then nodded.

Brood stepped to the doorway and peered inside.

A fire built of shredded tire rubber burned fifty meters away at the center of the warehouse's concrete floor. Farming equipment sat parked around the building's convex perimeter. Combines, threshers, fertilizer trucks, all rusted out. Fossilized monsters in the fire's vague illumination, prehistoric, covered by a century's dust.

"Count six asleep around the fire," Brood said. Slumbering bodies wrapped in burlap and canvas. He wrinkled his nose at the stench of dysentery. "One awake." A red-scarved *Chupe* sitting in a plastic chair and drinking from a ceramic pot. "That's it. Couple AKs on floor. We go fast and quiet, we should be good." Brood raised the bow. Hondo placed the flat of the carving blade against Brood's arm, halting him.

"Wait 'til he sets that pot down."

The *Chupe* took another long swig. Golden liquid ran from the corners of his mouth. Corn mash. He set the pot down. Brood exhaled. Released. The arrow thudded home. The *Chupe* grunted, keeled over. Hondo ran past. Brood dropped the bow, pulled the .32 and his blade, and followed. Quick, silent steps, the rubber souls of tire tread sandals padding across the concrete. He felt fast, light, the weight of the flack jacket forgotten.

They worked quickly, slitting throats.

Four *Chupes* never knew they'd died. A fifth stirred, rose to an elbow and spoke somnolent words at Brood. Then he seemed to register what was happening. His eyes went wide and he reached for a rusted AK that lay nearby. Brood extended the .32, fired three shots fast into the boy's chest. The *Chupe* fell back into his blankets like he'd never awakened. The last *Chupe* leapt to his feet, startled by the gunshots. He was older, near Hondo's age. His mouth made a perfectly surprised black circle in the center of a grey beard as he watched Hondo swing the Mossberg his way. The gun shrieked. The man rag-dolled away from the fire and lay still.

Brood blinked in the Mossberg's ringing aftermath. "Thought you said there were girls," he said.

Movement sounded behind him. He turned to find the *Chupe* he'd shot with the arrow still alive, squirming. High cheekbones, the dark mottling of burn scars. The *Chupe* went still as Brood moved to stand over him. The arrow quivered his chest as he struggled to breathe.

Brood stuffed the pistol and knife back into his pants. "Sorry, homes, I need that arrow." He placed a foot atop the *Chupe's* belly and gripped the shaft. He started to pull, but the big *Chupe* moaned in a way that made him feel all twisted inside, so he stopped and stepped back. Flecks of pink foam speckled the boy's lips. "Got you in the lung, *ese*."

"Richard."

"What?"

"Richard. My name's Richard."

"Richard." Brood considered the sound of it. Decided perhaps it was right that one's name be used when one was close to death. "You ain't got long, Richard. I can take care of you, you want." He drew the inverted blade and held it up for Richard to see. Richard stared at it for a tortured heartbeat, then closed his eyes and shook his head. "Alright," Brood told him, and felt strangely awkward, as though he were invading the *Chupe*'s privacy. "Alright." He left the arrow where it was and moved to where Hondo stood by the fire, stuffing fresh shells into the Mossberg.

"Don't see nobody else. Thought you said there were girls."

Something slammed into Brood's back. He tried to turn, but his body didn't respond. Instead he fell forward. Cracked concrete moved up to meet him. Pain erupted along his spine, spread through his ribs. He heard gunfire then, the unmistakable clang of an AK roaring out from some recess among the farming machines. Hondo yelled something, but the shotgun sang, drowning out his words.

Brood found himself staring into the dead eyes of a *Chupe* whose throat he'd cut. He tried to get his body to move, tried to breathe, and failed—just lay there gasping like a fish on a stone.

The gunfire went on for a long time, ripping the air, before abruptly ceasing. Footsteps approached, scratching across the concrete from where the AK had fired. The pain felt distant now, like watching someone else get punched. Brood felt calm.

A rough hand gripped his shoulder and turned him over. Brood heard a moan, realized it came from inside his own body. A *Chupe* stood over him, so astonishingly well fed that a pink lip of flab edged the perimeter of his chin as he gazed down at Brood. An AK with a broken stock dangled recklessly from one hand.

"What the fuck were you thinking?" He smiled as he spoke, and the words sounded tough. But beneath the low-pulled red scarf, his eyes looked sad and scared.

Brood found himself mesmerized by the boy's flab, wanted to reach up and touch it, prove to himself it was real. He opened his mouth to say something, but now the pain hit him. He let out a wet sob. The *Chupe*'s lip curled in disgust. He raised the AK. A sharp pop rang in the air. It didn't hurt—not at all. For an instant, the *Chupe* seemed confused. He turned, angry, looking for something. Another pop. His forehead opened like a dropped melon. He fell.

"Carlos?"

Brood smiled at the intimate sound of his real name. Pollo's gaunt face filled his vision. A face consisting almost entirely of concavities, deprivation. It made Brood sad, like he hadn't really looked at his brother—hadn't really seen him—in a long time.

"Pollo…" Brood said. The boy peered down, eyes wide and curious, fully there, connected…his rodential fist clutching Hondo's tiny pistol.

"Carlos, get up. I found the seed. There's lots."

CHAPTER 2

"This is corn." The mountain of seed, piled high as the spine of the nearby dirigible, glowed molten gold in the late afternoon sun. Pihadassa extended a long hand from beneath her simple cotton shift and waved languidly at the pile as though caressing its aura. A single helix, repeated a hundred million times, once for each individual kernel, danced in her head. A vision of uniformity, not a chromosome out of sync. "It can withstand temperatures as high as one hundred forty degrees Fahrenheit, as low as negative twenty degrees." A sine wave appeared in her mind, temperatures rising higher each summer, growing colder each winter. "Not anomalous extremes. I speak of sustained heat and cold. It needs one-tenth the water of the corn we produced six years ago."

The Special Liaison to the President seemed not to care. He grunted absently, sucked his lip, scuffed the sole of one gleaming leather boot impatiently against the tarmac. He kept glancing at the dirigible's pilot, who leaned in her black drop suit against the craft's rear hatch, arms crossed, exuding indifference.

"This," Pihadassa explained patiently, "is the best corn I have ever made. It will resist climatic flux worse than what we have seen. Worse than what we project for the next decade."

Ten Satori landraces—her children—worked the corn pile. Muscle rippled beneath skin the color of fecund soil as they leveraged stocky bodies against the sinew cords of a skeletal pulley crane—a bone raptor rising beside the pile.

"Corn," Pihadassa repeated. The Liaison's sharp face turned her way. He pointed a hard smile at her.

"Your goddamn clones were supposed to be gone by the time we got here." His lip curled in distaste around the word "clone."

The deep folds of the Liaison's coat fascinated Pihadassa. A cotton and maize weave, a dense thread count. It bespoke a concentrated resource expenditure. Satori seed flown halfway across the continent. Rows of grow lights burning in the subterranean fields of New D.C. Water drawn in from the Chesapeake, desalinated over algae diesel fires and pumped down furrows of seaweed foam flown in from Newfoundland. Crops harvested, their fibers ginned and spun into fabric, sewn and tailored. All for the sake of primate preening.

This, while spring migrants gathered already outside the bone-and-skin length of Satori's outer wall. They camped around detritus fires in the brick remnants of old Denver, wore old FEMA paper refugee suits. Turned their hungry eyes towards the broad back of Satori's dome, which enclosed the steel, brick and plexi of what had been downtown. They watched as the dome's winter fur sloughed away, exposing acres of pink skin. Watched as Satori children brought seed through the dome's luffing gates and piled it high on the tarmac, where it awaited the government zeps.

"You need not worry about my landraces," Pihadassa assured the Liaison. "The Fathers will discover soon enough that I have gone." Pihadassa's Satori children released cords; the crane's yellowed jaws plunged deep into the corn seed.

"They'll tell the Fathers *I* was with you. My people can't be connected to your defection."

His people. A government whose only real function was to distribute seed to a populace in a state of permanent migration. Seed provided exclusively by Satori, and which Satori could easily distribute on its own. A government afraid of its own obsolescence.

"To whom else would I run?"

"What's obvious and what Satori can prove are two different things." A scar moved above the Liaison's eyebrow. Anger flexed in his jaw. Pihadassa noted the broad structure of his cheekbones. She took a long, meditative breath.

The Liaison's helix unfurled in her mind, a map of his past and future. Solid musculature and military bearing belied bones not quite as dense as they should have been. A thin heart wall that would open up and cut him down before he was old. The offending chromosomes had unfurled, vulnerable as a hangnail along the helix's length. They might have remained latent if not for childhood malnutrition. A pity. Otherwise the Liaison was solid, strong. Pihadassa wished she could bring him along, could breed him. Sometimes all nature needed was a little management. Perhaps she could convince him to give her a sample.

"You need not worry about my children," she said, and smiled. "They will not relay any information to the Fathers. They are going with me."

The landraces heaved. The crane's head rose, swiveled to one side. Its jaws opened, vomiting seed into the beds of wooden carts with a sound like static. Five other Satori children put thick shoulders to bone and leather yokes, hauling the carts up the dirigible's rear ramp.

The Liaison stared at Pihadassa. Muscles worked in his jaw. Pheromones rolled off him in waves. Without a word he turned and strode towards the pilot. Pihadassa reached out a hand to stay him, but the Liaison shrugged it off.

The pilot watched impassively as the Satori landraces strained past her and up the steel ramp into the zep's hold. The Liaison moved up beside her, close enough to brush his chest against her shoulder. The pilot did not look at him, but Pihadassa smelled the abrupt flow of pheromones. A sexual response to most kinds of stress—anger, fear, excitement—it had always struck Pihadassa as an elegant primate survival trait. She smiled, watching. She would have to describe this to Sumedha—

Sumedha…Something cratered in Pihadassa's chest as she remembered she would not see him again.

"The mountains have nice weather this time of year." The Liaison stated this flatly, challenging. The pilot jerked her chin west, where beyond the tarmac, beyond the high skin fence separating the airfield from the ruins of west Denver, the Rockies rose, icy and dark in the February dusk.

"A good year for skiing," she said. It seemed a strange thing to say. Nobody had skied since before the first Hot Summer, since long before Pihadassa had come awake in Satori's warm embrace. The Liaison stepped back, nodded, satisfied that the tenants of some ritual had been met.

"So you're Rippert's girl then," he said.

"That's right."

"I know you. We met when you were a little girl. Back in Dubai."

"I remember." The pilot looked directly at the Liaison for the first time. "You and your troops had just come in from the desert. Dad was pissed that you got sand all over his Turkish rug."

"Sounds about right," the Liaison smiled. "How is he?"

"He's okay. Bored. Doesn't know what to do with himself without a war on."

"We might be about to solve that little problem for him." The Liaison glanced up meaningfully at the massive dome's animal expanse. Shoved hands deep into pockets, pulled his coat tight around himself, as though chilled by his thoughts. "He tell you anything?" The pilot shook her head.

"Just that I'd have extra cargo. And don't fuck up."

"Seconded." The Liaison briefly withdrew a hand from a pocket and jabbed a thick finger at Pihadassa. "That's your cargo." Pihadassa moved forward, the tarmac hard and cold against her bare feet.

"Hello," she told the pilot.

"She looks cold," the pilot observed.

"I do not normally get cold," Pihadassa said. The quick freeze that came with the fading light felt crisp against her skin.

"How's that?"

"My vascular system is efficient."

The pilot's eyes narrowed with understanding. "You're a clone."

"A composite," Pihadassa corrected. She took a breath, coming fully to the moment. The girl's helix unfolded. Pihadassa reached out, brushed the tip of the girl's tight pony tail. The girl swallowed involuntarily, caught somewhere between attraction and disgust. Pihadassa smiled at her.

The pilot slapped Pihadassa's hand away. Backed up a pace, screwed her shoulders back, military, defensive.

"Touch me again, you bleed."

Pihadassa smiled pleasantly. "I understand."

"We can leave as soon as these monkeys finish loading." The pilot gestured at the ramp. "Hop in."

"These landraces will be joining us. As will some others. I wait for them."

"We've waited long enough," the Liaison said. "Get in." Pihadassa said nothing, simply remained still. The Liaison's nostrils flared as he seemed to calculate exactly how much of his natural aggression to unleash on the situation. "You can get into the zep yourself, or I can assist you." He took a step forward, presented big hands, ready to execute his will. "Your choice."

"If you touch her, I will kill you."

Warmth spread through Pihadassa's body at the sound of the advocate's voice. The Liaison turned.

The woman had arrived silently. She stood a few meters away. Like Pihadassa, she wore a simple shift, but there was something different about her stance. Something loose, predatory. She watched the Liaison with pale eyes.

"I will." Her tone matter-of-fact, the flash of a sharp smile, eager.

"Mercy," Pihadassa said. At the sound of her name, the advocate's eyes flicked to the Designer.

"Mother."

"Be still."

Mercy sank slowly to her haunches, and balanced there, balletic on the balls of her feet. She looked again at the Liaison, who took a step back now, lowering hands. The pilot settled her palm on the butt of a ceramic pistol at her hip. Pale eyes following the movement—the advocate smiled.

"Mercy!" Pihadassa spoke sharply. "You will do only as I command." The advocate glanced at Pihadassa, then back at the pilot. Smiled again, the baring of sharp teeth, defiant, an expression of beautiful malice that struck Pihadassa as reptilian, rooted in some primordial stretch of the creature's helix. "Kassapa gave you to me," Pihadassa said. "You are mine. Obey." The smile faded. The advocate gave a barely perceptible nod, the slightest acquiescence. Pihadassa turned to the Liaison.

"This is my advocate, Mercy. She will accompany us."

The pilot kept her hand on the pistol. Pihadassa watched the pulse in the girl's neck, felt the sudden heat rolling off both her and the Liaison: their bodies sensed death. The Liaison shoved hands once more into coat pockets. Pihadassa wondered if he knew of the advocates. His tone grew conversational.

"How many of your friends will be joining you?"

Pihadassa smiled.

The Satori landraces rolled the last cart up the ramp. Abandoned, the crane fell limp, a macabre doll against the heap of corn seed. Landraces gathered around Pihadassa, some taller and graceful, others short and dense. They genuflected to her.

"Mother," each murmured in turn, and in turn Pihadassa affectionately touched the tops of their bald pates. She let the helix of each fill her mind, noting minute variations from one to the next. She knew each intimately. She'd made them.

"The females," she inquired.

"They are right behind me, Mother," the advocate said.

"Females?" the Liaison asked. Pihadassa gestured with a languid hand at the landraces.

"They are primates. Like you." Like Sumedha—her twin, her mirror, her Other…His face filled her mind and something inside Pihadassa tore. Her throat clenched with the need to sob. She breathed, putting her attention on the sensation until it passed. "Like me. They couple."

The females arrived then, a score of them jogging across the tarmac in the dusk, skittish as herd animals, their shifts wet with sweat. They pressed in close to their mates, touching fingers, foreheads, lips. Pihadassa noted the barest extra curve to three of the females' bellies. Their skin glowed in the fading light.

"Up the ramp," she ordered them. "Get aboard. We are leaving." She looked at the Liaison, then the pilot. "Now." The Satori children filed aboard and nestled into the seed filling the storage bays. The Liaison placed a hand on the pilot's shoulder.

"Tell your father he owes me a scotch." He nodded once to Pihadassa, then turned and stalked back towards the dome, shoulders bent against a sudden icy gust rolling down off the frozen Rockies.

"Mother." Mercy motioned Pihadassa up the ramp.

The pilot followed. The hatch squeezed slowly shut behind her.

Pihadassa nestled into a bed of corn seed with two Satori children, tall ones, and began stroking their shoulders, backs, necks. The female shuddered with pleasure as Pihadassa touched her ear—an ear that was a mere G and A switch from the gills through which the fetus in the girl's belly breathed.

"You are beautiful, child," Pihadassa whispered. She watched the pilot's hands rove the zep's control panel, hitting switches with deft jabs of her fingers as she went through her preflight. The quiet hum of electric props soon vibrated through the steel cabin. The landraces gave one another startled looks as the floor shifted beneath them.

"We are flying?" the girl asked, and her face filled with wonder. Pihadassa kissed her forehead. The girl smiled and gripped her mate's hand.

Pihadassa closed her eyes and began to meditate. She tried to open her mind to the helix, but it would not come. Instead her awareness fell into orbit around a void, an empty place deep in her chest that throbbed like the socket of a lost appendage.

Sumedha.

He would be thinking of her now, wondering where she had gone. Soon he would learn of her defection, and he would cast his mind puzzling down the chain of her choices. Perhaps he would understand, would reach her same conclusions. If not, he would be left alone. She felt cold absence.

"Are you alright, Mother?" the girl asked.

Pihadassa opened her eyes. The cabin was dark except for the soft glow of the cockpit's instruments. Sleeping children breathed softly. The girl watched Pihadassa with wide eyes. She reached out, touching slender fingers to Pihadassa's cheek. They came away wet.

"I am fine." Pihadassa nodded at the girl's partner. "I miss my mate." The girl glanced down at the male sleeping with his head against her hip. Her face went soft with immediate empathy.

Pihadassa touched the girl's cheek and stood. Nearby the advocate sat on her haunches, balanced on the rim of a storage bin. Pihadassa reached her mind out, touched the creature's helix. Kassapa had done beautiful work, had ripped code from everywhere—deep marine sources, insects, raptors, even creatures long extinct—and hammered it into human form. Vertical slits of irises watched Pihadassa. Pihadassa gave the advocate a tiny nod and moved up to where the pilot sat fiddling at a partially disassembled sat phone with a pair of needle nose pliers. The advocate lowered herself silently to the floor and followed.

"Where are we?" Pihadassa asked, sliding into the empty copilot's chair. The pilot set the sat phone on the metal floor beside her seat and leaned forward, squinting at the instrument panel. She tapped at a glowing readout, then peered into the darkness beyond the windscreen.

"Don't know exactly. Once in a blue moon you can pick up GPS out here, but not usually." She shrugged. "Western Kansas, on a heading for Fort Riley." She yawned, stretched, propped her boots up on the instrument panel and leaned back in her chair, lacing fingers behind her head. "Hope you're not in a hurry. These fatties don't exactly push Mach. Wind's with us though. We should hit Riley before sunrise." Pihadassa closed her eyes, breathed; the pilot's helix settled in her mind and began to slowly turn.

"You could come with us," she told the pilot.

"Come with you?"

"You have strong genes. Endurance, and resistance to disease. You would make a strong contribution. You would be welcome."

"No offense, but I don't speak Chinese."

Pihadassa opened her eyes. "What do you mean?"

"I mean I have no fucking clue what you're talking about."

"You are beautiful. And the Mother created you without any help at all." Pihadassa breathed, matched her heart rate to the girl's, which had begun to quicken. "We are starting a new life. You could join us, if you wanted."

The pilot took her feet from the dash and leaned forward. Her pupils dilated. Her nostrils flared. A wave a pheromones washed over Pihadassa. Anxiety, but…curiosity as well.

"What life?"

"A life where we are free. Where the Mother shapes the helix, as she has always done. With only a little help from me."

"I don't know what Mitchell told you back there, but I don't expect your pups are going to taste much freedom at Riley. More like the south end of a scalpel."

"We are not going to Fort Riley," Pihadassa said. She spread her hands, inviting.

A vein throbbed three times in the pilot's neck. Her hand dropped towards the pistol on her hip.

Movement flickered in Pihadassa's peripheral vision. The pilot's body jerked upwards. Something snapped. Blood sprayed the windscreen. The pilot rose slowly, then seemed to hover over her seat. Surprise shown for a moment in her eyes, then she went limp.

The advocate stared down the length of her arm at where her fingers—bones spliced with coral and dense as granite—disappeared into the pilot's throat.

"Are you injured, Mother?" she asked. Her pale gaze stayed on her kill. A slow smile crossed her face. Pihadassa watched the wolves, the snakes, the eels, the raptors—all the various killers swirling up out of the advocate's helix, reveling.

"I did not order this. You do only as I command. Next time you wait."

"If I had waited, Mother, she would have killed you. How, then, would you command anything of me?"

"You will wait!"

The advocate let her arm drop. The pilot slid off her fingers and collapsed into a heap on steel floor plates.

"Yes, Mother."

"Such a beautiful creature, and you ruined her." Blood pooled as the last vestige of life ebbed from the body. "Get rid of it."

"Yes, Mother." The advocate defiantly licked one bloodied finger with a dexterous tongue before she spun the wheel on the pilot's emergency hatch. The hatch hissed open. Frigid air flooded the dirigible. The advocate gripped the pilot's neck and, with a motion smooth as a breath, hurled the limp form out into the darkness. Then pulled the hatch closed, spun the lock. Pihadassa pointed at the yoke protruding from the cockpit's control bank.

"Fly. East-southeast. Land before sunrise."

"Yes, Mother." The advocate took the seat and Pihadassa returned aft.

"What happened, Mother?" The pregnant child and her mate lay nestled in corn seed, faces creased with worry. Pihadassa settled in with them.

"Do not worry. What is your name, child?"

"Name, Mother?" The girl looked confused. Pihadassa stroked her ear.

"We start our lives together now. Your life is yours to name." The girl thought about this, then glanced skeptically at the Designer, hesitant to reveal a desire, lest it be taken away. "Truly," Pihadassa assured her.

"What do you call the ring around the sun? That you can see just before it rises and after it sets?"

Pihadassa smiled. Love filled her.

"Corona."

CHAPTER 3

The Lobo sat like a matte black spider on eight burly run flats. It growled a mean, atavistic nuke growl.

It drew hungry eyes. Migrants crouched on stoops along the block of once well-to-do old Philly brownstones. They peered down the street through the acrid smoke of laminate scrap cook fires, over which they'd spitted rats and skinny dogs. None moved forward, but Agent Sienna Doss felt them watching.

She stood in the armored crook of the Lobo's driver's side door, arms crossed, right hand thrust not-so-subtly inside her Kevlar-weave blazer, palm on the carbon fiber Ingram slung beneath her arm.

"Tick tock, Emerson," she whispered, her vocal chords massaging the tiny mic collared around her neck. The Lobo idled at the stoop of the cleanest brownstone on the block, before which three barefoot boys stood guard: *La Chupacabra.* They wore red scarves tied over their heads. AKs dangled too casually from their fingers. Doss gave the rifles a less than even chance of firing, even if the *Chupes* had, by some miracle, scrounged bullets.

"Roger." Emerson's voice came back tinny in her left ear. "Boss man's gotta put on makeup before he goes to the dance."

Doss' teeth ground. She had taken four Go Pills an hour earlier. They'd already spiked, then mellowed to a steady, vigilant hum at the base of her skull. Great for focus, bad for patience. She seethed, checked her watch. Three minutes, thirty-eight seconds doing nothing but scratching her ass and waiting for bullets to find her.

"Bitch ain't the queen of England. Kick his ass out the door."

"Roger."

Sewage flowed in rivulets along the buckled sidewalk. It reminded her of Siberia. She'd spent six months in a frozen prison pit there, where the snow had fallen in an ephemeral column through a grated hole in the ceiling. Where dysentery had been as pervasive as frostbite. She found its reek almost comforting now.

What rankled, however, was that the shit had smeared her boots and the cuff of her slacks. *Real, machine-tailored cotton slacks.* The US government's notion of civilian dress: slacks that fit snug at the hips and hung stiff and neat at the ankles. Like they were made for her. White cotton blouse. Grey Kevlar-weave blazer and matching Kevlar scarf tied over her head. Like something a character would've worn in the flex vids Doss and her sister had watched as children. She felt civilized, even as the Go Pills punched at her heart.

She scanned windows for rifle barrels, for muzzle flashes. Windmills, cut from cloth and heavy PVC, churned on fire escapes up and down the block—but only on the upper stories. Proof of a siege mentality among the *Chupes.* Doss had seen the Chinese do the same thing in Dubai. Hole themselves up in the top half of those cartoonishly massive skyscrapers, blockading all the elevator shafts and all but one stairway. It had worked, too, until the Americans had decided to ratfuck their policy of limited damage to civilian property. With apologies to the UAE, they had fired in barrage after barrage of cruise missiles. Doss had watched from a cot set up in the middle of empty square miles of flat desert as the missiles screamed in from the night, their explosions imprinting afterimage novas on her retinas. When dawn came, a single

Dubai Tower rose like a tongue of flame over the rubble—all that remained of that strange theme park of a city. The Chinese had pulled out the next day. Two weeks later the UAE had admitted that its oil supplies had run dry, and within months had ceased to exist. All those missiles for a scrap of empty desert that was useless to anyone but the Bedouins.

La Chupacabra's rivals didn't have cruise missiles. But they did have AKs, and worse.

"Ass in gear, Emerson." She set her jaw, waited for bullets.

"Good to go." Emerson appeared at the brownstone's door.

Like Doss, he wore civilian garb, a trim dark suit with a blue tie that made him look like an old-time American businessman. Like he should carry a briefcase, hail a cab with a thrust of his chin, oblivious to the deep ambient thrum folding over him, because he was an integral part of it—a city alive with elevators, revolving doors that breathed air-conditioning out onto the street. A city raucous with thousands of ethanol engines, blaring horns, the murmur of a million pedestrians, all sucking the teat of impossibly complex supply chains.

He looked good.

Doss bit her lip, forced herself to stay On Task. Emerson stepped out into shit smell rising from the gutters, into the oppressive silence of the brownstones' vacancy, an Ingram propped ready against his shoulder. His eyes, hard and alert, scanned the block as he crossed to the Lobo.

Their assignment followed close behind. A white man with a thick neck. Burly shoulders protruded from a sleeveless robe— ostentatiously opulent leather, *La Chupe* red. He clutched Emerson's blazer and peered furtively over the agent's shoulder. Emerson ushered him through the Lobo's rear passenger door, slammed that shut, got in front and slapped the dash three times hard with his palm.

"We're good!"

Doss got in, slammed her door. She loved the Lobo. It was EMP proof, which meant no superfluous electronics and thus no computer-assisted pumps for brakes or power steering. And best of all, no pantywaist electric motor.

She punched the accelerator. The reactor roared. The Lobo twisted perceptibly under the force of its own torque, oblivious to the massive tonnage of its titanium armor plating as Doss threw it into gear and muscled out into the street.

She leaned into analogue steering with all her Go-Pill strength, wove around cook fires and detritus under the indifferent eyes of vacant-looking migrants. She aimed the Lobo south, out of the Flourtown squat, down empty and crumbling Stenton Avenue, onto Broad Street. Pulled heavy Gs up the ramp onto the Roosevelt Expressway, 1200 horses howling as they surged east towards New D.C., Kevlar run flats chewing pavement like breakfast.

"You drive well, Agent." Doss glanced up to see the assignment watching her in the rearview with unblinking grey eyes. He held his wide jaw at an angle that exuded self-satisfaction. Perfectly shaven skin, offensively healthy glow. Doss said nothing. She kept her face professional, impenetrable. "I find tall, black women very compelling," the assignment said. His voice had an irritating nasal quality. "What's your name?"

"None of your fucking business," Emerson snapped. "That's her name."

"I see." The assignment gazed out the window, where the sky-scrapers of old downtown Philly reached out of upper Delaware Bay. Titanic steel and concrete fingers glowing orange in the late February sun. Windmills and old reclaimed PV squares hung pre-cariously from open windows high up. Small boats floated on wa-ter brown with early runoff, trailing nets and fishing lines through glass canyons that had once been streets.

"It's like Venice," the assignment mused. "Or it could be, if you covered one eye. I wonder what it's like living there year-round. How do they survive the winters? I've heard the temperature tops out at twenty below in December and January. And those are the highs. And how do they fight off malaria in the summers?" He sank back thoughtfully in the seat, then looked from Emerson to Doss. "So you two are together."

Doss and Emerson exchanged a glance. Emerson turned and

glared. The assignment's thin lips turned up, a knowing smile.

"On task," Doss snapped. Emerson turned back around, letting his glare linger for a few seconds on Doss. Doss pushed the Lobo up to 150 kph. The empty expressway, cleared of detritus by the US Gov, unfurled like a lucid concrete dream.

"That's alright. It makes sense. Partners should be close." The assignment paused. "You don't like me much, do you?"

"No offense," Emerson said. The assignment blinked placidly.

"Yet it's your job to step in front of a bullet for me, should the need arise. How can you take a bullet for someone you don't like or respect?"

Doss thought of her sister and father, living in climate-controlled Gov housing in New D.C. Her sister studied biomechanics at school. Her father walked without a limp on a titanium hip, and never lacked for malaria meds. All because Doss had never Fucked Up.

That had been the secret to her success. Up through the army, through Rangers and Spec Ops, and now with Sec Serv: Don't Fuck Up. A simple, perfectly linear road, navigating the landscape of incompetence that defined every military operation she'd ever witnessed. Everybody fucked up, usually always. Just not her.

"Not you I'd be taking it for," she told the assignment.

"Ah, she speaks. Good. So for whom would you be taking it?" Doss said nothing. The assignment smiled. "What's your name, Agent?"

"Doss."

"I am Tsol. My people call me El Sol. Pleasure to meet you." He patted Doss on the shoulder with a beefy hand.

"Back in your seat," Emerson growled.

"Your name's Richard Davenport," Doss objected.

"My given name, yes. My chosen name, and therefore my *real* name, is Tsol. It's Aztec. It means…" He smiled again. "Soul. Also, sun. As in, El Sol. I am the soul and the sol of my people." Emerson snorted. The assignment ignored him. "Do you believe in fate, Agent Doss?" he asked. In the mirror, a wild crescent of white shone over the tops of his irises. Doss had once seen a man with eyes like that in Siberia. Alyosha had been his name. He'd convinced three other prisoners that the certainty of transcendence lay in discorporation. He'd facilitated it by strangling them, one by one. They'd lined up for him. One of them had been Doss' lieutenant. Afterwards Alyosha had chewed the flesh off his own hands.

"Our ideas feed us," he'd told Doss, and showed her teeth black with his own blood. "And we feed them." Infection had killed him. The bodies had lain for more than a week at the pit's center, going rigid in the pool of frozen northern light that fell through the ceiling grate.

Doss had lost things over the course of those days. God was the first thing to go. Then her country. Even her own name had slipped away from her. She'd known her fate then. She would die, but only after her soul disappeared, like Alyosha's body under a dusting of snow.

"I don't either," Tsol said, interpreting Doss' silence as an answer. "At least not for most people. Most people, they live, they die. That's it. They breed, get diseases, carve out some crops, beg, starve, whatever. The wind blows, the wind doesn't blow. It's all the same to them. There's no difference between living and dying. But some of us… *We* are the wind." His eyes filled the rearview. "I am fated."

"You're a pissant gangster," Doss told him. "A deluded one."

"Roger that," Emerson agreed. Tsol leaned forward in his seat.

"Gangsters sit by the roadside and rob people of their precious corn seed. I *provide* seed to forty thousand people. I lead those people south every autumn and north into the Midwest every spring. During the summer, the entire Midwest is *mine*."

"You keep your people hungry." Doss kept her eyes flat on the road, face expressionless as she spoke. "You force them into line and make them come to you for seed. You're a thug."

"Maybe." Tsol gave her a diamond-hard smile in the rearview. "But the difference between me and your President Logan is merely one of scale. Have you read your Hobbes, Agent Doss? No? Well, Logan has, you can be sure. He prefers to have forty thousand hungry refugees whipped into line by a thug like me than to have them descend on New D.C."

Doss aimed them east down the 202. Philly's deserted burbs spread out around them like crumbling termite colonies. They crested a rise and Doss saw the burned frames of two twen-cen cargo trucks draped across the road half a klick ahead.

"Could be company," she told Emerson.

"You. Down." Emerson reached back and shoved Tsol down behind the seat. The professional calm in his voice set Doss on edge. Adrenaline spiked her chest. For an instant her brain froze, then years of training took over. She let out a long breath through her nose. Adrenaline ebbed, flowed to her extremities. Her fingertips tingled.

Things slowed down, details stood out. Late afternoon sunlight gilding the skin of two zeppelins that hung like fat maggots ten klicks out over New D.C. A crack in the concrete freeway barrier as they whipped by at 150 kph. The way the truck frames overlapped, creating a solid, obviously intentional blockade. The boy in FEMAs, maybe ten years old, kneeling behind the concrete barrier beside the trucks. The AK he brought level with his shoulder—

"Definitely company!" Emerson bit the words out of the air.

"Yep." Doss saw another refugee to the left. He held what looked like a long piece of pipe on his shoulder. It flashed. Doss saw a cloud of smoke and fire blazing towards them, a black dot at its center.

"RPG left!"

"Yep." She stomped on the breaks with both feet. Run flats shrieked against the pavement. The missile hissed over the Lobo's nose, inches from the windshield. A cry issued from the back as Tsol crashed into the back of the driver's seat. Doss saw the young migrant fire his AK spastically in their direction. Two other migrants stood beside him now. One fired a pistol and the other merely waited, a cinder block dangling from his hand. A sound like hard rain on pavement came as bullets disintegrated against the Lobo's armor. Doss glanced left, saw the RPG shooter reloading. Another stood beside him, taking aim. She checked the rearview. Migrants flooded the freeway behind them. She noted at least three RPGs. "Shit." Tsol peaked over the top of the seat.

"*These* would be gangsters, Agent," he said. Doss was pretty sure she heard him laugh.

She let the Lobo coast, down now to 110 kph. She considered her options—simple on this narrow band of freeway: reverse, or forward. *Do not fuck up.* The familiar mantra focused her in a way Go Pills never could.

"Now's the time." Emerson's voice had gone ultra calm. "Left!" The RPG flashed. Doss grabbed a gear. The Lobo heaved forward. The rocket came in off center, clipping the vehicle's back corner and—

Blackness. She was back in Siberia. Naked, bent over a saw horse, her face submerged in a barrel of freezing water. A red flash as the Spetz officer struck the back of her head with his palm.

"We're breached!" Emerson yelled.

Doss came to with her hands still gripping the wheel, her jaw still set. The Lobo rode a straight line. Wind howled from a hole somewhere in the back. Emerson had his hand down behind the seat where the assignment had been.

"Status," Doss demanded.

"Think he shit his pants."

"That mean he's dead?"

"Nope."

"Too bad."

"Yep."

"Okay." Doss breathed. Angled the Lobo along the concrete barrier, aiming for the right end of the truck near where the boy with the AK stood. He fumbled now with a second magazine as he tried to reload his rifle. Doss kept the accelerator floored. The speedometer rolled higher. 190 kph. 210. 240. Emerson swore. The refugee with the cinder block let fly as they rocketed past him. The block crashed into the center of the windshield. The world disappeared as thick plexi turned into a galactic pattern of white impact rings.

The Lobo hit the truck. Everything turned to searing white noise.

It was like being in the vortex of a crashing wave—a wave of twisting, shrieking metal. Doss felt her body wrenched in impossible directions. Twice she saw blue February sky and black asphalt blur together. She saw the refugee boy standing upside down on the pavement—*above* her—his eyes wide and his mouth shaped like an "O."

Then, silence.

The Lobo's nose had curled up like a black steel tongue in front of her. The windshield was gone. Doss realized, after several seconds of trying to figure out what it meant that the sky was above them, that they were upright, faced back the way they had come along a trail of broken plexi, gouged pavement and miscellaneous fluids. She hoped vaguely that the nuke's containment had held.

The truck they'd hit was nowhere to be seen. Refugees streamed after them, a score or more. Doss saw muzzle flashes. The insect buzz of a bullet nearly touched her ear. Some distant part of her pressed the clutch, tried to find a gear. It caused angry metal to grind.

She noticed Emerson beside her. He had pulled an emergency handheld from the dash and was shouting into it. Blood ran from beneath the black hair at his temple. Doss could not make out what he said. She tried again to find a gear. Emerson shook her.

"We're out of commission," he yelled. "We gotta run." She nodded, more because it seemed like an appropriate response than because she understood what he was saying. He sat there watching her. He looked so worried.

"You're bleeding, baby." Doss smiled, reached out to touch the trickle of blood at his temple. Emerson cuffed her.

"On task!"

All at once the world grew dense and hard. Bullets whined around them, pecking against the Lobo. Doss blinked, nodded. She turned to the back seat to find Tsol watching her intently, grey eyes wild.

"You alive?" He gave one mute nod. A wide smile gripping his face. "Okay. Gotta go. Stay close behind me or Agent Emerson, understand?" Another nod. "Good. Out."

Doss moved to open her door. It was gone. She stepped out, immediately collapsed. She rose, steadied her legs. A bullet tore at her Kevlar sleeve. Migrants came on, closer now, only thirty meters away. A fierce hiss came from the opposite side of the Lobo as Emerson fired his Ingram. Two migrants disappeared in a cloud of red mist. Another hiss, another migrant went down. Doss reached back into the Lobo, pulled a single mag grenade from the dash compartment. She thumbed the grenade's safety switch, waited a few interminable seconds as the gang of refugees drew within range.

"Emerson, fire in the hole!" She pressed the fire button and hurled the grenade in a high arc. Pulled Tsol behind the Lobo, pushed him down, bent herself over the top of him. Emerson joined them an instant later.

Metal fragments came first as the grenade's electromagnet switched on, propelling its steel casing away in a perfect sphere of hypersonic razors. They cracked against the Lobo and arched overhead, evidenced by a thousand molten friction contrails and the firecracker peppering of tiny sonic booms. Next came the sound, a frozen bell shattered under a hammer.

Then came the screams.

Doss peered around the Lobo. The migrants had momentarily halted their charge. Those not shredded staggered in confusion. She looked east towards New D.C. The zeppelins hung impossibly far away.

"Can't stay here," she told Emerson.

"There." He pointed at a mostly intact strip mall a hundred meters beyond the concrete barrier. They would have to cross a hideously exposed stretch of broken parking lot, but it was their only choice.

"You take him, I'll cover."

Emerson nodded, grabbed the assignment by the forearm and rose. Doss pulled her Ingram from its sling, slapped his back with the flat of her palm.

"Now."

Emerson and Tsol began to sprint. Doss stepped out from behind the Lobo. A few of the migrants had noticed the agent as he darted across the freeway, assignment in tow. They raised their rifles. Doss leveled her Ingram and began firing short bursts. Two migrants flew apart, ceramic bullets exploding inside them. The others ducked and covered. Doss fired a final burst and ran after her cohorts. Over the barrier, down the median, onto the parking lot. She heard the far-off throb of chopper blades—the cavalry.

She hadn't gone fifteen paces across the lot when bullets began to smack into the asphalt at her feet. Ahead of her, Emerson staggered and grunted as bullets struck his broad back. He pushed the assignment forward, regained his footing and kept running. Doss stopped, turned, fired a long burst at the migrants lined up now along the barrier. A bullet smacked into her Kevlar blazer as she tried to reload. Pain lanced through her side and her legs buckled, dropping her to her knees. An RPG sailed past her head. It exploded somewhere behind her. The concussion steamrolled her.

She stared at the cracked pavement in front of her face. She had skinned herself on a hundred empty lots like this, playing with her sister outside tent cities from Chicago to Atlanta. She knew that if she cried, Olivia would laugh. Sienna Doss resolved not to cry. She stood.

A bullet hit her shoulder and she staggered. Gunfire roared from the freeway. Several refugees made their way down the median, firing as they came. Doss turned and saw Emerson and Tsol both down, side by side, thrown by the RPG. They struggled to rise. Blood exploded from Emerson's leg. Doss heard him scream.

"Neal!" She stumbled towards him. The assignment gained his knees and sat there dazed, shaking his head. Emerson writhed. The chopper's thud drew closer. Doss looked from Emerson to Tsol and back again. "Fuck." She staggered to Tsol, pushed him flat and lay herself over him. He pressed his lips against her cheek.

"I am fated," he whispered.

"You're shit."

Bullets rained down.

CHAPTER 4

Hondo's wagon—the wooden flatbed of a twen-cen cargo truck chopped free from its cab and driven by a series of electric motors geared to the back wheels by three heavy drive chains—jounced and rattled as they rolled west out of Amarillo along the broken track of the old interstate. Hondo sat at the front, calling directions to Brood, who heaved at the tiller welded to the rear differential, steering them around the worst of the freeway's craters. They made perhaps five miles per.

Brood shivered under his zarape in the morning chill. Flexed his bruised ribs beneath where the AK bullets had buried themselves in his flak jacket. Every few minutes he glanced behind them. Nothing back there but the slowly expanding pearl glow of predawn, smeared by smoke from a single early cook fire.

Pollo sat on a stationary bike situated at the wagon's center beside the 300-gal water tank. He'd stripped naked and his legs churned on the pedals, topping off the charge on a row of four Hercules batteries the size of five-gal buckets—scavenged two springs previous from an abandoned tank at Fort Bliss. Beefy as fuck. Brood glanced behind them again. Still nothing.

It wouldn't last. The three fifty-gal barrels of seed, wrapped in camo netting, rocked back and forth on the wagon's deck in front of him. People didn't forget a haul like that, especially not *La Chupes*.

"I'm good for some speed, homes," Brood called when it grew light enough to see the road. Hondo stood and unhooked the stack of ancient solid-core twelve volts off which they typically ran the motors. The wagon halted and he ran a cord from the Hercs through an adapter Brood had jerry-rigged from an old stereo amp, and plugged that into the motors. Immediately the wagon jerked forward. Hondo made his way back, joining Brood at the tiller. He pushed the throttle forward. The wagon built speed, the Hercs pushing serious amps from barium nitrate cores.

"*Rápido,* Pollo, *rápido!*" Hondo yelled. Pollo peddled faster; Hondo kicked the throttle up further. The motors whined. Pollo gave a delighted shriek as the wagon banged along at a solid thirty miles per. Hondo laughed. Together, he and Brood hauled on the tiller, wending down the freeway, putting real distance now between them and Amarillo. He slapped the cargo netting and laughed again.

"What a job!" He gripped the back of Brood's neck. Spittle wheeled off his gums and landed on Brood's cheek. "Proud of you, *homito.* Couldn't have done this with nobody else."

"Ain't done yet, *chimuelo.*" Brood turned to look behind them. Hondo, surfing the wagon's deck like it was welded to his feet, eyed Brood across the tiller's rebar shaft.

"Worry ain't nobody's friend, boy. Ain't never going to be done. Not ever." He smiled and slapped the barrels again. "*Mas rápido,* Pollo!" He inched the throttle forward.

....

Brood was six when he'd done his first job with Hondo. It had been in southern Kansas. He'd stood naked with Pollo by the side of the road in the lee of a stack of rusted irrigation pipe. Caravans of wagons and piecemealed trucks slowly rolled past, heading north to their spring planting, electric motors clogged and grinding with dust.

Pollo'd been barely more than a baby, barely able to stand. Brood had wrapped his arms around his brother's shoulders, tried to shield the boy's vacant, drifting eyes from blowing sand.

Some migrants rode in the backs of trucks, crammed in amongst makeshift hydrogen cells, battery packs, solar panels. Most walked, leaning into packs strapped to their shoulders and foreheads, eyes squinting against the dust and the unyielding yellow sun. Women sometimes turned gaunt faces at the two boys, and sometimes the hardness in them relented. They'd reached calloused fingers deep into soiled orange FEMAs and canvas robes. Pulled forth a few precious Satori seeds or bits of jerked meat and tossed them reluctantly into the dirt at the boys' feet. The regrettable price of keeping their own souls intact. Their men almost never looked, instead kept their chins jutting north towards the planting grounds of northern Kansas, Nebraska, Iowa, the Dakotas—kept their tire-tread sandals churning wearily along the broken asphalt.

It had been late in the day when a solitary wagon halted beside the boys, its electric motor wheezing fast towards death. A white man in tattered t-shirt and jeans had climbed down. Smiled, scratched his beard anxiously—held out a handful of dried apple slices. Brood recognized the hunger in the man's eyes. It hadn't been for food. The wagon hauled a trailer over which had been flung a burlap tarp. A child's sob came from beneath it. The man looked from the boys to the wagon and back. Shrugged, stuffed the apple slices into a pocket, stepped towards them.

"*Que pasa?*" Hondo'd said as he emerged from behind the stack of irrigation pipe. The man's eyebrows had gone up in surprise. Then the world had shattered around the shotgun's horrible shriek.

In the stunned silence that followed, Hondo had stepped casually over the man's shredded body and Pollo had begun to slowly rock his shoulders from side to side. He squawked like a chicken.

They'd found three children in the wagon, two boys and a girl, all near Brood's age. Hondo gave them each a handful of the dried apple slices scrounged from the man's wagon and sent them on their way. North into the prairie where they would scrounge, *perros de basura* at the heels of some caravan.

"Saddens me, little homes," Hondo told Brood as they'd rummaged through the battery stacks and heaps of rusted scrap metal on the man's wagon. He'd held up a horsewhip with a frayed tip. "Didn't used to be like this." He tossed the whip onto the road and pulled back a piece of corrugated sheet metal, uncovering a crate full of sealed mason jars. He pulled one out and held it up to the light, peering through the cloudy glass at what looked like shriveled fingers. He smiled black gums. "Green beans."

....

Around noon they cut the wagon off the freeway and aimed north across an arid flat, still etched with ancient irrigation furrows. The temperature had hit the high nineties and Hondo, who had stripped down to canvas shorts, switched battery packs. They rolled slowly so as not to raise dust and soon came to a wide draw. Down in it, concealed from the freeway, stood the sagging skeleton of a farmhouse. Exactly where the whiteboy had said it would be.

Brood pulled a pair of binoculars from a foot locker and scanned the house. Three boys stood in the house's shaded lee. Tattered FEMAs, red *La Chupe* sashes. Whiteboy waved.

"Just the three of them."

"Nobody *en la casa?*"

"Don't see nobody."

"Weapons?"

"Nope."

"Okay."

Brood and Hondo donned flak jackets, still wet from where they had scrubbed away the morning's blood. Hondo propped the Mossberg within easy reach against the water tank. They rolled wordlessly up beside the three boys.

"'Sup?" Brood said. The three *Chupes* shuffled their feet in the dirt, abashed, expectant. Hondo motioned at the cargo netting and together he and Brood uncovered the barrels. The three boys gawked.

"Goddamn," Whiteboy said. As Brood and Hondo duck walked one barrel to the wagon's edge, he smiled like he'd just seen the sun for the first time. "Ya'll don't fuck around."

"Don't fuck around," Pollo echoed from the stationary bike. His legs churned slowly on the pedals. His head hung low to his lap so only the top of his shaven brown pate touched the world. The smallest of the three boys aimed a finger up at Pollo.

"He ain't right, is he?"

Brood silently met his gaze, flat and unblinking. After a moment, fear crossed the small boy's face. He took a step back.

"Don't be rude, Todd," the third boy said. "He ain't no wronger than you."

Todd stared at the ground. White dust rose around him as he shuffled his feet. Then he sucked his lip and squinted greedily up at the wagon.

"That all corn?"

"Nah," Brood told him. "All kinds of shit." He sank a hand into the seed and lifted it to show the boy. It trickled through his fingers, flickering like gold in the high sun. A tiny disk caught on the tip of his index finger, crossed by a tiny, perfect barcode—not a lazed counterfeit, but smooth, sunken into the seed's flesh, an expression of its very DNA. Brood held it up. "Cucumber," he said. Todd reached up, touched the tip of his finger to Brood's thumb and the seed stuck to him. His eyes crossed as he brought it close to his face.

"Hard to believe this li'l fucker turns into a cucumber."

"Lots of cucumbers," Whiteboy corrected. "Help 'em with the barrel, Todd."

They wrestled the barrel to the ground and the three *La Chupes* gathered around it like it was a fire on a frozen January night. Brood watched as they dug their hands into it and laughed.

"Why you stealing from your own gang?" he asked after moment.

"Defecting," Todd said, buried up to his elbows in seed.

"Fuck, Todd." The other boy glared.

"What?" Todd withdrew his hands and raised them, as though he held two question marks. He looked from Whiteboy to the other ex-*Chupe*. "What?"

"Gotta make a living," Whiteboy said. The swirled tats on his face creased as he squinted at Brood. "Barely eat with *La Chupe*."

"Striking out on our own," Todd offered. "Starting our own gang." The third boy shook his head and turned away in disgust. "What?" Todd said. "Maybe they'd like to join. You know?"

"*Gracias, amigo.*" Hondo's face crinkled with mirth. "Maybe next time."

"What kind of vehicle you got?" Brood asked.

"Got nothing," Whiteboy said. "We carrying it."

Hondo gave Brood a long look. Brood scanned the distance. The empty brown of north Texas badlands stretched as far as he could see.

"Alright."

"*Diviértase con eso*," Hondo told Whiteboy.

"Yeah, we will." Whiteboy eyed the wagon. "Sure you don't want to come with us?"

"We got to be up north," Brood said. He pictured himself working a long furrow atop the Ojo ridge. Pushing corn seed three knuckles deep in dark soil. Rosa Lee following close behind with a ceramic jug, the long curves of shoulders growing dark under the sun as she poured each seed a birthing drink. Desire squeezed Brood's heart, made his skin burn. "Soon."

"Yeah, well." Whiteboy smiled. He turned and together the three ex-*Chupes* gathered themselves around the barrel of seed. They began inching it awkwardly north.

"Hold up." Brood pulled a tarp free from a stack of milk crates and rummaged. Pulled free a mason jar full of pickled radishes. He filled a second jar from the spout on the water tank and handed the two jars down to Whiteboy.

"Pleasure doing business with you," Whiteboy said.

"Luck, *ese*."

....

At first they travelled only at night, rolling slow with the deep cycles bats. Hondo sat up front, calling out directions while Brood handled the tiller. In the predawn they'd kick in the Hercs, making real miles westward for a couple of hours, then pull far off the road and shelter the day under a camo net.

Pollo disappeared those days while Brood and Hondo napped or swatted languorously at flies. They listened to prairie saints blather on an ancient dented Ham radio with dials the size of Brood's fists. Neither of them cared much for Jesus, but sometimes the prairie saints dispensed news. Rumors of what caravans were where, of what wells were finding water.

Pollo always returned at dusk, once with a tiny wild dog to spit over the fire, another time with a rattlesnake longer than he was tall and as thick as his thigh. They cooked most of the snake, enough meat for all of them for three days. The rest of the meat Brood cut into sections and pounded flat with a stone. He salted it and spread it to dry on a rock. The nights froze them while they rolled, but during the day February sun hammered down, hot enough to dry the snake in a single afternoon.

"Ain't worry keeps bad shit at bay," Hondo told Brood on their fourth morning out of Amarillo. Brood, his arm draped over the tiller, kept squinting over his shoulder into the rising sun. They'd transferred all their water to five fifty-gal drums they'd slung under the wagon, and hidden the seed in the water tank. Hondo sat against it, a man roosting on his hoard, jostling as the wagon rolled. "Foresight. A good plan. A little luck. That's all you need, young homey."

"Maybe," Brood squinted east. Rusted-out pump jacks and storage tanks, the last evidence that people had once carved a living out of the dry plains, had faded as they'd moved into New Mexico and the endless sagebrush of deep desert. Massive steppes loomed around them now, ghostly in the early light. A prairie saint droned on the Ham, talking salvation, the second coming. Talked about the Corn Mother, some bitch up in Kansas who'd come out of Satori and was going to save everyone.

"Maybe," Pollo sang from his perch on the stationary bike, his voice slow with concentration as though he were trying to decipher some hidden meaning in the sound. He'd wrapped a scrap of wool blanket over his shoulders. His skinny legs churned on the pedals.

"They think we gone north with the herd," Hondo said. "They thought otherwise, we'd know by now." He absently dug something out of the ulcerous patch on his cheek and held it up on a dirty fingernail to examine it, then stuck the fingertip in his mouth and sucked. "We be dead."

"Alright." Brood cast a challenging eye at the old man. "We keep rolling." Hondo met his gaze, and smiled.

"*Bueno.*"

"Alright." Brood halted the wagon, switched the motor over to the Hercs.

They rolled into the day, making good time along the broken freeway. Mean white sunlight charged the bats—hooked through a converter to PV paint slopped over the wagon's every flat surface—almost as fast as the wagon's motors drained them.

"I like this stretch," Brood said. Nothing but freeway, angling ever westward through picked-bone desert, marked every hundred miles or so by the crumbling shells of abandoned gas stations. As if the best civilization had ever managed here was to pass through on its way to somewhere else.

"Bandit country," Hondo agreed. He killed the power to the Ham and connected its cable instead to an ATM interface Brood had jerry-rigged to a car stereo amp and an ancient hard drive the size of a brick. A moment later the shrill vocals and heavy beats of mid-century Chinese dub spilled from a speaker cone bolted to the wagon's edge. Hondo settled back down, propped his dreads against a big twelve-volt battery and folded his hands priestly on his bony chest.

"Beats," Pollo noted. Brood bobbed his head.

"What I'm talking about." He leaned into the tiller, and with the beats passed miles.

CHAPTER 5

Mercy's body trembled. Balanced atop her extended toes, she seemed to occupy the exact center of the entire formless prairie. Every tendon, every strand of muscle sang with focus as she watched the tendril of ocher dust billow from the horizon.

Pihadassa smiled. She reached out, ran fingers lightly along the tense arc of the advocate's neck. The woman started. Turned, hissed—then smiled. Pihadassa breathed a centering breath, let herself fall down the advocate's helix. She diagnosed the war there. The need to lash out barely reined by the need to submit.

"Child," she chided. Mercy sank immediately to her haunches. Her raptor's arms encircled one of Pihadassa's bare legs. Her tongue unfurled, touched its warm tip to Pihadassa's bare knee, then her head sank between her shoulders, the way a dog's might.

"Mother," she whined. Her eyes shot again to the horizon. A migrant caravan, heading their way. "Let me have them, Mother." Pihadassa stroked the soft edge of one of Mercy's ears.

"No." She gazed down into a wide, shallow valley that lay before her. Her landraces worked there in pairs. Mates, laboring side by side. Furrowing the valley's contour with tools made from bits of cannibalized zep frame, or simply using their hands. Sweat shone on their sun-browned skin and they exuded contentment in their toil, fulfilling a base instinct to labor. An instinct Pihadassa had built into them.

A brown stream, thick with spring runoff, meandered the valley's length. In the embrace of one of its curves near the valley's center grew a ring of geodesic bone work. The nascent frame of a new dome, just large enough to support her landraces, a few hundred people. Just large enough for her to do her work.

The valley's beauty swelled in Pihadassa's chest, and she smiled. It was a good spot, fecund. It was the future.

Mercy whined again. The agonized sound of suppressed need.

"No," Pihadassa told her again. "They will come here. You will let them. They will help me make my children." She pinched Mercy's ear. The advocate emitted a low growl, part pleasure, part pain. The smudge of dust on the horizon grew.

. . . .

Sumedha slept, folded in flesh. The city's deep pulse throbbed the length of his body, soothing him, speaking its love. It whispered to him, told him the secret names of its exquisite children. Names even those children, living for the pleasure of service, did not know. It told him of the Fathers grumbling, how they turned, restless in their amniotic sacks, riding the visionary edge of perpetual sleep. It whispered of the skin stretched over its dome, contracting in the cold night wind cutting down out of the Rockies. Whispered of the warbling chorus sung by the wind turbines churning in their cartilage sockets out on the plain; of the corn digesting hot in its subterranean guts. Sumedha listened, rapt, dreaming the helix.

Or perhaps the helix dreamed him. It turned like slow prayer in his mind. He broke it apart, adding and subtracting, piecing it back together. A limitless puzzle that could never be wholly solved, but that could shape a solution to any problem. His faith was thus: Ask the question and the helix would answer. Life would answer. He felt his way along the helix's length, not analyzing, merely intending. The helix sometimes recombined itself, independent but in sync with him, a rebellious dance partner at whose insights he could only marvel.

Such moments were rare—and tonight was one of them. He lay thoughtless, hearing the city's dream and holding the helix in his mind for long minutes, nearly weeping at its beauty. Then, like all things, it would pass. He let it go and approached it anew, watching it turn and break of its own accord. He felt a voyeur, as though the helix had been recombining itself alone in a hidden part of his mind long before he had stumbled upon it to watch. It showed him things, pointed in revelatory directions. The particulars of transcendence, whole evolutionary culminations. But when he reached to comprehend, the visions evaporated. So he relented, breathing his way deeper, letting the dream come to him on its own terms. The helix danced, twisted, spun. Abruptly stilled itself and beamed epiphanic light through Sumedha's nervous system—

Pihadassa had gone.

Sumedha woke. The warm skin of his bed reluctantly parted, releasing him. He sat there, struggling to comprehend in his waking state what he had just witnessed. The floor's pale fur caressed the soles of his feet. The bed undulated invitingly. He stared across the small sleeping alcove at the flushed and puckered lip of Pihadassa's bed, ever ready to enfold Pihadassa's smooth dark weight. He longed for her. So often they had risen together and sat opposite one another in this alcove. Naked, a mirrored pair, the male and female of primate unity. A whole.

"I want to have a child."

She had said this upon emerging from her bed, face clouded with sleep. Dream noise, Sumedha had thought.

"No," Sumedha told the empty chamber, performing the memory, looking for clues. "You do not. Bearing young is not an imperative you are designed for."

"Of course." A single line had creased her tranquil brow as she struggled to phrase her thoughts. "I *wish* I could want a child."

Sumedha had watched her, curious at such a rare moment when their thoughts did not touch. Pihadassa sometimes saw things he could not. Perhaps she was smarter than he, perhaps simply more chaotic. Regardless, he loved her for it. He had waited, but she had said nothing more. Instead she had smiled and stroked his face with her thumb.

Sumedha leaned forward, felt the echo of Pihadassa's touch. The walls, sensing him stir, gurgled gently. Soft biolumes activated beneath their skin, setting the room to glow a soft underwater blue, revealing within a tracery of bone latticework, tendon, muscle, vein. The color matched Sumedha's mood.

He willed the lip of Pihadassa's bed to unfurl and produce her, newborn from sleep, smooth brown head bowed for him to stroke. How she must have planned. How much she must have kept from him. A puzzle, yes, one he could no more turn away from than he could command his heart to stop beating. He placed a palm against the wall, connecting once more to the rush and whisper of the city's metabolism, then rose.

The blue glow of the abode's walls followed him as he paced naked into the ovular center room and there stopped before a vertical slit in the wall. Feeling his presence, it irised open with a kissing sound, stretching taut a layer of epidermis, molecularly thin, transparent.

The city spread out below, an intermingled series of bending muscle towers and soft domes twined abruptly with the concrete, brick and plexi of the old city. Shadowy bone latticework showed through translucent skin. A thousand hearts beat oxygen and heat into a thousand buildings, pumped waste out onto the compost heaps along the northern fields.

Far beneath Sumedha a group of landraces moved slowly on their hands and knees along a snake-scale street. Their rough voices sang as their hands polished the scales with fur brushes. Sumedha closed his eyes and touched the wall, sure he could feel the city's pleasure at the touch of its children's brushes. A warm sensation spread through his body...*Love*. He opened his eyes and the helix danced. Each building a different expression of its strange and brilliant will, yet part of a whole that fed sensation down lush nerve matrices to the center, here, to Satori Tower, where Sumedha stood touching flesh, almost connected. Over it all stretched the dome, a mother's womb shielding the city and its children from the mad seasonal swings of a climate knocked from its axis. This was his dream; he was its architect.

Was this not Pihadassa's dream, too? Was *this* not her child?

"Satori," he said.

"Yes, Sumedha?" Satori's voice emanated from the walls and ceiling. Female, pleasantly flat.

"You have samples of Pihadassa's voice."

"Yes, Sumedha."

"Please assume her voice when addressing me."

"Yes, Sumedha." Pihadassa's voice now. Vertigo assaulted Sumedha. He wanted to put his forehead to hers, to sync his thoughts with hers, to join with her. He touched the wall, felt its life, let it steady him. He breathed—the sensation moved through his body and passed.

"What puzzle were you working?"

"I do not understand."

He breathed slowly, checking his impatience, letting the answer come. She had wanted him to understand.

"What did you foment among the children?"

"I do not understand."

"Why did you leave? What do you see that I do not?"

"I have not left. I am incapable of going anywhere. I do not see anything."

He let his mind follow the sensations Pihadassa's voice produced in his body. Heat mostly. Something less tangible that he could only describe as pain. It took him to a hollow place down in his belly, and there his mind settled. When it stilled, the helix rose once more behind his eyelids—

"You are awake."

Sumedha spun. Two other Designers stood in his abode. They had entered quietly through a large slit in the wall which now contracted behind them.

"Kassapa. Paduma." He nodded to each in turn. They were an identical mirrored pair, like Sumedha and Pihadassa. Hairless, dark, smooth. His siblings. Both wore white cotton shifts. The backs of their hands touched continually. "Welcome," he told them. "Sit." He motioned with a hand and three soft protrusions rose from the floor. He waited for his guests to sit and then settled himself cross-legged into the third seat's soft fur. "Is there news?"

Kassapa watched Sumedha, his face impassive. After a long moment he gave the slightest shake of his head. Sumedha closed his eyes. Tightness he had not been aware of lifted from his chest, replaced by a flood of endorphins. He breathed, let the euphoria pass.

"You are relieved." Kassapa's voice was as blank as his face. Sumedha looked from him to Paduma and back.

"She is my Other. I wish her no harm."

"Of course not," Paduma said. "But you understand the necessity of what we must do."

"Yes. I understand why you monitor me." Sumedha spread his arms wide, hiding nothing. Paduma and Kassapa exchanged a glance.

"It has never happened before," Kassapa said.

"We worry for you," Paduma clarified. Sumedha slowly inclined his head towards her.

"And about what I might do."

They sat in silence, one regarding the two, the two regarding the one, all working long puzzle strands. The bizarre and foreign logic of betrayal.

"One defects," Kassapa said. "The other broods when he should sleep."

Sumedha smiled at their suspicion—a new sensation for all of them. Kassapa pursed his lips, then closed his eyes and breathed. They knew not what to make of their bereft brother. Sympathy surged through Sumedha.

"Pihadassa's betrayal is as much a puzzle to me as it is to you," he said. Paduma appraised him for a moment, black eyes unwavering—so very much like Pihadassa's.

"Then you do believe her defection is a betrayal."

"Yes. But I do not believe she thought it a betrayal, whatever her rationale. She...loves us." Sumedha swept a hand about him, indicating that by "us" he meant all of Satori. His body trembled with sudden emotion. Kassapa's face softened.

"A difficult puzzle for you."

"For us all, I think."

"I see why you do not sleep."

Sumedha closed his eyes, breathed slowly until he found his calm. His attention moved over every cell of his body, fully in the moment.

"We will send advocates," Kassapa said.

"I know."

Kassapa continued to stare for a moment, challenging, then closed his eyes. Sumedha and Paduma followed suit. They meditated together. Their minds touched, all three immersed in Sumedha's grief. After a time Sumedha reached out to them, touching their knees briefly. Their faces lit with surprise.

"The helix dances for me tonight," he said. Paduma's nostrils flared. Pheromones rose from her.

"You have found a solution for the Fathers?"

"Perhaps." Sumedha fixed in his mind the new configuration the helix had shown in his dream. "Part of one. I will not know for sure until I test it. But yes, it may be a step."

"You are the architect." Reverence filled Paduma's voice. Her hand levitated, seemingly of its own accord, and came to rest on Kassapa's shoulder. Sumedha nodded his gratitude. He looked to Kassapa. Doubt creased his brother's brow. He probed.

"Does this solution come from the infected migrants you have been collecting?"

"No. It comes from one I made."

"Then perhaps you will eliminate the infected migrants." Kassapa breathed slowly. Sumedha watched his brother's eyes dim, a mind perpetually bent on the ever-shifting puzzle of Satori's security. "So many of them," Kassapa said. "Each with families. Others who might come to retrieve them. It is a risk."

"Not yet, brother. But soon."

"We will let you work," Paduma said abruptly. "Forgive our intrusion."

Intrusion. Kassapa and Paduma were his brother and sister, strands of the same braid. Intrusion was as foreign a concept to them as deceit and suspicion. Paduma stood and offered a hand to her Other. Kassapa took it and rose. Their seats sank back into the floor. Sumedha stood and followed them to the door. It spread open with a fleshy whisper as they approached. Kassapa turned.

"She must have told you something. Given you some clue."

"No." Sumedha kept his face blank. His body felt squeezed by the lie. Kassapa's pupils dilated: recognition.

"We want the order to come from you," he said. Sumedha nodded. He breathed, let the emotion flow through him. He did not suppress the tears streaming down his cheeks. Empathy filled his siblings' faces.

"Send them, brother," he said. "Send your advocates."

CHAPTER 6

"**A**gent Doss!" The knock came loud, persistent, formal. Too fucking early to be anything other than official. Doss ignored it. Kept her eyes shut, afraid if she opened them she would see snow. Falling like ash out of the frozen Siberian sky, down through the grated hole in the ceiling to bury her under mute drifts.

"Agent Doss!"

"Shit." She opened her eyes.

Her rack, like all apartments in Sec Serv lower-echelon personnel housing, was roughly the size of a footlocker. A sink, hot plate, wardrobe. She stretched the half-pace to the shower/toilette combo, swiveled the toilette from its hole in the wall, vomited a long string of bile. Thus began her morning routine.

The knock grew insistent.

"I do not fucking hear you," she yelled at the door.

Next in her routine: get up, stretch, hydrate. A quart of water. It took twelve seconds to make the bed—she counted off in her head. Anything under fifteen was acceptable. Finish by bouncing a 2038 Georgia quarter off the spread up into her inverted palm.

She held the coin in her fist, inspecting perfectly clipped nails.

Her father had seemed gigantic the day he'd given Doss the quarter. It was her first clear memory of him. An olive duffle slung over shoulders wide as a wagon yoke, heat shimmers rising off the Fort Stewart tarmac behind him. The end of a long tour in Saud. He'd grinned spectacularly in the roar of a four-prop angling for takeoff. Leaned down to press the coin into her tiny hand, his fingernails perfectly filed half moons. It was fate, he'd said, that a Chinese officer from across the world would end up with an old coin in his pocket from the very state where Sienna Doss was born. Fate that Doss' father should take it back and give it to her. Doss had watched her face reflected in the sheen of his boots.

"Agent fucking Doss!" Again, they pounded the door. They were definitely going to fuck her routine. "Agents Fiorivani and Dumont." Sec Serv then, but Doss had never heard of either of them. "We have orders to take you to the capitol."

"Fuck off!"

"Negative. Fucking off is definitely not within our mission parameters. Open the door."

"I have three more days of mandatory leave. Your mission parameters include a definition of the word 'mandatory'? I've already passed my psych evals."

"I have been fully briefed on the meaning of the word 'mandatory,'" the voice called. "It means you get your ass up, get functional and come with us. Now."

"Do me the favor, guys. Agent to agent?"

A pause. Then more knocking.

"Fuck, alright! Give me ten."

"You got five. And you're dining with sharks, so get tight."

She got herself Sec Serv tight: navy slacks, white blouse, Kevlar blazer, black boots polished clean as onyx, hair pulled into a severe ponytail. Carbon fiber .45 holstered at the small of her back. She opened the door.

Two agents in Sec Serv civvies stood in the narrow cinderblock hallway. White teeth split the coffee face of one agent as he looked Doss up and down.

"Didn't know you'd be such a tall drink of tasty."

The other agent stepped forward, spoke the statutory Gov greeting: "For the people." He stood several inches taller than Doss' six feet. She stared up at crew cut blond hair, crazy green eyes—*savage* was the first thought to enter her mind. "I'm Fiorivani. That's Dumont."

"For the people," Doss said. She took in Fiorivani's height. "I pictured you as a short Italian."

"You wouldn't be the first."

"Follow me," Dumont ordered. He turned and strode down the corridor, wiry and taut, a definite soldier beneath his Sec Serv suit. Doss followed and Fiorivani fell into step behind.

"Where we headed?" Doss asked.

"Not at liberty," Fiorivani said.

"What are you at liberty?"

Fiorivani said nothing. Dumont glanced over the shoulder of his Kevlar weave blazer. He chuckled, kept walking.

They ushered her down flights of concrete stairs, through a reinforced steel door, into rain. A black Lobo hunkered on the muddy street outside the building. Behind it, the hulking cinderblock squares of New D.C.'s Gov district, felt more than seen through the mist. The two agents herded Doss into the Lobo, then climbed in front, Dumont at the wheel and Fiorivani shotgun.

"Don't mind a little music, do you, Agent?" Fiorivani called back to Doss. "This dog's *executive*." He pointed and Doss saw blue LEDs glowing in the face of a rare stereo in the center console. Soft black leather surrounded her. Bottles of scotch, vodka, gin, along with old fashioned and highball glasses, secured by elastic holders inside a mobile wet bar installed in the seatback.

"Not at all," she said. "Make me feel a little less like an assignment."

Fiorivani hit a button on the stereo. Thick, Earth Mother thrash squalled from a dozen speakers. Dumont grabbed a gear and cranked hard on the wheel. They set off, heads bobbing. Out of the muddy core of West Chester and up onto the 202, rolling fast, making a hard target. For whom Doss had no idea.

"I know you from Dubai." Fiorivani propped an elbow on one towering knee and twisted to face Doss. "I know of you, I mean. I was regular army." He showed bright teeth. "My guys mopped up after your crew once or twice." Doss smiled politely, said nothing. She watched old Philly roll past in the rain.

Migrants walked both edges of the freeway, streaming out of the south, bent in the rain. They gathered to the east, squatting among government seed warehouses that wouldn't open until March. Waiting for a bare ration of climate-resistant Satori seed they'd take into the undulating hills of old Amish country or west into the plains. There, they'd plant, suffer the crippling summer heat, harvest and uproot southward before the first freeze. They peered through the rain at the Lobo. Doss saw a man's lip curl as he turned and spit. Another migrant staggered, clearly gripped by the Tet, her arms jutting straight as rebar from her shoulders.

"How's Emerson?" Dumont called over the strains of thrash. Doss shook her head.

"Still in the basement IC at Echelon B." Mummied up in paper blankets on an army surplus cot. Hooked to a saline drip and tended, as far as Doss'd been able to tell on her daily visits, by nobody. He seemed paler each morning. Seemed to shrink, to be slowly disappearing under winking low-load fluorescents. A fecal odor pervaded the place, and something worse, something faint and rotten beneath the antiseptic. "Still unconscious."

"Sorry to hear it. We were on assignment together a couple years back. Good man."

"Yes he is."

Dumont geared down, took an exit. The Lobo's reactor whined as though slowing pained it. They descended from the freeway into the Gov district's heart. Concrete and cinderblock cubes rising blank and windowless out of the old Philly burbs. They rolled past the capitol building, past the cabinet offices and Pentagon, each as square and implacable as the next, designed to hermetically entomb stable internal climates.

Dumont slowed as they came to a crowd of migrants pressing against a heavy steel gate, atop which ran a curl of razor wire. The entrance to Executive Park, around which stood the flat facades of the executive offices. From behind the gate, a phalanx of lower-echelon Sec Serv troops in full riot gear faced the migrants.

"Get tight," Dumont said. An Ingram appeared in Fiorivani's big hand. Dumont wove the Lobo slowly through the migrants, following a flatbed truck stacked with bricks of black algae. The migrants held signs overhead on sticks. FEED OR SEED! GOVERNMENT: BY THE PEOPLE, FOR THE PEOPLE, HELP THE PEOPLE! One simply read, STARVING. An old man who reminded Doss of her father put his face close to the Lobo's blacked out windows—seemed to stare straight into her soul, his eyes wide with the urgency of whatever it was he needed to convey. He pointed skyward. At the rain or the fleet of ghostly leviathan zeps hovering overhead, or at some angry god. Who knew? Something moist struck the rear window. Mud or shit. The gate swung open. Fiorivani let out a breath.

"Fucking mudfish," he said. Dumont kept quiet, just rolled the Lobo smoothly through the gate. Something rigid in his silence made Doss think the agent knew what it was to be hungry. Fiorivani cracked his window, extended a hand, gave the riot guards the shaka. They nodded.

Dumont steered them around the road circling Executive Park, pulled into the drive leading to the building at the park's center. The Lobo halted abruptly, tires hissing on wet pavement.

"You got to be fucking kidding me," Doss said.

"Told you," Dumont said. "Sharks." Beside them rose the White House, grey and rectangular as a tombstone in the rain.

....

The room smelled of cigars and scotch. Shelves along the walls held real books. Doss had never seen so much leather and dark wood. It felt like a museum.

"Agent Doss." The man stood tall beside a dark oak desk so massive it looked sea worthy. The sleek wool of his suit jacket flowed like mercury over his shoulders as he extended his hand.

"For the people."

"For the people," Doss replied.

"Bill Rippert." His greying flattop and rigid posture stank of old-school military. He gripped Doss' hand far too hard and stared into her face with shocking green eyes. Three gold stars gleamed on a single epaulet on his left shoulder.

"General Rippert," Doss said. "I heard of you in Saud. We were there at the same time. I think you were a colonel then."

"A long time ago." A hard glint shone in his eyes as he smiled. "I do my best to be a civilian now. An advisor." He glanced into a far corner. Movement there caught Doss' eye.

A white woman, ensconced in the plush folds of a leather sofa. Stocking-clad legs crossed in the pooled light of two wrought-iron lamps burning low-load fluorescents. Doss saw black ankle-strap heels, a smooth black dress ripped straight from an old flex vid. Lipstick. Skin stiffened by surgeries and plumping injections.

Doss nodded to the woman, who gave no response. Rippert did not introduce her. Instead he motioned Doss to a high-backed leather chair, then seated himself behind the acreage of oak desk.

Rippert stared at her for an unblinking moment, then picked a flexpad up off the dark acreage of his desktop and began wordlessly poking at it. Windows scrolled across the translucent screen.

"Too bad you ruined the Lobo." He spoke without looking up, with the sort of crisp enunciation cultivated among military school spawn. The sort who excelled at getting good soldiers killed.

"Sir?"

"We don't make those anymore. We can hardly maintain the ones we have."

"Yes, sir." Doss speared her fingers into the deep leather of her chair's armrests, made conscious effort to keep her teeth from grinding. Rippert watched her coolly, and smiled.

"You did fine work, keeping our little warlord friend intact."

Little warlord friend. Doss chewed on the phrase. Weighed it against the memory of Emerson laid out, bleeding, on cracked asphalt. He'd reminded her of a ruined bird, the fucked up way his limbs had moved. Frantic and weak as he'd struggled to cross the distance to where Doss had lain herself across Tsol.

"Just my job, sir."

The woman on the sofa snickered. Doss turned. The woman withdrew a cigarette—an honest-to-God manufactured one, the likes of which Doss hadn't seen in more than a decade—from a tiny leather purse. She tapped it delicately against a thumbnail, lit it with a tiny silver lighter. Her surgically stiffened face remained motionless, imperious, as her rictus lips pursed and she inhaled. She reminded Doss strangely of the ruins of Old D.C. Marble domes and columns, granite obelisks rising stately and useless out of the bloated Potomac. A totemic face, an idol of old elite. The woman exhaled perfumed smoke, winked at Doss.

"Hopefully your partner will pull through," Rippert said.

"Yes, sir."

"How are you feeling?"

"Fine, sir."

"No injuries?"

Doss shook her head. "Nothing got through the Kev." Rippert nodded slowly, as though after consideration he'd decided this was a good thing. He tapped a finger absently atop the desk.

"I crossed paths with your father in the first Saud war," he said after a moment. "Twice. Did you know that?"

"No, sir."

"We were both Spec Ops. I didn't know him well, but his reputation was solid. Almost as solid as yours. How is he?"

Doss had visited her father during her mandatory psyche leave. Sat with him on the tiny cot in his apartment while he drank bitter algae ferment and listened to the weatherman on a handheld radio predict rain, rain, rain. He was thin now, spoke very little. Black fertilizer ran like wood grain in the cracks of his fingernails, which he chewed constantly, his eyes red-rimmed from fumes in the algae-diesel plant where he worked in New D.C.'s tunnels. Occasionally he'd rise and stand gazing out the slit of a window at the zeps nosing in from the east. From Paris, Manchester, Madrid. The flooded and frozen capitols of countries that still tried to exist in some meaningful way.

"He's good, sir. He loves being retired."

The corners of Rippert's mouth turned up. "You're a shitty liar, Agent Doss." Doss kept her mouth shut. Behind her, the woman's cigarette hissed. Rippert abruptly punched a button on his desk intercom. "Brian. Two whiskeys. You like it neat, don't you, Doss? Neat, Brian."

"Yes, sir," came a voice through the intercom.

"It's too bad," Rippert said. "This country should have more to offer a man like that in his golden years." Rippert leaned forward, placed his elbows on the desk, steepled his fingers. His eyes bore into Doss.

"I knew you in Saud as well. Iran and Dubai, too. I became special assistant to the regional coordinator of Spec Ops about a month before the Chinese decided to wander back into the desert for round two. I followed you and your crew real close. Every time we ordered you sent out, something got blown up." He grinned. His eyes turned wild and predatory. "Sometimes not what we wanted blown up. Sometimes it was even better." He leveled his conjoined fingers like a plow at Doss. "You knew how to take a mission by the balls and make it work." Understanding wormed its way into Doss' mind.

"This is a mission briefing," she realized.

The door opened behind her and an enormous man moved noiselessly into the room. His nose had been smashed to one side and never reset. He carried two highballs, three fingers full on a silver tray—set one on the desk in front of Rippert, handed Doss the other. His white blazer remained Kevlar stiff as he moved.

"Thank you, Brian."

"Sir." The man exited. Rippert leaned back in his chair and raised his glass.

"Here's to the old world, Doss." His gaze stayed on her over the rim of his upturned glass. Doss sipped her whiskey. It shocked her, smoky and smooth, the best thing she'd tasted since…she didn't remember. Rippert smiled. "Good, isn't it?"

"Very." Doss crossed her legs and settled into her chair, chill now that she knew the meeting's purpose. She met Rippert's eye for several beats, then said, "You don't strike me as the coy type." Rippert picked up the flexpad, scrolled through windows until he found the one he wanted and peered down his nose at it.

"Seems you've been keeping to a routine." Green eyes flicked to her and waited, unblinking, heavy with implication. Twice a day she ran the stairs at Sec Serv housing until her legs felt wrapped in barbed wire. Twice a day she pumped iron in the basement gym. In between she did plyometrics and ate vat-grown chicken breast and weirdly perfect Satori vegetables. She had no visitors. She visited no one.

"Works for me," Doss said. Exhaustion worked for her. It kept her mind inside her skull, heavy and free of thought, anchored by her crushed metabolism. Rippert arched an eyebrow.

"Ask me, I'd say you're wound a little tight. Of course, I'm no expert." Rippert tapped the flexpad. "I have two psyche evals here that state you're fit as a fucking fiddle. The goddamn rock of Gibraltar." The woman on the couch snickered again. Rippert waited.

"What's the mission, sir?"

Rippert set the flexpad on the desk. He leaned back, lacing fingers over the smooth wool of his jacket, and looked to the woman on the couch. Doss turned, watched the woman give the slightest nod.

"If there were a mission, it would be classified," Rippert explained. "Executive One." Straight from the president. "It would be completely volunt—"

"I'll take it."

"Agent?"

"I love this country, sir." Doss drained her whiskey in a gulp. Leaned forward, placed her empty glass on Rippert's desk. "I'm good to go." Rippert nodded, the ritual complete.

"What do you know about Satori Corp?" he asked.

"Bio-architecture," she said after a moment's thought. She'd seen sat feed of the flesh amoeba covering old town Denver, but she'd never seen it in person. "They shifted their focus to agriculture sometime around the first Hot Summer." She shrugged. "They make the seed."

"They make the seed," Rippert affirmed. He pulled what looked like a folded piece of paper from a jacket pocket and tossed it to Doss. A flexpad. She unfolded it, found a window already tabbed up. A woman's face stared out, dark-skinned and hairless, placid as a cat. A face so perfectly proportioned it made the rest of the world feel distorted. "Specifically, *she* makes the seed."

"She doesn't look real," Doss observed.

"She is very real," Rippert told her. "Her name is Pihadassa. A creation of Dr. Prekash Gupta, President of Satori Corp's genetics division. One of his monkeys. She's Satori's number two geneticist. Designed specifically for that function." He paused, letting his next words gather weight. "She makes the seed. And she's defected."

"Defected?" The term felt strange, outdated. "To where?"

"She was coming to us. Our man at Satori put her on a zep headed for Fort Riley eight days ago." A muscle trembled in Rippert's jaw. "She never showed. The zep went off Riley's radar in eastern Kansas. We want you to find her."

Doss tabbed up an info blob on the flexpad's screen beside Pihadassa's face, began skimming it. After a moment she looked up. Brown rain had begun to spatter against a small window high on the wall behind Rippert's desk. Rippert waited for Doss to set the flexpad down before he spoke.

"We distribute seed, Agent Doss," he said. "Anymore, that's all we do. We no longer feel confident in our ability to bring Satori to heel. Soon enough they'll figure that out, if they haven't already. When they do…" An errant tendril of blue cigarette smoke drifted between them. Rippert's eyes went briefly to the woman on the sofa. The heat kicked on, hot air pumped through floor vents from algae fires burning deep inside the building's basement. The room grew instantly oppressive. "When they do, things will get very bad for us. For everyone. We need to be able to make seed, as efficiently as Satori does." He leaned back in his chair, crossed a burnished leather shoe over one knee. "You met Agent

Fiorivani. He's my man. He's going with you."

"Fiorivani." Doss regarded Rippert across the desk—saw now the same green eyes, the same geometric cheekbones and chin. She leaned forward, ran a long finger around the rim of her whiskey glass. "That his mother's name?" Rippert nodded once, his face rigid with sudden emotion.

"This mission has high personal value to me, Agent Doss. The pilot of the zep that disappeared. She's my daughter."

"I hear you, sir."

They let the moment settle. Then Rippert picked up his flexpad and tabbed at it.

"You've spent time at Fort Riley."

"A long time ago," Doss affirmed. "I did my jump certification there." Twenty-one years ago. She'd been seventeen.

"That's where you'll set up ops. Riley's resources will be at your disposal. You leave in the morning."

"I'll need a third," Doss told him. Someone to watch her back, whom she could trust. Someone good at fucking shit up. "Sergeant Javier Gomez. He was with me in the Middle East. Good soldier. Last I heard he was back here in D.C. working convoy duty."

"If I can find him, he's yours."

"Thank you, sir. I need one more thing. A favor." Rippert raised expectant eyebrows, so white they were nearly invisible. Doss hesitated, then turned and spoke directly to the woman on the sofa. "My partner, ma'am. Agent Emerson."

The woman's lips turned sour, betraying age through the layers of derma sculpting. She'd lit another cigarette. She pulled on it slowly, raised it before her face and squinted at it as though she held there the entire measure of Doss' worth. Then, very deliberately, she crushed it into a silver ashtray sitting on an end table beside her. Smoke emanated from her nostrils. Doss persisted.

"He's laid up in a meat locker out on the fringe. He'll die."

"I see." The woman's voice was as smoky as the whiskey churning hot through Doss' bloodstream. "He'll be transferred to the cabinet hospital adjacent to this building. Before the day is out."

A faint smile touched her lips as her gaze settled on Doss. "Will that suffice, Agent?"

"Thank you, ma'am."

"Welcome back to the army, Doss." Rippert slid a hand palm down across the desk towards her. When he raised it, metal gleamed on the dark oak. A silver eagle. "Congratulations, Colonel." He bit the syllables off, sharp and formal, then stood and extended his hand.

CHAPTER 7

Their ninth day out of Amarillo brought them to the small town of Las Vegas, New Mexico, little more than a few building foundations and the echoes of giant parking lots etched into desert hardpan, abutting the freeway. They didn't stop. Angled the wagon off the freeway and north along the trace of an old highway whose number had long been forgotten. Up into the New Mexico foothills, into an expanse of dead junipers baked grey by the heat.

It was quiet, the trickle of snowmelt running in muddy rivulets down deep gullies on either side of the road, the whine of the wagon's motor the only sounds. There was no grass to rustle in the wind. No small animals scurried out of their path or hid trembling out of sight. No hawks or vultures circled overhead. Tightness gripped Brood's gut as he worked the tiller. It was a dead forest.

"We're levitating," Pollo said. He lay on his back, eyes closed to the sun. A small rattler coiled languidly around his wrist. He'd spread a handful of Satori seed on his chest, mashed into a golden disk occupying the tattooless spot over his sternum. The black hieroglyphs of animals surrounded it. Deer, rats, turtles, lizards, most of which he'd X'd out. Goners. "Satori keeps us floating." He sat up suddenly, careful not to startle the snake, and let the seeds fall into a cupped hand. "That's lonely." He pulled his blanket over his head and folded in on himself. Began to hum, weird and tuneless.

Hondo punched up some Tijuana lounge on the stereo, but it felt wrong, laughter in a cemetery. After a few moments he killed it. He sat down and laid an arm across Pollo's shoulders.

At dusk they camped on the road rather than risk sinking the wagon into the muddy ditches. They built a fire as the temperature dropped and made a stew by dropping hot rocks into a pot with canned potatoes and the last of Pollo's snake meat. Nobody spoke.

The meal's warmth settled Brood. He lay on a blanket by the fire, watching desert stars blaze, so bright they seemed to sing. They were three days shy of Ojo Caliente. His mind wandered with visions of Rosa Lee. Her bracelets jingling as she knelt beside him in a long furrow, planting. Pollo and Hondo would be there, too. Settled and safe, the road's long miles vague in their memories. As his thoughts turned to dreams, Brood saw a life long enough to have a baby with Rosa Lee. A girl, with Rosa's black hair, who would smile and squeal and grip his fingers and call Pollo her *tio* and Hondo her *abuelito*.

He woke to find Pollo standing over him, chest bare to the chill night. Pollo's little snake wormed slowly over the boy's knuckles, lethargic in the cold. Brood shivered, glanced at the sky. Orion had set, but dawn had made no overture yet at the eastern horizon.

"Pollo? *Que onda?*"

"Time to go," Pollo said. His voice was strange, mild but insistent. He stepped over Brood, hopped the gully and disappeared into the woods.

Brood heard whispering. He squinted, glimpsed movement off the road opposite from where Pollo had gone.

"Hondo!" he hissed.

Lightning flashed a few feet away. Everything went white.

Thunder pounded the air. The smoldering remains of the fire exploded beside him. Hot ash showered him.

He leapt to his feet. Something hit his shoulder. He staggered. He saw people now, dark shapes running out of the trees. Pain shot down his arm. He screamed Hondo's name, heard nothing besides an awful ringing in his head.

Another impact, this time against his sternum. It knocked the wind from his lungs. He gasped, wretched. A shadow loomed before him, wielding something over its head. Brood's palm tightened on the .32. He didn't remember picking it up. He raised it, fired three times. The shadow staggered back, dropping what Brood now saw was an aluminum bat.

Another strobe of white light. This time Brood felt the concussion in his bones. Dirt kicked up at his feet. He looked in the direction of the flash. A girl stood a few feet way, eyeing him down the barrel of an ancient bolt action rifle. He backpedalled. Three men struggled on the other side of the fire. Brood leapt, driving his shoulder into a body. It dropped. Dreadlocks flew.

"*Cojer!*" Hondo yelled. Brood ducked as somebody swung at him. He pulled the old man up by the arm.

"Sorry!"

Gunfire popped like heat lightning in the trees. Brood grabbed Hondo and yelled into the old rat's face.

"Run!" And they both did, in opposite directions.

....

He found Hondo the next morning, naked except for his sandals, sitting cross-legged atop a boulder up on a hillside overlooking the spot where they'd camped. He had his eyes closed, his face turned contentedly into the low morning sun. Sweat and dirt streaked his ribcage. Below, the wagon sat where they'd parked it. He nodded as Brood approached.

"You hurt?"

Pain throbbed in Brood's shoulder, stabbed his chest with every breath. He shrugged.

"Nothing serious. You?"

Hondo shook his head. "Just catching some sun. That your *gringo?*" He pursed grizzled lips at where a body in stained FEMAs lay face down beside the extinguished fire. Brood recalled firing the pistol, which now dangled empty in his right hand.

"Might be. You seen Pollo?"

Hondo smiled, inclined his dreads towards the wagon. Pollo sat there against the water tank. He held his snake in cupped hands and appeared to be having a serious conversation with it.

"Pollo!" Brood called. "*Esta bien?*" Pollo did not look up. He transferred the snake delicately to one hand and with the other raised a thumb high. He continued talking at the snake.

They found everything intact. Brood's bow and quiver hung where he'd left them on the tiller. He inspected the batteries and motor, checked the food crates, the drive train.

"Everything's good," he told Hondo. Hondo wrapped a knuckle along the water tank, checking the seed, then slid under the wagon to check the water barrels. He reappeared a moment later and stood, brow furrowed, picking the scab on his cheek.

"We good?" Brood asked. Hondo said nothing, instead stepped to the spot where he'd slept. He pushed the blanket aside with a toe, revealing the Mossberg.

"*Que pasa?*" Brood demanded. Hondo bent with a long groan and picked up the shotgun, then turned to Brood. Gave him a look like he'd forgotten his own name.

"Think it's all good, *homito.*"

Brood scanned the dead trees on either side of the road. Fat black flies had begun to gather on the body beside the fire.

"*Que coño?*"

"We chased them off," Pollo explained, as though this were the most obvious thing in the world. Hondo thought about this for a moment, then his naked ribcage puffed out like a lizard's throat. He placed a hand on a hip, showed Brood slick black gums.

"Course we did."

"*Sale vale.*" Brood found his sandals beside the fire where he'd left them, slipped his feet inside. "Ain't *La Chupes*, though.

Chupes would've had us."

"True." Hondo sobered. Propped the Mossberg on one shoulder, eyed the surrounding forest. "Who you think then?"

"*No se.*"

....

Brood killed the motor, let the wagon coast to a halt. He leaned across the water tank, squinting at an intersection a half-mile down valley where their road crossed another, barely more than a game trail. A small band of people had broken camp there and now trudged slowly east in the dusty wake of two grinding trucks, one water and one cargo.

"*Cuantos?*" he asked.

"*Cinco.*" Hondo stood at the wagon's bow, scoping the intersection through binoculars. "They got a dog," he said after a moment. Brood squinted again, saw a dog trotting beside the second truck.

"They our friends from last night?"

"You seen anyone else out here?" Hondo pushed back dreads and gravely sucked a thumbnail. "They look hungry."

"Hide or roll?"

"Roll," Pollo sang. He sat on the wagon's edge, feet dangling. He stared out at where cloud shadows scudded like apparitions across the valley floor. The last stretch of desert before the mountains. "They got a dog."

Brood and Hondo exchanged a look. Hondo shrugged, picked up a flak jacket off the wagon's deck and tossed it to Brood.

"*Chale,*" Brood muttered.

They met the group just east of the intersection. A girl with aviator shades and a rifle slung over one FEMA-clad shoulder spotted them, yelled something to the others. The trucks jerked to a halt, heaving on their chassis. Motors spooled down.

Brood pulled the wagon in a long curve through the brush and hardpan, parking across the trail behind the small caravan. He killed the throttle, kept the motor switched on. Gripped his bow, an arrow already nocked.

The lead truck consisted of the teardrop of an ancient helicopter cockpit cobbled atop a heavy tractor chassis. Welded, bolted, tied with wire. Its door cracked open, caught for a moment on rusty hinges, then swung wide as someone inside kicked it. The unmistakable fuzz of a Ham radio issued forth.

A *gringa* stepped out. Brood saw grey hair pulled back tight, a sleeveless denim vest over FEMAs. She raised a tentative hand in greeting, her face pinched in the morning sun.

"See?" Pollo whispered urgently. He pointed at the small dog, which wiggled, skinny and nearly hairless, around the woman's shins. It spasmed with pleasure as she leaned down and scratched it behind the ear.

"Who the fuck got a *dog?*" Brood wondered. Hondo shook his head.

From the other side of the truck emerged a tall man dressed all in denim. He stood there, a pistol held partly visible behind one hip.

The girl with the aviator shades said something to the group. They idled for a moment, wrapped against the sun in filthy canvas blankets. Then, one by one, they sat, exhausted heaps on the broken road—all except the girl and a square-jawed boy with cornrowed hair. They unslung rifles.

"Where you out of?" Hondo called.

"Baja." The woman's voice sounded choked, as though dust caked her throat. She coughed, stepped slowly forward, palms open. "Baja," she repeated, narrow jaw thrust forward, vibing defiance, determination, need. Brood guessed her to be a little older than Hondo, maybe fifty.

"First we've seen from Baja," Hondo said. The woman swallowed hard, clutched her throat with fingers thin and gnarled as a raven's claw. Her face stretched as she did this, outlining her skull. "You try to rob us last night, *chica?*" Hondo asked.

The woman glanced at her small troop. They watched with hollow faces, their eyes fevered and unfocused. They had the look of people with few miles left in them. The woman gave Hondo a frank look.

"Sorry about that," she said. She eyed the wagon's water tank. "Spare any water?" Hondo looked her up and down, head tilted speculatively to one side.

"Shit." He looked from the woman to Brood and back, then his lips stretched over his gums and he rasped out laughter. "Shit," he said again, and turned serious. He pointed his gaze at the small group's water truck—so rusted it looked like it had been dredged from the sea floor. "You out?"

"Just about," the woman said. They eyed each other. A hiss of static came from the Ham in the woman's truck. Wind kicked dust out of the trees. Finally Hondo's dreads swayed as he nodded.

"*Homito.*" He gestured at Brood.

Brood reached into the footlocker, withdrew a jar full of water and tossed it to the woman, who snatched it deftly out of the air. She uncapped it and drank, long and desperate, throat flexing. Paused eventually to breathe, then kept drinking. When the jar was empty she held it up to Hondo, childlike with both hands.

"Got any more?"

"Shit," Hondo mused.

"Shit," Pollo echoed.

They filled a galvanized gallon bucket and gave it to the woman. She gave it to her people. She policed it, making sure no one drank more than their share before passing it on. Her hands trembled as she passed Hondo the empty bucket.

"Thanks, *amigo*," she told him.

"*De nada.*"

"They got any food?" called a boy with a black ponytail. He was Brood's age, maybe a little older.

"Shut up, Raimi," the boy with cornrows told him.

"Billy..." the ponytailed boy started to say, but the cornrowed boy gave him a hard look and he went quiet. The woman stared up at Hondo, held out her hands like she had no cards left to play.

"Well?" she asked. "Can you spare any food?" Hondo's dreads swiveled from side to side.

"I could skin up that dog for you, you want," Brood told her.

The dog, panting at the woman's feet, canted its head to one side as though considering the idea. "That'd get you a few miles at least." The woman went rigid.

"Touch my dog, I'll skin *you*."

"Just a suggestion."

The woman turned to Hondo. Her face softened.

"I'm Anna."

"*Mucho gusto*." Hondo's tone made clear his indifference.

"You could roll with us. We could help each other."

"You mean we could help you," Brood said.

"Where you headed?" Hondo asked.

"Kansas." The woman tilted her head towards the truck's cab, where a distorted voice now squawked from the HAM. "We're going to find the Corn Mother. She's building a permanent colony. Going to recrop the entire state."

"We heard." Hondo gave the woman a sympathetic look. Motioned at the road north. "We heading that way."

"Nothing up that way but snow and more of this…" The woman held up her hands and with a sweeping look took in the surrounding forest, grey and empty.

"They're not levitating," Pollo mused. His eyes came alive— something long sunken rising to the surface—and stared at Brood. "Satori don't carry them."

"You could come with us," the woman insisted. Her eyes, scared now, pleading, pinned Hondo. Hondo shook his head. The woman stepped forward, hands reaching. "Please, *amigo*." Hondo leveled the shotgun at her face.

"Ain't your *pinche amigo*, girl."

"Don't," the girl in the shades called. She sounded tired. Both she and the corn rowed boy raised their rifles.

Everything froze like that. The woman reaching. The mouth of Hondo's shotgun parked the width of a bead of sweat from her nose. Pollo, emergent, staring at Brood.

A gust of wind peppered them with needles of sand. Brood rubbed his eyes. Reached once more inside the footlocker. Produced a jar of pickled radishes. He tossed it to the woman, who caught it tightly in both arms.

"We ain't going with you."

"Please."

Brood cranked the throttle. Hondo staggered as the wagon lurched forward. The woman said something else, but her words evaporated beneath the motor's whine. Brood pulled hard on the tiller, steering the wagon in a wide u-turn and away.

"Please!"

They kept rolling. After a moment came the mosquito buzz of a bullet winging past, followed by a single rifle report. Brood looked back. The woman sat on her knees, the jar cradled close to her chest. Beside her stood the girl in aviator shades, now slowly lowering the rifle from her shoulder. Brood raised his arm, extended his middle finger.

"Ain't floating," Pollo mumbled, his eyes vacant again. He wrapped his arms around himself, bringing the snake close, and began rocking back and forth.

. . . .

The air turned cold that afternoon. White clouds built over the mountains. Brood tasted metal in the wind, then the snow came.

They holed up at the leaning remnants of a gas station. Brood gathered dry-rotted juniper and built a fire in the corner of what had been two walls. He passed around a jar of eggplant, which canned had the consistency of axle grease. They scooped out black globs with their fingers and sucked them. Pollo tried to feed some to his snake, which coiled and rattled.

"You keep that thing away from me, *manito*," Brood told him.

"*Esta bien*, Carlos. He's *friendly*." Pollo held the snake up as though to show Brood its true, benevolent nature. It rattled and struck. Brood flinched and Pollo laughed, eyes bright and fixed on the cracked concrete wall behind Brood's head.

"Ain't kidding," Brood said. "I ever see that thing out of your hands I'm gonna stomp it and eat it raw. *Entiendes?*"

Pollo's face darkened. "No, you ain't. You *good*, homie."

"*Claro.*" Brood looked to Hondo. The old man still wore his flak jacket. He hadn't spoken since they'd put the beleaguered caravan behind them. He sat staring into the fire, the Mossberg cradled upright in his lap, his cheek pressed to its barrel in way that made Brood feel lonely.

"*Por qué tan pensativo, viejo rata?*" he inquired. Hondo kept his eyes on the oscillating firelight.

"Sometimes I pray." He aimed the words at the flames, as though he'd rather they burned up than touch the world. The confession hung in the air. "Those poor motherfuckers," he said after a moment. "Desert going to take them. They going to watch each other die, and ain't nothing none of them can do about it." He spread his hands open on his lap and stared down at the tough leather of his palms. "Didn't used to be like that."

"I pray," Pollo sang. Maybe the boy meant it, maybe he was simply parroting. He'd settled by the fire and now stirred charcoal with spit in his clamshell. As Brood watched, he began etching something with his needle along a bare hipbone. His snake lay coiled in his lap, soaking up heat.

"Momma prayed," Brood said. She'd prayed incessantly at the end. Staring up at the empty white sky, watching day turn into night and back again. Fever had burned through her, beading her skin with sweat and turning it yellow as the Oklahoma hardpan on which she'd lain. Her mouth had been stretched open when Brood had awakened that final morning. Her face wrapped her skull like leather, as though her last breath had pulled taut a thread, drawing her flesh tight as it escaped. She'd bloated in the heat. Her eyes had milked over and flies had covered them. Brood gazed flatly at Hondo in the oscillating firelight. "Can't say as I do, though."

"That shit today," Hondo said. "I'm sick of it." Brood tossed a piece of juniper on the fire and settled in beneath his blanket, using his flak jacket as a pillow. The snow had quit and stars shone through the clouds.

"Ojo Caliente," he said quietly.

"Ojo Caliente," Hondo agreed. Brood closed his eyes, tried to conjure Rosa Lee's face. Instead he recalled the fear in the *gringa's* eyes as they'd rolled away from her. Bitterness gripped him.

"Who the fuck got a *dog?*"

. . . .

The weather had cleared by morning. The air felt clean. The sun warmed Brood's face as they ascended further into bone-picked foothills. Pollo held the snake in his cupped hands and clucked at it happily while Hondo quietly sang old *corridos* at the wagon's bow. If the road held, they'd make Ojo sometime the next morning.

It was afternoon when they smelled the cook fire. The road cut low through a swath of dead juniper between two long, low ridges. They rounded a bend and found two boys sitting beside a fire pit they'd built in the road's center.

They wore red sashes tied over their heads, red splashes on their FEMAs. Hondo swore, made chopping motion with one hand.

"*Alto!*"

Brood killed the throttle, but it was too late. The *Chupes* rose to their feet, faced the wagon. One of them put fingers to his mouth and whistled. The sound pierced the dead forest like a stiletto.

They swarmed over both ridge tops. Thirty-odd *Chupes*, brandishing machetes, iron rock bars, clubs and five or six AK-90s, banana clips curling obscenely forth. They yelled and whooped, red sashes flying. Pollo rose to his feet and moaned. AKs barked, spitting up droughted clay all around the wagon. In seconds, *La Chupes* had surrounded them.

"Kill that fucking motor," one of them ordered. A spindly girl with strings of teardrops tattooed down her cheeks. She eyed Brood down the smoking barrel of an AK. Brood switched off the motor.

Hondo'd stood, but hadn't bothered to grab the Mossberg. He wheezed quiet laughter.

"Fuck you laughing, old man?" Brood asked. Hondo shook his dreads and held up empty hands, black gums gleaming.

"Ojo Caliente," he said, the punch line to a sad joke.

Brood put a hand on Pollo's shoulder. The boy trembled, moaned.

"He hit?" the *Chupe* girl demanded. "Goddamnit, we're supposed to shoot *near* them, not *at* them. Who fucking did that?"

"He ain't hit, *chica*," Brood said. "He just like that." The girl squinted up at Pollo, then at Brood. She pointed at the ground near her feet.

"Come down off there."

Brood looked around at the glowering faces, the eagerly brandished weapons. So many of them.

"How I know you all don't tear us up, we come down there?"

"Don't matter." The girl brought the AK up. "If you don't I'll just shoot your ass. Your choice."

"You ain't supposed to shoot us. You just said."

An AK fired close by, three sharp rounds that sounded like a hammer hitting bone. Everyone jumped. In the stunned silence Brood looked down at himself, to Pollo, to Hondo. Saw no blood.

"Sorry!" called a young boy, maybe eight years old, sunburned and freckled. The AK in his arms made him look tiny. He stared wide-eyed at a furrow the bullets had just plowed into the dirt inches from his feet.

"*Bunny!*" A larger boy stood beside him, clearly his brother. He snatched the AK, thumbed the safety, shoved it back into the smaller boy's chest. "Knew you was too young for a rifle." Bunny seemed about to respond, but fell quiet as a deep voice spoke from behind the *Chupes* crowding the wagon.

"Get off the fucking wagon." A big *Chupe* moved forward through the other gang members pressing around the wagon. He stepped gingerly, wincing each time his sandals touched the dirt. A makeshift rope sling bound his left arm close to his left side, where on his bare chest a spot of blood stained a fresh white bandage.

Brood recognized high Indian cheekbones, burn-mottled lips. Fear twisted in his guts.

"*Hola*, Richard," he said. A name he'd last spoken when the

Chupe had lain trembling on the warehouse floor in Amarillo, Brood's aluminum arrow protruding from his chest. Brood figured first names were no longer appropriate, since the boy was no longer about to die. "*Hijo de puta,*" he amended.

Richard's head bowed in greeting. "Bitches."

"Fuck'd you find us?"

Richard's eyes narrowed. A shrewd smile curled misshapen lips. "You told me. Got some Tewa friends up north."

Brood digested this for a second, then clenched his teeth and let out a long hiss. Richard's smile broadened.

"No worries, *homito,*" Hondo said.

Brood shook his head. "Never seen anybody live through something like that." Richard's smile faded. His jaw tightened.

"Wasn't what I'd call easy. Or pleasant." He beckoned with his good arm. "Get down off that fucking truck, or I let these boys climb up there and chop you all to pieces."

"It's a wagon," Pollo corrected, then began once more to moan, an empty sound that reminded Brood of a dead Ham station. Disconnected.

"Do it," Hondo said. He hopped off the wagon, and stood before Richard, looking up into the big boy's face. Brood cursed, and climbed down. Pollo followed. Richard leaned forward, put his face close to Hondo's.

"I got one question for you, old man. I think you know what it is."

Hondo didn't hesitate. "Water tank." Richard's eyes moved languidly to the tank, then to the small freckled boy with the AK.

"Bunny, you ever want to touch that rifle again, you get your ass up there and see if my seed's in that tank." Richard moved close to Brood. Slipped his good arm around the small of Brood's back, found the bone hilt of the hooked blade. Pulled it free and held it up, smiling as he inspected it. "Looks familiar."

Bunny slung the AK over his back and climbed nimbly atop the wagon. He unscrewed the tank's lid and stood on tiptoe to peer inside. His eyes widened; his mouth formed a black circle.

"Goddamn!"

"Watch your mouth, Bunny," his brother scowled.

"That mean it's there, Bunny?" Richard inquired mildly.

"Fucking hell," Bunny affirmed.

"*Bunny!*" his brother growled.

"Good." Richard stared down into Brood's face. "Take off your sandals." He waved Brood's blade at Hondo's feet, then Pollo's. "You two. Sandals."

Brood felt suddenly cold. He squinted in the sun, glanced around at the dead junipers, felt their silence. Knew his body would rot slowly here, uselessly, because there were no scavengers to feed on him. It made him strangely sad. He kicked off his sandals.

"I had a son," Hondo said.

Brood blinked. "You never said nothing."

"Nothing to say." Hondo eloquently lifted one shoulder. "Didn't like him much. He was lazy. Real stupid, too. Made me sad. *Me daba verguenza*, like I couldn't believe he came from me, you know? I was real mean to him."

"Sandals," Richard repeated. Hondo kept his eyes on Brood.

"Wish he'd been like you, *mijo*."

"That's real nice." Richard smiled and nodded like everything was good. Like he had patience to the moon. He pointed the blade at Hondo's nose and spoke slowly. "Take off your goddamn sandals, old man."

Hondo glanced down at his feet, pursed his lips as though considering. Then squared shoulders, pushed dreads back with a palm and looked calmly at Richard.

"No, young *puto*, you ain't getting my sandals."

Richard glanced around at his *Chupes*, then tilted his head to the side and gave Hondo a beseeching look. Hondo stared back, intractable.

"Alright," Richard said. He stepped back, slid Brood's blade into the waist of his torn denim pants. Then snapped fingers and pointed at Hondo.

Hondo's head whipped to one side like he'd been slapped. It spit red mist. He dropped like a sodden rag. Blood pooled instantly on hard clay around limp dreads. Brood saw something white, thought it was skin, then realized it was *inside* Hondo's skull. Bunny's older brother peered over his AK's sights, smirking as he admired his work, the crack of his AK still reverberating in the inert desert air. Bunny cussed appreciatively.

Pollo went quiet. A spatter of blood the shape of a bird covered his cheek. Brood watched his own hand slowly rise, watched his thumb wipe the blood from his brother's face.

"Bacilio," he whispered

"Get his fucking sandals," Richard ordered. Hondo's body jerked as the *Chupe* girl with the teardrop tats knelt and yanked his sandals free. Richard took a step towards Pollo, who had wrapped tattooed arms around himself and now trembled. "What's wrong with him?"

"Please," Brood whispered.

"He got Tet." Richard withdrew the blade once more, placed it gently under Pollo's chin and lifted the boy's face.

"No," Brood pleaded. His hands shook at his sides. He noted with strange detachment that he couldn't feel his own skin. "Told you back in Amarillo, homie. He just like that." Richard squinted at Pollo down the length of his arm. His face went sour with distaste.

"Nah, he got Tet. We're taking him." He motioned to the teardrop girl, from whose hand Hondo's sandals now dangled. "Tie him up. Get him on the wagon."

Brood lunged.

His fist found the wound on Richard's chest. His teeth found skin, tasted hot blood. Richard screamed and the two of them went down, Brood on top. He sat up, rained down punches. Richard's hands pressed against his face. Brood snapped his teeth at them. Something hit his back. He snarled, bit down on a finger. Something hit his head—the world exploded, *La Chupe* red.

He found himself on his back. Richard stood over him. Pain distorted the big *Chupe's* face. He held the hand of his bad arm to his neck, which trickled blood. In his other hand he held a small pistol. He glowered at Brood, brought the pistol up, fired.

Brood felt a thunderclap inside his body. Felt like he'd been ripped in two. Pollo cried out, an unwavering howl as though he'd just burst into flames.

"Jesus, would somebody shut him up?"

Breath refused to come. Richard turned and walked out of sight. Pollo's squeals muted as someone covered his mouth. The wagon's motor spooled up, whined high as some *La Chupe* cranked the throttle too hard, then faded, tires crunching over the cracked earth, back the way Brood, Hondo and Pollo had come. With it receded the pitiful sound of Pollo's wail. Rage filled Brood for an instant. Then pain buried him, localized now to his left side. His body curled involuntarily around it.

The *Chupes* dispersed, chuckling. All except Richard, whose face reappeared overhead.

"Does it hurt?"

Brood tried to speak, couldn't. He nodded. Richard winced, whether at Brood's pain or his own, Brood couldn't tell. He held something up for Brood to see: the hooked blade. It winked white in the sunlight.

"You want me to take care of it?"

Brood wondered how bad it was to die of thirst, then figured he'd bleed out long before that happened. He hesitated. Then shook his head.

"Alright then." Richard nodded once, a score settled, then turned and disappeared. Brood listened to his footsteps fade.

A few minutes later came the hum of a quiet motor. A shadow passed briefly overhead. A small zep, its side marked by smeared red paint, the letters LC. Then it, too, disappeared, and Brood knew only pain, the sound of his own labored breathing, the infinite blue of New Mexico sky.

CHAPTER 8

Sumedha watched the tattoo—a black cobra winding up Snake's sternum between etched ribs—and wondered why a boy who had never seen a cobra would adopt it as his personal totem. Why, indeed, did people adopt totems at all?

"*La Chupes* bringing in tons of Tet bitches." Snake waved his arms effusively when he spoke, in a way that seemed to have nothing to do with the rhythms of his speech. Sumedha kept a step between them as they walked the mud path between rows of newly constructed chain link pens.

The stench of dysentery and rotting meat assailed him. He stepped gingerly on bare feet, holding aloft the hem of his white shift, lest muck and filth stain it—the crude stuff of the world outside Satori's clean, smooth flesh.

"More'n Snake can house," Snake informed him, his voice high, not yet pubescent. He flicked a manic hand at the bodies. They packed the pens, some stiff with the Tet, others stiff with rigor mortis. Some, those yet to fully succumb to the Tet's grip, leaned against the chain link and watched with despondent eyes as Sumedha and Snake passed, trailed by the Designer's entourage:

six muscled Satori landraces, plus six riot-clad security, wild-born humans with military resumes.

Snake shielded his eyes from the late winter sun and motioned at a long row of collapsing steel-and-brick buildings a few hundred meters beyond what had once been a park—a park now covered by mud huts, corrugated tin shanties, a few tiny vegetable gardens, trucks sprouting solar panels and wind turbines at strange, makeshift angles. Yellow-FEMA'd migrants filled the squat. They sat around small fires, stewed rats and dogs together with Satori vegetables. Toyed with old radios, or simply lay there, too hungry and sick to move. Every so often they cast their faces towards Satori's dome, as though waiting for it to awaken. It loomed over them, still patchy with late-winter fur, covering the whole of old downtown Denver. Perhaps, Sumedha mused, they hoped it would excrete seed straight from its pores. Snake motioned around them at the pens.

"Haven't been able to keep 'em all in there since three weeks ago. They bringing more in every day. Look." A multi-axle truck, emitting a bad grind noise, had just limped around a corner of the park. "They got a bad CV joint," Snake observed.

The truck made its way towards them, towing a long trailer built high with rough-hewn boards. A cage on wheels. Faces peered out from between wooden slats. Sumedha turned to face his entourage.

"Bring carts," he ordered the landraces. "Sort through the pens. Take the dead inside the dome and give them to Satori." In unison, the landraces nodded and took off at a stiff jog, heavy shoulders rolling. A seam formed in the pink skin of Satori's outer wall as they approached. Bone framework shifting, joints articulating, popping as the seam split and spread open before them. They entered and the gate sealed shut behind them.

"Snake gotta joke for you." The boy tapped Sumedha's shoulder with the back of his hand and winked, making a tiny star tattoo dance beneath one eye. "You know what the worst thing about fucking a girl with the Tet is?" Sumedha stared blankly into Snake's face.

"No."

"She stiffer than you are. You know what the best thing is?"

"No."

"When you done you can stick tires on her and use her as a wagon."

Snake grinned. Sumedha stared. Someone in one of the pens coughed. Snake's smile faded. His shoulders sagged slightly.

"Never mind," he said. One of Sumedha's security detail snickered behind a black riot mask.

"This is completely unacceptable," Sumedha said. Now it was Snake who stared. Sumedha pointed at the pens. "These people need shelter."

"Why? They got the Tet. They dying."

"Yes. But I need them to die of the Tet. Not dysentery. Not pneumonia. Do you understand?"

"What's the difference?" Snake spread his palms in incomprehension. "Dead be dead."

Sumedha closed his eyes, breathed. Snake's helix spread open to his mind. Sumedha ticked his awareness along the switches, sensing the shape of the boy's future. It wasn't much. A suspect heart valve. A high probability for childhood stress to express itself as lymphoma. Sumedha opened his eyes, noted for the first time the slight but unmistakable grey tint to Snake's skin: heavy metal poisoning. Snake's immune system would crater long before any cancer presented. Sumedha spoke slowly.

"What if one of these people survived the Tet, but died of parasites, or exposure?"

"Then they be fucking dead," Snake insisted. He crossed arms over the reared cobra head on his chest. "My point being."

"Yes, but then I would not *know* if someone survived the Tet."

The truck had backed its trailer up to a pen and now four boys, tattooed, malnourished and wearing red *La Chupe* sashes stood around, eyeing Snake, Sumedha, the security detail. Snake stared sidelong at the Designer, then held up a hand, palm forward as though to stop time.

"Hold on a sec. Snake gotta deal with these boys." He turned and stalked though the muck to the trailer. Pressed his face to the slats and squinted inside. "How many live ones you got?" he asked one *La Chupe*. The *Chupe's* chest puffed with primate bluster, which Sumedha took to mean he was about to lie.

"All of them," he claimed. He leaned awkwardly on his left leg, hips strangely canted. Sumedha projected himself along the *Chupe's* helix, saw genetic cratering brought on by malnutrition—felt pity, disgust.

"Shit," Snake said. "I ain't blind. Half of them bloating."

The *Chupe* glared at Snake. Snake glared back, unbending. It fascinated Sumedha. Two complicated mammals reading in one another the signals of dominance, understanding only the summation. Finally the lopsided *Chupe* deflated.

"Half then. I'm guessing ten."

"Fine," Snake told him. A man inside the trailer cursed and spat.

"You can't sell me! I'm not some piece of meat, boy!"

Snake ignored him. He pulled a pencil and pad of paper from somewhere down the front of his topless FEMAs and wrote on it.

"You boys unload your live ones into that pen right there," he said, pointing with the pencil. "Keep the corpses. They your problem." He ripped the page from the notebook and handed it to the *Chupe*. "Take this to Juice over in front of that building you just drove past. He give you your seed."

"Your mother's a whore!" the man in the trailer cried. Snake smiled at him. The star tat danced as he winked.

"That she was."

Satori's exterior wall flexed open once more with the snapping of bone-and-cartilage framework readjusting. Sumedha's landraces reemerged with a score of their muscled brethren, towing bone carts. They began rooting through the pens. In pairs they dragged out bodies, heaved them onto the carts while Sumedha and Snake looked on. When they'd filled the carts, they towed them back through the outer wall.

"Satori fed these people," Sumedha mused. "Now they feed Satori." The symmetry pleased him. Snake stared, said nothing.

The *Chupes* had finished herding their stiff-legged Tet captives into Snake's pens. A metallic whine came from their truck as its motor spooled up. It ground slowly away, then halted and quit, apparently broken down. Sumedha gestured at the pens which, occupied now by only the living, seemed spare and empty.

"These people need better shelter."

"It was your people built these cages," Snake protested. "You tell me where to put them, that's where Snake'll put them." Sumedha spread his arms, indicating an entire edifice of brick and steel, the edge of old downtown, which Satori's dome had not subsumed.

"You need not limit yourself to one building. You may use—"

White light coruscated through Sumedha's mind. He sensed impact, pressure squeezing every cell in his body. Gravity disappeared. The earth itself screamed.

Satori's dome turned upside down, a pink flesh egg resting on soft blue sky. A security guard flew past it, limbs flung wide.

A helix rose in Sumedha's mind. His own. It hung there, separated from him, glowing, then flew apart before a wall of fire.

Everything went still. Sumedha thought perhaps he rested, nascent in an amniotic sack deep in Satori's womb, ready to be born. Pihadassa would be there awaiting him, newborn, her skin glistening with amniotic fluid.

Muffled voices came to him. His body shifted painfully. Daylight crashed into his head.

"You alright?" A riot mask hovered over him. The security guard's gloved hand pawed Sumedha's bones. The helix reformed in Sumedha's mind. It sank into his body. He breathed deep. Everything hurt.

"Are you injured?" The guard's hand probed.

Other members of his security team stood over him now. He smelled their pheromones. Fear, mixed with an always present revulsion for Sumedha. He didn't mind. They couldn't help their aversion. They were animals, the crude produce of nature's raw hand, and he was strange to them. They did their job, and they were well fed for it.

"I have no significant injuries," he told them.

He pushed the hand away and tried to sit up. Weight held him down. He shoved, realizing it was the body of one of his security team. A piece of two-by-four the length of Sumedha's arm protruded through the soy epoxy armor on the man's back—a piece of the trailer.

"Holy fuck!" Snake walked up, eyes wide. Dirt caked him, pressed deep into his pours. Blood trickled from a cut on his head. He motioned at the truck and trailer, now nothing more than a twisted hunk of chassis and splintered wood from which flames rose. Bodies lay in a ring around it like scorched flower pedals. "You fucking see that?" He poked the impaled security guard with a toe. "Holy fuck!" The rest of the security team coalesced around Sumedha, their riot masks pivoting vigilantly.

"Time to get the Designer home," one of them commanded. A woman. Terse, in control. The others took hold of Sumedha's arms.

"Stop," Sumedha ordered. They hesitated. "Let go of me. I am not finished here."

Reluctantly, they unhanded him. He shoved the body off his chest and sat up. Mud and excrement covered his shift, and something else. Charred flesh.

Sumedha rose, stepped forward, grabbed Snake by the chin.

"Focus. I need your mind present in this moment. Are you with me?" Snake blinked, nodded. "Good. I want these people housed. I want their deaths documented. I want every symptom listed. That is why they are here. Do you understand?" Again Snake nodded. "Good. Whatever you need to make this happen, you will have." Sumedha turned to the nearest Satori landrace, who stood gaping over the smoking body of what was probably his partner. "You," Sumedha commanded. "Get back to work. Round up more landraces. Clear the dead from the pens first. Then clean this up." He motioned at the bodies and mangled pens surrounding the crater. The landrace let out a long, low moan, then chuffed and nodded. Sumedha nodded to his security detail.

"Now we may go. I have work inside."

. . . .

"Will it hurt?" The girl stood naked, knees together, arms crossed tight over her breasts. She trembled, completely hairless, her skin almost as pale as the biolumes glowing opalescent within the ovular room's flesh.

"It will." Sumedha did not look up as he spoke. He stood at the room's center beside a long bone table, atop which lay a meaty cocoon the wormy color of viscera. He pulled up the sleeve of the fresh shift he had donned. Pushed a hand through a slit at the cocoon's end. Fished around inside, felt the nipple tip of the gland at the cocoon's center, and massaged it. The cocoon flexed intestinally around his arm. When he withdrew his hand, viscous yellow liquid covered a forefinger. His gaze fixed on the girl. "How do you feel?"

"I do not want it to hurt."

"It is inevitable. The retrovirus will affix itself to your cell nuclei. If the splice works, you will begin to change on a cellular level. There will be pain. It will last for perhaps two or three days." He watched her for a few seconds, searching for viral symptoms. "How do you feel?" he repeated.

"Cold."

"That is fine. Do you have any aches? Any nausea?"

The girl shook her head. Then asked, "Will it kill me?"

Sumedha considered for a moment. Overhead hung five glistening amniotic sacks, red as the back of an eyeball. Just three months ago the girl had been no more than a microscopic nub of splitting cells floating in such a womb.

"Your predecessors presented with problems," he said. Flipper arms, scoliosis, progeria, swollen hearts. "They did not survive. But you have developed more rapidly." In the past week her hips had widened. Her face had taken on an adult angularity. "The indications thus far are that you are a more stable platform. And this is a new version of the graft." The form the helix had taken in his dream pulsed in Sumedha's mind. "It contains a protein that will respond only to direct environmental stimuli. This should avert previous problems of cascading mutability. I am optimistic you will survive."

He moved forward, proffering his wet fingertip. The girl watched with wide dark eyes, shook her head, retreated until her back pressed into the wall's soft meat.

"I do not want it to hurt."

Sumedha noted her fear, and smiled. The helix never failed to surprise.

"Your situational comprehension far exceeds expectations. Your brain has solid neurological cohesion despite your rapid growth. I am indeed optimistic." He leveled his finger at her face. "Open your mouth." The girl stared at the cocoon's yellow bile. Her face registered disgust. She clenched her jaws shut. "Open," Sumedha commanded. The girl mutely shook her head.

The walls vibrated suddenly, a warm but insistent hum. Satori spoke.

"Sumedha." Pihadassa's smooth voice. "The Fathers wish to see you."

Sumedha closed his eyes, pleasure spreading through his mind. A hot vortex of longing opened inside his chest as the last vibrations of his partner's voice faded. He breathed until the feeling passed. When he opened his eyes, the walls, which had gone briefly, intensely violet, were turning pale once more. The girl trembled before him.

"I will only be a moment longer, Satori," he informed the room. "But first I need a steady table, please."

Immediately, a section of floor stretched hard and flat. It rose beside the girl, snapping and popping as bone framework articulated into place.

"A little lower," Sumedha told it. It settled slightly. "Good." He motioned to the girl with the mucused finger. "You will take this. Step forward, please." She did so. "Good. Lean across the table." The girl hesitated, then lay face down on the table. "Restraints, please." A pair of digits rose out of the table and wrapped themselves like an enormous thumb and forefinger around the girl, and squeezed. The girl cried out. "Not so tight," Sumedha said.

They loosened; she quieted. Sumedha moved around the table until he stood directly over her. "Relax," he told her. With one hand pushed open her rump. "Relax." He slid the mucused finger sharply into her rectum. She grunted, whimpered. Sumedha waited, breathing, two helixes turning in his mind. The girl and the retrovirus. Slowly, warmly, they merged.

When he'd finished, he crossed the room and inserted hands into a small opening in the wall, shaped like a bowl. Thick saliva poured over them, cleansing.

"It hurts." The girl squirmed against the restraints.

"Hold still. You will expel the retrovirus before your system absorbs it." The wall began to undulate, tonguing Sumedha's hands dry. "Only another moment." He withdrew his hands, placed a palm against the wall and closed his eyes. His heart rate slowed, syncing with Satori's. He counted ten slow beats, then said, "Release," and opened his eyes. The restraints retracted and the girl stood. Sumedha looked her up and down, wondering vaguely if the splice would crack her bones, buckle her organs, force her immune system to implode and begin devouring her. For the moment, she looked healthy. "Assistant," he called. A door stretched open in one wall, revealing an ovular hallway. A thick-shouldered landrace stood there, naked and grunting quietly with each patient breath. "Take her back to her pod," Sumedha ordered. The assistant nodded, entered the room, gripped the girl by the arm. "I'll monitor you periodically for the next few days, girl." He stepped towards the door.

"Minerva," she said. Sumedha hesitated, turned.

"What did you say?"

The girl gazed at her feet. She spoke quietly.

"My name is Minerva."

"You...have a *name?* Who gave you a name, girl?"

"Pihadassa."

Sumedha's mind tilted inside his skull.

Pihadassa. Sister. Wife. Sumedha had often puzzled over the primate pair bond. He had toyed on occasion with trying to isolate and eliminate it, but found it too entwined with innumerable other evolutionary functions. Social structures, hierarchies. Tweaking the pair bond sent ripples through the entire group organism, where the effects became too complex to predict. Better to work with it.

The Fathers had reached the same conclusion. Had created him as half of a unit. He touched the wall once more, felt Satori's slow, strong heartbeat—one for every five of his own. Together he and Pihadassa had been part of Satori. Now…Sumedha was less so. Longing coursed through his chest, the need to connect. He reached out his mind, tried to bring the entire city, throbbing with life, inside himself. He could not.

The walls hummed again.

"Sumedha, the Fathers wish for you to join them now," Pihadassa told him. No, not Pihadassa. *Satori.* Sumedha pressed palms hard against his eyes. An animal sound escaped from his throat. He took a breath, stood upright, saw the girl and assistant both watching. The assistant chuffed, agitated. Sumedha faced the girl.

"When did she talk to you?" he demanded. "Where?"

"She came to my pod," the girl said, backpedalling.

"I see. What did she tell you?"

"She gave me my name. She said it was a wise name."

Sumedha said nothing for a moment. He breathed, letting his heart slow. The landrace grunted impatiently. Sumedha leveled a finger at it.

"You be still." To the girl he said, "She told you more." The girl's face creased with fear. She looked at the floor, where her bare white feet sank into spongy snake scale, and shook her head.

"No."

"You should barely be able to follow simple directions. And yet you know to lie." Sumedha slowly shook his head, marveling. "The helix dances." Its beauty calmed him.

"I do not want you to hurt me," the girl whimpered. Sumedha moved close, took the girl's face in his hand and forced her to look up at him.

"Tell me what Pihadassa told you, girl."

"Minerva." A current of defiance ran beneath the fear in the girl's voice.

"Minerva." Sumedha said it slowly, trying out the sound of it. "You have identity attachment. This is very good." He let his hand slide down her throat. Settled thumb and forefinger on the nerves behind her jaw, and squeezed. The girl mewled. Her pulse quickened under Sumedha's palm. "Tell me what she told you."

"She said she will have a child."

Sumedha released the girl. His mind brought forth the memory of Pihadassa emerging from her bed, her body languid with sleep.

"I want to have a child," she had said. Then touched her lips to his head, and mounted him. Their day had begun as it was meant to—joined—and it was as though she had said nothing, simply whispered dream noise.

But she had said it, and meant for him to hear it. A seed planted.

The girl started to say something, then cried out. She doubled over, wrapped arms over her stomach.

"It hurts," she gasped.

"The graft is taking effect." Sumedha addressed the assistant. "Take her to her pod." The assistant grunted obediently, took the girl under the shoulders and ushered her towards the wall. It flexed open before them. "I will check on you shortly," Sumedha told her. Then, as the landrace hustled the girl out of the room and the door began to shrink behind them, he called: "Do not worry." Immediately, he wondered why.

The walls hummed once more.

"Sumedha," spoke Pihadassa's voice. "The Fathers demand you cease whatever you are doing and join them at once."

"Satori, inform the Fathers I will be there momentarily."

. . . .

Sumedha counted his steps. Four times four across the blood-hued Temple floor. His mind touched each number with the same pressure as his foot touching cold flagstone.

Strange objects stood station across the Temple's empty space.

An ancient, fat motorcycle, polished red. An ornately worked leather saddle with silver pommel. A square bed the size of Sumedha's entire abode, piled with silken pillows. A worn leather chair, beside it a standing brass lamp with green glass shade. Artifacts from the Fathers' lives, totems to what it had once meant to be human. Sunlight filtered incarnadine through the dome's flesh, spilled ambient through granite-arched plexi windows twice the height of a man. A stuffed hunting dog, a Labrador, seemed alive in that light, poised as Sumedha stepped past it.

He reached the Temple's center. Took his station there at one point of a four-pronged star lazed black into the floor. Kassapa and Paduma had already taken up their positions, Paduma at the star tip to Sumedha's left, Kassapa directly opposite. They wore white shifts. In unison, they nodded their greeting. Sumedha nodded and together they silently waited, breathing—totaling three.

Sumedha's mind, unbidden, touched the number: *four.*

Four was a balanced number. The vacant star point to his right felt like a distortion in the fabric of things. Pihadassa's station. It bent around his mind like a helix missing code, a puzzle whose pieces he could not move: *three.* Sumedha reached out, touched his mind to his siblings'. Sensed their mute tension, as though the air between them had changed shape. They were three. An imbalanced number.

"Sumedha."

The voice came from everywhere, four harmonized layers. The song that breathed life into the universe, the sound of the world's own beating heart. Sumedha bowed deep, every nerve afire with fear and love. Reverence hushed his voice:

"Fathers."

They hung high overhead at the center of the Temple's vaulted marble ceiling, the very top of Satori Tower. Four amniotic sacks attached to thick umbilicals. Occasionally one sack or another gurgled, and Sumedha could see the outline of a limb or torso as an atrophied body shifted within.

"You've made us wait." The voice said.

"I apologize, Fathers." Sumedha took a meditative breath, let his heart rate drop, smoothed the tremor from his voice. "I came as quickly as I could."

A Father shifted overhead, a pod gurgled. Sumedha waited, listening for the quiet rush of Satori's metabolism. He could hear it, barely. Intestines, veins, nerves running behind the dead materials of the Temple's old-world facade, pumping life and information into the Fathers' bodies.

"We've waited." The Fathers' voice pitched up. "Too long."

"Yes, Fa—"

"Results!" Plexi windows shook. Sumedha fell to his knees. The voice softened. "Poor child," it cooed. "Shh, poor. Frightened… Stand, child." Sumedha hesitated, then rose. "The bomb. Were you injured, Sumedha? Poor child?"

"No, Fathers."

"You were…the target?"

"I do not believe I was directly targeted, Fathers."

"Fathers," Kassapa said. He bowed until the silence implied permission for him to continue. "My people tell me the bomb was meant to breach the outer wall. The wild-born posing as members of the *La Chupacabra* organization intended to try and gain access to seed. The bomb malfunctioned and detonated early, killing all those involved in the attempt."

"Sumedha," the Fathers said after a few beats of silence. "Why do you make us wait?"

Sumedha sensed Kassapa's eyes, knew his brother's mind—bent always on Satori's security. He worked the puzzle of Pihadassa's defection. How could Sumedha not have known?

Sumedha breathed. Sensation played through his body, as immediate and fleeting as weather. Guilt, fear, anger.

"I was at a critical moment in my work, Fathers," he explained.

"Your work." A moan resonated through the Temple. "So slow."

"It is slow work, Fathers. The helix dances unpredictably."

"The helix…" The words trailed off into a long chord, as though the Fathers had decided to contemplate their own voice. It went on, grew louder until it reverberated, rattling the windows, filling Sumedha's skull like a cosmic event. Sumedha counted heartbeats, had reached thirty-four when the voices began to warble. Their harmony shattered, became an animal squeal, then ceased. Sumedha glanced to Kassapa and Paduma. Saw his siblings' faces gone brittle with fear. From the silence, a single voice emerged:

"Shit."

Sumedha had not heard the Fathers' voices singly since before he had been born. Individually, they had whispered things to him in the womb. Imprinted their minds on his in limbic dream he had known before birth. He had always loved them. He recognized the voice of Father Bill, the Father who had brought Satori into being.

"Doped up retard in a wheelchair would work faster'n you, boy." Pain, or something like it, warped Father Bill's voice, distended its vowels. Sumedha parsed the phrase for meaning, found none, so simply bowed.

"Father."

"Your analogy's…lost." Father David, Bill's brother. His voice, too, sounded the result of great labor.

"Yours especially, Bill." Father Prekash, the one who had created Sumedha and his twins.

"That's what makes them…such damn good company." Father Bill's words trailed off in a long wail. A pod overhead bubbled and shook. "Fucking…Buddhist lemmings."

"Told you." Father Prekash's voice strained through the words. "*Buddhian*. Methodology. No religious—"

"Christ. Hurts my soul listening to you." A baleful hiss sounded through the Temple. "*Years!* Prekash. Prick. Ass."

A long silence ensued. The amniotic sacks overhead stretched as the insectoid outlines of the Fathers' bodies twisted within.

Pihadassa's absence pulled like a vortex at Sumedha's attention, drawing it to the empty star point where she should have stood. Nearby, the stuffed yellow Labrador also seemed to regard the spot, its glass eyes empty with melancholy, its pink tongue lolling, frozen on the verge of a yearning howl…

Sumedha caught himself. Breathed, closed his eyes, concentrated on his sudden urge to anthropomorphize. No, he decided, simply to externalize. He opened his eyes, saw Kassapa watching him, unblinking, calm as a mirror. The serene antithesis to Sumedha's turmoil. Sumedha nodded. Detected something hard in his brother's smile.

The Fathers began to vocalize once more, the bent sounds of animals achieving sentience. The voices coalesced, harmonized.

"Sumedha."

"Yes, Fathers."

"Results. Tell us."

Sumedha bowed once more. His mind travelled the unspeakably difficult puzzle of random genetic variance.

"A genetic configuration should exist naturally," he said, "that is stable enough to maintain organism identity when combined with a splice causing heightened adaptability. It is a statistical inevitability, given a large enough population."

"Crop Graft 3," groaned the Fathers.

"Yes, Fathers. It should reveal in the consuming population those who hold the markers we seek. Thus far it has yielded no results."

Another moan filled the Temple.

"How will you know? When there are results?"

"Anyone with the proper genetic configuration who contracts the graft will survive," Sumedha said simply.

"Results!"

Sumedha hesitated. Kassapa met his eye, waiting.

"I have concluded, Fathers, that the configuration is less common than first thought. We have increased our sample size this year by incorporating the graft into a larger percentage of seed."

"How much?" The question echoed through the chamber.

"This year, all of it."

"Good." The pods overhead shook as the bodies within spasmed. "Years. *Years!*"

Empathy washed over Sumedha. He closed his eyes, imagined the Fathers' pods lying on the Temple floor before him where he could stroke them under his palms, shush them, comfort them. He breathed. The sensation passed. He opened his eyes and spoke.

"Fathers. In the event that a stable configuration does not present itself in the wild-born population, I have begun building one from scratch."

"Results!"

"She is my fifth attempt." Sumedha recalled fear in the girl's eyes, her attachment to the name Pihadassa had given her. "She has developed more rapidly than I expected, but I believe her quick development indicates stability. I am also testing a new version of the graft on her." To his left, Paduma tensed. Sumedha saw her pupils widen, sensed her heart quicken. "I am optimistic."

"How long?"

"Soon. Two days for preliminary indications. Gauging the long-term effects will take much longer."

"How...*long!*"

"Only a few months longer, Fathers."

The Fathers let out another low chord. Soon its harmony shattered.

"I want," Father Bill hissed. Overhead appeared the outline of a hand against pod membrane. It pressed outward, skeletal, clutching. "I want...*Out.*"

....

Back in his abode, Sumedha stripped off his shift and stood before the undulating window, watching the city. Walls everywhere had begun to molt in the late February heat. A breeze blew through the dome's open flaps, pimpling the city's rosy new flesh with goose bumps. Fur drifted like black cotton down to the streets, where far below Satori's landraces, its children, worked, bent behind push brooms, sweeping the fur into floppy cartilage buckets.

Pihadassa had loved the shedding. An animal release, she'd called it, the moment when the city was most alive. Sumedha turned from the window.

"Lotus," he said, and a flat mound blossomed from the floor. He settled himself into its fur, bringing his feet up onto his thighs. He meditated.

"Satori," he said after a time.

"Yes, Sumedha?" answered Pihadassa's voice.

"Explain the phrase, 'doped up retard in a wheelchair.'"

"I am sorry, Sumedha. I do not understand the phrase."

"Neither do I." He opened his eyes, stood and began to pace. "Satori."

"Yes, Sumedha?"

"Tell me about lemmings."

"Lemmings were small rodents, found usually in the Arctic, in tundra biomes. They are subniveal animals, and together with voles and muskrats, make up the subfamily Arvicolinae…" When Satori had finished, Sumedha sat on his fur stool, thinking.

"I do not understand," he concluded. He recrossed his feet and resumed his mediation. "Satori," he said after a time.

"Yes, Sumedha?"

"I love you."

CHAPTER 9

Titanium strutwork the size of a small city shrieked in sudden wind sheer as Doss nosed the zep down hard beneath the roiling press of a derecho that moved in from the west. She toggled the heads-up display to the sat map.

"We should be there." She watched as the white dot representing the zep blinked towards the center of the Fort Riley Military Reservation, a red blob in the upper half of a larger, rectangular blob labeled "Kansas."

"Elections," Fiorivani said. He sat beside Doss in the zep's co-pilot seat, fatigue-clad knees rising like camouflaged mountain peaks on either side of the half-wheel yoke. "You imagine that shit? Fucking mudfish making decisions?" His mouth soured with distaste.

"This country was all about the vote before '72, homie," Sergeant Gomez told him. The sergeant huddled behind Fiorivani in the zep's nav/gunner seat, cradling a blue plastic sandbox bucket in both arms as though it were something precious. "Emergency Climate Act of '72 suspended all elections. Supposed to be temporary." The zep bucked in the wind and Gomez leaned his face close to the bucket. Almost casually, he wretched. "Motherfucking democracy," he said, a tendril of bile dangling from his bottom lip.

Two black-helmeted guards had produced Gomez the previous morning. They'd kicked him—shackled ankle and foot and wearing a yellow prison jumpsuit—from the back of a stockade truck onto the cold tarmac of the D.C. airfield. They'd handed Doss a release form to sign, cautiously unlocked Gomez's cuffs, then climbed back into their truck with the air of having unburdened themselves profoundly.

"Temporary," Fiorivani scoffed. He craned his head over one big shoulder to peer at the sergeant. "I prefer it this way. Stable, you know?"

Gomez said nothing. Doss met his gaze sidelong and he smiled, a fake diamond flashing in one tooth. His cheek curled around a deep scar: a wound Doss had watched him take in Iran when he'd tried to toss a Chinese grenade back in the direction from which it had come. It had exploded a foot from his face.

"Stable's stable, I guess," he said finally. In the fingers of one hand he clutched a worry bracelet, a leather thong threaded through small bones, which Doss happened to know were human finger bones. Sudden turbulence shook the zep and Gomez put his face once more to the bucket and wretched.

"Looks mean, Colonel." Fiorivani leaned forward, peered through the windscreen the way a child would, both hands pressed to the glass, watching the black wall of oncoming thunderhead. A new lieutenant's bar gleamed on the collar of his pressed fatigues.

"You got anything, Gomez?" Doss asked over her shoulder.

"No beacons, Boss."

The yoke vibrated in Doss' hands. She squinted again at the glowing heads-up, then out at the prairie dusk, which had abruptly turned to night beneath the storm.

"We should be there."

White light flashed close, blinding. Fiorivani laughed.

"Never seen lightning so close."

"That ain't lightning," Gomez said. "That's anti-AC fire."

Another flash. "See? Tracers." Doss cursed.

"Charge up the RAM, Gomez."

Gomez set the plastic bucket carefully on the plate-steel deck and began punching buttons on the gunner console, his face glowing demonic in the instrument panel's red lume. A heavy clunk sounded through the floor plates as the rail gun on the zep's belly came online and began to swivel, searching for targets. Doss put the headset to her ear and began shouting codes into the mic. More tracers flashed, closer this time.

"They aren't very good," Fiorivani observed. "How hard can it be to hit this whale?"

"Zero on the source," Doss told Gomez. "Aim thirty-five degrees off. Fire when ready."

Gomez immediately thumbed a red button. An electric sizzle filled the cabin as the RAM spooled up. Then came a tearing sound as the gun spit a needle of depleted uranium the size of a small suitcase out into the Kansas darkness at seven times the speed of sound. A white sun rose instantly off the prairie floor a few kilometers away, searing Doss' retinas. Before she looked away she saw the rounded concrete hummocks of tornado-proofed hangars and out buildings, concrete strangely naked in the harsh blast light: Fort Riley. The storm overhead, abruptly illuminated, churned like flame.

The anti-AC fire ceased. Voices shouted frantically through Doss' earpiece. She smiled.

"That did the trick." She put her mouth to the mic. "Riley, this is Army Exec flight one. Clear my flight path. Elvis wants in to Graceland."

. . . .

"I'm sorry for firing on you," General Lewis said. They'd settled at the end of a long table row in an olive drab cafeteria deep beneath Riley's surface. A prairie saint squawked from the tinny speaker of a Ham somewhere back in the kitchen, where a black kid in an apron manned a buffet of steaming stainless bins.

Lewis gestured at the aide who stood a pace off his right shoulder. A blond boy, maybe sixteen, tall and rangy from a recent growth spurt. Stiffly at ease, fatigues starched and tightly buttoned, gleaming sergeant's chevrons on the shoulder.

"My kids are a little jumpy. We don't get a lot of traffic out this way." Lewis' overfed cheeks broadened in an avuncular smile

Doss said nothing. For uncomfortable seconds she took in Lewis' sharply pressed uniform. The three polished stars on his shoulder. The orders from Rippert—handing Fort Riley over to Doss—which Lewis had folded with furtive hands into a tiny paper brick and now worried with his fingertips. The schoolmarm spectacles that clouded his eyes as he watched Doss. The tension trembling at the edges of his smile.

"The Designer," Doss prompted.

"Yes." Lewis inclined his head agreeably. "My orders were to get her to D.C. once she arrived here."

"She didn't make it."

"Chen, our radio operator, had her on radar. Her GPS beacon was pinging us every five minutes. Then it stopped. She veered south and disappeared."

"Where?"

"East of Garden City. That's how we know she defected. Intentionally, I mean. Garden City's far south. Way off her flight plan. There was no weather, so no reason for such a wild deviation from her course."

"You sent out recon parties?"

Lewis' expression turned troubled. "No."

Doss let out a long breath, heavy with contempt: typical fucking Army. Watching her, Lewis seemed to wither a little. He leaned his thick torso back on the cafeteria bench as though he were afraid she might reach out and strike him.

"Why not?" she demanded.

"We lack the capability—"

"To send out a recon party two hundred miles into territory you control?"

"We...I..." Lewis glanced around the room. His gaze settled

on Gomez and Fiorivani, who sat a discrete but vigilant distance down the row, wolfing down rehydrated vegetables, turkey and gravy. Heaped so high it had breached the corrals of their molded plastic trays and coalesced into a watery stew. They gazed flatly back at Lewis as they ate. Lewis looked at Doss and held up a plump, pink hand, at loss. "D.C. didn't brief you?"

Doss pulled the flexpad Rippert had given her from a hip pocket and tossed it, still folded, onto the table. She leveled an accusing finger at it.

"D.C. seems to know fuck all about what's going on out here, General. They thought Riley would be prepped and waiting for me. They thought you'd have a bead on where the Designer might be. They seemed to think you'd have troops primed and ready to jump." She pinned Lewis with a violent look. "What they did not think, General, was that you'd light up my zep with double A's on the way in."

"Yes. I see." Lewis peeled off his specs, laid them on the table. He seemed to deflate. "Jingo," he said, looking at the middle space between him and Doss. The unwavering young aide stiffened a touch.

"Sir."

"Would you please go and ready some quarters for Colonel Doss and her men?"

"Sir." The boy turned crisply on a heel and strode out of the cafeteria.

Lewis peered at Doss, eyes vulnerable now without his specs. A little too intent. Made Doss think of reclaimed POWs who hadn't yet come right in their heads, of downed pilots lost too long in the blinding heat of the Saud deserts.

"I'm a scientist, Colonel," he said, and gave Doss a small, hurt smile. "I used to be. Agrigenetics. I was doing field research here when…" He held his palms towards Doss, like the only way to convey what had happened was to physically hand it over. "Zeps just stopped coming. I got stuck here. I waited an entire winter for a chance to get back east. One day in the spring a zep came, and I thought I had a ride home. I was wrong. Instead I got orders, informing me I'd been promoted to major." Sad humor filled Lewis' face. "I wasn't even in the Army. That was over ten years ago. Now D.C. sends one zep a year, for resupply. That's it. I brief them quarterly on the sat link. And I have the distinct impression they don't care whether I do or not." He canted his head, gave Doss a look that begged for understanding. "We no longer factor into D.C.'s sphere of influence out here, Colonel. I'm afraid we've been written off."

Doss leaned back on her bench, laced fingers behind her head. Her eyes absently scanned ancient recruiting posters, faded by time and torn at the edges, that lined the cafeteria's walls. Square-jawed commandos glowered, faces streaked with photo-perfect camo paint. Tank operators squinted winningly into the targeted distance. A drop-suited pilot, goggled helmet tucked under his arm, glanced over his shoulder at an attack chopper backlit by an explosive sunset. *The Russians Need Company. Iran: Vacationland. Be All You Can Be.* Captions so familiar that Doss no longer rendered any meaning from them.

"What's Riley's status, General?" she asked.

"In terms of?"

"Combat readiness."

"My kids…" Lewis smiled again, exuding the fond resignation of a parent who knew his children lacked potential. "My little soldiers. They're orphans. Their parents died, or deserted them because they couldn't feed them. They sneak onto the base at night and we give them uniforms. They drill. They keep order. They get fed. That's it. They're good kids." He looked at Doss. "All Riley's real soldiers deserted a long time ago, Colonel."

....

Insertion planes sat parked along the underground hangar's length, tails to the wall, aggressive raptor lines muted by heavy grey storage tarps coated with dust. Flylights, big enough to carry a solid platoon, small, agile and heavily armed enough to chew a battlefield into mulch. They seemed limitless, disappearing into a far darkness where a bank of fluorescents had failed.

"That," Gomez noted, twirling the string of bones around a finger, "is a shitload of resource." He'd changed from his stockade jumpsuit into fatigues so new Doss could smell the sour odor of the vacuum pack in which they'd been sealed. Gomez whistled into the hangar's vastness. There was no echo. "You can't tell me no one in D.C.'s keeping track of this shit."

"Drop suits look okay," Doss said. The suits, lining the cinder-block wall opposite the Flylights, hung upright in racks. Kevlar, ceramic, titanium. Matte black, sucking up light like holes in the air. The scars on Gomez's cheek twisted with hard mirth.

"Fills me with an acute need to buttfuck a small dictatorship."

"Roger that," Doss told him.

They wandered the hangar's length, came to a Flylight where a fatigued rump and long legs extended from beneath a tarp to the top of a maintenance ladder. Somewhere under the tarp, a battery-powered socket wrench whined.

"Lieutenant," Doss called. The wrench ceased. The tarp fluttered. Fiorivani emerged from beneath, smiled, ran a hand over the Nazi glow of his crew cut.

"Colonel. Sergeant."

"Got an inventory for me?" Doss asked.

"Most of it." He set the socket wrench atop the Flylight and pulled a sheaf of papers from a cargo pocket on his pants. "Not finished yet, but…" He flipped through the papers until he found his page, ran an index finger down it as he read.

"We got four medium zeps, not counting our own. Forty-two of these babies." He lovingly touched the titanium lip of the Fly-light's delta wing. "I've only been able to check a few of them over, but so far they seem mechanically solid. Haven't had a chance to really dig into them. Been tarped up for god knows how long. Gaskets and lines tend to crack in this dry heat. What's very good news…" White eyebrows gained sudden altitude as Fiorivani held up an eager finger. "Reactors all show green lights. We got plenty of fuel rods in storage beneath Hangar Two. Also good, we got a whole warehouse full of M-8s. Seventeen Barrette railers. Haven't found ammo for those yet, but where there's a rail gun, there's fire. A fuckload of P-40s, both frag and incendiary. A bunch of old LAWs. Total garbage. Probably just pop in their tubes. Enough ordinance for the Flylights to carry on an air war. Everything you want. Sonics, bunker-busters, air-to-air." His eyes stayed on the page while one finger pointed at the blunt beak of a Gatling gun protruding from the Flylight's nose. "Days' worth of 30-mil for the rattle guns." He grinned, folded the papers and stuffed them back into his pocket. "We are good on fuckpower," he concluded.

"Alright." Doss gave Gomez a cruel look. "Find me some soldiers, Sergeant, and I'll let you build me some chalks." Gomez didn't flinch.

"Might need some pilots, too, Boss."

....

Riley had been crowded once. Too crowded. Doss' sergeant yelling into her face like they did in flex vids. Thrusting his chest against her tits, spit flying from lips wounded by overly aggressive shaving. Word was, he'd never seen combat. And he was short. A seriously bad mix for a drill sergeant. But at least then Fort Riley had been alive.

Now Doss wandered the haunted silence of its underground. A labyrinth of hallways, meeting rooms, barracks, all empty. Fluorescents flickered every fifty yards or so. She felt herself disappear in the darkness between, kept extant only by the hollow scuff of her boots on concrete.

Her first deployment, she'd stood on the plastiform deck of a submersible troop ship, watching a destroyer, half a mile long, slide grey and predatory as a shark across the Persian Gulf's slate surface. A hundred sat-guided missiles a minute had shrieked from its ballistic tubes. Up into the stratosphere and out to the Birjand plain, where they'd hammered down on Chinese positions six hundred miles distant. Doss had been seventeen, and it had been like watching Jesus himself breathe fire. It had filled her with rapture. "God bless the US of motherfucking A," she'd yelled at a nearby soldier.

And now…Now Kansas was barely even on the fucking map. Her footsteps echoed back at her. Nothing here but time.

Emerson would've made it seem okay, would've joked about it. Pushed that button that made reality go all rubbery, made Doss laugh. These past days Emerson had come to Doss' sleep, eidetic visitations at the edges of dreams. His rough palm lightly running the muscled length of her hip. How his switch could flip, the scary laser calm that came over him when he drew the Steg from the small of his back and brought its sights in line with his eye.

"I'd love to have kids someday," he'd told her once. They'd lain, pressed close together, in his cot, barely wide enough for one. Doss cupping him in her palm, Emerson's arm pillowing her head, his strangely spicy scent warm around her. He'd said it like he was just some guy, and she was just some girl, and the world was just turning. Said it like he couldn't sense her terror—or if he could it didn't worry him. She'd watched him, staring up at the fiberboard ceiling of his quarters, musing, and known. He was the right kind of stupid.

Doss worked her flexpad as she walked. Tabbed through cabinet personnel files, old society profiles, scanned old journo feeds.

She found only a single pic of the anachronistic woman from Rippert's office. A young version of her. A smile, lush with vanity, beamed into the paparazzi shine of some black-tie cabinet function. Porcelain shoulders rose from a sleeveless black gown. A hand clad in a black opera glove lightly held the tuxedoed arm of a broad middle-aged white man whose jaw thrust forth, exuding authority. President Logan. Doss squinted at the pic's caption.

"Ellen Vokle," she intoned aloud. The hand on Rippert's leash. Doss kept searching. Found no records of the woman, either government or civilian. The phrase "plausible deniability" came to mind.

A crease of light emanated from beneath a doorway ahead. Doss folded the flexpad, in the darkness put her nose close to the door's stenciling. INFIRMARY #3. She palmed the latch and pushed it open. Saw cots with clean paper sheets, stainless IV stands gleaming under fluorescents.

A Latino boy sat at a long table side-on to Doss, chin propped on fists as he stared at the flat screen of a data port. After a moment his head slowly turned. His eyes landed on Doss.

"Oh!" he blurted, and leapt to his feet. He stared, frozen, his arms out to either side like an insect pinned to a board. "Who are you?" He blinked at Doss for a second, then his eyes settled on the silver bird pinned to her chest. Meticulously shined boots clicked together as he saluted. "Ma'am!" Doss waved the salute away.

"At ease. I'm Colonel Doss. Who are you?"

"Corporal Henderson, ma'am."

"Why so jumpy, Corporal?"

Corporal Henderson's eyes shifted from side to side. His cheeks reddened.

"It's dark down here."

"I was noticing that myself. It didn't used to be. Things do change though, don't they?" The kid's brow creased along the path of a long scar the shape of saw teeth. He said nothing. Doss ran a finger along the edge of the stainless table. "What do you do, Corporal?"

"I'm the base doctor, ma'am."

She looked him up and down. Guessed him to be no older than twelve.

"You're shitting me. Been to med school have you?" The kid's face darkened. He glanced defensively at the data port.

"I read a lot."

. . . .

"Why Denver?" The question came from the flexpad Doss had unfolded across one knee. She'd taken typical officer's quarters. Blank concrete walls. A metal desk and chair, a metal footlocker. A toilet and sink, open as a prison cell. The cot, upon which she now sat cross-legged.

She pinched the bridge of her nose, squinted at the translucent screen: an aerial view through the eyes of some amateur newsfly peering out through a chopper's passenger window. A jumble of old monoliths below, skyscrapers whose empty black windows exuded the same vacancy as dead termite mounds.

"You can see its *bones!*" The view grew jittery—an early model iris cam embedded in untrained eyes—then gradually focused on a stretch of crumbling freeway between downtown and the remnants of an enormous stadium. A series of megalithic bones slanted forth, each a tower of Pisa, implying a long curve. What looked like spider webs stretched between them. Sinew. The first stage of Satori's dome.

"Well, first things first," another voice said. Male, a lilting Indian accent. The view blurred past a helmeted pilot, settled on a man sitting in the back seat. He wore a plush blue suit. Doss recognized the round face from the Satori files Rippert had provided. Prekash Gupta, Satori Corp's lead geneticist. "Denver was cheap. It gets incredibly cold here now in the winter. Most people had already left when we moved on it. It's close to the Rocky Mountain snowpack, and therefore close to water. But even more importantly, Denver is incredibly sunny, even in the winter. Satori's dome will be a composite, meaning her DNA is built from many different sources, some of them plants. She will derive a significant percentage of her energy from photosynthesis. So you see, sunshine is vital." Gupta stroked a vermillion tie, beaming. "This was Sumedha's idea." He placed his hand on the dark skin of a bare shoulder beside him. The view blurred, refocused on a smooth caramel face, features balanced as easy math. A face identical to Pihadassa's, only male. Black eyes watched the newsfly with spectral calm. The view blurred, settled once more on Gupta.

"You're Indian, right?" The newsfly's voice sounded young, barely pubescent.

"Yes."

"Why'd you name it Satori? That's, like, Chinese."

"Japanese." Gupta's smile tightened. "Your Uncle Bill chose the name. He thought it might market better than something more appropriate."

"Mute," Doss ordered the flexpad. "Show me the file on Bill

Coach." The file expanded on her screen. She tabbed to the bio, opened the section labeled "Education and Career, Overview:"

Bill Coach, founder and CEO of Satori Corporation. Born in Houston, 2016. Graduated from the University of Houston with a B.S. in climate science, 2036. M.S. in climate science from Bard, 2038. Elected CEO of The Monsanto Company, 2063. Voted out that same year. Appointed President's Special Liaison to Amalgamated Iranian Oil, Public Relations division, 2064. Appointed Chair of Pentagon Council on Climate Change and Foreign Policy, 2068. Founded Satori, 2072.

"Interview," Doss said. The window reopened. Now Bill Coach occupied the newsfly's view. His hands made chopping motions as he spoke across a geographic expanse of conference table. "Unmute."

"—santo, DuPont, Pharmacia, those assholes got it all wrong." He spoke with a thoroughly Texan accent, wore a suit so black it seemed to create its own gravity. "They're way behind the curve. Their production's still oil-based, for Christ's sake. And they're still talking in terms of drought-resistant crops." He shook his head. "Five degrees Celsius in under half a century, that's not a goddamned drought. We're talking a completely different ballgame. A new environment. And it's only getting worse. Better crop production's just a baby step. Short term. And it won't ever be anything more than a stopgap. The endgame is, we need to change ourselves." His face, lean as a scalpel, turned square with the cam. His eyes lazed the newsfly. "You getting what I'm telling you, Andy?"

"Yeah, Uncle Bill," the newsfly said. "We totally got to make better choices." Bill Coach's lips clenched with thin patience.

"I'm saying we need to change ourselves. Not morally or ethically." He pressed an index finger to his sternum. "*Fundamentally.*" The view wobbled briefly as the newsfly nodded his head.

"A totally new philosophy. I get it."

Bill Coach stared. After a moment his lips parted, releasing a long, constricted breath, then he lay his head against the back of the high leather chair in which he sat.

"I love you like the sunshine, Andy, but goddamn. You did

collect your daddy's shit for brains."

"Close interview," Doss said. The window disappeared.

She tabbed open another file. The four Satori Designers floated up her screen. Skin the color of black tea, almond eyes gazing out with the placid curiosity of birds. Doss expanded the bio of the Designer named Pihadassa.

...specializing in recombinant agriculture with specific aim towards crops resistant to extreme climate variance. If she is alive, Pihadassa will most likely look for a situation where she can fulfill compulsions to practice agricultural eugenics and—

A quiet knock came at the door. Doss folded the flexpad with one hand and laid it on the cot. Her other hand closed unthinking around the .45 she'd stashed beneath the thin pillow.

"What's up?" she called.

"Friends." A boy's voice. No one Doss knew. She moved to the door, held the .45 behind the small of her back. Slid back the small deadbolt and stepped away.

"Enter," she called. The door swung slowly open.

Two boys stood there, one white, the other taller and black. The acne of early adolescence speckled their cheeks and necks. Both wore tightly pressed camo. The taller boy raised a hand. Doss raised the pistol.

"Fear not, beautiful lady friend," the boy said. He slowly finished a salute-like gesture, except instead of his brow he touched a red band tied around his fatigued bicep. "I'm Jake. This is Casanova." The smaller boy nodded, touched fingers to a red band tied around his own bicep. Jake smiled. "We *La Chupacabra*." He squinted at Doss' pistol. "You don't need no gun with us, lady. We friends. El Sol sent us." Both boys reverently touched their red bands a second time. "We here to express for him his eternal gratitude. You save his life, lady. El Sol's in your debt. He tell us to tell you: *La Chupacabra* your friend. For life."

"For life," Casanova echoed with gravity.

"Also," Jake's face grew somber, "El Sol sorry about your man who got hurt. Sorry beyond all measure."

"Beyond all measure." Casanova solemnly bowed his tow head.

"He sends a gift. Taken from the thug who planned the attack that got your man hurt." Jake reached to his chest, produced from a breast pocket a small rectangular parcel wrapped in red tissue paper. He held this out to Doss, leaning far forward without moving his feet, as though her personal space was something too sacred for him to touch. Doss eyed him down her pistol sight for a moment, then lowered the gun. She took the parcel and the boy leaned back.

"Also," he said, and looked at Casanova. The blond boy nodded encouragement and Jake thrust his chin forward. "Also, we yours. You need protecting, we protect you. You need food, we feed you. You say it, we do it. You get it?" Doss stared. "Alright," Jake said. "You need anything, we right here." He gave one awkward nod, then turned and, ushering Casanova out before him, egressed and shut the door.

Doss peeled open the parcel, found a small wooden box inside with a tiny hand-written note affixed: *Fated.* She opened the box and tipped out what looked like a blackened piece of pork. Turned it in her palm.

An index finger. She mulled it over for a moment, then tossed the finger into the toilet, hit the flush lever with a boot.

....

General Lewis' young sergeants paraded Fort Riley's soldiers on the airfield. The late morning sun cooked heat waves out of the cracked tarmac as the troops marched impetuously, all three hundred and fourteen of them, tight and buttoned, lockstep.

"They march nice," Fiorivani said. He stood, massive arms crossed, and spit sideways towards General Lewis' boots. Lewis, who stood between Doss and Chen, Riley's radio operator, seemed not to notice. He chewed his lip and every so often glanced at Doss over the top of his specs. Doss kept her face blank.

Gomez leaned in close. He pointed at where, on the prairie beyond the perimeter chain link, a smattering of migrants had set up squats made of mud and corrugated tin. Early spring crops sprouted from uneven plots near a collection of muddy wells.

"Think their parents are watching?" Many of the young soldiers bore the fragile look of migrants, bodies scored with hunger and parasites.

"Nobody here got parents, man," Jake said. He stood vigilantly behind Doss, shoulder to shoulder with Casanova. "Our daddy's the army." Gomez cast a long gaze at the boy.

"Shit." He turned to Doss. "They follow you home?" Doss said nothing. The scar furrowed along Gomez's cheek. "You didn't feed them did you? Can't get rid of them once you do that." Doss tried to suppress a smile and failed.

Out on the tarmac, the troops about faced and began to run in place. Doss turned to Lewis.

"You've done a remarkable job with discipline, General, all things considered." General Lewis swelled at the compliment. "Got any pilots for those Flylights we found in the basement?" The general deflated.

"I'm afraid not, Colonel." He gestured at the rows of kids, who had now dropped to the tarmac and struggled to do pushups. "What you see is unfortunately what we have."

"Actually, Colonel…" Chen, who wore a button-up denim shirt over FEMAs, pushed thick sunglasses atop his head. His black ponytail reached the small of his back. Definitely not Army. "There's a simulator down in Hangar Three. Some of the kids and I spend time on it during the winters."

"A simulator." Doss raised her eyebrows at Gomez, whose face narrowed with contempt.

"I know five or six kids who are pretty good," Chen said. "They can fly straight into Shanghai under heavy fire. On night mode."

"Five pilots sounds about right," Doss figured. She faced Gomez. "You've got a week. I want five Flylights airborne and attack ready. Find me enough Rangers for five chalks."

Gomez shifted his eyes across the tarmac, where Lewis' troops now spun plastic rifles, barrels tipped with red safety plugs. He worked his tongue over his diamond tooth, exuded doubt.

"It'll be easy," Doss told him. "Just grab the ones tall enough for the drop suits." She placed a hand on his shoulder and her voice turned serious. "One week, Gomez. Ready to kill."

"Ready to die, more like."

"That, too." She pointed her chin at Fiorivani. "Lieutenant, gear up. You're with me. Gear up."

"Gear's in the zep, Boss," Fiorivani said. "I'm good to go."

"General Lewis." Doss regarded the neatly pressed man. "You'll remain in charge of general logistics and training. But Sergeant Gomez will take whatever he needs, whenever he needs it. That includes personnel, weapons, gear, fuel, food, everything." The general nodded affably to Gomez.

"He'll get whatever he needs."

"Have your troops unhangar my zep." Doss turned to Jake and Casanova. "You two ready for a trip?"

"Where we going, lady?"

"Hunting."

CHAPTER 10

When his mother died, Brood sat beside her with Pollo in the white Oklahoma dust. Heat rose out of the world in shimmering waves, alive and hateful. It gripped Brood's skin and he wanted to cry, but couldn't because some animal part of him feared the lost moisture of tears. Pollo sat naked and tiny on his haunches, head limp against Brood's shoulder. He spoke their mother's name over and over, his small mouth working carefully, ritualistically, over each syllable. Lupia Maria Escadero.

Her family was from Chiapas, generations back, when people still tried to live in the jaundiced desert south of Mexico City. In the greenhouse's flat light, she'd told Brood stories of how the great kings of Palenque had spawned her line. She'd proven this by holding up her hands, palms inward, for him to see: middle fingers the same length, pinky and forefinger the same length. The indisputable symmetry of old jungle royalty.

Brood had stared at the symmetry of his own hands as the heat rapidly turned the blanket-wrapped body before him into something other than his mother. Lupia Maria Escadero. The name turned to a jumble of noise as Pollo repeated it. The body turned to bloating meat.

Caravans rolled past. Refugees struggled through dust kicked up by wagons. They held aloft blankets mounted on sticks to shade them, too bent on their own waning chance at survival to spare a glance towards the bereaved boy in the faded Mickey Mouse shirt and his tiny, whispering brother. Other children trailed the caravans, trotting like skinny-legged dogs.

Eventually the body's stench overwhelmed Brood. He slid a hand under Pollo's arm and rose.

They walked north. Bodies lay beside the caravan track, some obviously cared for, wrapped in blankets and made comfortable. Others had simply been dumped, tongues swollen from fever and thirst.

Pollo made perhaps two miles before his legs gave out. Brood pulled him up piggy-back, and kept on until his own legs refused to move. Then sank to the ground and lay there, too weak to scream as the sun pealed the skin off his face. Beside him Pollo moaned, a sound as empty as the sky.

Sometime later he heard the whine of an electric motor. It stopped close by and footsteps approached. A toe prodded him. A dry rasp issued from his throat as he tried to beg for help.

"Still alive." He heard disappointment in the wheezing voice. Rough hands turned him over and he found himself staring at a grizzled beard, dreadlocks. Bright dark eyes stared down at him. A toothless smile gaped. "Mickey fucking Mouse. Classic." The hands yanked Brood's shirt up and off. Footsteps receded. Brood tried to form the word *please*, but his tongue didn't work.

The footsteps returned. Brood smelled water. A plastic gallon milk jug appeared beside his head, sloshing, nearly full of brown water.

"Fair trade, little *ese*. Don't try following me. You ain't a dog and I ain't gonna give you another treat. *Te llenare el culo de perdigones.*" Then the man was gone.

Brood drank. Strength surged through his body. When he looked up he saw a flatbed wagon bouncing away to the north, the grizzled man standing like a ship's captain at its tiller. Brood put the jug to Pollo's lips. The little boy's vacant eyes went wide and he drank. When he could stand, they started north again.

They caught up with the wagon well after dark. The man had steered it way off the caravan track and now sat propped against one of its tires. Brood's Mickey Mouse shirt wrapped his bony shoulders, tight as a surgical glove. Across his lap he cradled a fat, pistol-grip shotgun, which he leveled over a knee as Brood approached.

"Told you, *homito*. Happy pack you full of buckshot as have you anywhere near me." He thumbed off the safety, a bone-snap sound in the dry night air.

Brood stopped, set the empty water jug down and pointed at the Mickey Mouse shirt. Laughter croaked from the man's throat.

"*Cojones* for brains, little *ese*." He lowered the shotgun, stood and offered his hand. Brood reached to take it. The man cuffed him hard on the temple. Brood fell and the man kicked him in the stomach. "*Cállate!*"

Brood cried out and Pollo moaned loudly. Brood felt his brother's tiny hand gripping his wrist, pulling him. They fled together into the darkness.

They snuck back shortly after dawn. The man lay asleep beneath the wagon, shotgun beside him, Mickey Mouse logo still tight against his torso. Brood silently helped Pollo up onto the wagon, then climbed up behind him.

Immediately Brood gravitated to the assortment of batteries, some lithium, some deep cycle. He knew electrics. His mother had taught him. He traced his hands along fat rubber wires running from bats to electric motors, to a converter connected to thick photovoltaic paint slopped atop the water tank at the wagon's center. A portable charge detector hung on a leather thong from the tiller. Brood took it and began testing circuits.

An hour or so later the man rose with a start beside the wagon. Dust flew from his dreads as he gazed wildly around. Brood and Pollo sat against the water tank. They'd filled the water jug once more and Pollo cradled it tightly in his arms. He hummed a strange and directionless tune as the man stared. Brood stared back, chewing a dried apricot he'd found in a footlocker near the tiller.

"Thought you was a goddamn shark walking around on my boat." The man pressed a hand to his head as though to squeeze out the dreams. "Fuck you want, little cuz?"

Brood pointed at the Mickey Mouse shirt. He tried to explain that his mother had given it to him, but his mouth refused to form words.

"*Madre*," Pollo said. He rubbed his cheek along the jug's textured plastic. "She give Carlos that shirt." The man gave them a dark look.

"*Tu madre*," he said.

"Lupia Maria Escadero," Pollo intoned, and this seemed an answer in the affirmative.

The man lowered his head. Dreads hid his eyes. He rested hands on jutting hips and for a few seconds seemed to do some hard mental lifting, then his mouth turned bitter and he shook his head.

"Can't take you on, young homies."

Brood didn't move. He kept his gaze level, implacable. The man shook his head. In one quick motion he stripped off the t-shirt, revealing sun-leathered ribs. He tossed the shirt into Brood's lap. "There. Even up." He waved a hand. "Now get the fuck off my wagon."

Brood pointed silently at the rewired batteries. The man's withered face narrowed. He clambered up onto the wagon and crawled about on all fours, face close to the wires. Finally he looked at the boys.

"You do this?" he asked. Brood nodded. The man eyed them sidelong. "*Cuántos años?*"

"*Cinco años*," Pollo sang, and then, staring into the sky above the man's head, began chanting the words over and over. "*Cinco anos. Cinco años…*" Brood held up eight fingers.

"*Me llamo* Hondo. Hondo Loco." The skin around his eyes crinkled. He seemed relieved.

"*Me llamo* Bacilio," Pollo said. "*Mucho gusto, rata.*"

Brood tried to speak, failed, shook his head.

They rolled north that morning through churning dust devils and past the bodies on the roadside. Hondo stood at the tiller, singing songs to himself in a way that reminded Brood strangely of Pollo. Brood and Pollo sat at the bow, knees curled up under their chins. Every so often Pollo quietly sang: *Mama Lupia*. Tears traced clean tracks through the dirt on his cheeks.

"Dónde vamos nosotros, Carlos?" he asked the air near Brood. Brood stared at the prairie stretching hot and empty before them, and shrugged.

"You pensive, homes," Hondo called from the tiller. "Brooding and shit. You let me know when you think up something useful." Without turning around, Brood raised his hand and gave Hondo Loco a thumbs up.

．．．．

Fever gripped Brood the first night. His body burned while the desert around him froze in the dark. He woke screaming every few minutes. Each time the silence of the dead forest made him moan with terror. He closed his eyes against it, sank back into sleep.

Dreams shattered him. Hondo rose and peered down at him, dead eyes blackened with hemorrhage, face broken, dreads matted with blood. Pollo, up to his neck in an enormous pile of golden seed. Swimming his arms, trying vainly to stay afloat, drowning. The echo of his long moan hung in the air. Brood's mother lay on her back beside him, stiff. Her death grin gleamed in the cold starlight. Her teeth parted and she tried to sing lullabies—emitted only the sound of empty wind bending itself over long Oklahoma hardpan.

Thirst forced him finally, completely, awake. Grey dawn light made the forest seem insubstantial, a memory he couldn't quite grip.

He sat up. Pain made him vomit. He checked his wound. A poultice of pressed clay, which he barely remembered applying, had staunched the bleeding from two holes above his hip bone. A through and through, around which spread a deep flush. What was bruising and what was infection Brood couldn't tell, and he figured it didn't matter. It would all be infection soon enough. He crumbled more clay in his palm and pressed it home, shivering under a wave of pain and fever.

Hondo lay nearby. A dry black stain haloed the parched clay around the old man's dreads.

The body's stillness terrified Brood. He crawled over to it, reached out to touch it as though he might somehow bring comfort. His fingers drew up short, hovering a few inches from one leathery shoulder.

"*Chale!*" He spoke this at the corpse, astonished at the utterly totality of its death. "Fuck, Hondo."

Pollo's snake lay curled nearby, crushed and discarded by the *Chupes*, its white belly exposed to the sky. Brood gathered it in his hands. Leaned back on his knees and, with no one around in the crushing vastness to see him, wept.

"*Sale vale. Sale vale. Sale vale.*"

After a time his eyes cleared. The sun rose above the trees, baking him. He realized he'd pissed himself. Unthinking, he pushed a foot forward, braced himself against the pain, stood.

He collected pieces of roadside junk. A blue vinyl tarp, strips of which he tore up and tied around his feet. A ten-foot strand of barbed wire. A tin can. A broken jar. A piece of some ancient car's rearview mirror. Pollo's snake hung limp from his fingers.

The roar of a snowmelt wash roiling out of the Sangre de Cristos drew him. He knelt in the mud beside it and sank his head into water cold as an electric shock, but did not drink. Instead he piled up a small mound of dry crabgrass. He fiddled with the convex jar bottom and the mirror until a tiny white spot of sunlight smoked and the crabgrass caught with near-invisible flames. Then he added dry juniper branches until a steady fire crackled, and set water to boil in the tin can. He used the jar's sharp edge to gut the snake, which he set to cook on a flat rock beside the fire.

When the water had boiled, he splashed his wound gingerly.

Crumbled more clay in his palms, pressed it home. Pain had become as much a part of his body as breath. As such, Brood ignored it. He drank the rest of the water. Refilled the can and put it back on the fire. He ate half the snake, even though the fever had stolen his appetite. The water boiled and he drank again.

His mind fell adrift in fever. Regular waves of heat and chill rolled up his back. When he returned to himself, the fear had left him. He figured he may as well die walking.

The sun hammered him. He tried not to think of the dark adobe rooms of Ojo Caliente, of Rosa Lee wrapped naked around him in the cold waters of a stream's deep eddy. The Tewa would run him off or shoot him if he arrived a beggar. So he turned east, away from Ojo. Towards the desert, burning white as a muzzle flash far below, and the caravan track of the old freeway.

His feet moved him through the day. Then it was night. Visions came to him in the dark. Snakes under foot. A giant black spider skittering beside him down the rocky slope. A raven perched on his shoulder.

"I pray," it whispered with Hondo's voice.

"Then you pray for me, *Chimuelo*," Brood replied.

Pale light filled his head. He thought he'd died, entered the realm of *espiritu enojados*, become one of them, a hungry ghost, no longer even a mouth to feed. Then the sun rose. He found himself standing amid dead sagebrush on the broken remains of an asphalt lot, staring at the sun-faded logo of a cartoon coyote. It adorned the rim of an old truck stop portico that had collapsed over the rusted shells of a dozen gas pumps.

"Freeway," he told the raven, but the bird had disappeared with the night. Behind him, a raised track stretched across the desert. "*Sale vale*," he said to the coyote, and crawled into the portico's shade.

He lay on his back, trembling with fever. His wound stank and oozed puss. Red tendrils of infection had spread across his belly and chest. Thirst wracked him. He considered looking for water, but knew he could no longer move. Better, he decided, simply to close his eyes.

He woke to something wet pressing his cheek—over and over. It made a smacking sound. A dog whined.

"One of those fucking *cholos* from the wagon," someone said. A girl's voice. Brood opened his eyes. Found the dog's wet snout wiggling eagerly, inches from his nose. Someone stood over him. Brood squinted, discerned the tiny twin mirrors of aviator shades.

CHAPTER 11

The forearm lay, pale and stiff, atop the undulating surface of the bone-and-muscle worktable. Three ear-sized hooks lay beside it.

Sumedha watched as Minerva eyed the arm uncertainly. She'd grown three full inches since he'd given her the splice.

"How do you feel?" he asked her.

"Cold." Taut muscle rolled under downy skin as she ran a tentative finger along one of the hooks. She crossed her arms over her breasts.

Sumedha turned to where Kassapa and Paduma stood, watching from the hallway outside through a transparent film of skin.

"Note the increased musculature." He pointed to the girl's arm, then at her hip. "Also increased height. Both indicate increased growth hormone. I have periodically changed the temperature of her pod over the last ten days, ranging from thirty-three degrees to one hundred and fifteen. Her body fat, hair growth and vascular efficiency have all fluctuated accordingly." He turned back to the girl. "Satori. Operating table please."

A second table articulated from the floor with the machine gun pop of shifting bone, cartilage, sinew.

"I don't want it to hurt," Minerva said. "It always hurts."

"Lay down," Sumedha ordered. Minerva hesitated. "Do not worry. I will make it painless," he promised. Minerva nodded and lay on the table. "Satori, restraints please." Fat digits extended from the table and gripped her.

"You told me—"

"I told you it would not hurt. It will not. Satori, general anesthesia." A bone needle extended from the tip of one of the restraining digits and jabbed the girl's neck. She cried out once, then went still as the injection took hold. "Satori. Amputation. Left arm, two inches below the elbow." A skein of wet viscera unraveled from the ceiling. Coalesced into a single boneless cord that coiled and shifted as though it could barely contain the force of its own life. A flat head, all muscle and teeth, opened at its end, wide as Sumedha's spread hand. The cord, an attentive snake, followed Sumedha as he moved to Minerva's side. He took hold of it. It felt alive in his hand as he steered it towards the girl's forearm.

"Cut...*here*." Muscles flexed, teeth clamped down. Blood spurted, stark in the room's pearl glow. Bone snapped. The arm broke off, easy as an aloe stem. The snake's mouth held the arm for a moment, suctioning blood. Sumedha smiled.

"Satori. Epoxy please." Another skein unfurled, this time forming a tube with a hollow end. Sumedha took the forearm from the worktable and held it up before the window for his two designer siblings to see. "This is the forearm of one of our workers born outside Satori. Wildborn. I harvested it this morning. It belonged to a male."

Sumedha placed the dead arm to Minerva's, stump to stump. Took one of the hooks from the worktable and deftly speared it through the flesh of each arm, joining them. Squeezed the hook closed, a metal link. He did the same with the two remaining hooks, then pulled the dangling tube over the arm's length. The tube pulsed wetly, oozing amber sap, which soon encased the girl's arm from shoulder to fingertip.

"Assistant." The door flexed open and a thick, female landrace lumbered inside. Sumedha motioned at the severed arm. "Take that. Feed it to Satori." The landrace chuffed, nodded. Picked up the arm and left with it cradled to her breasts as though it were her own child.

Kassapa and Paduma entered the room. Sumedha felt their minds, warm, admiring—but something kept his mind from meeting theirs. A difference of emotional geometry, the sensation of hard angle.

Together they gazed down at the unconscious girl. Her helix turned in all their minds, already morphing, absorbing the new material of the wild-born arm.

"Beautiful," Paduma said.

"Yes, brother," Kassapa agreed. "Beautiful work. What is the next test? If the arm takes?" Sumedha mulled this for a moment, then said simply:

"Free her."

Kassapa and Paduma exchanged a glance.

"You grow reckless," they observed in unison. Sumedha looked from one to the other. He smiled. Laughter rang out of him. Kassapa's face creased with doubt. Pheromones rose from him; his eyebrows arched, signaling primate dominance. Sumedha met his brother's eye, felt the challenge there, returned it.

"The world is not a controlled experiment, brother," he said. "We cannot duplicate its complexity." He ran a loving finger along the girl's throat, felt the vitality of her pulse. "If she cannot survive the world, then neither will the Fathers when they emerge."

....

A cloud obscured the sun. The temperature dropped. The dome, having shed the last of its winter fur, began to shiver. A tectonic quaking through mountainous flesh. Its skin turned pink as chloroplasts retreated from its cooling surface.

The same shift occurred within Sumedha's skin. He lay naked at the dome's peak, chest to the sky, skin to skin with Satori, heartbeat to heartbeat. Satori shivered; Sumedha shivered.

His mind retreated from the cold, retreated to the place he had shared with Pihadassa. They had often spent sunny days up here, feeling Satori's skin gurgle with photosynthesis. They would bask in steam as the dome opened her pores and exhaled sweat. Pihadassa would mount him, her skin glowing green in the sun as the chloroplasts did their work. Her body arching as energy surged through her. Her pupils would dilate and Sumedha would peer into her, open himself to her, meet her in their own personal Bardo of moment and mind, flesh and heat.

Sumedha breathed, turned his attention to the sensation of his solitude. The agony of it surprised him. His throat squeezed tight, producing a long keen.

The sound of footsteps silenced him. Bare feet padding lightly over the dome's spongy skin. They halted at a respectful distance. Sumedha stilled his thoughts, nodded assent. Paduma approached, seated herself lotus position beside him. She smoothed her white shift over dark thighs and gazed out over the dead sprawl of the old city. Heat shimmered where the sun hit the plains. Thunderstorms congealed like bruises.

"There will be tornadoes," she observed after a moment. "I would like to try and harness one."

"A tornado?" Sumedha watched a train of black government zeps angling in beneath the storms, noses pointed at Satori.

"Yes. The energy from one of decent size, if I could store it…I imagine it would equal what the wind fields generate in a year." To the north, among square miles of black factory ruins, churned several fields of bone-bladed windmills. They flashed white, slow and graceful in their cartilage sockets, as though they existed in a different sort of time. "But the preconditions are far too complex to predict exactly where and when one will form."

The first of the black government zeppelins nosed up and settled with surprising grace onto the airfield beside the secondary dome. Pihadassa's dome, where she had produced her seed. A hatch opened at the aircraft's rear, revealing a wide storage bay, out of which black-clad soldiers marched. A group of burly landraces stood waiting, wagons in tow full of seed.

The sun emerged from behind its cloud and the temperature immediately shot up. Chloroplasts surged to the surface of Sumedha's skin, of Satori's skin. Pores the size of bomb craters opened around them.

"It feels good," Paduma said. She pulled the shift over her head and lay down beside Sumedha. He did not reply. He watched, where down below the landraces began loading the zep.

"The government's third run this spring," he said. They would unload the seed at distribution stations across the Midwest. From there scatter it to the subaltern migrant wind. "Sometimes I can almost see them out there." The maggot-white dots of humanity scratching at the dry earth, laboring to reap the harvest of their own obsolescence.

"You have grown strange without her," she said. A fat black fly buzzed Sumedha's head. He remained still. "Kassapa thinks so, too."

"Kassapa sent you to visit me."

"He knows. But I chose. You do not connect to us anymore."

"Perhaps it is you who does not connect with me."

"Perhaps, but..." Paduma turned her head and eyed Sumedha as though he were a puzzle. "You are not forthcoming."

"I think we have all grown strange," Sumedha decided. "What do you want?"

"We want you back in the fold."

"I want that, too." Sumedha rolled onto his side, facing her. The moisture of Satori's steam glistened in the long concavities of her skin. "I want to connect." He reached out, touched her leg. Found her skin hot, boiling with chloroplasts. Heard her breath quicken. Slid his hand between her thighs. Found her wet.

"I know," she whispered. She rolled close to him, lips parting against his ear. Her fingers circled his member. She rose up, slid down. Sumedha's mind compressed, collapsed into its dense, primate core. He pulled Paduma to him.

She locked her eyes on his. Photosynthesis buzzed like carbonation beneath her skin. Sumedha felt it against his chest, beneath his fingers. Satori throbbed, alive beneath him, in rhythm as he moved against Pihadassa—no, *Paduma*. He linked his breath to hers. In as she exhaled, out as she inhaled. Joining them in primordial loop. Round and round, up the burning helix. She placed her forehead against his. Her lips parted, her skin seared him. Her pupils swallowed her eyes. A tiny white sun formed somewhere down in Sumedha's brainstem, grew. Filled his skull until he knew nothing but light. He saw Pihadassa there, glowing. He wanted to warn her: Kassapa's hounds tracked her. She smiled and he heard her voice...*I want to have a child.*

He opened his eyes. Paduma stared down at him. His hand went to her cheek—she looked so much like Pihadassa.

"You cannot connect anymore," she said, and looked confused. She watched him, separate, other.

"Not with you, it seems."

Sadness quietly touched her face. She leaned forward, touched her forehead to Sumedha's for a silent, empty moment, then leaned back.

"I'm sorry for your loss, brother." She pulled herself off him. He watched his seed trickle out of her.

"We have all lost," he said. "Three is an unstable number. We have collapsed into our individual parts, but continue to try and behave as though we are one." He ran a finger through the smear of semen on her leg, drawing a figure eight. Useless seed, sterile as a patch of alkali on the plain. An instant of acute melancholy overcame him. The primate urge to plant his likeness inside Paduma's belly, stymied. Her wombless belly, his own dead seed. "We have never been exactly what we are," he said. Paduma regarded him, her expression now blank, meditative. Sumedha wondered what she saw. It seemed a long time since he had known his siblings' minds.

"Did the splice succeed?" she asked after a time.

"It is still too early to tell."

"The girl appears healthy. Vigorous even."

"She was very sick at first. I thought she would die like the others. But then she recovered. Now she seems very strong. Very healthy, yes."

Paduma rolled onto her back. Smiled up at the blazing spring sky.

"This is good news," she said. "The Fathers will be happy."

Sumedha ran his thumb along the smooth verdance of her cheek. He touched her chin, pressed his thumb to the softness of her lips.

"You and Pihadassa are alike," he told her. She turned her face to him.

"We are similar. In some ways."

"I begin to see the puzzle Pihadassa works," he said. Paduma's pupils widened. Sumedha noted the barely perceptible flare of her nostrils. He watched the air between them, as though the words hovered there and he could gather them back in.

"You withhold much," Paduma said. She stared at him. "Kassapa is right not to trust you."

"You are right to be open with me about the fact he does not."

For an instant realization flashed in her eyes, then they went flat. She placed a palm to the dome's gurgling skin and took a deep, stilling breath.

"He does not believe you could fail to know your partner's mind. He has concluded your loyalty to Satori is as tenuous as Pihadassa's."

"And you?"

Paduma breathed again. Her hand rose, pressed itself lightly to Sumedha's cheek.

"I want to understand. Could you fail to know Pihadassa's mind? Is it possible?"

She lay back down and closed her eyes. They lay like that for a time, meditating together under the life-giving sun, each respecting the other's turn of mind.

"He will kill you," Paduma said finally. Sumedha saw the desolate place her puzzle had led her, a place he well knew.

"He has already tried."

Paduma sat up. She hovered over Sumedha, filling the sky, her body rigid. She closed her eyes, breathed. Sumedha sensed her mind bent hard on the puzzle. Her eyes snapped open.

"The bomb," she concluded. Her heart hammered audibly. The sour stench of fear rolled off her.

"Yes," Sumedha said. Paduma's face went slack—the vertigo of desolation, the inescapable end to a puzzle that could do nothing but damage. Empathy swelled in Sumedha.

"Now you know what it is not to know your partner's mind." He placed his hand flat to the sweating skin over her solar plexus, the place where he knew it hurt. Felt the muscle there clench as a single sob worked its way up through Paduma's body. It escaped her throat with a strangled sound.

"Yes," she nodded. "I am sorry for you, brother." She lay back down and closed her eyes. Sumedha breathed, reached out with his mind, felt the slightest flicker of connection.

"Random variance," he said. "It fevers my dreams."

"And mine," Paduma agreed.

"We touch a genome's every switch. We monitor each chromosome as an organism develops in its amniotic state—"

"And yet any organism can exhibit the unexpected—"

"For no discernable reason." This last they spoke in unison. Sumedha rolled to face his sister. Lost himself for a moment in the moist line where her cheek met Satori's skin, the touch of mother and child. He spoke once more.

"Pihadassa is my twin. She solves problems just as I do. Only she does it better." Understanding spread over Paduma's face.

"She is smarter."

"Yes. But I begin to see. And so do you." Sumedha closed his eyes. Pictured snowmelt raging down out of the Rockies, funneled into Satori's canals through a series of massive cartilage turbines. Paduma's turbines. He listened to the far-off whistle of bone windmill blades carving the air amid the factory ruins to the north. He placed a palm to the dome's skin. Satori's nerves sang with electricity.

Paduma's work.

He opened his eyes. She glowed in the sun. Verdant. Brilliant. He touched her brow, ran a finger along the curve of her ear.

"You *are* like Pihadassa. You see what she saw. Do you not?"

"I do not understand it." Paduma's face relaxed as the confession emerged. "But I feel it." Their minds touched, wound together, the mirrored double helix of twins.

"The Fathers' plan—"

"Is wrong. Yes."

"When they are whole, they will abandon Satori."

"Abandon us."

"Satori will die—"

"—and the Fathers do not care."

Fear welled up inside them. Together, they breathed, stilling their joined minds. They came to the moment. Observed the effervescent sensation of sugars combining inside their skin. Observed heartbeats synchronized with each other, with Satori.

"It feels good to connect."

"I feel your urgency. Sumedha, you must not—"

"Complete the Fathers' graft. I do not know if I can stop myself. It is—"

"What you do. Satori must live."

"We must live. Pihadassa—"

"Knew."

"Satori—"

"Is her child."

Sumedha slid his hand over Paduma's smooth scalp. He pressed his lips to hers. Their tongues met—joined like their minds. Paduma rolled onto her side and Sumedha pulled her hips close. Slid himself inside her. Their twinned helix spun, expanded, the blazing center of a universe belonging entirely to them. Sumedha ran his hand up Paduma's belly, over a breast to her throat.

"You and I—" he whispered into her ear.

"Have secrets."

"Are connected."

"What about—"

"Kassapa. I keep one secret—"

"We can keep two."

CHAPTER 12

Doss wrapped the coarse burlap of her shawl across her nose, filtering out dust. She sat hunkered, dressed in migrant rags, at the edge of a firepit dug into the powdery dirt of a field in the lee of a collapsed overpass. Acrid smoke rose from a hunk of burning plastic, over which several other migrants had spitted rats.

"Anything?" she asked.

"Lots of chatter about a permanent colony," Fiorivani reported. Like Doss, he'd wrapped himself in soiled cotton and burlap. A makeshift hood cowled the broad expanse of his well-fed face. Despite the disguise, the sallow migrants who shared the fire sensed the big man wasn't one of them, gave him too much space.

"Somewhere in Kansas," he told Doss, "but nobody knows where. She may as well be Santa Claus." He paused, listening. The telltale wire of an earpiece ran the edge of his cowl. "Chen says Gomez has five Flylights up and flying. They did their first training jump today."

"And?"

"Four dead."

Doss sucked her teeth, cursed. Still…

"Could be worse. He got a line to D.C.?"

Fiorivani mumbled into his throat mic, listened, shook his head. "Sat link's still fucked."

Doss gazed skyward through yellow topsoil haze. Imagined a net covering the sky, a com satellite sitting at each juncture. There were a lot of holes in that net these days. No sat link meant no coms with Rippert. Which meant no news on Emerson. It made Doss feel homicidal.

She peered out at the ruins of downtown Wichita, crumbling foundations protruding like rotten teeth from drifts of fine topsoil. Caravans rolled in from the south along I-35 and from the west along Route 400, overlapping to give the crossroads the illusion of permanent settlement. Long lines of bone-thin migrants limped along, wrapped in homemade burlap or torn FEMAs, tailing cobbled-together trucks and wagons that whined with disrepair.

Doss and her crew had camped here for five days, watching for some sign of the Designer, waiting for some definitive word. So far…nothing but rumor.

Across the fire, a migrant girl shuddered, stricken with obvious Tet. Doss' hand, filled with dark longing, touched the molded-plastic remote hung on a cord around her neck, hidden beneath her rags. Her eyes moved to the zep, which zombied ten miles out, a black finger pointing its way along the eastern horizon. She could hit the dead-man switch. Cause the rail gun to fix on her location. Do all these miserable fucks the favor, just vaporize this place. She keyed her throat mic.

"Puppy dog."

Across the field stood a miraculously intact motel, where *La Chupes* had set up shop. They cooked food out front, rancid stew bubbling in an old heavy-rig fuel tank they'd torched in half and set over a big fire. The other half of the tank held cornmash. Migrants gathered there, handing over pinches of seed to the well-fed *Chupes* in exchange for cornmash, for stew, for time in one of the motel's rooms. Speakers the height of a man stood either side of the motel's entrance, and the migrants soaked up fat dub like it was a long lost vitamin, the echo of civilization. Some feebly danced.

As Doss watched, a small gang member led three naked orphans, two girls and a boy, roped neck to neck, in a line up to the motel's second floor. The orphans looked scarcely younger than the gang member, maybe nine or ten. The *Chupe* ushered them into one of the rooms.

"Puppy dog," Doss repeated. She spotted Jake throwing dice against a stack of cinderblocks with three other *Chupes* near one throbbing speaker. He rose and stepped away, touched fingers in salute to the red scarf around his head.

"Boss Momma." He kept his back to her, eyes on the dice, his voice needling through strains of dub in Doss' earpiece. He'd ditched his army uniform for cutoff FEMAs. Doss watched his delicate shoulder blades. Wondered when, exactly, children had begun doing the nasty business of adults.

"Don't salute," she told him. "Gives you away."

"Nothing to hide here, Boss Momma. *La Chupacabra* loves you."

"No more signals. Got anything for me?"

"West," he said authoritatively.

"Revelatory. Anything new?"

"Everybody talks, nobody knows. Just west." He hesitated. Beats thumped in Doss' ear. His shoulders bunched as he struggled to form words. "They call her Corn Mother. Lot of people looking for her. Think she can save us."

"Don't worry, puppy dog. Nobody's going to save you."

"You'll save me, Boss Momma."

"Don't count on it. Out."

The migrant girl across the fire moaned. Her back arched with a sudden spasm. Fiorivani stared, something tormented in his expression.

"She's dead, you know," Doss told him. "Your sister."

Fiorivani's eyes—the same shocking green eyes as General Rippert's—settled on Doss for a second, then he turned and stared out at where a massive wall cloud rumbled over the plains to the north. His chin dipped to his chest.

"Yeah."

"Our mission is clear," Doss said. "We collect the Designer. Alive. There's no room for vengeance. Either yours or Rippert's."

"Sure, Boss." Fiorivani kept his gaze far away. Doss reached out, gripped his chin in between her fingers. Turned his face to hers, saw the loss there. Empathy stabbed her chest. She spoke gently.

"Alive, Lieutenant. Get in my way, I'll kill you."

"Understood, Boss."

"Good."

They took turns monitoring radio chatter, listening for any clue as to the Designer's location. Nothing. Just prairie saints and caravan updates. The afternoon waned. The storm to the north swelled, turned the nasty green color of an old hematoma. Then, as the day began to go dark, Doss saw what they'd been waiting for. She nudged Fiorivani with an elbow.

"There."

A flatbed truck pulled up beside the motel. Its cab had been shaped from heavy duty greenhouse plastic wrapped over a PVC frame; it carried three 100-gal water tanks.

"Damn." Fiorivani's jaw hung open. "Is that...a clone?"

The girl, skin the color of charcoal, sat naked at the truck's back end. A spiked collar circled tight around the svelte length of her neck. A thick log chain ran from it, clasped to a steel ring bolted to the flatbed's deck.

"A landrace," Doss affirmed.

The truck ground to a halt and the girl stood, phantasmal and glabrous—a collection of supernaturally precise ratios. Eyes to ears to mouth. Hips to waist to breasts. Shoulders to fingertips to ground. Devoid of chaos, randomness, imbalance. The back of Doss' neck tingled. Fiorivani gaped.

"She's perfect."

Three men climbed from the truck's cab. Doss noted cowboy hats, jeans, t-shirts, muscle. All three slung plastic assault rifles on their backs and stood surveying the scene.

"They've been eating," she observed.

"Jesus," Fiorivani said. "Could you maybe find some a little bigger?" Two of the cowboys were obviously twins, and enormous, pushing seven feet. Doss glanced sidelong at the lieutenant.

"Don't be a pussy."

The third cowboy, shorter than the others but thick, moved to the back of the truck. Cords of muscle worked in his forearm as he unhooked the girl's chain, handed its end to one of the big twins. They moved to the motel entrance, the twins' hats floating like boats sailing a sea of migrant heads as they shouldered their way through the crowd, the landrace girl in tow. The third man brought up the rear, his hat bobbing to chunky dub.

The *Chupes* at the motel entrance exchanged looks, reached for weapons as the cowboys approached. Doss saw one twin's mouth twist into a satisfied smile. He held up a small leather pouch, and spoke. The gang members relaxed, laughed. One took the pouch, said something and pointed towards the stairs. The tall cowboy tipped his hat.

"Puppy dog," Doss told her mic.

"Boss Momma," Jake answered. Doss spotted him near the *Chupes'* cooking vats, winced as he saluted.

"That's our crew. With the cowboy hats. Got it?"

"Got it."

"Where's Casanova?"

"Upstairs."

"Alright. Give the cowboys ten minutes to settle in. Then you two clear everyone out you don't want shot. Understood?"

"Got it."

Doss turned to Fiorivani. "Gear up."

La Chupes had cleared away from the rooms. They milled with Jake and Casanova at the bottom of the stairs, leaning against the railing or standing, arms crossed with obviously practiced nonchalance. They nodded respect as Doss and Fiorivani approached. A thick *Chupe* girl, nearly Doss' height and with a viciously crushed nose, stepped forward. An LC tat covered most of her dark face.

"Savior of El Sol. I'm Jill. I run this place. What you need, you get." She reverently touched fingertips to the red band wrapped around one bicep. Doss nodded to her, and beckoned Jake.

"What you got?" she asked him. He stepped forward, assuming some approximation of soldierly attention.

"Girl and one of those big fucking twins in room 124," he reported. "Other twin and his buddy are next door, room 122." Doss considered this, then addressed the *Chupe* girl.

"Jill, what do you have in room 122?"

"One slut."

"What's in room 124?"

"Two sluts."

"Nothing else?"

"No, ma'am."

"Okay," Doss said. "You're going to hear some noise, Jill. Ignore it."

"Yes, ma'am." A cruel smile distorted the LC on Jill's face. Behind her, the other *Chupes* somberly nodded.

The metal staircase squealed and tilted on its bolts as they started up it, Doss with the silenced .45 drawn and held low, Fiorivani following close behind. At the top, they paused. Doss eyed the motel's long exterior corridor, its row of doors facing out to what once had been the freeway and nonstop auto traffic. A thin metal rail lined the walkway, dangling in places from bolts corroded clean through. Below, the gathered *Chupes* watched, their faces upturned and young.

"We want the girl alive," Doss told Fiorivani, "and the twin with her, too. We take the other twin and his buddy out first. I'm on door. We go on three. Copy?"

Fiorivani nodded once, his face hard. "Copy."

Doss moved quietly up to the door whose chipped brass numbers read: 122. Pressed her ear against it, heard a young girl's voice, then a man's laughter. She carefully tried the knob. Unlocked. Fiorivani got behind her, pistol low, ready. Doss nodded the silent count, turned the knob.

Deep training kicked in. She went in low and fast, turning

right, following her pistol's front sight.

A kerosene lamp lit the room with smoky light. Two men sat on their knees, naked, the shorter cowboy and one of the twins. A small white girl lay naked between them on a heap of soiled blankets, one tiny ankle viced in the big twin's fist. He turned just as Doss squeezed the trigger. The pistol hissed, jerked twice in her hand. Blood sprayed the wall. The big cowboy collapsed, utterly limp.

Doss brought her sights to the shorter man, whose brows had just managed to go up in surprise. Fiorivani's bullets caught him just as Doss fired. The man's body collapsed around impacting rounds. He fell back. Doss swept her sights across the remainder of the room…Nothing. Just the lamp, stained blue carpet, decades of dust, the young girl. Doss moved into the room, poked each body with a sandaled toe.

"Deader than shit," Fiorivani judged. The girl sat up against the wall and casually eyed the bodies of her abruptly deceased clients. A spray of blood dotted her forehead. Doss guessed her to be eleven.

"You gonna kill me, too?" The indifference in her voice stirred strange and deep kinship in Doss. In her mind, she saw a single snowflake descend out of the grey light through the ceiling grate of the Siberian pit, settling against the frozen cheek of a corpse.

"You want me to?" she offered. The girl blinked wide eyes and shook her head, calmly.

"We're good," Doss told Fiorivani, and turned for the door. The girl was already rifling pockets.

They moved to the next door, room 124. Doss listened. Holstered the .45, drew the composite tube of the fuckstick from her belt. Rapped knuckles against the door three times hard. A few seconds passed, then the door opened. The cowboy, massive and naked, his erection stabbing in Doss' direction. On the floor behind him lay a boy and girl, wrapped naked around each other but motionless, as though posed. The landrace sat cross-legged in the corner, still collared. Doss smiled broadly at the cowboy.

"Hi," she said. He looked her up and down. Scars crisscrossed his face. His lip curled into a hungry smile.

"You're a tall bitch."

"You, too."

The fuckstick thumped. The cowboy flew back into the room, smacking against the opposite wall. He slid to the floor, his entire body quivering with volts.

Doss moved through the door, sweeping the fuckstick about the room. Fiorivani followed, tight behind his pistol. There was nobody else, just the kids and the landrace girl. Doss leveled the fuckstick at the cowboy. Figured he was a big fucker, and thumbed the trigger. It thumped a second time, spit a sizzling blue ball across the room. The cowboy arched. Only the top of his head and the points of his toes contacted the carpet.

Fiorivani closed the door. Kept his pistol on the kids and the landrace girl with one hand, with the other withdrew a roll of piping tape from within the folds of his burlap. This he tossed to Doss. She caught it, holstered the fuckstick, went to work.

It took the cowboy several minutes to fully revive. He strained instinctually, futilely, against the tape binding his limbs, muscles flexing. Then, consciousness fully achieved, he went still. His eyes peeled with fear as the situation registered—Fiorivani sitting Indian style on the floor beside him, tape dangling from one hand while Doss stood against the wall, .45 trained absently in the cowboy's general direction. The cowboy spoke mutely against the band of tape covering his mouth. Doss and Fiorivani watched, blank, until the cowboy began to scream, rage and panic, muffled.

Doss spoke mildly. "You can yell all you want. Your boys are dead. What we want is very simple." She pointed at the landrace girl, who now sat, also bound with tape, against the wall. She watched, her smooth face unconcerned, curious even. Up close, she looked carved from obsidian. "*Her*," Doss said. "I want to know where you got *her*."

"They took me at a crossroads to the east," the girl said. "They killed Rat." Her face fell, a child's uncomplicated sadness. "I miss Rat."

Doss and Fiorivani exchanged a glance. The cowboy nodded

emphatically. Doss gestured and Fiorivani ripped the tape off the big man's mouth. The cowboy sputtered, trying to form words.

"Pratt," he said. "We grabbed her near Pratt." He started to say more but Doss waved a hand. Fiorivani ripped a fresh strip from the role of tape and mashed it against the cowboy's lips. Doss stepped forward, knelt before the landrace girl.

"Honey, do you know where the Designer is?"

The landrace girl smiled. "My name is Dry Grass, not Honey."

Doss let out a long breath, a thin strand of patience drawing taut. "Okay," she said, conjuring each syllable slowly. "Dry Grass. Do you know where the Designer is?"

"Pihadassa?" The girl's gleaming pate swiveled slightly, indicating she didn't. "We split into three groups when we landed. My group went south. Pihadassa took her group west. The advocates found my group. We thought we could fend them off." The symmetry of her features cratered as the memory twisted her face. "We could not. Only Rat and I got away." She glanced at the cowboy, who watched her with wide eyes, no doubt calculating the odds of his survival with every word she spoke. "I miss Rat," she repeated, and tears welled in her eyes. "He was my mate."

Doss gently insisted. "Where is the Designer?"

"I do not know. I do not imagine she is anywhere. Not if the advocates found her, too."

A loud beep sounded from Doss' fatigue pocket. She blinked, holstered the .45, drew forth the flexpad. It beeped again in her hand. She unfolded it.

A face, square as a piece of steak, peered out from the translucent screen. He wore a *Chupe* red scarf tied over his head.

"Tsol," she said. He showed teeth.

"Agent Doss. Such a pleasure."

"It speaks." Dry Grass' eyes went wide. Her mouth formed a circle and she reached out to touch the flexpad. Doss stepped away.

"Rippert gave you this line" she guessed. Tsol's smile broadened.

"I'm his favorite little warlord."

"I'm a little busy at the moment."

"Indeed. My kids tell me you're enjoying Wichita." He chuckled. "They're good kids. Two of my favorites. Did they deliver my package?" He waited. Doss said nothing. "I'll take that as a yes. The digit's previous owner didn't give it up quietly. I wanted to assure you of that."

A clear bottle of something appeared in the feed, obscuring Tsol's face as he upended it. He swallowed, seemed for a moment to be close to retching, then held the bottle up, toasting.

"Indiana's finest. So I'm told. Tastes like you'd expect anything from Indiana to taste."

"Right." Doss began to fold the flexpad.

"I know what you're looking for, Agent Doss." Doss hesitated. Tsol gave her a shrewd look. "Just north of a littled town a hundred miles west of you. Burdock."

They regarded each other for a moment through the screen. Then Doss folded the flexpad closed and stuffed it into a hip pocket. She glanced at where Fiorivani towered over the cowboy, and shrugged.

"West."

"What about him?"

Fiorivani pointed a sandaled toe at the cowboy, who shook his head and pleaded mutely through the tape.

Doss thought of Emerson. A man so full of decency it had sometimes enraged her to be around him. It'd occurred to her that it was his decency that appealed to her. If a man like that could stomach her...

She glanced at the two children, who stared vacantly back, and decided decency in this situation was simple. She drew the .45. It hissed twice and the cowboy's chest burst. He went still.

Doss holstered her piece, cut the tape binding the two children and the Satori girl. They didn't move. Doss pointed at the door.

"You can go."

The boy shook his head. "*Chupes*'ll fuck us up."

"They won't. I promise."

"They feed us," the girl said. Doss started to say something else, but the girl's implacable stare stopped her. She turned and walked out the door.

Outside, night had fallen. Lightning strobed the prairie as the storm rolled by to the north. Thunder growled. Dry Grass emerged from the room. Leaned against the upper walkway's railing, turned her face into the electric wind, completely unconcerned with her nakedness.

"I like the storms," she said. "They're alive." She'd left the collar in the room.

"What now, Boss Momma?" Jake called up from below.

"Yeah, Boss," Fiorivani said. "What now?"

Doss eyed the cowboys' truck. It sat canted hard to one side, and pinged, the sound of an overheated motor cooling in the night air.

"West," she said.

"Shit," Jake grinned. "I told you so."

"Roger that."

CHAPTER 13

Brood woke to the sound of a dog barking. A small wind turbine whined somewhere close and for a while he thought he'd fallen asleep in his mother's greenhouse. In a moment she would come and carry him to bed. But it was too cold to be San Antonio. And there was a girl, naked and warm against him.

All at once he remembered the world. Dread, absent for that one instant, sank into his body, as integral as bones. He opened his eyes, saw his breath.

"You're awake," the girl said. They lay wrapped in a wool blanket on broken checkers of linoleum, what had once been a grocery store on the outskirts of some little Oklahoma shithole. A white beam of sunlight cut across the room from a high window.

"Fucking hate Oklahoma," Brood said. He bet they weren't fifty miles from the spot where his mother had died.

The girl rose to an elbow and smiled at him, missing teeth. The girl who'd worn the aviator shades. She was slightly younger, thirteen, maybe fourteen, so skinny he could see blue veins beneath the translucent skin of her cheeks. Her eyes, without the shades, pointed in slightly different directions, and Brood didn't know which one to look at. But she had frizzy hair the color of ripe corn and she was warm, and she seemed to like getting naked.

Brood couldn't remember her name, so he kissed her. She tasted like dust. He slid a thigh up between her legs. She pushed her hips close. He felt bones. He ran a hand down her back, his index finger ticking over each protruding vertebrae.

"Wait here," he told her. He kissed her on the forehead, extracted himself, stood.

"Where you going?"

"Nowhere, *chica*." His canvas shorts lay in a heap on the floor. He pawed through them, retrieved something from a hidden pocket, then stood naked for a moment in the sunbeam. It warmed him, made the wound in his side tingle, but in a good way. The infection had receded. The hole had almost healed shut.

"Probably hit eighty today," he said. For a week the caravan had holed up in this shell of a strip mall at the little town's edge. Snow had been so thick the night before he couldn't see a foot out the door. "Probably be one ten tomorrow."

"You're so skinny," the girl said. "Nothing but bones. Maybe the Corn Mother can fatten you up when we find her."

They'd changed course, backtracked, changed course again in the week after they'd picked Brood up. He thought of Anna, sitting in the helicopter bubble cab of the lead truck. Holding broken headphones to one ear while she tuned the dial on the ancient Ham mounted with wire to the dash. Trying to divine the Corn Mother's sacred location as her people grew hungrier.

"Ain't no Corn Mother," Brood said. "Just a ghost you all chasing around the prairie."

"We," the girl corrected. "*We* chasing."

"*Supongo*." Brood smiled at her. "No need to fatten me up. *Más rápido que un* rattler." He pointed at her, one eye closed, his hand a pistol. "I can put an arrow through a rabbit's eye at a hundred meters. On the run." He watched the girl to see if she was impressed. She smiled kindly. Her hunting rifle lay pieced out and rolled up in a cloth on the floor nearby. He'd seen her nail a rabbit at a quarter mile. He lowered his hand. "How come you missed me that night?" he wondered.

"Didn't want to kill nobody. And we been watching you all that day." She lifted a coy shoulder. "I liked you. It was cute the way you talked to your brother."

Brood held his breath, swallowed hard. Pushed a palm against one closed eye, as though he could physically force thoughts of Pollo out of his skull, thoughts of what his own life now had become. He was nothing, *espiritu enojado,* a hungry spirit, a mouth wandering the dust, trying to feed itself. Emptiness swelled in his chest. His body tightened against it, locking it inside. After a moment he registered the girl, still watching him. He slid under the blanket beside her.

"You're skinny," he told her, and his voice quavered. He swallowed again, stuffed the emptiness down, down, down inside. Ran a hand up the girls ribs, over her breast. "Way skinnier than me. Here." He opened the fingers of his other hand. The girl's eyes widened.

"Seeds!" A dozen of them, plump lentils resting like tiny eggs waiting to hatch in his palm.

"No, *chica*. I soaked them." They'd grown fat with juice and aminoes. He pointed at their nascent tails. "They sprouts now."

"Where'd you get them?"

"Raimi gave them to me."

The girl gave a sly smile. "He *likes* you," she said.

"Yeah, he's okay."

"No, he *likes* you. Everybody knows he likes boys. He wants you to be his little bitch." Brood considered this for a moment, decided it was possible and laughed. The girl knitted her brow. "He shouldn't have gave you seed. That's for planting." Brood held the sprouts close to his face.

"Hope they ain't frozen."

The girl carefully took one between a thumb and forefinger, placed it like a fat emerald on her tongue. Her eyes grew distant with pleasure as she chewed. Brood tossed a few into his own mouth. They were perfect. Tasted like he imagined sunlight would taste. His body, cratered by vitamin deficiencies, instantly began sucking nutrients from them, a sort of electric feeling in his gut. He let the rest drop into the girl's hand. "Our secret, Bev," he told her. She gave him a cold stare.

"*Viv.*"

"Viv. That's what I said." He held her chin between his thumb and forefinger, forcing her eyes to meet his—he was pretty sure. "Promise. That *culero* Billy'll give me all kinds of shit if he finds out."

"Our secret," Viv nodded.

"Okay. Don't know what his problem is. He ain't liked me since he first saw me."

"He just don't like stray dogs. You're another mouth to feed." She furtively placed another sprout in her mouth. "And he's my brother."

"*Coño.*" Brood stared at her. Shook his head, marveled at his own stupidity. "No wonder." Viv laughed, a leering sound.

"Don't worry. He only looks mean. Once Anna takes you in, you're family. Anna's big into family." Viv propped herself on an elbow, let the blanket fall away. Her hair frayed out like lightning. She gave Brood a look with implications. He leaned in to kiss her. She leaned away.

"Who's Rosa?" she asked. For an instant Brood let himself imagine it was Rosa who lay there, dirty blankets tangled around her. But to think of her was to think of Hondo. And to think of Hondo was to think of Pollo. He shut his eyes. "You talk about her in your sleep," Viv said. "She's your girl, huh."

"Not no more. She won't have no beggar." Brood met Viv's eye. Then her other eye. She looked away.

"My eyes are broken. I know it."

He reached out, cupped her face in his hand, felt malarial heat in her cheek. He made her face him, met each eye in turn, forcing her to endure it.

"*Nada roto, chula. Muy bonita.*"

She grew hotter against his hand. She aimed an eye at him, reminded him of a crazed bird.

"I can see why she dumped you," she said, and her eye travelled down his body. "You're so skinny." She pushed the last sprout into his mouth. Then her hand moved south, wrapped itself around his cock. "Don't look so sad. I like skinny boys."

....

They emerged from the store to an explosion of blue sky. Deep snow covered the flat acreage of an old parking lot fronting the strip mall. Three men stood nearby, warily eyeing a huge satellite dish they'd propped over a fire and filled with snow to melt.

"Think about it like a pie," Raimi said. He had long black hair hooked behind his ears and the front of his FEMAs were soaked through, evidence of the problem at hand. "Three pieces. Three of us lift. On three." Billy ran a hand over cornrows, seemed to concentrate for a minute, then shot a sly look at Raimi. He winked at the third man, Jorgen, who was tall and wore shredded jeans.

"You lost me there," Billy said. "On what?" He looked again at Jorgen, who kept his face straight.

"On three," Raimi said.

"You count to three, then we lift on four?"

"No, we lift on three."

"Right. You count to three, then we lift."

"We lift when I *hit* three. *On* three."

"So do you mean on two?"

Raimi took a step back, pushed a strand of long black hair delicately behind an ear. He raised a hand, shading his eyes from the brittle post-storm sunshine, and began patiently to explain himself once more.

"We stand around the dish. Equal spaces. I count to three. When I hit three, we lift. Together." Billy suppressed a smile. Sunshine turned Jorgen's blond crew cut white as he turned and snickered up the sleeve of his stained denim shirt.

"Got it," Billy said. "We spin around three times…"

"Oh, fuck you guys."

Billy and Jorgen laughed. Then Billy spotted Brood. He went silent and his face darkened. Brood grinned.

"*Que onda?*" He stepped out of the building's shadow and stretched ostentatiously, letting the sun warm his bare torso. Billy's eyes wandered between Brood and Viv. He turned to Raimi.

"Let me ask you a question, since you know so much about pies. Can a pie have four pieces?"

"Course," Raimi said. "It's a circle. It can have as many—"

"Get your skinny ass over here, *Cholo.*" Billy motioned at the dented satellite dish. "Take a piece of pie." Brood stepped up, his bare feet punching holes in the melting snow. He cautiously placed a finger against the dish's edge, making sure it wasn't too hot, then sidled up and gripped it with both hands. Raimi counted.

"One. Two. *Three!*" Gallons of newly melted water sloshed as they lifted.

"*Dónde?*" Brood asked.

"There." Raimi jerked his chin at where the two trucks sat nose to nose, half buried in snow drifts a good fifty yards across the lot. A tiny plastic funnel no wider than his hand stuck from the opening atop the water truck's rusted tank, perhaps fifteen feet off the ground.

"Got to be fucking kidding me, homes."

"Why don't you just use a hose and siphon it?" Viv suggested. Brood and the others paused, looking at one another. They set down the dish. Viv shook her head. "Idiots." She turned and stomped off across the lot. Jorgen grinned.

"She ain't wrong."

"A complete lack of foresight ending in failure." Billy narrowed his eyes at Raimi. "Imagine that."

A sharp whistle pierced the air. They all turned, found Anna headed their way, short legs pistoning through the snow. The dog loped up to her and barked, bouncing happily. She whistled again and it went quiet and heeled.

"I'm sure you could do much better, Billy," she said as she approached.

"I'm sure, too," Billy replied, but now he didn't sound very sure.

"You." Anna pointed at Brood. "Come with me." She turned and pressed once more through the snow, back the way she had come. As Brood moved to follow, Billy reached out and gripped his arm. He leaned close enough for Brood to see the acne-pitted geography of his face. Brood smelled something sour and hungry emanating from his skin.

"Viv's into you," he said. "The second she ain't, you be rotting in a ditch." Brood took in the older boy's broad frame, the ropes of thin, underfed muscle. His wound throbbed. He felt weak. He smiled pleasantly up into Billy's face.

"You talk a lot."

....

Anna prodded delicate fingers around the puckered red dot above Brood's hip where Richard's bullet had pierced him. The swelling had disappeared, the bruising had turned the color of corn mash.

"Sensitive?" she asked. Brood shook his head.

"*Poquito.* Not bad."

"One more shot of Cipro, just to be safe." Anna turned. Brood watched the eagle, made of multi-colored plastic stones, sewn into the back of her denim vest as she bent through the chopper bubble's open door, rooting for something.

She'd cleared snow away beside the lead truck and set up a long metal worktable in the sun, and beside it a metal folding chair. Atop the table the Ham radio hummed hotly. A cinderblock-sized hunk of aluminum hooked to a block of stacked lith bats, whose cords ran through a converter, up a high PVC pole. There, in an impossibly blue sky, whirled the blades of tiny wind turbine.

Anna emerged with a steel box, red with a white cross on it. From this she pulled a hypo gun into which she loaded a vial half-full of amber liquid. She pressed the gun against Brood's side. It hissed, a quick bee sting, and he winced. She peered at him then, searching, the creases of long years on the road mapping her face.

"How do you feel?" she asked.

"Okay. *Gracias, Madre.*"

"*De nada*." Anna repacked the hypo gun, put the med kit back into the cab and withdrew something else. She glanced around, made sure nobody saw, and placed a handful of dried apple slices in Brood's palm. Brood bit into one. It tasted alive. Anna smiled, pressed a finger against her lips. "Don't tell anyone where I keep my treats." She watched with obvious satisfaction as Brood chewed. After a moment she asked, "What happened to your brother?"

Brood stopped chewing. He started to say something, then simply shook his head. Anna rubbed the back of her neck beneath her grey ponytail.

"How?"

Brood's jaw clenched. All his muscles tightened, tried to deflect the memory, keep it somewhere outside his body where he wouldn't feel it. He gazed over the snowed-under remnants of the little town. It looked almost like nothing had ever been there—just the hollowed out strip mall and the steel frame of an office building. White smoke curled on the horizon. The cook fires of another caravan.

"*La Chupes* found us," he said. "They thought Pollo had the Tet."

Anna nodded. Abruptly she turned and whistled. Brood saw movement across the parking lot. The dog. It emerged from the shadow of a doorway and hopped through the snow along the strip mall's edge. Anna whistled again and the dog stopped, hunkered in another doorway, utterly still, barely visible.

"Smart dog," Brood observed.

"Smarter than most humans. They're bred to herd sheep."

"How come you don't eat it?" Brood asked. Anna fixed him with a hard look.

"Because we're civilized."

Across the parking lot, the tall man named Jorgen trudged through the snow and settled beside a small fire, where a hollow-looking woman and small girl huddled together beneath the old portico of a vacant storefront. He pulled a Satori carrot from beneath a fold of burlap, produced a small knife and began cutting the carrot into sections. Carefully, like it was gold.

"It's a *dog*, *Madre*," Brood said. "You get miles off that meat."

"That dog is my friend." Anna leaned with one hand on the table and placed the other on a defiantly cocked hip. "I don't eat my friends." Anna stared. The moment hung. Finally she turned and whistled.

"Viv likes you," she told Brood, her eyes on the dog now loping through the snow towards them. "Maybe you could stay with us."

"Got nowhere else to go," Brood admitted. "Don't think her bro would be happy about it if I stayed, though."

"Billy." Anger touched Anna's face and she looked at Brood. "He's not much help to her."

"Qué quieres decir?"

"Viv, hon. She has the Tet."

"Nah." Brood shook his head. "She ain't stiff or nothing."

"She is. Watch her at night."

Brood searched his memory. Found Viv there, working her shoulder in circles, easing a cramp. The emptiness welled up inside him.

"She know?" he asked.

"She's known for weeks."

"What about..." Brood's mind froze with the thought. His hands went involuntarily to his chest, as though he might detect the Tet worming its way through him, cranking his muscles tight, stiffening his joints.

"You're fine," Anna told him. "It comes from Satori." She aimed her eyes pointedly at where Jorgen squatted beside the fire with the woman and her daughter, parsing out small hunks of carrot to the woman and girl. "You get it from eating, not fucking."

"How you know?"

"The Mother told me."

"The Mother?" Brood looked at Anna like she'd spoken gibberish. "Whose mother?" Anna smiled.

"The Mother. She tells me all kinds of things. Maybe you'll get to meet her."

Brood made a mental head count of the small troupe. There

was Anna, Jorgen, Raimi and Billy. The strange woman and her daughter, who spoke neither English nor Spanish, and whose names he didn't know. Himself and Viv. That was it. No one he hadn't yet met. No Mother.

"*Esta loca, Madre?*" he inquired, and quickly held up a diplomatic hand. "It don't bother me none if you are. Just like to know, you know?"

Anna laughed. She whistled over her shoulder. The dog halted, stood rock still in the snow fifty feet away.

"I keep my family alive," she said. "Beyond that, what difference does it make?"

Viv settled herself at the fire with Jorgen's group. Her smile flashed at Brood beneath the aviator shades as she reached out to tickle the girl. Tiny laughter rang across the lot. It sounded strange, incongruous with the hunger pressing down on them all, heavy as time.

"How long she got?" Brood asked.

"Who knows? It's different with everyone." Anna's hand settled atop the Ham. "The Corn Mother came from Satori. If I can find her, maybe she can help."

"Hope ain't nobody's friend, though, *Madre*." Brood hawked and spit something black into the snow. The hint of a smile touched Anna's face. "You laughing at me, *madre?*" he asked.

"Absolutely not, hon," Anna said, her tone making it clear she was. "It gives me comfort to see you make her happy. I think it does Billy, too, even though he won't say it." Silence held them for a beat, then she said, "You don't strike me as the farming type. How'd you and your friends get by?"

"We're traders," Brood told her. Anna nodded.

"Thieves. That's what I thought when we saw you on your wagon. A bunch of thieves." Brood thrust his chin defiantly forward, remained silent. Anna stepped forward, reached out. Touched cool fingertips to Brood's cheek. "The Mother told me you would come to us. She told me you would help us." Brood caught a glimpse of fear, of need eddying just beneath the leathery surface of her personality. Her tone grew frank. "We've eaten the last of the food we canned last fall. We won't last another week, let alone until we harvest. We won't even find a place to plant before we starve. I need to find the Corn Mother. I need more time." She brushed his cheek with her thumb, then let her hand fall until her finger aimed at Brood's healing wound. "Am I your friend?" she wondered. Brood watched her narrowly, gave a noncommittal gesture of his hand. Anna inclined her chin to the east, towards the smoke of the distant cook fire. "How far you think that caravan is?"

"Six miles," Brood figured. Anna looked him up and down.

"You a good thief, Brood?"

"Better than you," he said, and then began to understand. He crossed his arms, eyed Anna down the length of his nose. "We don't do no stealing from the hungry."

"Who's we?" The corner of Anna's lip curled. She pinned Brood with a complicated look, then let her gaze wander the flat empty miles of shimmering snow. "There's only us. Or there's only you."

She turned abruptly away. The jeweled eagle on her back winked in the sun. She whistled and the dog came running. It wiggled between her legs and under her hands. She reached into the truck's cab and brought forth a piece of jerked meat.

"Good dog!" she cooed. It whined. She fed it. It lapped its tongue at her hands and she rubbed its white face. "Who's a good dog!"

....

Brood pretended he was a clump of mud in the moonless dark. He slithered, wending around vestigial patches of melting snow, through wet clay, over asphalt.

It was a small group. Two families, as far he could tell. They'd circled three wagons—flatbeds like Hondo's, with electric motors bolted to them—nose-to-tail, forming a vehicular fortress on the blank lot adjacent an empty, monolithic foundation. They huddled around a fire in there. Brood caught glimpses of them through wagon undercarriages. He smelled rabbit, and tomato sauce. He heard children's voices.

He pulled the last soft brick from his knapsack. He knew nothing about Semtex, beyond that it blew shit up. When he'd asked where it had come from, Anna'd smiled and told him simply, "Dallas." It felt dense in his hand, weighed too much for its size, like it had cut its own deal with the laws of physics. He placed it atop the concrete base of a dead light pole protruding out of the lot.

A wire dangled from the open back of an old walkie Jorgen had taped to the brick. Brood held his breath. Wound the stripped copper end around a hook in the detonator, a gleaming metal stick that protruded from the brick. Pinched the knob atop the walkie between thumb and forefinger. Held his breath. Turned the knob until it clicked. A tiny LED came awake on the walkie's front. Brood exhaled.

It took a long time to crawl back to the ditch, where the others waited. As he moved, the fire inside the ring of wagons burned low. Voices went quiet, except for two men who muttered in the dark. Brood imagined he could see the palest implication of dawn to the east.

"You're shivering," Viv told him when he slid into the ditch beside her. She opened the blanket she wore and pulled Brood into the warmth she shared there with her rifle.

"Let's get it done," Brood said. He looked down the ditch at the line of faces, turned silently his way. Billy, Raimi, Jorgen and Anna. "Get on them like you mean it," he whispered to them. "Loud and mean. Scareder they are, less likely we'll have to fuck them up." He nodded to Jorgen. The scrawny man held up a walkie and switched it on.

"Here we go," he said, and thumbed the send button.

A flash lit the prairie. For a strobed instant, Brood saw one wagon hovering, an inverted V, its back broken.

The blast wave hit. A wall of blank violence that turned everything white. Then came the tornado howl of the sound wave. When it passed, Brood found himself against the ditch's opposite side. Mud caked him.

"Jesus!" Billy shouted, blindly, rhetorically, at the space in front of him. "How much of that shit you use?"

"Here we go," Jorgen repeated. This time Brood dove for the ditch's bottom and covered his head. Jorgen changed the walkie's channel, thumbed the button a second time.

Another blast, a digestive rumble Brood felt well up through the ground. Mud rained down.

"Last one!" Jorgen called. He thumbed the button. This time Brood heard within the concussion the shriek of twisting metal: the light pole upending, elevating, coming down on asphalt. Brood waited for the rain of debris to cease. When it did, he stood.

"*Vamonos!*" he yelled. He ran, slipping across greasy clay, a heavy wrench in one hand. The others ran beside him, all holding old rifles or pistols.

"Oh shit," Raimi exhaled when they reached the camp. One wagon had been obliterated—nothing where it'd sat but a deep cavity in the broken asphalt, already collecting water. The other two wagons lay on their sides. Anna drew to a halt and stood surveying the obliterated camp.

"Don't think we'll have to shoot anybody," she concluded. She lowered the hunting rifle she carried, slung it over a shoulder and stepped over a body that had been pounded into the earth, as though it had fallen from very high up. Other bodies lay about, some of them in pieces, mixed in with crumpled chassis parts.

Billy wheeled his rifle around one-handed. He gestured at the crater.

"Shit, I hope their food wasn't on that wagon."

Brood saw movement. A woman sat near one upended wagon, her arms wrapped around a toddler. Their eyes shone white through a plaster of blasted mud. Both watched Brood blankly as he approached, as though they'd been frozen in time the moment before the blasts.

"Here it is," Jorgen called from the other wagon. "Seed, too."

Anna stepped up beside Brood. Looked from him to woman and her child, then around at the destruction. She laid a hand on his shoulder.

"A good plan. None of us got hurt."

Brood watched the woman and her toddler. They gazed back, silent, empty. Ghosts staring into the stunned predawn. Brood figured it was something like what Hondo had seen, those years before when he'd found Brood and Pollo. Two starved boys withering in the Oklahoma sun, broken by the refugee road. Something churned in Brood's gut, like hunger but worse. A terror he couldn't quite fathom. A darkness at the center of things, a shifting of the scales. Hondo had left them water.

"You don't need their seed," Brood told Anna. "Leave it."

Anna's gaze lingered on the woman and child. She seemed to make a hard calculation of her own, then nodded.

"Half the food, too," Brood said.

"Jorgen," Anna called.

"Yo."

"Leave the seed." She hesitated.

"Fuck that." Billy stalked up beside them. Propped his rifle on his hip as he regarded the muddy tableau. "Fuck them," he decided after a moment. Anna ignored him. She turned to Jorgen, who moved to her side. He slid an arm over her shoulder, quietly took in the catatonic woman and child.

"Bad luck," he said, and shrugged like that was all it was. Behind him, Raimi and Viv had laid out a heavy tarp and begun filling its center with jars of canned Satori vegetables.

"How much food we got?" Anna asked. Jorgen let out a breath between tight lips as his face pinched with mentation.

"Four days," he guessed. "A week if we stretch it real hard."

"Alright." Anna looked at the two survivors. "Leave a little for them."

"If you say so."

"I do."

"Alright. You're the boss." Jorgen leaned in close. They kissed, briefly but deeply. Then he turned and joined Raimi and Viv. Anna turned to Brood, eyed him like a tool she'd just figured out how to use.

"The Mother was right about you." Smiling as she said it.

"Give me your rifle," Brood told her. Anna's eyes narrowed. "Give it," he insisted, and held out his hand. "They can maybe hunt." Anna hesitated, face pinched with calculation, then slowly unslung the rifle. She laid it reluctantly into Brood's upturned palm. Brood knelt.

"*Lo siento*," he said, and placed the rifle gently before the woman and her child. They seemed to neither hear nor see him, just stared into the night.

....

He sat huddled in the rear wheel well of Anna's truck, a seized-up CV joint pieced out on a tarp before him. There was nothing in the world except heat and wind and dust. Topsoil turned the day a perpetual brown dusk, as though all of Oklahoma had risen in a wave and folded over on itself. Grit caked the insides of Brood's lips beneath the rag through which he breathed. His lungs felt like two muddy turds in his chest.

He dipped his fingers into a jar of yellow corn oil, spread it on a rag and wiped it into the worn grooves of a small differential. The metal glistened for an instant, then went dull again, caked with dust.

It had been a week since the raid. Anna had spent the bulk of that time in the cab of her truck, monitoring the Ham. Now the stolen vegetables were mostly gone, and the little caravan hadn't yet left Oklahoma. Brood pulled the rag from over his mouth and spit.

Dust to dust. His mother had whispered it near the end, over and over. *Polvo eres y en polvo te convertirás*. He considered the phrase, felt the truth of it as he began piecing the joint back together. The dust would take them.

A hand touched his shoulder. He turned, found Viv's goggled face peering down at him. She said something, but the wind stole her words. Brood gazed mutely at her. He tried to speak, but his mouth remained inert.

It had been like this since the raid. Like the silent weeks after his mother's death, riding Hondo's wagon. Words formed in his mind, but he couldn't voice them. Viv leaned close.

"Ceremony," she yelled. She started to walk away, then turned and beckoned. Brood rose and followed. He saw the stiffness in her shoulders now that he knew to look for it, the awkward reluctance of her knees to bend as she walked.

They'd already gathered in the truck's lee, every member of Anna's little tribe. They sat in a tight circle, wrapped in their blankets and tarps against the dust. The dog wiggled among them, moving from one to the next, receiving love. A fire—hunks of rubber tire and bits of laminate siding—burned at the circle's center, belching black smoke.

Anna sat beside it, a ragged blue scarf tied around her face. She'd spread a blanket before her. On it sat an ancient bullhorn hooked to a frothing old twelve-volt battery. A gallon water jug. A dented steel pot. As Brood watched, she reached into the pot and withdrew a leather pouch. She held it up for everyone to see, poked fingertips inside withdrew what looked like a piece of shriveled tree bark. This she placed in the pot. Viv leaned close to Brood.

"They're from down south," she hollered in his ear. "The Mother doesn't make them anymore. They're extinct." Brood poked her shoulder, raised shoulders and hands, miming confusion. "For talking to the Mother," Viv said.

Anna rose to her feet and shed her denim vest. She unzipped her FEMAs, let them fall to her ankles. Stood there naked, a shocking white apparition in the blasting dust. She spread her arms. Her people beheld her. After several beats, she squatted over the pot and pissed. When she'd finished, she dressed, poured water from the jug into the pot and placed the pot against the fire. Occasionally she shook it, mixing its contents. The little tribe waited. When the fire'd burned low, she scooped out a handful of ash and moved around the circle. She knelt before each person. Pressed her index finger to the ash in her palm, then marked a dark comma on each waiting brow.

"Mother guide us," intoned each person in turn.

Anna knelt before Brood. Ain't much for praying, he tried to tell her, but nothing came out. He regarded her silently. She smiled.

"The Mother brought you to us. You brought us food. You brought us time." She pressed her finger between his eyes. "Today we welcome you to the family."

When she'd marked them all, she returned to the fire. She raised the pot, held it aloft like a religious artifact, letting her tribe bear witness.

She drank. Her face twisted, like the stuff burned. When it passed, she carried the pot to the small girl who sat on the opposite side of the fire from Brood. The girl's face turned sour as she brought the pot to her lips, then she passed it to her mother, who sat beside her. Next came Jorgen. He drank, passed the pot on. Soon it came to Brood. He peered down into the steaming brew. It stank like diesel fumes.

"Drink," Viv insisted. Brood looked around at the covered faces of the migrants around the circle. Felt their eyes on him, felt desperation, thick as the wind. Figured it didn't matter one way or the other what he did. They were out of time, a family bound by dust. He silently intoned his own prayer, *Que se chinque* Oklahoma, and drank.

It tasted dark, like something fetid from out of a swamp. Bile rose, but he suppressed it.

"Welcome to the family, Brood," Raimi called from down the line.

"Welcome to the family," Viv told him. Brood passed her the pot.

Anna brought the bullhorn to her lips. A squeal of feedback cut through the wind, and then she spoke.

"Tonight we ask for guidance to our destination. Let us move to the light." She paused and for a second the wind swallowed them all. "Let the dead be dead."

"Let the dead be dead," the small clan echoed as one. Ann began to sing, a lilting, wordless tune, crunchy with the bullhorn's static.

Other migrants picked it up and after a time Brood realized he, too, had begun humming the tune, but silently. The song turned sad. It pulled his mind like a long thread out of his skull—suspended it before his eyes. It looked like stained glass. As he watched, it shattered in a shriek of feedback.

He saw a snake, long as all the roads he'd travelled. It hissed, a sound like heavy rain on hardpan. He fell down its spiraling coils, down the hole out of which it rose. A hole straight to the world's core.

Pollo came to him there, a skinny boy standing in a scorched forest. Ash fell like snow around him. Little stick figure animals danced across his skin, a parade of the dead. His empty eyes, old as the world, watched Brood. They were the snake's eyes, Brood realized, and for some reason this broke him. He wept.

He saw Hondo Loco in the forest, too. He saw his mother.

Time passed, but strangely. He found himself dancing, a rattlesnake held tenderly in each hand. They coiled around his wrists. Their diamond eyes stared into his. He'd mesmerized them, or they him.

"These snakes in my hand, *Madre*," he said to his mother's bloated face. "*Son mi amor para usted.*"

"Let the dead be dead," someone said, and his mother's face turned to ash.

"Let the dead be dead." Hondo Loco's face turned to ash.

"Let the dead be dead." Pollo's face turned to ash.

They all blew away in the wind.

"Fucking *cholo*," he heard cornrowed Billy say. "Don't know drug real from real." From somewhere out on the prairie came the rattling tin sound of Viv's laughter.

"Let the dead be dead." Brood had never felt so alone.

. . . .

He woke, walking. The rhythmic crunch of his sandals along worn asphalt, muffled by the occasional drift of powdery dirt, wore a groove into his mind.

The quiet struck him. The wind had ceased. The dust had dropped from the sky as though it had never existed, leaving the world so clear it seemed fragile—which was how Brood felt inside, empty as a shard of polished glass. And that was alright, he decided.

"Where the fuck are we?" he asked the person walking beside him. The sound of his own voice startled him. They were the first words he'd spoken since the raid.

Billy happened to be the person walking beside him. Dust wafted from him with every step as he walked hunched beneath the rifle slung over his shoulder. He leered at Brood. A strip of dirt caked the area around his eyes that hadn't been covered during the wind, except for clean white crow's-feet that made him look surprised.

"You just get back?" he asked. Brood blinked. Billy nodded. "First time's like that for some people. Lose yourself, you know? My first time, I couldn't remember my own name for a week." His laughter felt like a washboard against Brood's brain.

Anna's rusted trucks lumbered a hundred paces ahead along the worn track. Behind them the road stretched, a grey thread across table-flat topsoil all the way to blue, blue sky. He saw Anna and Jorgen back there, marching hand in hand. They wore soft expressions. Viv and Raimi, the mother who spoke the strange foreign tongue and her daughter, they all walked easy, free of worry.

"*Where* are we?" Brood asked again. Billy angled his head up the road towards whatever destination awaited.

"Half a day out." He eyed Brood. "You see the snake?" Brood thought about it.

"*Sí*, homes. I saw the snake. Saw the whole fucking world die." He gave Billy a pinched look. "Half a day out from where?"

"The Corn Mother's place. Friend of Anna's is already there. Uncle Jessup. Anna got him on the Ham last night during the ceremony. Got directions."

"So we..."

"Home," Billy grinned. Brood struggled to comprehend this, and failed. He marveled at his own marching feet.

"Shit," he managed. Billy laughed.

"Talk to the Mother, brother, and shit happens." He watched Brood as they walked. A metal bead at the end of one cornrow glinted in the sun. Brood saw honesty in his face. "Welcome to the family, bro," he said, and placed a hand on Brood's shoulder.

CHAPTER 14

A body fell. Twelve stories of silence, then a heavy clap as organs imploded and bones shattered.

"Love that sound," Snake laughed. "Sound of work getting done."

Sumedha ignored him, ignored the dozen helmeted men and women pressing close—his new security detail, expanded since the bombing. Kassapa's orders. He inhaled deeply, taking in the stench rising from Snake's new Tet pens. Turned a long stretch of Satori's helix in his mind, searching for possible tweaks in the timing of the dome's seasonal shedding.

The storm had come like a white wall down out of the mountains and socked the city in for a week—then, in a moment, had evaporated. The sun now shone yellow and dense in a sky gauzy with tundra methane. Cold rivulets trickled down Satori's skin, wending through goose bumps the size of anthills. Runoff from a rapidly melting cap of snow at the dome's peak.

The storm was nothing she could not handle. She had been designed to thrive in aberrant weather. She was mammalian, kept warm by her own metabolism. Yet Sumedha shivered with empathy at the—

She.

This proclivity to anthropomorphize was new to him. He sensed its roots in his isolation, his need to connect. Knew it hampered his acuity. He knew, too, the only way to cease compulsive thoughts was, simply, to cease them. He went still, brought his mind to a state of disciplined rigidity, felt nothing but heat spreading his pores.

Snake cleared his throat politely. His two helper boys shuffled impatiently, one tall and broad, hollow-chested, the other small and gaunt beneath his FEMAs. Another body thundered to the ground.

"Alright," Sumedha said. "Show me."

They stood on the twelfth floor inside the steel-and-concrete skeleton of a high-rise just outside Satori's perimeter wall. Pairs of thick landraces ranged through the pens, checking pulses. They stacked pale bodies onto wagons and hauled them to the building's crumbling edge, where they pitched them over the side. Far below, landrace teams gathered around the spot where the bodies cracked the earth. They gathered them onto more wagons and shuttled them inside the dome.

Snake cocked back his shoulders and rubbed his bare belly—an unconscious display of primate musculature his undernourished frame entirely lacked. Lifted his chin, peered over the press of bodies cramming one chain-link pen. He pointed.

"That one."

An adolescent boy hunkered in a corner, so thin he seemed about to disappear. A chaos of tatted hieroglyphs covered his naked torso. He stared emptily at a spot of chipped concrete.

Sumedha motioned to the four landraces he had tasked for help. They nodded heavy brows, and muscled into the pen, hauling bodies aside until they could reach the tattooed boy. As their hands gripped him, the boy moaned, a long empty sound punctuated by the smack of another body hitting the ground.

"Take him to my work chamber," Sumedha ordered. The landraces chuffed obediently. They marched their way past the security detail with the tattooed boy, still moaning, held between them.

Sumedha turned to Snake. "Are there any others?"

Snake gave an apologetic shrug and shook his head. "That's it." And now Sumedha noticed dark circles shadowing Snake's eyes. Snake's face looked pinched. As Sumedha stared, the young jailor grew visibly uncomfortable. He looked away, and back at Sumedha, and rubbed a hand against the back of his neck. "What's up?" he asked after a moment. Sumedha said nothing. He breathed, ran his mind down Snake's helix. Found a combination of switches there as familiar as his own name. It felt like music ticking through his mind. Crop Graft 3. The Tet. Sumedha turned to the head of his security detail, a big woman with a heavy jaw.

"Take him. Put him in the pen."

The woman hesitated. Sumedha sensed her pulse quicken behind the soy epoxy riot mask. Another body hit the earth, the sound reverberating like a gunshot. Sumedha pointed at Snake, who glanced from the Designer to the security guard to his two helpers. He ran an absent finger over his cobra tattoo and smiled, puzzled.

"Snake's cool," he said. "It's all good."

"Take him," Sumedha repeated. "Put him in the pen." The security head nodded once. Took a stun stick from her belt and leveled it at Snake. It sizzled. A blue bolt shot forth. Snake dropped, convulsing. His two friends backed away, open-mouthed.

"Lucky. Bruce," the security head ordered two of her troops. "Put him in the pen."

The armored security guards moved forward. Gripped Snake by wrists and ankles, swung him—counting one, two, three—and on three flung him into the pen. He hit concrete with a thud. Four sick men, to whom Snake had been jailor, eyed him narrowly as he continued to twitch with volts.

"You have the Tet, boy," Sumedha explained, and then turned to regard Snake's two helpers, both of whom now looked on the verge of bolting. Sumedha breathed. DNA unfolded. He parsed through it until the better strand revealed itself. He opened his eyes and addressed the taller of Snake's helpers, who stood shirtless in torn denim pants.

"Your name?"

"Uh…" The tall boy looked to his FEMA'd companion, who offered no help. "Juice," he said, staring at the concrete at Sumedha's feet.

"Do you understand the operation?" Sumedha asked him. Juice hesitated, then nodded. "Tell me," Sumedha commanded.

"He…uh, we collect folks sick with the Tet. We pay the *Chupes* to bring 'em to us. We pack the sick ones into the pens and shoot 'em up with antibiotics and antivirals. We feed 'em, and watch for anybody who recovers." Again, he shrugged.

Sumedha nodded. "Juice." Committing the name to memory. "You are now in charge of this operation. It is very important we spot anyone who recovers from the Tet. Do you understand?" The tall boy nodded. "Good. I will check in periodically. If you need anything, send one of my landraces."

Sumedha turned and strode away without waiting for a reply. Bodies thundered to the ground outside, in rhythm with his footsteps.

. . . .

There was something strange about the boy, something crucially absent. He pressed his cheek against the wall's smooth skin. The swirl of his tattoos drew Sumedha close, his nose nearly touching the line of tiny animal figures up the boy's shoulder. The boy caressed the wall with his fingers. He smiled with his eyes closed and made contended noises.

"You feel pleasure," Sumedha observed. The boy kept his eyes closed, but nodded.

"*Hermosa*."

"What is?"

"She floats above the world." The boy kept his cheek once more to the wall, nuzzling. The mammalian echo of both nursing and mating. *She*, the boy had said. Sumedha placed his hand on the wall, closed his eyes, felt the city's warm pulse.

"Satori," Sumedha said.

"Yes, Sumedha," spoke Pihadassa's voice. Sumedha breathed it in. "Nothing."

"Very well, Sumedha."

"Satori," the boy echoed. His voice turned singsong. "Satori keeps us afloat."

"You feel an affinity for Satori," Sumedha observed.

"Satori," the boy echoed again. Empathy stirred Sumedha. It struck him that the boy felt no pain. He considered bringing a table up from the floor and having Satori restrain the boy, but the boy sank to his knees, his face still pressed to Satori's skin. Sumedha stilled his mind, let the boy's helix come into focus.

The Tet configuration revealed itself immediately. Yet…it lay dormant.

Sumedha opened his eyes. He paced the ovular room. He stood over the boy.

"Do you have a name?"

The boy turned until his back rested against the wall. His face rose towards Sumedha. His eyes failed to engage.

"Do you have a name?" Sumedha calmly repeated.

"Bacilio," the boy said to the space beside Sumedha's head. "My brother calls me Pollo." He assumed a doll-like posture, palms flat on the floor, legs stuck straight out before him.

"Do you feel any pain, Bacilio?"

"Not in Satori." Bacilio spoke the last word carefully, as though not to offend it. "She's complete." For an instant his eyes met Sumedha's, then looked away. "Not you, though, homes. *Usted no es completo.*" Sumedha breathed, puzzling.

"Satori. Restraints, please." Digits articulated forth from the wall and floor, wrapping the boy. He looked surprised for a moment, but seemed not to mind. Seemed in fact to settle himself into the restraints, an infant being cuddled by its mother.

Sumedha pressed his index finger against Bacilio's shoulder joint. The boy exhibited no pain. Sumedha moved his hand down to the boy's elbow, then his wrist and fingers.

"Any pain in your joints?" Sumedha inquired. Bacilio shook his head slightly. Sumedha furrowed his brow. "You have the Tet.

But it does not present."

He lowered himself lotus position on the floor, facing the boy. He recalled the boy's helix, turned it with his breath. The Tet was there, precise and elegant. Pihadassa had designed it, and it bore her grace. Key switches designed to turn, to destabilize the entire helix. Love flooded Sumedha whenever he looked upon it. He let himself slip into deep meditation, going over Bacilio's helix switch by switch. As he worked, Bacilio's breath gradually synced with his. He felt invited, welcomed.

He saw something. A configuration he had seen only rarely before, and in his own failed designs, never in a wild-born human. Such a configuration did not survive long in this world. He opened his eyes, took in Bacilio's placid face. Bacilio's eyes stared into nothing. A puzzle opened up before Sumedha, and with it, wonder.

"You are autistic."

....

The door to Kassapa's work chamber flexed open and Sumedha found himself staring into the vertical irises of an advocate. The soiled cotton and burlap she wore stank of dust, sun, blood. For an instant her helix spun, beautiful and vicious, in Sumedha's mind.

"Sumedha," Kassapa called from within. "Enter."

Inside, Kassapa sat naked, lotus position on a furred cushion protruding from the floor. Brown skin briefly gleamed as he bowed in his seat, leaning forward into an amber pool of dome-filtered light falling through the open window. To one side, leaning against the skin wall, stood a wild-born man. He wore military fatigue pants tucked into combat boots crossed at the ankles, an old-world flak jacket over his bare chest. He and the advocate eyed one another, the man exuding pheromones, the stench of fear and contempt, the advocate smiling, salacious and predatory. Sumedha faced Kassapa and bowed.

"Brother."

"Satori," Kassapa commanded. "Cushion." A fur mound rose from the floor and Sumedha settled into it. The two of them meditated for a moment. Love filled Sumedha as his mind briefly touched Kassapa's, a hand touching a mirror. His brother. His enemy. Then Kassapa opened his eyes and motioned to the tall wild-born.

"One of my security liaisons to the outside." Sumedha greeted the man with a nod. The man regarded him with flat eyes. Licked something out of the space behind his bottom teeth, said nothing. He crossed his feet and leaned with a hand against the wall near a rendition of Pihadassa's face, which Kassapa had lazed from memory into the flesh.

"I am glad you are here, brother," Kassapa told Sumedha. "You will want to hear this. Pihadassa has been establishing colonies. My advocates found one." He smiled. Biolumes gurgled as the chamber's walls turned abruptly violet, then green with excitement.

Blood filled Sumedha's ears in a hot rush. His throat tightened.

"She is dead?"

"She was not there," the advocate said, her voice a malevolent singsong. She skirted the room's edge, her movements preternaturally smooth. The security man eyed her. His palm settled on the butt of a ceramic pistol holstered at his hip. The advocate glanced at him, smiled and quietly hissed.

"Pihadassa lives?" Sumedha asked her. The advocate's eyes flashed to him.

"I do not know."

Tension flowed from Sumedha's muscles. Something akin to a sob tried to escape his chest. He let it out as a long, slow breath. He met Kassapa's eyes.

"That is disappointing," he said. The lie hung in the air between them until a thin smile tightened Kassapa's mouth. He turned to the wild-born man.

"You say you know the government agent who searches for Pihadassa?"

"Doss?" The man showed humorless teeth. "I worked with her in Siberia."

"She is persistent?"

"Oh yeah. She's a dog with a fucking bone. She'll find your girl."

"You trust your man at Riley?" Kassapa asked. The man's eyes narrowed as he considered the question, then he nodded.

"I think we've pushed the right buttons. He'll be reliable. He's blocking their coms as we speak."

"Very well." Kassapa's gaze shifted to the advocate, who had sunk to her haunches and stared, seemingly entranced, at the raptor claw fingers of one of her own hands. She flexed the fingers slowly, one at a time, as though marveling at each one's precise strength. "When can you and the other advocates be in place?" Kassapa asked.

The advocate's hand went still. "They are already in place, Father."

"Good." Kassapa addressed the liaison. "Coordinate your man at Riley with the advocates."

"Will do." The man did not wait to be dismissed. He strode quickly from the room, the advocate's eyes tracking him the whole way. Kassapa spoke the advocate's name.

"Grace." Her eyes snapped to him. "Make sure your advocates are ready."

"We are always ready, Father," she told him, and her lips peeled back, unsheathing teeth refined from a thousand predators.

"Go."

The advocate stood, moved to the door with the fluid strength of a tidal surge, disappeared. Kassapa watched her go, and smiled. The walls turned red with pride, lust. He reached out, touched Sumedha lightly on the shoulder.

"We will let the government woman bring Pihadassa home."

Sumedha breathed. His mind emptied. He cast his eyes to the likeness of Pihadassa lazed onto Kassapa's wall.

"You obsess, brother," he said. Three deep breaths swelled Kassapa's chest before he answered.

"I wish to know her."

"You do know her. She is like us."

"She betrayed us!" The words flashed from Kassapa's mouth. His hand moved between himself and Sumedha, tracing an imaginary cord connected to both their hearts. "She betrayed our bond. No, brother, I do not know her. I have yet to understand." His face contorted with pain, then smoothed. He stared intently at Sumedha. "Do I know you, Sumedha?" Their eyes locked. In unison, they breathed. Their minds briefly touched, electric and fierce.

"We must go, brother," Sumedha told him.

"Where?"

"To observe Minerva. The graft's final test." He smiled. "I left her unguarded. She attempts to escape."

....

"I wonder if the city was alive when it was like this." Sumedha's hand moved over a section of early twen-cen brick, coarse and dead under his fingers, then rode a lip of skin where the living flesh of the new city had subsumed the old wall. Ambient sunlight shone pale through the dome's translucent skin, backlighting a chaotic lattice of bone and vein overhead. "Maybe it knew itself even then. Maybe it always aimed to evolve." He tickled the lip of pink flesh, felt the current of life there. "Perhaps it is the city who made the Fathers, not vice versa."

"She is in the park," Kassapa said, seeming not to have heard. He stood a few paces ahead of Sumedha, peering around the building's corner, his shift clean and white against the dark skin of his shoulders. Eight of his landraces stood in a row behind the two Designers, swaying idly back and forth on broad bare feet as they awaited his command.

"What is she doing?"

"Watching a duel."

"A duel?" Sumedha moved up to peer over Kassapa's shoulder. Saw Satori children gathered in a square of blue algae-grass the size of an old city block. Landrace varieties, some erect and regal, pale faces symmetrical and blank. Others short and thick, peering from beneath heavy brows. They wore simple cotton shifts, like the Designers, or red robes, or nothing at all. Sumedha's breath caught.

"They *learn!*"

Two landraces faced off, one tall and thin, the other short and covered in patches of dark fur. They aimed long pieces of rusted rebar at one another, rapier-like. Two deep cuts ran the length of the tall landrace's muscled chest. He grinned. A female in the crowd barked laughter. Another hooted encouragement. The two landraces went at each other. The rebar clanged. The combatants laughed. Love surged through Sumedha.

"They learn too quickly," Kassapa said.

Sumedha spotted Minerva standing at the edge of the crowd, wrapped in a simple white blanket, watching. He had left her unlocked, unsupervised. She had run. They had followed.

"This is dangerous," Kassapa said. Impatience made his words tight, made muscles work in his arms and jaw. "We should take her now." Sumedha laid a hand on Kassapa's shoulder.

"Calm, brother. She will not escape."

"Your improvisation is reckless. You could do this in your laboratory."

"Not everything in life can be studied under controlled conditions." Kassapa turned to gaze at Sumedha, his brow flexing with weighty calculations. Sumedha made calculations of his own, and smiled. "You are wrong, brother. I do not take this lightly. I will not let the splice go to the Fathers until I know it is safe. "

"It is not just this that you take lightly."

Sumedha watched as one of the dueling landraces lunged forward, slicing downward and drawing blood from his opponent's face. The bloodied Satori child staggered, grinned, attacked.

"You know of what I speak, Sumedha. You know of *whom*."

Sumedha laughed. Then shot forward. He took Kassapa beneath the chin and pushed him hard against the wall.

"Pihadassa destroyed our balance when she left us." He glared into Kassapa's face, then leaned his head forward until their brows gently touched. His voice softened. "It cannot be put right. There is only acceptance." He released his brother, stepped back. Kassapa breathed, achieving a coiled stillness. Sumedha swept his arm to encompass all things. "The world is change, Kassapa."

"You grow wild."

"I acknowledge what is. Things change and that is all. We must change with them." He glanced at where Minerva stood at the crowd's edge, clutching the blanket around her with the newly transplanted arm. "I know Pihadassa. I know she saw something the rest of us cannot. She brought change, and she foresaw its consequences. I do not understand it. But I trust her." Sumedha held up a hand, flat and empty. "The past is nothing."

"You risk the Fathers' plan." Pain returned to Kassapa's face, pain Sumedha intimately knew: a puzzle that wouldn't click. "I do not know you." Laughter rang once more from Sumedha—something extra for his brother's calculations.

"The Fathers' plan…Do you truly not see it, Kassapa?" He searched Kassapa's face for doubt, for hesitation. Saw none. "If the graft succeeds, the Fathers will emerge, glorious and mutable. A new thing, fit for this world. Made for it."

"And we would facilitate that," Kassapa implored. He grew emphatic. "We *serve* them. It is what we are."

"Yes. And whom do they serve, brother?" Sumedha placed a hand to Kassapa's chest as though to press understanding straight into his heart. Kassapa's eyes grew distant. He breathed. Sumedha could almost hear the puzzle shifting in his fellow Designer's mind. "That's right, brother," he said. "See it. They will leave Satori to rot under the sun. Satori will die. Our children will die. We will die." Cruelty edged his smile. "And then whom will we serve?"

As he spoke, he let the shape of things rise in his own mind. It hung there, a glowing whole, the path clear. A puzzle solved.

"Satori," he told Kassapa, "would shelter our children. She would shelter us. If she knew herself." He extended his consciousness. Felt Kassapa's mind, surging with fear and uncertainty. "The graft would let her know herself."

He looked into his brother's eyes, identical to his own, and opened himself. It was like stepping through a mirror. He let Kassapa see everything.

Rebar clashed. The crowd murmured as a hit once again drew blood. Kassapa slowly shook his head. Turned his back, faced the duel.

"They will fight to the death, I think."

"It is sad." Sumedha said, and breathed grief through his body. He let his hand fall from Kassapa's shoulder. "But beautiful. They are beautiful."

"Yes."

They fell silent, watching. The tall duelist lunged forward, thrusting his rapier at chest level. The short landrace parried, spun, countered. Then stepped back, admiring his work. His rebar protruded, trembling, from the tall landrace's chest. The two landraces regarded each other. The impaled duelist grinned. He staggered. He fell. The crowd cheered.

"She does not look well," Kassapa observed. As they watched, Minerva teetered. She knelt, placed a hand on the ground and vomited. Landraces backed away from her. She rose. "She is moving."

She meandered, staggering away from a group of statuesque Satori children, making her way gradually towards the dome's gate.She limped. Her shoulders lurched heavily under the blanket. Then, as the Designers watched, Minerva pulled herself upright. Her shoulders squared. Resolution steeled her face.

She ran.

A burst of preternatural speed, legs flickering as she ducked under the shadow of a fat building the shape and color of a kidney, whose roots clutched the ground like muscular fingers. For long seconds, nothing. Then, a bone-wheeled wagon rolled slowly past, hauled by four squat Satori landraces and piled high with compost. Minerva made for it, rolled underneath, disappeared. The dome's gate wafted open, admitting a blast of dry air that smelled of the sun-beaten plains. The wagon rolled through, past a dozen wild-born human guards armed with clubs and plastic assault rifles that Sumedha found crude. Soy epoxy breastplates shone white in the sudden sunlight, then grew dull as the gate flexed shut behind the wagon

"Even ill she is quick," Kassapa said. "We should grab her now before we lose her."

"If she evades us I will consider that further proof of the graft's efficacy."

"You would lose her?"

"We have the graft," Sumedha said. He smiled as a thought occurred to him. "Perhaps the helix expresses itself through the girl's desires. Perhaps we should let her go." The dome's gate buffeted slightly, the complicated idleness of a living thing. Sumedha thought of the humans in the hot wilds who scavenged for their meals, who fought over their seasonal ration of Satori seed. Humans who had been produced by *mating*, born into the misery of hunger and the elements. Forged by chaos. At their center: the glowing, pristine helix, paring away its own random edges, sharpening itself like a flint spear-point against the stone of predation, disease, war, starvation. It filled Sumedha with wonder. "The helix dances, brother. Perhaps we should allow it room."

Kassapa's expression turned grave. "You have become very strange," he told Sumedha, and Sumedha sensed something cold beneath his brother's apprehension. "Outsiders could puzzle through her helix, if they caught her. They could discern the Fathers' plan."

Sumedha waved the thought away. "Your advocates will find her, if we fail. We should see where she goes. We may learn something."

. . . .

Minerva emerged from beneath the wagon a half-kilometer south in the lee of the old state capitol building. Sun shimmered off the gold-flecked dome. The Designers watched from across a weed-cracked boulevard as the girl sprang with animal speed up granite steps, taking them three at a time. She disappeared through granite arches at the building's entrance, blowing past migrants huddled in the building's shadow. Yet beneath Minerva's strength and speed, Sumedha sensed weakness, barely suppressed.

"She falters," he observed. He spun her helix in his mind, searching for the flaw. "It seems she is not a stable platform after all." Relief ballooned in his chest.

"Do not lose her." Kassapa motioned for his landraces to fan out. He raced after her. Sumedha followed. Migrants scattered as the two Designers and their entourage of grunting landraces surged up the steps.

They entered the capital dome. The ashes of cook fires littered the cracked marble floor. A fecal stench assaulted them. Muted shapes huddled around them in the hollow darkness.

"There." Kassapa's voice echoed in the cathedral space. He pointed. Minerva stood opposite them, watching. Kassapa's landraces made for her. She bolted up a flight of wide granite stairs. Kassapa followed, face rigid with sudden urgency.

Sumedha watched his brother go. A wet film covered his eyes. He wiped at it. He stared at his fingers, puzzled by the moisture there.

Tears.

He paced slowly across the floor, poked a bare toe at the ashes of a cook fire, saw rat bones and scorched insect husks. Ashes clung to his feet, stained his white shift black. He felt cold.

Landraces reached the floor above, a balcony circling the open capitol floor. Minerva cried out. Sumedha slowly ascended the stairs. Found landraces surrounding the girl. They had her pinned against a crumbling granite wall between rusted femurs of protruding rebar. Kassapa stood a few paces away, face aglow with triumph as he watched.

"Bind her," he ordered. His landraces brought forth corn-fiber ropes, pressed the girl to the floor, trussed her with rough hands.

The girl abruptly seized, a convulsion working its way in a slow wave up and down her body. She vomited. Muscles violently contracted. Skin split open. Sumedha saw grey tendrils of intestine. Blood poured from Minerva's nostrils, then her ears. She vomited a second time, and cried out once, then lay still. The two Designers silently regarded the body.

"She is indeed not a stable platform," Kassapa concluded after a moment. A hint of satisfaction glinted in his eye as he watched Sumedha. "You have failed, brother."

The landraces stood there, confused. They looked at the body, looked at one another. They parted as Sumedha stepped forward. He bent over the body. Its abdomen had ruptured. Its limbs had filled with fluid. He poked it with a toe, then closed his eyes. Turned the girl's helix, saw the entropic cascade. He turned and faced Kassapa.

"For now." His voice was calm, but his hands had begun to tremble. The moment, he realized, had come. "For now the Fathers will remain in their pods. But there is another option. The Tet has revealed a second platform. The correct one, I believe." He stepped close to his brother. Grief churned suddenly, unexpectedly, in his chest. "But I will not give it to the Fathers. I will keep it for Satori."

Tears had begun streaming down Sumedha's cheeks. Kassapa's wide brow furrowed with questions, then his eyes lit with understanding, and fear.

"Now?" he whispered.

"Now, brother."

Sumedha gripped Kassapa under the arms. Reached out his mind, let Kassapa feel his love. Then lifted and drove forward with all his strength.

Kassapa shuddered as his body hit the wall—his pain bleached Sumedha's mind. Together they screamed.

Sumedha stood there for a time, his forehead pressed to Kassapa's, their minds joined and reverberating with horrible knowledge. Finally he returned to himself and stepped back.

Kassapa hung from the wall, three bloody rebar fingers protruded from his chest. He reached out for Sumedha, eyes wide. Savage empathy drove Sumedha to his knees. He retched. The landraces chuffed, agitated.

"Sumedha?" Kassapa reached out. Sumedha rose, took his brother's outstretched hand. Felt the life force there, erratic, ebbing. He spoke softly.

"You are not alone." He closed his eyes, reached his mind out, stroked Kassapa's ragged consciousness. "You should have joined us, brother."

"Us?" The word came out jagged, flecked with blood. Sumedha nodded. Kassapa's face buckled with grief. "Paduma." His lips parted, emitted a long wail. It echoed in the capitol's dome. Sumedha regarded his dying twin.

"You were always the slowest of us," he said.

"I was designed to maintain security. Not to create, the way you were." Kassapa smiled weakly. "I hope you have solved the correct puzzle brother. I should have supervised the bomb personally." He glanced down at the rebar protruding from his chest. "It hurts," and this fact seemed to surprise him.

"Are you ready?" Sumedha asked. Kassapa nodded. Sumedha touched his forehead once more to Kassapa's, then gripped his brother and pulled. Kassapa moaned, foamed blood as he slid off the rebar.

Sumedha dragged him to the balcony's edge, held him upright, nodded farewell. Then heaved him over the railing. A long second of silence, followed by a dull crack as Kassapa hit the marble floor twenty meters below. Sumedha looked down, saw blood pooling in the ashes around his brother's broken body. He sank to his knees and wept.

CHAPTER 15

I t was so much more than just the suit. Emerson was fundamentally an optimist. What some regarded as the end of times,
the climate apocalypse, he saw as nothing more than a brief
glitch on the implacably upward trajectory of human progress.
Listening to him talk was like watching the crowd give up amens
at one of the sweltering Georgia tent revivals Doss' mother had
taken her to. It made her hot.

Emerson had liked to fuck her rough. He'd pulled her hair and
bit her neck. Grabbed her by the throat and fucked her hungrily,
like his life depended on it, like there was nothing anybody could
want more. When they were done he would lay on his side, his
arm under her head, and lightly trace constellations with an index
finger among the cigarette scars on her back.

And Sienna Doss would let him.

She woke sweating, wet, empty. The smell of a cook fire came
to her, and the stink of home-stilled corn diesel that hung perpetually around the dead cowboys' truck. Dry air turned her lungs
to dust, made her cough, and she remembered: fucking Kansas.

She lay on a wool blanket spread in the dust beside the cowboys' truck. They'd driven it from Wichita. Two days across the brown flats of southern Kansas, empty but for the occasional crooked postage stamp of green Satori crops rising from drought-stricken soil. The lean-to settlements of migrants adjacent to these plots had vibed like civilization, had seemed almost permanent, rooted. But Doss knew these were the ones who had run low on canned stores, who had been forced to plant too early, too far south. Come May the temperatures would hit a hundred and twenty, and even the robust Satori yield would wilt. The migrants had watched Doss and her crew roll slowly by in the cowboys' truck. Some silently nodded. Doss had nodded back. It'd felt like an acknowledgement of what they all knew: the migrants had reached the site of their graves.

"Morning, Boss Momma."

Doss sat up, found Jake squatting beside a small fire in the nearby crook of a concrete foundation. He wore cutoff fatigue pants, his red *La Chupe* sash tied over his head. He watched her, a skinned jackrabbit spitted on a length of rebar in one hand, a K-ration cracker in the other.

"Why aren't you at the blind?" she asked.

"Big lieutenant got it under control." Jake set the rabbit across the fire, popped the cracker in his mouth and chewed contentedly. "Looking for his sister."

"El Sol say we stay with you, Boss Momma," Casanova said. Doss saw only the top of his head as he spoke. He sat cross-legged in the dirt a few paces away, poking intently at Doss' flexpad. He'd discovered a cache of porn on it during the drive from Wichita. The unpurged files of some cabinet staffer who'd used it before the military had co-opted it. Or perhaps it had been Rippert's. Whatever, Doss figured it was good for morale.

"That's right," Jake said. "We stay with you." He poured the saved juice from a spent K-ration bag over the rabbit. It hissed in the fire. "Breakfast be ready in ten."

Doss rose, stretched, regarded the two young *Chupes*. Tough boys, but boys all the same. Orphans who had found a mother.

She opened the valve on the truck's water tank and stuck her head beneath the lukewarm stream, then cupped her hands and drank. Her hair stuck to her face and she tied it wet into a tight ponytail, then fished through her blanket until her hands closed on the holstered .45 and her radio. She inserted the radio's earpiece, throated the mic.

"Lieutenant," she said. A pause.

"Boss," came Fiorivani's hushed voice.

"Report."

"Not much. I see…" Doss imagined the big man curled fetus-like inside the camo'd womb of the small blind they'd set at the edge of the Designer's valley. Imagined him leaning forward, fitting his face to the molded rubber end of the spotting scope. "Migrants toiling in the fields. Many weird clones. Also toiling. And…yes, there she is, that creepy fast bitch slinking around the dome."

"The advocate," Doss prompted. Satori's combat design, according to her briefing files. A genetic aggregate of predators, honed to kill, stuffed inside the barest human camouflage.

"Affirmative."

"Any sign of the primary?"

"Negative on the primary, Boss."

"Alright. I'll relieve you in an hour."

"No hurry, Boss. I'm a tick in shit."

"I think you mean pig."

"Whatever. I know only happiness."

"Out." Doss turned to the *Chupes*. "Stay here."

She wandered down a row of decayed building foundations. Slipped behind one and came to a pile of crumbled cinderblocks. Her toilet. She checked for snakes, dropped her pants and shat. Then moved to an open patch of hardpan. Jackrabbits skittered through the grass around her.

She started with yoga, then did pushups and, holding a cinderblock over her head, squats. Followed that with supersets of burpees and crunches. She worked until blackness closed around the edges of her vision, until her limbs went noodly and vomit rose, a teaspoon of white bile from her empty stomach. She retched, then stood, a warm flood of endorphins blotting out the visceral dream memory of Emerson.

The sun rose behind her. She spread her arms, watched her shadow encompass the little ruin of a town. It looked like it had been abandoned since the days of Egyptian pharaohs. Foundations protruding like tombs from a sea of grey cheat grass. The tiny town of Burdock, barely a memory. For one clear instant Doss understood it made no difference whether or not she Fucked Up. She could do everything right, could be perfect, and the world would still go whatever way it wanted.

"Gear up," she told the boys, back at the truck. "Bring water."

She donned desert camo Kevlar vest, tied a Kevlar scarf around her head, grabbed her M-8 and extra clips from the truck. She bent, snatched the flexpad from Casanova's hands, folded it, stuffed it into a fatigue pocket.

"You need breakfast, Boss Momma." Jake, grinning, handed her a hunk of scorched rabbit meat stuck to the tip of a rusty kitchen knife. "Boner appetite."

....

Two miles of naked cheat grass prairie lay between them and the Designer's valley. They moved fast and kept low. Still, Doss felt the crosshair tickle of bad exposure on the back of her neck. A half-hour brought them to a long low ridge, atop which sat a line of dilapidated vehicles, backlit like bison carcasses against the morning sky. The discarded trucks and wagons of migrants who had found the Designer's valley. The smell of water hit Doss, clean and sharp.

Her flexpad beeped.

She cursed, withdrew it, unfolded it. Tsol's face peered at her, flat and square as a totem head. He smiled.

"Camouflage becomes you, Agent. You look like a sidewinder. Or some sort of nasty desert tick."

Doss saw plush red pillows, something that looked like peacock feathers. Heard the faint tinkling sound of a young woman's laughter, the quiet thump of bass.

"Busy," Doss said. She folded the flexpad and knelt to gather her bearings, scanning the ridge for the blind.

"El Sol!" Wonder hushed Casanova's voice. "That was El Sol!" Jake shushed him. He pointed to a cottonwood stump three hundred meters off, where a deep gully cut the ridge.

"There," he said. Doss rose and led the boys towards it.

The flexpad beeped again. Doss hissed through her teeth, folded it open.

"The prairie is so magnificent," Tsol mused. "Don't you think, Agent Doss? I'm in Dakota right now. I don't know which one."

"South," came a girl's voice.

"South Dakota. Not that it matters. I'm on the prairie. Like you, Agent Doss. I am where I am fated to be."

"Two kinds of people believe in fate," Doss told him. She reached the gully's lip, sank to her rump and slid down. "The arrogant and the weak. I have no patience for either."

Tsol's laughter crushed the flexpad's feeble speakers, emerged as an abrupt hiss of static weirdly out of sync with his bobbing Adams apple. He showed both rows of teeth, distorted and gigantic on the flexpad's flat plane.

"Guilty as charged, Agent Doss. On both counts, I think." For a moment he seemed proud of this. Then his face turned serious. "The prairie was barren like this once before, Agent Doss, long ago. They called it the Dust Bowl. All the soil blew away. It blew east, all the way to old D.C. People had to migrate then, just as they do today. But Roosevelt saved the prairie. Do you know how he did it?" Doss said nothing. She motioned to Jake, who produced a gallon jug of water from his backpack. "He planted." In the flexpad, Tsol beamed. "Trees. Thousands of rows of trees. From Texas to Canada. It was one of the biggest undertakings this country's ever seen. And it worked. Trees saved the soil. The rains came and the prairie grew again." Casanova leaned close to Doss, his face rapt as he peered down at El Sol. "Do you know what my fate is, Agent Doss?" Doss uncapped the water jug, took a long swig. Then:

"Some pissed off migrant plants an AK round in your brain after you rob his mother into starvation?" She shrugged. "Just a guess. You have anything interesting to tell me?"

Tsol raised what looked like a fat grape between a thumb and forefinger and popped it into his mouth. His eyes went half-lidded as he chewed.

"Inch by inch, row by row," he sang. "I'm going to make this garden grow." He smiled. The girl giggled in the background. "I'm going to save this world, Agent Doss." His eyes widened, showed white above his irises. "For the peop—"

Doss folded the flexpad closed. She passed the water jug to Jake.

"Let's go."

They crawled single file along the gully's dry bottom until they crested the ridge. There they came to a screen of low-slung desert camo netting. It smelled like piss.

"*La Chupacabra,*" Doss whispered.

"Red sash," came Fiorivani's voice from behind the screen. Doss and the two boys slipped into the blind. They found the big man propped on an elbow, face pressed to a spotting scope mounted on a short tripod and aimed downslope through the netting. A Longshot lay beside him, the front of its fat barrel propped on a bipod and pointing the same way as the spotting scope.

"I'd avoid that corner." Without taking his eyes from the scope, Fiorivani pointed at a muddy spot. "Pair of mudfish came up here to have their breakfast. Sat about ten feet away. I had to take a leak."

The two *Chupes* worked their way around the Longshot's awkward length and settled themselves into the corner farthest from the one Fiorivani had indicated. Doss withdrew the flexpad, tossed it to Casanova. He opened it deftly with one hand and began rapidly tabbing at it with the other.

"Water," she said. She took the jug from Jake's pack and handed it to the lieutenant, who took it and gratefully drank. Dirt streaked his face and even in the blind's shade his eyes looked glazed. "Head back to camp," Doss ordered him. "Get some rack time." Fiorivani shook his head.

"Negative. I'll stick for a while if you don't mind."

"Suit yourself."

"Got snacks?" Fiorivani asked.

Doss pointed a thumb at Jake's pack, then situated herself against the Longshot. Thumbed its power switch. It came alive with a quiet but lethal-sounding electric hum. She put her face to its scope.

Below, half a kilometer away, lay the Designer's shallow valley, maybe three hundred meters across. A small stream wound along its bottom, bloating every so often into a series of ponds that shone like coins in the morning sun. Furrows raked the valley's contours. Beneath each pond grew a different crop. Strange land-races—some statuesque, some squat and muscular—wandered the rows side-by-side with migrants. Doss pinned their faces with the Longshot's scope, scanning for the Designer's smooth dark face and placid almond eyes.

"No sign of the primary," Fiorivani told her. Doss settled the Longshot's crosshairs on the dome. The round living heart at the valley's center—a tiny replica of the living dome that covered old Denver. Its skin had tanned in the days her small band had sur-veilled it. A green tinge edged its eastern side, chlorophyll surfacing in the early sunshine. Doss spotted a place near the dome's top where the skin trembled, rhythmically. A pulse.

"That thing freaks me the fuck out," she mumbled. Nobody said anything and she knew it freaked them out, too.

They waited. The sun climbed. They began to sweat. They sipped water, chewed burned rabbit meat. Flies buzzed.

"El Sol like you, Boss Momma," Casanova declared late in the morning.

"Lucky me." Doss had the Longshot trained on the woman outside the dome's concave wall. She wore FEMAs and sat with weird grace on her haunches.

"You could be his woman," Jake agreed. "He treat his women good. Like from the old world. Everybody know. He treat them like *ladies*."

"Uh-huh." A migrant boy crossed Doss' scope a few paces from the woman. The woman's lips peeled back, bared barracuda teeth. Her tongue flicked out like a snake's. Wide nostrils flared.

Doss mentally ticked down the bullet points in the flexpad's file on the Satori combat designs. Genetic splices drawn from multiple sources, mostly predatory. Increased bone and muscle density. Enhanced senses of smell and sight. Enhanced strength and speed. Originated as a government military contract, but rejected due to the designs'—Doss relished the phrase—"unpredictable disposition." As Doss watched, the combat design raised her face and seemed to stare straight into the Longshot's scope. Doss saw pale, wolfen eyes, irises that were vertical slits no wider than a fingernail. Skin tingled the length of Doss' spine. "That bitch is a killer if I've ever seen one."

"Hey, what's this?" Fiorivani squinted through the netting, then pivoted the spotting scope to point at the valley's far rim. Dust rose there a kilometer out on the plain.

"Big caravan," Doss observed through her own scope. A dozen wagons and trucks limped in from the east. PV panels, tiny windmills and kite turbines waved like antennae.

Fifty-odd migrants trudged among vehicles, cloth bundles balanced on their heads, scarves tied over their faces against the dust. As they neared, commotion spread through the valley. Its residents began to scramble. Some climbed the valley's rim and simply stood watching. Others produced old rifles, slingshots, pistols.

"Looks like the home team don't want to share its cereal," Fiorivani guessed.

"Should be interesting," Doss concurred.

The standoff ensued. Doss kept her eye to the scope. Four hundred valley residents barred the caravan's way. Words were exchanged. Fingers pointed, then guns. The combat design stalked the gathering's edge, then loped, panther-quick, back to the dome. She stood before it, face upturned, a penitent before an altar.

"Boss, look." Fiorivani said.

"I see it."

A vertical slit appeared before the combat design in the dome's wall. It widened, two flaps of wall folding over with muscular effort. Doss saw within what looked like a snakeskin floor. Loops of glistening viscera hung from somewhere above. It reminded her of a gigantic abdomen that had been cut open.

A woman stood there. She wore a clean white shift. Doss zoomed her scope.

Saw smooth skin the color of black tea, preternaturally regular features. Recognized almond eyes that gleamed with a bird's empty intensity.

"I believe I have eyes on primary. You second me on that, Lieutenant?"

"Fucking aye," Fiorivani confirmed.

"About time," Casanova said.

"Shut up." Jake chucked the blond boy's shoulder with a fist. "Duty, man. *Duty.*"

"You right. I apologize."

"Don't sing it to me."

"You right. I apologize, Boss Momma."

Doss turned, looked from one *La Chupe* to the other, let her gaze linger on Jake's resolute face. She recognized, not for the first time, something ardent in the kid's nature. Concluded this was a good thing.

"Learn from your friend," she told Casanova. Jake's chest swelled with pride. He smiled at Casanova. "Now shush," Doss said.

She put her eye back to the Longshot's scope. Watched the Designer touch the combat design atop the head. The combat design squirmed with pleasure, something between a child being praised and a dog being scratched.

The Designer strolled calmly up the valley's side, the combat design following at an agile pace behind. When they reached the gathering, the Designer moved to its center, raised her hands and spoke. A moment later, guns lowered. Hands calloused from tilling soil clasped those dusty from the plains. Together, new comer and valley resident descended to the fields.

"Guess they have enough to go around," Doss said. "Wonder if those crops'll bear up once the heat comes."

"I have a recommendation, Boss," Fiorivani said.

"Let's hear it."

"We wait until just before dawn. Then run a sneak-and-snatch."

Doss folded her hands over the scope and rested her chin atop them, digesting the notion. "How do we breach the dome unde- tected?" she asked after a moment. "That's where the Designer will be." Fiorivani thought for a minute, shook his head. "My thoughts exactly," Doss said. She tabbed her mic three times, channeling Fort Riley. Several minutes ticked by. Finally Gomez's voice, laced with the static of distance, sounded in Doss' earpiece.

"Boss?"

"What's the status of our freshly minted Rangers, Sergeant?"

"Wouldn't call them Rangers, Boss. They can't fight for shit." A pause. "They do obey the laws of gravity, though. They'll scare the hell out of anyone they land next to."

"Lost any more?" asked Doss.

"Three more. Some of these old suits..." Doss heard a long stretch of static as Gomez let out a breath. "They're for shit."

"How about pilots?"

"Six pilots," Gomez said. "All officially now with flight time under their belts."

"Combat functional?" A long silence ensued. In it, Doss could almost hear the concept of "combat functional" groan as Gomez stretched it to the point of snapping.

"Affirmative, Boss," he decided finally.

"Alright. Sergeant, I want four birds, four chalks ready to roll in two days."

"Copy."

"We're on our way home. See you for breakfast. Out." Doss tabbed off her mic, turned to Fiorivani. "We wait until dark, ren- dezvous with the zep, head home."

"Maybe..." Fiorivani hesitated.

"What is it, Lieutenant?"

"Maybe we could use a prisoner. For interrogation. We wait

until dark, then snatch one of those mudfish to take home with us. Wouldn't be hard. I could do it myself." His tone grew officious in a way that reminded Doss of Rippert, and squared his chin at her. "I volunteer." Doss shook her head.

"I'm sorry about your sister, Lieutenant. But you are not going down there. Copy?" Fiorivani glared. Muscles pulsed in his jaw. Doss held his gaze. After a moment, he looked away and nodded. "Good," Doss said. She checked the sun, then checked her watch. "Just past thirteen hundred." She lay back, propped her head against the injection molded carbon of the Longshot's stock. "Who brought the cards?"

"Right here, Boss Momma." Jake produced a red-backed deck of cards from his pack. Then poked Casanova with a finger. Pointed with two fingers at his own eyes, like: eyes on me. "You learning yet?" Casanova's face turned sour.

"Only what your mama taught me."

CHAPTER 16

Was it summer yet? It didn't seem like it. The sun felt like a friend. It pressed red through Brood's eyelids, filled his skull with soft warmth. Something skittered beside his head. He opened his eyes, saw a fat blue beetle scrambling over a clot of earth and wondered for a moment if the creature was edible. Then remembered he didn't have to eat it, even if it was. Viv stirred beside him, slid a tanned thigh over his hip.

They lay naked beside a cold pool where the stream meandered in a broad arc downstream from the strange flesh dome that turned green in the sunlight. The clean scent of water rolled over him. His skin tingled as it dried. Laughter echoed faintly up the valley. Pleasure stirred in Brood's soul and he smiled. Things had been worse.

"I feel like the fat lady," Viv murmured. Brood let the memory of recent meals trickle through his mind. Eggplant cooked together with tomatoes. A tomato-and-corn soup made in peanut shell broth. Soft meatballs spit forth from a series of fat vines hanging down the dome's side. Prepared by the Corn Mother's strange and beautiful people. Brood felt like a stray dog found.

He felt full.

"What fat lady?" he asked. Viv rolled onto her side. Her lips moved close against Brood's cheek as she spoke.

"She used to sit at the crossroad by Hermosillo. We used to see her every spring when we come north. She was huge. Gigantic." She held a hand out far, indicating girth. "*Fat.*"

"Never seen a fat person," Brood said.

"She was fat. She would just sit there at the crossroad, naked. Huge. Kind of beautiful, though. People'd leave her food. Like religious offerings, all heaped up in front of her. Nobody never stole nothing, neither. Not that I ever heard." Viv's fingertips ran up Brood's belly, which actually bulged with food. "She never said nothing. She stared in front of her like you weren't even there. We always left her corn, and whatever meat we could spare. Anna was big into that. Offerings to the Mother. She wasn't there this year." Viv paused. Her brow creased for an instant with troubled thoughts, then she shrugged. "We still left offerings for her, though." She lay on her stomach, propped her chin in her hands and watched Brood. "You remind me of my dad," she said. Brood's eyes drifted closed.

"Ain't no old man," he murmured, and ran a finger along Viv's back. Her spine no longer protruded. She felt profoundly clean.

"No. But you're mean like he was."

"*Gracias.*"

Her voice turned serious. "No, it's a good thing. He saved me. We were in Houston when the levees broke. He had to fight an entire crowd to get me and Billy onto a boat. I was young but I remember. He did it. He had a pistol, and he shot people. He got us on that boat." She went quiet. Brood lifted one eyelid, found Viv staring into the space between them, her jaw clenched with grief. "Let the dead be dead," she whispered. "I remember his face."

A Tet spasm worked its way suddenly up her arm. Her jaws clenched tight, her back arched.

"Don't look at me like that," she told Brood when her body finally relaxed. "I ain't dead yet."

"Maybe we can get her to see you," Brood said. He'd seen

the Corn Mother only once since they'd arrived. She'd stood beside the stream at the valley's low end, hairless and ghostly in a white shift, supervising as her people planted a bone lattice in the ground—the foundation of a second dome. She'd spoken with no migrants; her people had let no one close. Viv shook her head.

"She don't see nobody she don't summon."

"Maybe people ain't tried hard enough." Brood ran fingers through her wet hair. Pulled her close, kissed her forehead. They lay quietly. A hot breeze blew down the valley, rustling a nearby field of weirdly dense corn.

A shadow fell across them. Brood squinted, saw two of the Corn Mother's strange people. Landraces, the migrants here called them. A tall slender woman, a short burly male.

"Hello." The woman's voice was so smooth it sounded greased. Brood sat up. The two were naked—the man rectilinear, the woman all perfect circles and fluidly curved lines, a landscape of soft skin-dunes in the late afternoon sun. "My name is Corona," she said to Viv. As she spoke, Brood saw the woman's sleek belly protruding, a pregnant sphere. "Pihadassa would like to see you."

"Pihadassa?" Viv asked. The woman regarded her with a pleasantly blank expression.

"The Corn Mother," she said. "You have the Tet. Pihadassa will help you."

The heavy-browed man grunted once, amiably. Viv smiled at Brood and kissed him, then stood and gathered her FEMAs. The two landraces led her away along the pool's edge, to the edge of a cornfield. Viv looked back and smiled once more, then disappeared between thick folds of supernaturally green corn.

. . . .

Brood waded into the mud. He'd tied his hair back with a leather thong. His nakedness had become so natural he'd forgotten it. The topsoil turned easily under his hoe as he dug and pulled. The earth smelled musky, fecund and alive. Pink earthworms, suddenly exposed, flexed and cowered as his hoe turned their burrows inside out. He worked apace with the landraces, steady but unhurried. They did not joke or laugh or sing but seemed fixed on their tasks.

An emptiness came over Brood as he labored. Hunger did not distract him. No worries tightened his chest. He knew only the rhythmic chop of the hoe's blade into the mud, the sting of blisters forming on his palms. He worked and sweat. The earth turned.

"Hey!"

Brood looked up. A pale kid stood over a fresh furrow a few feet away, leaning on a shovel. Tats covered his face.

"I know you from Texas," he said, grinning. Brood stared for a few seconds before it clicked. He chuckled.

"Yeah. *Que onda*, whiteboy?"

"Nothing, man. Just working the good work, you know?" He extended his hand and Brood shook it. Whiteboy looked around them at the valley, still grinning. "Fucking Eden here, man. Fucking Shangri La." He gave Brood a speculative look. "How'd you wind up here?"

Brood thought about it for a moment. His fingers absently touched the still tender wound on his side.

"Just did, I guess."

Whiteboy's smile faded a notch. He nodded, his eyes pinching around some hard memory of his own.

"Yeah. Me too, I guess." He smiled again. "The road don't matter, though. Just the destination."

"I guess."

They stood there for a moment, both of them thinking to say something, neither of them knowing what. Finally Brood extended his hand again.

"Catch you around, homie."

"Alright then." Whiteboy took Brood's hand and shook it with heart.

. . . .

"Five harvests before September," Raimi said. They sat with Anna, Billy and Jorgen in a small field of dense grass situated directly east of the flesh dome. The valley's migrants had gathered there, unwashed and weary from the fields, for the evening meal. "They've already had one," Raimi said. "They're almost ready for a second." He motioned at a burly crop of nearby corn, geometric in its uniformity, then held his hand extended as though gauging the weight of an invisible object. His face had thickened in the past days.

Two naked landraces—the tall kind, a male and female, as identical to each other as corn plants—cooked at a bulky stone hearth that rose incongruous, crude, beside the dome's suntanned skin. They moved fluidly, like tricks of the long evening light. Poked at nets of vegetables set to steam over a heavy iron cauldron. Stoked a fire burning in the hearth with hunks of gene-tweaked grapevine that grew along the valley's rim, thick as Brood's forearm.

"Plenty for us to take south come October," Billy said. He lay propped on an elbow, vibing serious contentment, the new meat of his chest bare to the waning light. He poured something amber from a ceramic jug into a tin cup, passed it to Brood. Brood drank. The corn ferment burned through him.

"You make this?" he asked. Billy smiled proudly.

"Set up a still out by the trucks."

"Taste like shit," Brood said, and held the cup out for Billy to refill.

Wind gathered up dust to the west, turned the sunset red. The alcohol warmed Brood's guts and brought on a sweet mellow. Chatter rose like soft static from migrants gathered on the field around them. It was a strange sound, an easy sound that Brood had heard only a few times in his life. Up on the Ojo Caliente ridge top, where the Tewa had roasted heirloom vegetables over open fires and danced and drank in the chrome light of the desert moon. It was a good sound.

"Five harvests," Jorgen mused. He ate with his fingers from a dented steel bowl. Sliced tomatoes and onions. Soft meat boiled in eggplant broth. Carrot and lettuce salad with sunflower seeds sprinkled over the top and flavored with grape vinegar. "That's more than enough for the winter." He gently held out a tomato to Anna, who opened her mouth for it. "Enough so we don't have to plant down south."

Anna shrugged a sunburned shoulder, causing the jeweled eagle on the back of her denim vest to flex a wing. She said nothing. The dog lay beside her and she dropped a hand to stroke its exposed belly. Its tail thumbed against the grass.

"We can trade for what we need if we have a surplus," Raimi said.

"How many more years you think we can keep that water truck rolling?" Anna asked. Brood sipped from the cup and coughed.

"Be lucky to coax it as far as Oklahoma," he told her.

"That's right," she said. "Every mile is a miracle. How many more trips do you think we have in us? I'm tired of giving our dead to the road. We need a home." Anna's jaw, which had thickened and grown softer during their days in the Corn Mother's valley, took on a resolute edge. "We winter here."

"All of us?" Billy wondered. He glanced around at the press of migrants.

"No, not all," Anna said. "But I've looked at the ground where the Corn Mother's growing the second dome. It's bigger than the first. Big enough for some of us." She plucked a cherry tomato from her bowl and fed it to Jorgen.

"Will they let us stay?" Jorgen asked, chewing. The glimmer of a smile touched Anna's lips.

"We're family. We need a home." She planted her index finger like a flagpole in the grass. "This is it. I'm not going to trouble myself over whether or not we're allowed. We're staying."

Nobody said anything. Nearby a young *ese*, no older than ten, settled a guitar into his lap and tilted his ear to it, testing its tune. Satisfied, he expertly plucked the first strains of a sad *corrido*, one Hondo had used to sing.

"Family," Billy declared. He raised the ceramic jug in salute, and drank.

"Family," Raimi echoed. Brood held his empty cup out to Billy.

"*Dónde está* Viv?" Billy asked as he poured.

"Still with the Corn Mother." Brood looked at the dome. It seemed to pale as the sun set. "In there I guess." As he watched, muscles rippled under the dome's skin and a split appeared in its side. Flesh furled, a living curtain.

The strange woman with the sharp smile emerged, the one the other landraces called the advocate. She wore denim pants, a dirty yellow t-shirt—wore them in a way that seemed too intentional. She sidled along the dome's side, something feral, kinetic, held in check. Her tongue flicked her teeth as she sank innocuously to her haunches. Her fingers twitched. Her eyes, half-lidded, watched the migrants gathered on the grass. The skin prickled on the back of Brood's neck. Billy's eyes narrowed.

"No news is good news, I guess," he told Brood.

"I guess."

The little *ese's* voice rose politely over the crowd, as though asking permission. A commotion drowned him out.

"It's unconscionable!" A wiry man stood from the midst of a large group not far from the dome. He wore a black suit coat over his FEMAs, and something about the fake pink flower pinned to its lapel made Brood suspect he was crazy. He faced two pretty landraces. "My daughters are not your…" A few wisps of grey hair fluttered along the man's pate as he sputtered. He motioned at the two white girls who huddled over their plates at his feet. "Not your *breeding stock.*"

"Settle down, Uncle Jessup," Anna called to him.

"I will not!" Jessup's chin thrust defiantly toward the dome. The strange woman in the t-shirt now rose to her feet and *hissed.* "It's unholy," Jessup yelled. "God did not intend for us to be *cattle.*" He motioned at his daughters to stand. Ten nearby migrants—all white and all wearing either tattered suit jackets or aprons over their FEMAs—stood with them. Jessup's eyes panned, wild and gleaming, across the surrounding migrants. "My people are leaving. Anyone who wishes to join us will be welcome in our Lord's grace."

"You going to die out there, man," someone said. Uncle Jessup shook his head, raised a finger to the sky.

"My defense is of God, which saveth the upright in heart."

He waited. Everyone stayed huddled over their plates. No one said anything. Jessup's lip curled. He turned and spat into the grass, then stalked through the crowd. His small entourage followed. Past the two landraces who stood before him. Past the dome and the stone hearth where stew simmered in a giant cauldron. The strange advocate woman in the t-shirt and jeans smiled sharp teeth, watching him go.

"Shame," Anna said. "Uncle Jessup doesn't see the long view." She plucked a piece of lettuce from Jorgen's plate and placed it in her mouth. Her fingers worked against the dog's belly as she chewed.

"The long view." Brood mulled the notion. It felt strange, to imagine thinking past the next haul, the next deal, to plan beyond even the next day. It made him suspicious. It implied hope.

"Civilization, hon," Anna said. "This is it. This is our valley." She leaned in against Jorgen, who wrapped a long lean arm around her and pulled her close. "Not theirs. Ours."

The young *ese* strummed his guitar again. His voice rose softly over the migrants as they resettled.

"That's real pretty," Jorgen said, hesitant, like he wasn't quite sure. "My Mexican's for shit, though."

"It's an old song, Cuz," Brood told him. "Real old." Older than this age of bad weather. Older than the country that had collapsed around them. A song Brood's mother had sung. "About a peasant boy who falls in love with a landowner's daughter. He takes her off to get married, but this *culero* landowner, he finds out. He sends his son out to kill the peasant boy. But the son fucks it all up. He kills the daughter instead. So the peasant boy kills him. He ends up *bandito*. Stealing, killing, running from the law. But he's always sad, 'cause he always thinking of the landowner's daughter." Brood translated as the young *ese* crooned the last lines, melancholy but strangely uplifting. "'She's the light of my life, she's my dark memory. I run for her, but I go nowhere. There is nowhere to go.'"

A crease appeared down the center of Jorgen's brow as he

thought about it. "That is real pretty," he decided.

Brood lay back in the grass and laced his fingers beneath his head. The sky had gone pink, the air cool. The corn alcohol warmed his heart. The *ese* with the guitar moved into a new song and it made Brood think of his mother, humming her lullabies while she worked her little garden. It sounded like home.

CHAPTER 17

Paduma thrust her tongue inside Sumedha's mouth, wrapped her legs around his hips and pushed her pelvis against him. He thrust deep. Satori hummed around them. Paduma's bed engulfed them like a gentle mouth, working over their bodies in slow undulations, moving with them, soft where it needed to be soft, firm where it needed to be firm. Satori's loving flesh.

Peace. Sumedha sought peace. Union. He thrust hard, grasping for it. He reached out, dug his fingers into Satori's skin as though he could claw his way into it, join it, meld. Closer, Paduma's breath hot against his cheek. He pushed her face away with his palm. He reached. The helix swirled in his head, glowing, showing him maps of creation. Pihadassa cried out—no, Paduma. Sumedha shoved a thumb into her mouth, dug in with his fingers. Her eyes, primordial black, swallowed him. For an instant he projected himself, into her, into Satori, into everything. His senses travelled an infinite glowing matrix of DNA—

Life!

The entirety of it throbbed to the rhythm of his own heart. Stars floated in his cupped hands, whole galaxies, spinning away within the spiral strands of the helix. He pulled them to his lips and drank—

And fell back to his body. To sweat, to confinement. Satori pressed against him. He opened his eyes, found Paduma staring up at him. He saw grief in her face, and stillness as she regarded the sensation. Sumedha touched a finger to her lips, touched his mind to hers.

"I know your loss," he said.

There had been kindness in Kassapa's face, even as the life had ebbed from his eyes. Sumedha's mind recoiled from the memory. He put his forehead to Paduma's. Tried to touch her mind once more, felt nothing but the confines of his own skull. He pushed harder, as though he could physically force his mind into hers. Pihadassa cried out. She pushed him away.

No...*Paduma.*

A growl escaped Sumedha's throat. He clawed his way free of the bed. He breathed, trying to place his attention on the sensations in his body.

Rage owned him. The walls of his abode went kaleidoscopic, attempting to gauge and soothe his unfamiliar mood. He paced. The window flexed open, then shut, then opened again. Mounds rose from the floor, offering themselves. He kicked one and they disappeared. He turned, saw Paduma watching. She gleamed. A bead of sweat trickled down her dark throat. Her chest swelled, tears rolled down her still face. Sumedha sneered.

"'I want to have a child.' That is what Pihadassa told me. It was no more possible for her to want a child than it is for me." Biolumes gurgled, refused to settle. These walls did not know him. He looked at Paduma. "We are not what we are."

"What makes you so angry?" Paduma wondered. Her breathing calmed. Understanding lit her face.

The room keyed on her mood, looked for an appropriate color, failed to find one and simply went dark. She rose. Sumedha felt her move close and turned. The biolumes defaulted to a pale glow, silhouetting her, head cocked to one side, waiting. Sumedha spoke softly.

"I am sorry for your loss."

Paduma stiffened. "Why?"

"I know what you endure."

"Do you?"

"I, too, have lost—"

"I know exactly what you have lost, Sumedha. I mourned for you." Paduma gave him a fierce look. "I fear you have lost your way. Will you kill me, too?" Sumedha hesitated. His mind tumbled down calculations, looking for possibilities, finding only inevitabilities.

"I do not wish to."

"Then tell me."

Sumedha's heart raced to the point of distraction. He breathed, observed the heat in his limbs, the tightness in his chest. His ribs felt clammy with sweat. This, he realized, was the state described by the word "terror." He had never felt it before.

"Say it," Paduma demanded. The grief had receded from her eyes and she watched Sumedha now, serene, implacable. Sumedha breathed. The terror did not subside. His voice wavered as he spoke.

"I killed him."

"You killed my Other. Say it. Tell me what you did to me."

"I killed your Other."

Paduma leaned in close. Her lips trembled. Sumedha thought she would attack. Instead she doubled over, arms wrapped around her gut. She collapsed to the floor. Sobs wracked her body.

She wept like that for over an hour. Sumedha stood over her, watching, silently meditating. When she finished, it was as though a switch had flipped. She simply went quiet and stood. She put her face close to Sumedha's, looked into his eyes, and together they meditated.

"Ruin," she said after a time. "This is Pihadassa's child." Sumedha shook his head.

"No. She seeks our salvation."

Paduma's hand snapped out and snared Sumedha's throat. Sumedha made no move to stop her. She squeezed. He kept his eyes on hers, peered into her. And now, finally, their minds touched. Paduma lowered her hand.

"You killed my Other. Tell me how."

Sumedha told her. When he'd finished, Paduma stared into the space between them. The walls turned violet.

"He felt intense pain, then."

Sumedha bowed his head. "Yes."

"You killed him to save us."

"From the Fathers. Yes."

They watched each other, each allowing the other time for calculation. Paduma cocked her head to one side, and again Sumedha saw Pihadassa.

"I am bound to Kassapa," she said. "I am bound to the Fathers." Sumedha shook his head. He gestured and the window flexed open. Revealed through its shimmering membrane the half-flesh city. Landraces wheeled carts piled high with golden corn through the dome's open flap. Others played in the parks, or scrubbed Satori's streets.

"*Apsara*, sister," Sumedha said. "The helix dances. Satori lives. No matter what the Fathers intended for her, her life is her own. Bind yourself to her." Paduma shook her head, smiled kindly.

"I will tell the Fathers, brother. I cannot help myself. It is how I am made." She leaned close. Her lips pressed lightly to Sumedha's cheek. She took his hand in hers, caressed it, raised it, kissed it. Then brought it to her throat.

"I do not want this," Sumedha said. "I do not want to be alone."

"*Apsara*," Paduma whispered. She held Sumedha's hand to her throat, insistent.

Sumedha's own throat tightened. A sob wrenched its way forth. He squeezed his hand tight. Paduma's eyes stayed on his, even as her face turned colors, even as her tongue swelled. She reached up, touched his cheek gently, then went slack.

Silence made Sumedha's skull ache, seared his chest. He eased Paduma's body to the floor. It lay there limp and empty, a mammalian husk. Urine leaked from it. Biolumes effervesced suddenly inside the walls, flashing strange colors as they sought an appropriate expression for utter desolation.

....

Sumedha watched the tattooed boy, who stood naked with his back turned, the entire front of his body pressed against the laboratory's flesh wall, even the flats of his palms, skin to skin. Murmuring, a simple little song, what sounded like a lullaby, strange and repetitive. After a moment Sumedha realized it was the boy's own two names. "Bacilio, Pollo, Bacilio, Pollo, Bacilio, Pollo…" Sumedha stepped forward, spun the boy by the shoulder and grabbed his throat. Pollo's eyes widened, but refused to look directly at Sumedha.

"Show me," Sumedha commanded. He shoved Pollo against the wall and closed his eyes. His mind burrowed for Pollo's helix—found it, turned it, probed the autistic switches. "Show me," he hissed. Pollo moaned, the empty sound that paused only when he ran out of breath. He inhaled, moaned again. Sumedha kept digging. "Show. Me." He found the Tet, sought the connection between its dormancy and Pollo's autism. He saw nothing. "Show! Me!" Pollo went quiet. His helix trembled in Sumedha's mind. Sumedha opened his eyes, saw Pollo's eyes dimming, going bloodshot. He released the boy's throat.

Pollo slid to the floor, gasping. He turned away from Sumedha and pressed his cheek once more to Satori's flesh, an infant seeking its mother.

"Satori."

"Yes, Sumedha?" Pihadassa's voice, the voice of the dead. Sumedha screamed. Pollo moaned.

"Satori!" Spit flew from Sumedha's mouth.

"Yes, Sumedha?"

"Table!" The table articulated into place. Sumedha grabbed Pollo under the arms and threw him face down across it. "Restrain him." The digits rose, joined, contracted. The boy struggled to breathe. Sumedha took Pollo's chin in his hand and squeezed until the boy's mouth puckered.

"Show me. Show me. Show! Me!" The helix held its secret. Sumedha released his grip, then reeled back and struck Pollo hard across the temple. The helix showed nothing.

"Satori!"

"Yes, Sumedha?"

"The cocoon. Graft design number seven."

A second table articulated into place before Sumedha. A slit opened in the ceiling and through it the cocoon emerged, suspended on a thick umbilical. It came to rest on the table. Sumedha slid his hand inside, tickling forth the graft. Pollo trembled. Sumedha held his finger, glistening with thick liquid, in front of the boy's face.

"You will show me!"

....

Sumedha went to the park where he and Kassapa had watched the duel. There, he sat in the grass and meditated. A warm breeze oscillated through the dome, kicking up every time the gate flexed open to allow in a wagon, dying off when the gate closed. It occurred to Sumedha that he could stroll right out that gate, disappear into the scalding detritus of the old city. He considered this, and tears rolled down his cheeks.

Satori children approached him. Sumedha did not open his eyes, but he felt them. He projected his mind to the living buildings, travelled their nerves to Satori Tower, spread his awareness out through the bone framework holding up the dome. Every cell his mind touched, he loved. The children placed offerings in the grass before him. Flowers, corn, blood from pricked fingers.

"Father," they whispered to him, each in turn. Light filled him. The light of love. The children placed their offerings and whispered, each in turn.

"Father."

"Father."

"Father."

CHAPTER 18

"What do we do with her?" Brood stood knee-deep in the muddy water of a drainage pond at the valley's lowest end. Sunshine scalded his back. Humidity shimmered from the pond in waves.

"We can't kill her," Anna told him.

She handed Brood the swollen end of a fat hose, flat as a tapeworm and made, as far as he could tell, from shiny intestine. One of many strange things the landraces had produced from inside the dome. The dog, which lay in the shade of a nearby row of torso-high onions, stood, padded over and sniffed at the hose. Brood shooed it away. He passed the hose to Raimi and Billy, who together dragged it to the pond's deep end.

Beyond it, the circular framework of the second, larger dome protruded from the earth. Cartilage and nascent muscle growing between bone spires, connecting them. A ribcage decaying in reverse.

Anna picked up a shovel and with a few quick jabs carved a groove into the pond's bank. Into this Brood aligned the hose. Anna stuck the shovel in the ground, placed her hands on her

FEMA'd hips and stood upright, stretching a kink out of her back.

"Must be a hundred and ten today," she said, and wiped sweat from her grey brow.

"*Casi.*" Brood climbed out of the pond, turned, undid the drawstring on his shorts and let loose a long stream of piss into the pond. "Hundred and five. Humidity makes it worse."

"It's not even summer yet." Anna shaded her eyes and squinted up valley at a field of green lettuce heads the size of baby mesquite, leaves large enough to use as blankets. They seemed to drink in the heat like it was a vitamin. "Things might get worse," Anna said. "In two years or five. Maybe ten. We may need her to design better crops."

Billy and Raimi emerged from the pond. Their faces had filled out. Their torsos had thickened with regular food and the elimination of parasites—accomplished, a friendly landrace had explained to Brood, through enzymes in the meat produced by the strange vines hanging along the dome's side. Billy eyed Brood as Brood tied his drawstring.

"Could've waited," he said. Brood winked.

"Could've."

The rest of the hose lay coiled around a foot-long piece of rebar. Billy hefted this and slowly the group made their way through thick crops towards the valley's upper rim, unwinding the hose as they went. The dog trotted behind them.

A dam marked the valley's upper rim, behind it a pool deep enough for Brood to dive into. Atop the dam sat...an organ, something that looked like it had been chopped from inside a massive animal.

A pump.

"Looks like a heart," Brood observed. "How we supposed to get it going?"

"Plug the hose in," Anna said. "Supposedly it'll sense it and just...start."

Billy brought the hose's lipped end to an aperture at the pump's side and shoved it home. The aperture flexed tight around it. For a while nothing happened. The group exchanged glances. Then the pump jiggled, throbbed, flexed down to a third its original size and released. Flexed again, produced a deep sucking sound. It continued to do this, contracting and releasing every five seconds or so—long enough between each pulse to convince Brood it had gone dead.

"*Pinche espeluznante*," he said.

Billy nodded. "Seriously." He rubbed the back of his head. "Should we prime it?"

"Let's see if we get water," Anna said. "If not…"

They waited. The sun hammered them. Brood gazed down the valley's quarter-mile length, imagined from high above it would look like the outline of a girl in a dress. A tiny shock of green in the brown Kansas wastes. The stream spun around her like a ribbon, her heart the dome, green with chlorophyll in the sun, laced by red veins. As he watched, a pair of thick landraces escorted a bare-chested boy up to the dome. They stood there, waiting. Brood recognized the swirling tats on whiteboy's face.

"People go in," Billy said. "They don't come back out."

"I got a friend," Raimi told them. "He was one of the first ones to arrive. He said nobody ever comes back out." He lowered himself beside the flexing pump, picked something from his teeth with a fingernail and with that same finger pointed towards the dome. "Heard that weird snaky bitch killed Jessup and his crew after they got out on the plains." Brood eyed him.

"Who the fuck would know a thing like that?"

"Just what I heard." Raimi inspected the tip of his finger, then stuck it back in his mouth. "Corn Mother doesn't want anyone to find our little oasis, I guess."

"We found it," Anna said.

A trickle of water began seeping from a sphincter on the pump's far side. Then all at once the hose thickened and water gushed forth in fat pulses. Brood traced the stream with his eyes, from the highest irrigation pond to the drainage pond out of which ran the hose. The pump throbbed, tying the valley together in a watery loop. It made the whole thing seem eerily alive.

"I went to see her about Viv yesterday," Billy said. He gave

Brood a tense look. It'd been four days. "Those stocky mother-fuckers wouldn't even let me close."

Anna sat in the dirt and the dog wiggled its way onto her lap. Her hands worked the scruff of its neck, but she kept looking at the dome.

"We should've heard something by now," she figured.

As they watched, the dome flexed open. The two landraces escorted whiteboy inside. The opening contracted behind them. It gave Brood the same cold feeling he got when he watched a rattler work its jaws around a rat.

"I'm going in there," he decided.

"She's family," Anna agreed.

....

The Corn Mother stood nude atop the dome, facing the sun with her hands spread as though beckoning the world into existence. Her skin glowed green. Four landraces—the thick kind, the strong kind—stood by the dome's entrance, naked as babies, faces intently blank. They watched as Brood approached. He smiled at them.

"*Que pasa?*"

They lumbered forward, blocking his path. One landrace chuffed, bared its teeth in what Brood had come to understood as an expression of conviviality. Brood pointed up at the Corn Mother.

"Got to talk," he said.

In unison, the landraces scowled. Their leader gave a second friendly chuff—shook its head.

"*Sale vale,*" Brood smiled. He took a step back, cupped his hands around his mouth, and yelled. "Corn Mother!" The landraces started. Migrants and landraces in a nearby lettuce field ceased their work and stood, watching.

"Away," grunted the landrace who stood before Brood. Strangely precise musculature worked in its forearm as it lifted its hand and pointed back the way Brood had come.

"*Chinga tu culo*." Brood took a running step forward, aiming a kick for the landrace's dangling balls.

Something hit him before he got close. Hit him hard. He found himself on the ground, gasping, staring up at a sky pale with sunlight.

A woman's sharp face appeared. Needle teeth gleamed. Irises contracted, vertical slits in pale eyes. The woman laughed, a flat hiss. Her hand drew back. Long fingers extended towards Brood's throat. Brood thought for an instant of his mother. Her fevered lips whispering prayers up at the sky as death bore down. No prayers came to him. He simply wondered how badly it would hurt.

"Mercy!" A calm voice, commanding. The hand hesitated. "Mercy. Release him."

The woman, Mercy, regarded Brood with all the sympathy of a bullet for a bone. The hand stayed poised. Her other hand tightened around his neck.

"Now," the voice ordered.

"Your command, Mother." Mercy smiled sweetly at Brood, then abruptly released him and moved away, ten paces in what seemed a single, easy step. She turned and bowed to the Corn Mother, who still stood atop the dome. Backlit like some deity descending from the sky. Her head angled towards Brood.

"Are you hurt?"

"No," Brood said. He stood. A dark blob of piss spread hotly across the front of his canvas shorts. He eyed the predator woman as he dusted himself, his hand trembling. She'd sunk to her haunches and sat like that, balanced and watching—wearing a pinstriped suit coat over her t-shirt, a fake pink flower attached to its lapel.

"I am glad," the Corn Mother said. She took a step forward, plopped onto her rump in a way that seemed strangely childlike. Slid down the dome's side to land lightly on her feet. She stood there naked, arms spread as though awaiting applause, her body so perfect it struck Brood as somehow wrong, unnatural, something transcendent that had no right to take animal form. Two of her landraces stepped forth and pulled a sleeveless white shift over her head.

"Come." She beckoned. Sweat glistened on shoulders etched with fine muscle. Behind her, the dome's flesh curled open with the staccato popping of articulating bone and sinew. Brood hesitated. "Come, boy." The Corn Mother turned, and strode inside the dome. Brood cursed, and followed.

Sunlight filtered red through the dome's flesh like a flashlight through a palm, casting strange shadows through geodesic bonework. Brood stepped carefully behind the Corn Mother, the floor smooth and dry beneath his feet. He saw only a few yards ahead, but sensed motion in the far darkness. The Corn Mother halted a few paces inside, motioned at a collection of intestinal vines dangling overhead.

"Would you like meat?" She placed the tip of a delicate finger against one of the vines—vines like the ones outside, Brood realized. He held up his hand and the Corn Mother squeezed. The vine contracted, produced a few ounces of the grey meat in his palm.

"*Gracias,*" he said.

Two thick male landraces stood nearby. They watched Brood, muscles trembling with anticipation every time he moved. He smiled at them. They chuffed quietly.

"This is one of my favorite designs." The Corn Mother ran her thumb down the length of one thick vine. "It is simple. Its base is a common Argentinean grape that once grew in nearly every semi-arid temperate zone on the planet. I combined it with a fowl, turkey that was unique to North America in the early part of the century, and also with an Asiatic, freshwater eel. It thrives. It produces even more than I had intended."

Brood sucked the soft meat off his fingers. It tasted salty and light.

"It's good," he told her. The Corn Mother's smile exuded calm self-satisfaction. The precision of her face transfixed Brood. Up close, it seemed geometric.

"Sometimes the helix makes its own choice. It dances." She

looked to the ceiling, where high overhead hung what looked like giant livers. Sacks, Brood realized, large enough to hold a small child, slick membranes stretched tight over…whatever they held. "It is my hope that the helix will dance here. That this valley will come alive in unexpected ways." She brought her attention to Brood, so keen his eyes went involuntarily to the floor. It bore the same pattern as a diamondback. Brood's spine tingled. The Corn Mother closed her eyes, breathed deep, as though testing Brood's scent.

"My friend," he said. "She got the Tet—"

The Corn Mother's eyes snapped open. She reached languidly forth, her fingers encircled Brood's jaw. She brought his face close to hers, began to examine him.

"You are dynamic. Well-formed. Small, but your aggression expresses peak primate functioning. Your helix drives you to the forefront of your breeding population. It wishes to reproduce itself. This is good."

She closed her eyes again, her hand still lightly cupping Brood's jaw. Her chest rose and fell sedately as she breathed four deliberate breaths. Her smooth brow rose as though, behind capacious eyelids, she found something intriguing. She peered once more at Brood.

"Malnourishment and parasites have inhibited your highest genetic potential. But you have…" Black eyes perused the space over Brood's head, searching for the correct distillation of some broad idea, then clicked back to him. "Endurance."

Brood gripped her wrist and forced her hand away. The landraces stepped forward, but the Corn Mother shook her head. They stilled.

"I'm looking for my friend." Brood told her. "She got the Tet."

"The Tet. A wild-born word, derived no doubt from the design's physical symptoms, which resemble tetanus. Its process is nothing like tetanus, however. Its correct name is Crop Graft 3. It is more akin to multiple sclerosis. It causes entropic cascade in the human genome, beginning with the nervous system."

Brood eyeballed the Corn Mother like maybe she'd just said

something and maybe she hadn't. Sucked a lip, pinched his chin between thumb and forefinger.

"My friend," he repeated. "She got it."

"It is not statistically uncommon. Between two point four and four point eight percent of the wild-born population has it. Those were our estimates given variables in crop yield and seed reharvesting over the past three seasons. I feel anything over four percent is optimistic, but Sumedha…"

She reminded Brood of people he had encountered on Texas badlands. People who had wandered too long alone, whose conversation felt like a valve venting pressure, the righting of a mind tilted by solitude. Brood hung on that word: "optimistic."

"How you know that?" he asked. The Corn Mother's eyes refocused. She regarded him keenly.

"Because I incorporated that particular graft into precisely five percent of all seed Satori distributed over the past three seasons." Her head canted to one side as she made a quick calculation. "More this year."

"You?"

"Yes."

They watched each other. The Corn Mother's face glowing with a child's naked pride, Brood standing very still, hardly breathing.

"You made the Tet." Barely more than a whisper.

"Yes," the Corn Mother said. "I designed it. It was difficult to discern exactly how to—"

"You put it in the *seed*. In the crops. People ate it. It came from you."

"Yes," the Corn Mother said. Utterly matter-of-fact. Brood's mind worked to comprehend. The countless bodies. Muscles binding up so tight they broke bones. The agony people felt before they died. The *Chupes* who collected them, who had collected Pollo.

"*Why?*"

The Corn Mother's eyes darted back and forth, tracing in the space between her and Brood some strange chain of logic. The air around her seemed to go inert as she breathed.

"For the Fathers," she said. "They wanted to evolve. They wanted to adapt to this world so that they might enter it anew. Everything was for them. Nothing was for Satori. Nothing was for us."
She smiled at Brood. Tears rimmed her eyes. "I miss Sumedha."

Brood's fists clenched at his sides. He took a step towards her.

"My friend," he said. "Your people brought her here. Where
is she?"

The Corn Mother seemed not to hear him. She reached up,
ran fingers along rough bark of the turkey-grape vine. It seemed
to comfort her. Her face relaxed, went dim as she lost herself to
some unfathomable memory. Brood took in the exactness of her
proportions, the acute grace of her neck. Watched the insectoid
quickness with which her fingers inspected the vine. His spine
tingled as though he'd just stepped on a snake.

"I miss him," she whispered. Tears streamed down her cheeks
now.

Brood hollered into her face: "*Dónde está* Viv!" The landraces
started, began to move forward. The Corn Mother's face snapped
back to the moment. She regarded Brood placidly, like she had
never been gone, the tears still wet on her cheek. She peered into
him, seemed pleased by his sudden aggression. She stilled the
landraces with a gesture, and smiled.

"She is back here. Come. Let me show you." She turned, and
Brood watched the aqueous motion of her body recede into the
dome's murky reaches. He followed.

Shapes emerged from the gloom. A thick female landrace
stood beside a heap of newly harvested corn. As Brood watched,
she took two thigh-sized ears in each hand and dropped them
through a hole in the floor. The hole puckered with a sucking
sound as the ears disappeared. Through the soles of his feet Brood
felt a deep and rhythmic throb, like heavy bass from a big speaker.
A heartbeat.

"She is there." The Corn Mother swept an arm before her.
Brood sensed they were close to the dome's wall. Several small
forms occupied a floor. He stepped forward, squinted.

Saw babies.

A score of them. They all sat upright, their naked bottoms buried in an expanse of thick fur growing from the floor. They seemed to sense company. In unison their wide faces turned and they stared, silent and weirdly attentive, at Brood. Umbilicals ran from their bellies towards the ceiling, where hung fat pods.

"*Dónde?*" Brood demanded. "*Dónde está* Viv?"

Confusion creased the Corn Mother's brow. She took a step forward, placed her hand lightly atop one baby's head. It looked her in the eye and grinned wet gums and cooed.

"Here," she said. She moved to another baby, fondly touched its cheek. "And here."

"That ain't her."

"But it is. Both these children bear portions of that girl's helix."

"But that ain't *her*."

"Perhaps not as you knew her."

Heat rose in Brood's chest. He struggled to breathe.

"You killed her."

"The weak die." The Corn Mother said this in the same tone as she might have said the sun rises. "This strengthens the greater expression. It has always been thus." She pointed back the way they had come. "Your people out in the wild, they are merely one of the helix's expressions of what human is. And far from the best one. They are the raw material from which my people awaken." She smiled. "The girl of which you speak, she *lives*." Her hand dropped close to the infant whose cheek she had touched. It reached up, blindingly quick, gripped her index finger. "I have taken the best of her, and improved upon it."

Brood sensed motion to his right. He took a step that way, peered into the shadows.

Saw a low table made of bone lattice. A body splayed upon it. Skin peeled back, ribcage exposed. Viscera and organs exhumed and precisely arranged beside the body. It took him a moment to recognize the swirl of tattoos on the boy's face.

Two of the tall landraces, a man and woman, knelt beside the table. Their hands buried deep inside whiteboy's abdomen. The man noticed Brood and smiled in greeting.

"He is beautiful, yes?"

Brood retched. His knees gave out and he vomited across fur and scale.

"Did you not like the meat?" the Corn Mother wondered.

A sob wrenched its way from Brood's gut. He stared at the tough skin of his knees, at a grey patch of fur, at his palms. At anything besides the body cut up on the table.

"Pollo." The word filled him like cold cement. He raised his eyes to the Corn Mother. "That what your Satori people do to him? *Lo picaron?* Like he a piece of fucking meat?" The Corn Mother stared. Beside her, the babies stared, too. Recursive, implacable intelligence.

"I do not understand to whom you refer."

"My brother. *La Chupes* take him. Thought he had the Tet."

"If he contracted Crop Graft 3, then he most likely died in one of Sumedha's pens." The Corn Mother said it like it was easy math. "Nobody would dissect him. They would simply let Satori metabolize the body. Human remains can be used to produce considerable energy, when used as fuel."

"He didn't have it, though." Pollo's desolate moan as the *Chupes* had loaded him onto the wagon—it filled Brood's skull, emerged from his throat. "No Tet. *Chupes* just thought he had it."

The Corn Mother's eyelids fluttered. Two precise blinks. She laughed—a sound that reminded Brood of wind chimes hanging outside his mother's greenhouse.

"Then why would he die, if he did not contract it?" For a moment she stood completely still. Brood saw the pulse in her neck, a heart rate slower than the movement of planets. She turned, spoke to the shadows. "Mercy." The quick woman who had attacked Brood slid from out of the nearby darkness. Hips swiveling, efficient and predatory. Pale eyes pinned Brood, and he froze with animal terror. Mercy grinned.

The Corn Mother gestured at Brood. "This one is sicklier than I thought. I do not need him after all." Rage flashed across Mercy's face, and she receded into the gloom. The Corn Mother turned and beckoned Brood. "I will take you back outside, boy. It is almost your evening feeding time."

....

Brood stared at the food in his bowl. A robust lettuce salad with cherry tomatoes that looked like perfect little red planets. Peanuts. Crescent slices of gleaming cucumber. Sprouts. A dollop of pale meat from the turkey-grape vines.

Beside him, Billy wept.

"Kill those motherfuckers today," the boy sobbed. "Kill 'em *now*." He started to rise, but Anna, who had folded herself around him, held on tight. She whispered into his ear. Shushed him when the sobs wracked him.

Raimi sat nearby with his friend, a short white kid with a shaved head. They watched Billy and touched each other tenderly. Beyond them sat Jorgen, vacant and stony.

Brood stared at his food. The happy din of mealtime rose from the field around them, migrants reveling over their full bellies. The evening had turned pink and the kid with the guitar sang his sweet songs and Brood's food seemed to laugh. He hoisted the turkey meat with two fingers, flipped it in the air. The dog caught it with a snap of its jaws.

"Motherfuckers," Billy sobbed. "Kill that bitch now." Anna kept her arms tight around him.

"We don't have the numbers," she said. "But we will. Soon." She stroked Billy's cheek. "Soon." Brood pushed his bowl away and turned to Anna.

"I'm heading west, *Madre*."

"To Denver," Anna said, and Brood nodded. "When?" she asked.

"*Mañana*. First light."

Billy fell to quiet weeping. Anna ran a hand over his cornrows, stroked his cheek, lightly kissed the top of his head. Tears welled in her eyes. Grief turned her face hard. She met Brood's eye.

"Your brother's dead, honey."

"Probably," Brood admitted. "But the Corn Mother say there's a chance he ain't."

"You're with us now."

"*Sí*, I am. But I got to go. I'm all he's got." Brood scanned the western horizon, where, far away, heat lightning flashed white against the dusk. "He all I got."

"You have us." Anna reached out, placed a strong hand on Brood's knee. "We're your family."

"If I find him, we'll come back here."

The *ese* with the guitar began a jaunty tune about a rodeo clown. A man nearby danced to it, slapping his FEMA'd knee. Nearby, someone laughed an easy laugh. The sound of the well-fed, the unworried.

"We're your family," Anna told him. Her grip tightened on his knee. "The Mother brought you to us. You stay with us." Their eyes met for a beat, then Brood looked away.

"*Sale vale.*"

....

Brood woke in the dark chill of predawn. Two tall rows of corn between which he lay rustled, weirdly sentient, in a light breeze. He crawled from beneath his canvas blanket, rolled it up, tucked it beneath an arm. Bent, and with one hand picked up a shoddy plastic bag full of fat Satori vegetables, a plastic gallon jug of water with the other.

He made his way quietly to the valley's rim. The Kansas plains shone chrome as far as the eye could see beneath a sliver of moon. He wandered among the abandoned vehicles until he came to where Anna's trucks had settled like rusted behemoth ticks into the dust.

He moved to the back of the cargo truck, crawled beneath its tarp—began rooting through heaps of scrap metal, rusted engine parts, folds of dusty canvas, tools, pieced-out electronics, searching for what he knew had to be there.

He found it buried deep under a pile of camo netting. A long duffel bag. Five smaller satchels lay packed inside it, identical to the one he'd used in the raid on the caravan in Oklahoma. He pulled one out, reached inside. Felt soft, plastic-wrapped bricks. Outside, he held one brick up in the moonlight. Faded block letters ran the length of a peeling label: SEMTEX.

"That's nasty stuff."

Brood started. A shadow stepped from behind the rusted hull of a nearby water truck. Brood saw scarecrow limbs in the moonlight.

"Jorgen. Fuck, *ese*, about made me piss my pants."

"What're you doing?" Jorgen stepped closer, motioned at the brick in Brood's hand. "Going to make us some pudding?" His easy drawl sounded wry, but his face remained humorless.

"Nah," Brood said. "I'm stealing it. For trade."

"That won't get you a ride to Denver."

Brood turned. Anna stood there, wide-hipped and tiny beside a truck twice her height. The black length of a fuckstick dangled loose in her hand. Brood looked from her to Jorgen and back.

"I got to go, *Madre*," he said. "He's my brother."

"We're your family now, Brood." Anna's face took on the pained expression of a parent doing what needed to be done. The fuckstick swung wide as she opened her arms, beseeching. "The Mother gave you to us. We need your help."

"The Mother." Brood laughed, a callous sound. "You knew where this place was before we drank that *humedo*." Behind him, Jorgen moved close. Brood aimed his gaze at the fuckstick. "You my family, you'd let me go."

"You could choose to stay," Anna said.

Brood nodded. "Yeah. Alright."

He spun. Slammed the water jug across Jorgen's face. The tall man staggered back. Brood threw the duffle of Semtex. Anna watched, calmly, as it arced towards her in the moonlight. It fell with a thud into the dust at her feet.

"It's very stable stuff," she said. Her head canted to one side, like, *what did you expect?* The fuckstick rose in her hand. Brood heard it sizzle, saw a flash of blue light. Then everything turned into fire.

CHAPTER 19

The assault was fucked, right from the get go. Falcon 2 went down, with its full chalk of troops, four minutes south of Riley. Thirteen kids who, for a week, had called themselves Rangers, plus two more who had called themselves pilot and gunner.

Doss experienced the crash as an abrupt spike in coms chatter, shrill and incoherent, as green pilots in Falcons 1, 3 and 4, along with Ops at Riley, tried to sort out what had happened, succeeded, then panicked.

Forty-year-old nuke-powered jets wailed. Hard Gs yanked Doss against the shoulder hooks of her drop seat as Falcon 1 fell into a trajectory towards the crash site. She craned her neck to peer down the Flylight's length, past the reflective visors of her young Rangers in their drop suits, through the cockpit's windscreen. For a moment, nothing out there but predawn blackness. Then a brief glimpse of flame smeared across prairie, a white-hot nuclear star burning at its center. A containment breach in Falcon 2's reactor. It would burn for months, vaporizing everything, leaving only a glass bowl the size of a small stadium carved into the prairie floor. An untouchable, radioactive marker for a mass grave. Doss had seen a hundred craters like it pocking the deserts of Saud and Iran, and the vast refinery cities of Siberia. Nothing left for a family to bury except a printed honorarium that looked like a high school diploma, placed with great ceremony into an empty coffin. Doss tried to remember the name of the kid Gomez had put in charge of Chalk 2. Tried to remember the Falcon's pilot. Recalled only that they had been children.

The pilot's mouth moved fast against her headset mic in the instrument panel's bile-colored loom. The Go Pills, which Doss thought had leveled off, resurged. She clenched her teeth, suppressing an insane urge to scream, chinned her mic.

"All players, this is Lead." It frightened her how chill and far away her voice sounded in her head set. "I want radio silence unless I specifically address you. Repeat: Shut the fuck up." Coms went quiet. "All Falcons, give me a sitrep."

"We're solid, Boss." Doss watched her Falcon's pilot set her jaw, resolute. She sounded young. Tense, but steady. "Combat functional."

"Ah..." came Falcon 3's pilot. He sounded like he'd barely reached puberty. "Ah," he said again. Fiorivani's voice cut in.

"Falcon 3 is combat functional." Hard as a knife point. "Mos def."

"Falcon 4 is combat functional," came Gomez's voice. "Fucking A." Within the red combat glow of her drop suit, Doss smiled.

"Riley," she said. "Report."

"Falcon 2 is definitely down," Chen stated. "He reported trouble with his controls, then we lost him."

"Hostiles?" she asked. A pause.

"Nothing on scope."

Doss wasn't surprised. Sketchy gear, raw troops: the whole enterprise begged for disaster. Maybe an ancient seal in the Flylight's engine had cracked in the dry heat of a half-century of storage. Or a bearing had failed. A green pilot had gotten scared of the dark. Whatever. Thirteen kids playing Ranger, plus a pilot and gunner, gone. Doss bit her lip, tasted the rust tang of blood.

"Riley, what's General Lewis' position?" She imagined Lewis, head tilted back, reading the tiny info scroll along the bottoms of his specs, patiently awaiting an opportunity to appear useful. He'd taken a zep out ahead of the Falcons. To ferry out refugees he'd said. Doss had set her own zep to zombie a holding pattern fifteen miles off objective, but Lewis had insisted on helping. And technically speaking, he was a general, so what could Doss really do?

"Lewis is holding steady at fifteen K feet, ten miles off objective."

Doss made a hard calculation, weighed the diminishing odds of success against the ever looming specter of Fucking Up. Chinned her mic.

"All players, mission is still go. Chalk 1, we're taking the objective by ourselves. Chalk 3, you take over perimeter from Chalk 2."

"Copy that," Fiorivani said.

"Chalk 4, you're still overwatch."

"Copy," came Gomez.

"Chen, make sure Lewis stays out of my way."

"Roger that."

"All Falcons, resume assault formation. Missiles hot, scopes cold. Don't paint any targets until we're close enough to bite." Pilots acknowledged.

Doss' guts heaved as her pilot dropped the Falcon, close enough to the deck to drag cock, and punched burners. A red LED in Doss' visor ticked backwards from nine minutes. The time it would take the Falcons to rail their way supersonic across Kansas.

Her mouth felt dry. The titanium hull vibrated through her drop suit. Go Pills tickled her nerves. When the LED hit two minutes, she chinned her mike.

"Chalks ready," she ordered.

"Yes, Ma'am!" all Rangers chorused. It made Doss smile. She'd armed them with fucksticks, side arms, stun grenades. Toys with which they'd have a difficult time killing themselves. Rangers indeed.

The LED hit one minute. An orange light appeared on jump bay's ceiling.

"Falcons, paint your targets and fire."

A second passed. Several loud bangs sounded in the hull. Missiles detaching themselves. Doss craned her head, watched through the cockpit window as fingers of yellow flame screamed away over the prairie. Suppression ordnance, a combination of concussion and sonics that would detonate over the valley.

Her stomach lurched as her Falcon abruptly climbed, then leveled. The light in the ceiling switched to red.

"Rangers are go!" she called. She patted hands over her gear. M-8 strapped across her chest, Mark 30 G-launcher slung underneath. Fuckstick on one hip, .45 on the other. Two frag grenades on her drop suit's left breast, two stunners over the right. Pig sticker on her left forearm. Cookie cutter charge packed against the small of her back.

Compression joints hissed as she moved. Seven of her young Rangers had died in training jumps the past two weeks because of fucked suits. Hydraulic shocks, stale from storage, failed to perform—suits had crumpled like beer cans. The kids inside…

Fear didn't touch Doss. Maybe it was the Go Pills, maybe just the fact that she loved this shit too much to care. She wanted to tear somebody's throat out with her teeth. She laughed…realized a split second later she'd forgotten to chin off her mic.

The light flashed green. Drop seats slammed open with a metallic crack, ejecting Rangers.

Freefall. Creamy dawn light poured for five silent seconds through Doss' visor. It was the best thing she'd felt since Emerson had—

Impact. It rang her bones like a bell. Readouts on her visor fizzled, came back to life. Doss flexed fingers, bent knees, mentally stated her own name—decided she was still alive. The suit had done its job, a thousand nano-hydraulic joints compressing, absorbing terminal Gs.

She stood in a cornfield, in the nadir of a knee-deep impact crater. Two Rangers stood close beside her, red *Chupe* stripes visible on their shoulders. Jake and Casanova, already oriented and intent on protecting her. She spotted the dome two hundred meters off.

"Rangers, sound off," she ordered. They did, one through seven, nine through thirteen. "Eight?" No answer. "Eight?" she repeated.

"Down," somebody said. Doss spied a heap of crushed metal through a row of chin-tall corn stalks. They had no medics.

"Twelve and thirteen, you're on eight. Everyone else, on me." Rangers gathered around her, titanium-and-ceramic drop suits shimmering silver as the day came on, mirrored visors hiding the children inside. "Lieutenant?"

"In position," Fiorivani said. "Got your six." Doss gripped the M-8 with her right hand, drew her fuckstick with her left.

"Let's go."

Hydraulic legs pumped. Doss lead her Rangers hard and fast towards the dome, ten meters at a step. A new readout appeared in the bottom left of her visor: an overhead view of the valley as Falcon 4 took up overmatch and began to transmit. Superimposed blue dots showed friendlies, red dots anything else with a pulse.

The suppression ordnance had done its job. Sonics still hovered overhead, wreaking limbic havoc with vicious feedback loops, which the drop suits squelched with dampening frequencies. Hundreds of red dots covered the valley. None of them moved.

Doss saw bodies everywhere as she ran. In the fields, in a large open space beside the dome, up amongst the vehicles parked along the valley's rim. Beautiful landraces and weathered-looking migrants all lay commingled, unconscious where they'd slept. Her chalk met no resistance, reached the dome without so much as sparking a fuckstick.

Doss moved to the dome's wall. The blue dots of her Rangers automatically spread out to cover her. Quick learners. For an instant Doss let herself feel pride. She let the M-8 tangle from its sling, took the cookie cutter from its slot at the small of her back. Peeled its adhesive strip and stuck it to the dome's strange skin. She thumbed the safety switch, hit the hot button.

"Fire in the hole!"

She leapt away. Young Rangers sank low. The charge detonated with a hard thud. Meat and bone erupted as a ragged orifice, large enough to walk through, appeared in the dome's side. Four Rangers hurled stun grenades through it. More thuds. Flashes illuminated the dome's bone work frame through its flesh.

"Inside," Doss commanded. "Fast and tight."

She led the way, following the front sight of her M-8. Through the hole, into the dome: a round space the size of small zep hangar. Rangers behind her unleashed their fucksticks to either side, just on principle. It sounded like glass shattering.

Nothing moved. A dozen bodies lay across the floor. Doss moved to them one by one, prodding them with a titanium boot tip. All were unconscious landraces, thick as pack animals. She moved further into the dome, her Rangers tight on her ass. Fleshy sacks, suspended from the ceiling, pulsed overhead, as though the dome itself squirmed with pain. White smoke from the stun grenades obscured her view. She switched her visor to thermal, saw the red outlines of bodies ahead.

"Movement." She yanked a stun grenade from her chest and hurled it. "Fire in the hole!" The thumper detonated like a hammer strike. An inhuman shriek followed. Movement still showed in the thermals. Something coming towards her, hard and fast. Doss knew what it was.

She sank to a knee, let loose two short bursts with the M-8. Another shriek as explosive ceramics found their mark. Still, the advocate came. It emerged from the smoke, a thin woman showing teeth. Doss' bullets had torn off an arm, ripped a cavity in the thing's chest. She fired two more bursts. Jake and Casanova came up beside her, firing pistols. The advocate flew apart.

Doss rose, slapped a fresh mag into the M-8. She moved forward, inspecting pieces. There wasn't much left. The woman's head lay away from the rest of her. It smiled dimly, exposing shark's teeth, then went vacant.

"Chalk 1," came Fiorivani's voice. "Everything okay in there?"

"We're solid, Lieutenant. Maintain your perimeter." Doss ordered her Rangers to fan out, and paused, marveling at the delicate ferocity of the advocate's inert face. "You weren't all that," she told it.

"Found her!" came Casanova's voice a moment later. Doss moved to where the boy stood over a limp form splayed out on the floor—a floor consisting, Doss now saw, of some sort of fish or snake scale. She rolled the body over with her foot, saw the unmistakable symmetry of the Designer's face. She bent, touched her palm gently to the woman's throat. An intermittent red dot appeared in her visor. A pulse.

. . . .

"That her?" Fiorivani's massive drop suit leaned over the Designer, who lay in the dirt trussed, head to toe, in an interrogation net.

"Affirmative," Doss said. They'd converged at the rally point on the valley's western rim, beyond a clog of behemoth caravan jerry-rigs. Falcons circled in the long morning sunlight. "We're good to go, Falcon 1," Doss told her radio. "What's the hold up?"

"General Lewis, ma'am," her pilot said. "He says he has priority to land. He wants to…ah…pick up refugees." Doss turned, saw Lewis' zep growing fat as it approached from the east.

"Fuck that. I've got mission priority. And I've got wounded to evac." She glanced at the crushed drop suit they'd peeled from the cornfield. Blood leaked from ruptures in the folded metal. Not wounded exactly, but still.

"Ah…" came Falcon 1's pilot. "Lewis says negative on your mission priority. He says the refugees have priority." Doss looked down at the valley. It brimmed with irrigation, swelled green and gold in the morning light, its crops bursting for harvest. Nobody would leave this place—not willingly.

"There are no fucking refugees. And why is he not talking to me directly? Tell him to patch his ass directly into my coms. And you land, Falcon 1, I don't care what he says. Get us the fuck out of here."

"Yes, ma'am."

The Falcon came around the valley and charged hard for the LZ, but Lewis' zep had already bulled in too close. It was like watching a hippo outmuscle a humming bird. The Falcon veered away. Doss cursed.

"Boss, this is Falcon 1," came the pilot. "General Lewis says he can't patch into your coms. He doesn't know why. And I...ah... don't feel comfortable...ah, I mean the space is too tight for me to land, ma'am."

"Roger that." Inside her drop suit, Doss seethed. "Falcon 1, tell Lewis to hurry the fuck up. All Falcons, cover the general's landing. Anything moves near us, kill it."

"Roger," came each Falcon pilot in turn.

"Nothing moving down there, Boss," came Gomez's voice. "You should be good for a while."

As he finished speaking, the sonics hovering over the valley abruptly lost their charge. Their props ceased spinning and they crashed one after the other onto the valley floor. Doss eyed her troops, totaling less than thirty on the ground, arrayed around the LZ's perimeter, fucksticks leveled outwards. Their visors mirrored the reddening dawn.

"Rangers, stay tight," she ordered. "We have some very unhappy people waking up soon." She cursed again. Watched the zep slide its fat ass over the LZ, casting her Rangers in shadow. Glaciers moved faster.

"Where's my sister?"

Doss turned. Fiorivani stood straddling the Designer.

"Armor," the Designer observed, calmly. Fully awake, blinking up at the big lieutenant. Animated, her features were so righteously proportioned it gave Doss vertigo, as though the whole world was crooked, always had been, and she'd never known it until she'd set eyes on this woman. Fiorivani leveled the muzzle of his M-8 at the Designer's face.

"Not going to ask you again, freak. Where's my sister?"

Doss stepped forward. "Lieutenant!" Fiorivani ignored her. The Designer's wide eyes stared serenely up into the lieutenant's visor.

"I cannot see you through your armor," she said. "I do not know who your sister is."

"She was the pilot on the zep that you took out of Satori."

The Designer's face creased momentarily with thought, then

turned pleasant, as though she were about to be helpful.

"Yes," she told Fiorivani. "She is dead. Mercy killed her."

Doss' fuckstick cracked. Fiorivani staggered back, blue lightning rippling across the titanium scales covering his chest. He recovered quickly, the drop suit dampening the charge's effect. He raised the M-8. But Doss was on him. She gripped the rifle's muzzle and held it low and away. It fired rounds harmlessly into the Kansas dust. She slammed her armored palm into Fiorivani's visor, shattering it. She hit him again, this time crushing his unprotected nose. He fell. Doss followed him to the ground. Placed her knee in his chest, pressed the muzzle of her M-8 to the center of his broad forehead.

"She's my sister." Blood poured from Fiorivani's nose. His eyes watered.

"Shut up," Doss spat. "I don't give one ratshit who's son you are or who your sister was. You stand in the way of my mission, I'll kill you deader than shit. Clear?" She leaned on the gun. Fiorivani winced. His eyes crossed, fixing on the black polymer barrel.

"Ma'am," he whispered.

"You're relieved, Lieutenant." Doss grabbed Fiorivani's rifle by the sling and tossed it into the dust, then did the same with his sidearm. "One and Two," she commanded Jake and Casanova. "Guard the lieutenant. He tries anything, you shoot him."

"Ma'am!" Jake picked up Fiorivani's rifle, Casanova his pistol. They took up position a few paces away and leveled the weapons at the lieutenant.

Lewis' zep fired four landing harpoons into the brown hardpan nearby. Winches whined, reeling the zep reluctantly groundwards.

"It is not what I thought would happen."

Doss turned, found the Designer watching her from within the net's folds, black eyes unblinking. It occurred to Doss that the woman was beautiful, in the way finely balanced things were. Everyone she'd ever met, ever even seen, she now realized as she took in the Designer's face, was a puzzle with a piece missing. "I thought you would not find us. I thought I would have time to work. It is unfortunate."

"You'll have plenty of time to work in D.C.," Doss told her

"No." The Designer smiled in a way that made Doss think the woman's thoughts were as symmetrical and uncomplicated as her face. "No, there is no more time. There is only one harvest remaining."

"What do you mean?"

The Designer cocked her head slightly. "Open your face armor. Let me see your face." Doss hesitated. "I would like to know you," the Designer insisted. Doss pressed a button on her helmet twice and her visor hissed open. The Designer closed her eyes for a moment, breathing, then regarded Doss with a smile. "You are beautiful. Your helix is beautiful. It would have added much to your species. Do you have children?"

"Not exactly the mothering type," Doss said. The memory of Emerson cut for a bitter second through the Go Pills and adrenaline humming through her system. His laughter had made things seem less serious, made the world seem made of rubber.

The Designer craned her neck against the net, taking in the surrounding Rangers. She laughed, a diamond sound in the Falcons' ambient throb.

"But you are, child. You exhibit strong parental traits." She turned suddenly sad. "Perhaps it is for the best." Doss cocked an eyebrow at the Designer.

"Why's that?"

"The Fathers seek the completion of their adaptation. They have grown urgent. Before I left Satori, they commanded me to incorporate Crop Graft 3 into all of the seed distributed outside Satori's walls this spring."

"Crop Graft 3?" Doss asked. The Designer smiled.

"The Tet. The Fathers will either find their adaptation, or they will not. Either way, your kind will soon cease to be. As will Satori." Her eyes turned skyward. "I had hoped Sumedha would eventually join me here. We would have continued our work together." She looked, her face suddenly mournful, at Doss. "Let my children keep this place. Do not destroy it."

"You're the only thing I'm after, lady."

The hatch of Lewis' zep cracked open with a heavy hydraulic moan and began to lower while the zep still floated ten meters off the ground. Doss saw movement inside. Migrants, dressed in FEMAs.

"What the fuck." She lowered her visor, chinned her mic. "Falcon 1, ask Lewis what the fuck he's up to. It looks like he's already got a load of refugees."

"Stand by."

The zep's hatch yawned wide. The migrants inside were women, all of them. Their FEMAs glowed yellow—clean, fresh out of vacuum packs. They moved towards the edge.

"Oh shit."

It was the way they moved. Too fluid, too fast. One by one they dropped the last ten meters to the ground, easy as panthers. Doss chinned her mic to fully open coms.

"Rangers! Fire everything you have on the women coming from the zep. Now!" In one smooth motion she jacked a mag grenade into the Mark 30 and fired. It detonated a half-second later with a familiar magnetic crack, shredding the half-dozen advocates who had yet to drop from the zep. Metal keened as the ramp tore loose from its hydraulic hinge. It dangled. The zep listed. "Gomez, I need back up, pronto."

"Copy that."

Twenty or more advocates had already hit the ground. With fleet strides they covered the fifty meters to Doss' Rangers. The Rangers leveled fucksticks.

The women tore into them.

They attacked savagely, leaping, hissing. They peeled drop suits open with clawing fingers. Tore out throats, ripped away limbs. Doss' Rangers screamed, the sounds of terrified children. The way all soldiers sounded when they died. A few managed to fire their fucksticks. The blue lightning seemed only to enrage the advocates. They howled, leapt upon those who had fired.

Doss sighted her M-8, firing burst after burst. Three advocates disintegrated under her bullets. Jake and Casanova fired their guns wildly beside her.

"Rangers on me!" Doss hollered at her mic. "Drop your fuck-sticks! Fire your pistols!" They were beyond hearing her. The advocates tore the Rangers apart, hurled their drop suits away like broken toys.

Doss fired, reloaded and fired, reloaded and fired. She fired until she'd used all her ammo, then drew the .45 and kept firing. Beside her, Fiorivani cracked a combat design's skull with his armored fist. The woman simply smiled needle teeth and drove raptor fingers through his face. He twitched and fell.

"Falcons 1 and 2, I need your guns." Doss' voice sounded like someone else's in her headset. Someone calm, and very far away. "Fire on my position. Repeat. Fire *on my position.*"

She didn't hear the pilots' responses. Heard only the echo of her own gunfire, the screams of her Rangers, the advocates' terrible hissing. One tackled Casanova. Doss gripped its writhing form beneath the shoulders. Hydraulics whined in her suit as she flung it. Casanova, helmetless, stared up at Doss from his back. He tried to speak through the gaping wound in his throat. She spied Jake nearby, swinging his empty pistol wildly before him.

Doss had never seen so much blood. It coated drop suits like so much excess grease, pooled beneath bodies in the dust. Some quiet part of her mind registered the violence as somehow strange, unclean in the clear morning sun.

The advocate she'd thrown leapt back at her, shrieking, its whole body rolling with smooth, malevolent motion. Muscle memory propelled Doss. She stared over the .45's sights into the creature's slit irises. Saw its predator's teeth part, watched its pointed tongue extend with glee. She double-tapped, aiming for the black pit of its mouth. Its head erupted in red mist, then it was gone. Piss ran warm down Doss' leg, pooled in her boot.

Explosions ripped the air around her. Bodies flew apart, advocates and Rangers alike. Falcon 1 hovered a few hundred meters off, the Gatling in its nose growling, spitting fire, burning a molten trench across the LZ.

It didn't matter. Her Rangers were already dead. The Falcon's Gatling went silent, its ammo spent. Doss wondered fleetingly where Falcon 4 had gone. Where was Gomez?

Advocates circled her. She counted seven. She moved forward, straddling the Designer, and raised the .45.

"Kassapa's children," the Designer mooned, "are so beautiful."

"Bitches be bitches," Doss said.

They came all at once. Doss fired. Felt herself lifted, thrown, then lifted again. Slit irises peered through her visor. She felt the pistol still in her hand, squeezed the trigger again. Heard a hiss. Something impacted her suit, pierced it, dug into her shoulder. She screamed, felt herself lifted again. Her helmet came free. Warm sunlight coursed across her face. She hovered, feet dangling in the air, staring into the face of the advocate who held her aloft, its fingers buried in her shoulder. Doss' arm went numb. She raised the pistol, but the creature slapped it deftly away.

Doss looked to where the Designer lay. An advocate straddled her. It sank to its haunches. Put its nose close to the Designer's neck and inhaled deeply. The two of them gazed into each others eyes. They smiled like lovers reunited.

"Mother," the advocate said. The Designer smiled.

"Beautiful child. Kassapa will be so proud."

"Kassapa is dead, Mother."

The Designer's big eyelids fluttered. Grief twisted her face.

"Was it Sumedha?" she asked. The advocate nodded, once. It raised its hand, fingers extended, then waited. The Designer breathed. Her face calmed. She smiled once more, and nodded. The combat design's hand thrust forward. Its fingers sank into the Designer's slim throat.

Doss thought of her father, her sister. She thought of Emerson. Rage burned through her.

She screamed into the face of the advocate who held her— drove her armored fist into the thing's face. Once. Twice. It hissed at her, showing blood and broken teeth. Doss drew her fist back a third time. The advocate caught it. Doss spit into its face, then slammed her forehead into its nose. It fell backwards, dragging Doss down with it.

Doss landed on top. Her hand came free. She drew the pig

sticker from its sheath on her numb forearm. Raised it, hammered down through the creature's sternum. The advocate regarded her with naked surprise. Doss stabbed again. And again. The creature gripped the blade, holding it fast. Doss let the knife go and grabbed the advocate's throat. Squeezed with all the hydraulic might her suit could muster. Cartilage compressed. Bone cracked. The creature's eyes widened. Its slit irises dilated.

It smiled.

Doss saw frank admiration. For a moment, she almost believed the thing to be a beautiful woman.

Clawed hands gripped her. The remaining advocates tore at her like sharks feeding. They smiled and laughed. They broke her drop suit off in pieces. One sank its teeth into her suddenly bare arm. Another struck her in the face with its fist. The inside of Doss' skull turned red. She saw hot blue sky, half-filled by the fat ass of Lewis' zep.

It reminded her...

She reached a hand up to her neck. Found the chord. Let fingers follow it down until they touched hard plastic. She clutched the remote like something holy against her sternum.

Thumbed the dead-man button three times, hard.

Somewhere, miles away, she could almost hear the thunk-and-clack as the rail gun on her zep's belly chambered a block of depleted uranium and swiveled, coming to bear on her coordinates. She smiled.

CHAPTER 20

Brood dreamed fire. He saw the faces of those he'd loved. His mother. Hondo Loco. Viv.

Pollo.

An ember of pain seared through him when he saw his brother's face. Intently blank, staring into some off-center space, eyes pushed away from Brood's like magnets unable to meet their same charge.

Something tickled Brood's face. He tasted smoke. Felt soot permeate his being. Something tickled his face again, persistently.

He opened his eyes: blackness. He moaned. Everything hurt.

He tried to touch the wounded places…Couldn't move his hands, couldn't move his feet.

Something wriggled in the darkness beside him. Intuitively he understood it to be a small dog. Anna's dog. It whined and licked his face again.

"*Perro perro perro.*" His voice rasped as he cooed at it.

He lay there and breathed, gathering his senses. Nylon upbraided his wrists. He recalled Jorgen, Anna, the fuckstick: he was tied up. A seam of light grew apparent along the ground. He lay beneath something.

Patiently, he began working his hands free. Thirst charred his throat. His mind and time tilted in the dark. The smoke smell began to frighten him, made him feel as though his lungs had been packed with ash. Finally his hands came free.

Pain forced him to move carefully. He felt deep bruising, basically everywhere. The entire left side of his body felt as though it had been cooked for days under the sun. The bullet wound over his hip ached. He probed it, found it hadn't reopened. All his joints worked. Nothing seemed broken.

He sat up, hit his head on something. Ran his hands along it, discovered a corrugated truck bed...*overhead.* The dog wiggled urgently, licking him.

"*Sí, sí,*" he told it. "We going." He stroked it. It felt hairless and wet.

He heard a roaring sound, like thunder but constant. It reverberated, filled the entire world, then faded.

Detritus lay all around him. His hands found things as he crawled. Engine parts. Electronics components. A small kitchen knife, which he tucked into the waistband of his canvas shorts. Lengths of pipe. He was under Anna's truck. He found the tarped edge, moved along it until he found a flap, squeezed through and rose shakily to his feet.

The world had gone grey with ash. He stood ankle-deep in soot. Caravan trucks, trailers, wagons lay scattered, upended and crushed. Anna's truck lay on its back like a giant dead insect. Tendrils of acrid smoke rose from its undercarriage.

Yellow heat blisters covered Brood's left side. He touched one, and the skin sloughed. He moaned. The dog wiggled against his shins. He looked down.

A sob caught in his throat. The dog had been horribly burned. Skin had peeled away, exposing spine, ribs, skull. An oily sheen covered what skin remained. The dog wagged a tail that no longer existed, and panted at Brood. Like any friendly dog. Like it had no idea.

"Fuck, *perro.*" For some reason it reminded him of Pollo. "*Perro perro perro.*" He took the kitchen knife from his waistband and knelt. The dog licked him and wiggled happily. Brood pet it and cooed at it, told it "Good doggy, good doggy." He cut its throat. It didn't seem to notice. Brood kept petting it as it bled. It wiggled happily under his hand until it went limp.

Brood stood, weeping. He spotted bodies now, most of them charred, some of them simply pieces. His feet shuffled forward. The stench of scorched meat made him gag. A few other people staggered about, either burned or covered with soot, Brood couldn't tell. None of them seemed to see each other, or know where they were going. They simply walked, unblinking, their mouths agape, their eyes empty.

The roaring sound came again. The sweeping raptor lines of a military plane appeared through the haze. Fat jets swiveled at the tips of its delta wings. It hovered for a moment over the monolithic and smoking bones of a crashed zep a few hundred meters away, then it sped off and disappeared behind a wall of smoke that rose out of the valley.

Sweat ran in white streaks down Brood's arms and over his bare chest, like a fever breaking. His feet moved; he thought of nothing.

He found himself down in the valley beside the stream. It had diverted along a line of black impact craters that ran the valley's floor. Water, choked with shining ash, pooled in the craters. One crater occupied the space where the dome had been.

He walked the edge of what had been a cornfield. Its stillness frightened him. Stalks protruded now like lines of scorched bones from blackened furrows.

A woman stood at the field's center. Mud and ash caked her ponytail. The plastic jeweled eagle on the back of her denim vest had melted in lurid streaks.

She stood gazing at one corn plant that still stood, perfectly intact, magnificently tall. Except it was black.

The metal falcon screamed overhead, disappeared again.

"Think it's the army," Brood said. "Maybe they give us a ride somewhere." Anna didn't look at him. She stared at the corn. "*Vamonos,*" Brood implored.

"Think I'll stay here," Anna said. Her gaze remained fixed on the plant.

She reached out slowly and touched it. The tip of her finger sank into ash. The stalk trembled and then, with a luffing sound, collapsed. A grey cloud lingered for an instant, then dispersed like an exhalation.

....

The dog lay where he'd left it. It looked like it had never been happy, or hurt, or anything at all. Brood tried not to look at it as he pushed his way back into the inverted bed of Anna's truck. He rooted in the darkness, fumbling things through burned fingers. He found the duffle bag packed with its satchels of cold soft bricks. A hunting knife, along whose six-inch blade he could feel nubs of rust. He tucked that into his waistband beside the kitchen knife and kept rooting until his hands closed around an empty plastic water jug.

He dragged the duffle out of the truck, stood, slung it over his unburned shoulder. Roaring jets rattled his bones as the plane reappeared overhead. It circled the smoking zep. Hovered there, low and tentative, kicking up a cloud of ash, into which it slowly descended. A second jet could be heard somewhere out in the smoke, not far away.

Brood meandered through the strewn vehicles until he found what seemed to be a water truck laying on its side, its frame blackened and twisted. Fluid trickled from a crack that ran the length of one of the tank's seams. It smelled swampy, but it was water. He put his mouth to the crack and sucked. Rust ground against his teeth. He didn't care. Strength flowed into his limbs as he drank. When he'd finished, he took the hunting knife and slid it into the crack and pried at the seam until water guttered forth. He filled the jug.

"That's my truck."

Brood turned. A man stood there watching him with blood-shot eyes. He seemed somehow off balance. Brood realized he lacked an arm.

"My truck," the man said again. He held something in his hand and gestured with it. The missing arm, still clothed in a scorched FEMA sleeve.

"*Lo siento*," Brood croaked at him. The man nodded. He leaned against the truck as though suddenly weary.

"You go on, have a drink." He wiped his forehead with the back of the detached hand. "Sure is a hot one."

"Yes sir." Brood stuffed the water bottles into the duffle.

A second jet shattered the sky overhead. It hovered over the zep and descended near where the other plane had landed. Brood shouldered the duffle and started in that direction.

"You have a good one," the water truck man called. Brood didn't look back.

The jets idled, black and sleek as vipers' heads at the edge of what appeared to be a bomb crater, their nuke plants throbbing, a meaty sound in the haze. The front half of the zep's skeleton seemed to have been severed at the crater's lip, and carried away somewhere.

Survivors had gathered, a dozen of them. They stood absently, as though they didn't know where else to be, and gingerly touched one another's burns. Brood scanned their faces, searching for Billy or Raimi or Jorgen or the foreign mother and her little girl. Saw none of them.

The crater was about fifty meters in diameter and Brood circled along its far side. The zep's ribs, honeycombed titanium from which hung ribbons of shredded foil skin, stabbed into red sky.

He discovered the two soldiers standing beside the zep's crushed cabin. A big *ese* and a tall black woman. Matte black armor, scorched and hammered, half-covered the woman. The *ese's* armor looked smooth and intact. They regarded the cabin's twisted chaos as though it were a puzzle.

"Nobody alive in there, Boss," the man said. He held a bent helmet with gleaming visor tucked under one arm. A scar puckered his cheek.

The woman ignored him. She reached out with one hand and

tugged at a titanium girder. Her other arm dangled uselessly. Brood saw blood trickling from gauntlet fingertips. The girder gave way with a metallic squeal.

"Give me a hand, Sergeant."

The man reached out, seemed about to set his helmet on a flat length of titanium girder, then eyed it with pursed lips and simply dropped it. He spotted Brood.

"'Sup, homey?"

"*Nada. Como esta?*"

"*Muy* fucking *bien,*" the *ese* said. His scar made him look both mad and like he was about to laugh.

"You soldiers?" Brood asked.

The woman turned. Brood blinked. She'd been burned, like the dog. Armor dangled off her shoulder, exposing blistered flesh, a bloodied white tank top. Half her hair was gone. The other half afroed out in a perfect semisphere that made Brood think of an eclipse.

"That's right," she said. Teeth showed through burned lips, a permanent, melted sneer. Her enunciation had suffered. "Soldiers." She turned back to the zep's cabin and grabbed a sheet of bent steel.

"Look like you lost."

A diamond flashed in one tooth as the *ese* grinned. He looked Brood up and down.

"Don't look like you done much better, homie."

"I been worse," Brood said. The *ese* looked skeptical, then shrugged inside his armor.

"Sorry to hear that."

"You with the jets?"

"That's right." Overstressed hydraulics in the *ese's* armor wheezed as he pulled a hunk of steel the size of a small table free from the cabin. It teetered, then tipped and slammed with a thud into the dust.

"Why you do this?" Brood asked.

"We didn't." The sergeant pointed at a wrecked body, little more than a broiled torso, that lay not far away. Brood recognized the sharp features of the Corn Mother's strange snake woman. "They did."

"I see him," the woman said, and then growled. She grasped a lip of bent metal with her good hand, grunted savagely, tore it free. Glass shattered as tension inside the cabin released too suddenly. The sergeant reached in, dragged free a body. A man. Brood saw grey hair, a uniform jacket. Brass stars on the shoulder. A cloud of soot rose as the sergeant let the body flop onto the ground. The man groaned.

"Fucking knew it." The burned woman took the man's face in her hand. "General Lewis. Are you in there? Look at me, General." The man groaned again. Eyelids fluttered. "That's it. Look at me, you sonofabitch." The woman smiled, grotesque with her burns.

"He going to make it?" Brood asked. A sly smile crossed the *ese* sergeant's face.

"Doubtful."

"Those were your kids, General." The woman sounded sad, her voice weirdly gentle. "Your boys and girls. You understand what I'm telling you, General?" The general gave a feeble nod. The woman stared down at him for a long moment. "Why?" she asked.

"Satori gave me seed. Enough for the future." The general tried to say something else, but the strain proved too great. He let out a pained breath, then simply said, "My kids." The woman pawed at her forearm, seemed to realize something was missing. Extended her hand towards the sergeant.

"Knife," she ordered.

The sergeant drew a short dagger from a sheath on his forearm. Flipped it deftly in his armored hand and passed it to the woman handle-first.

"Here's your future, Lewis." The woman pressed her blade to the general's neck. Cut it open with the deftness of a practiced butcher. Brood took an involuntary step back.

"*Coño*," he gasped. The sergeant glanced at him.

"He had it coming."

"Most of us do," Brood figured. He steadied himself. Sucked sour ash from his lip. "Just thought you was trying to save him." The woman grabbed the general's face once more.

"Look at me," she commanded. Gurgling sounds came from the general's gaping neck. His blood soaked the ash around him. He went limp. The woman rose, staggered slightly. Her height astonished Brood. The sergeant reached out to support her.

"You okay, Boss?"

"Never better." She handed back the knife, then hawked and spit very deliberately on the general's corpse. She looked towards the survivors. They'd begun gathering near the idling jets, their vibe distinctly unpleasant. They pointed at the planes. Some held rocks. "Time to dust the fuck out of here."

"Seconded."

Together the two soldiers stalked through the zep's teetering skeleton, rodents bee-lining through a mammoth corpse. Brood hesitated, then called after them.

"Dónde es dirigido usted?"

"Fort Riley," the sergeant replied without turning around. Brood hurried to catch up.

"Think I be able to catch a ride to Denver from there?"

"Doubtful."

A side hatch on the nearest jet popped open with a hiss, lowered as they neared until it became a ramp. The two soldiers clambered up it, the woman growing obviously unsteady. Survivors pressed close, but jets kicked up suddenly and as a group they backed away.

"You killed her!" Someone yelled. A fist-sized hunk of twisted metal flew out of the crowd and clanged off the plane's hull. The hatch began to close. Brood took in the survivors, looked over the scorched valley. Nothing but ash. He chucked his duffle into the jet and heaved himself aboard.

The two soldiers sat side by side in carbon-molded seats that ran the length of a long cargo bay. Ergonomic hooks clamped down tight on their shoulders. Another soldier lay on the floor, his armor twisted. A black boy, unconscious or dead. The sergeant and the woman eyed Brood as he picked himself a seat.

"Ain't nothing left here," he explained.

"We'd take the rest," the sergeant said. "They don't seem to like us much." Something banged against the jet, emphasizing his point.

"Good to go," the woman mumbled, her words slurring now.

"Good to go!" the sergeant yelled at the cockpit. An ambient moan filled the cargo bay as the hatch sealed and the cabin pressurized. Brood's ears popped. He saw two pilots up there, speaking into mics beneath their visors.

Jets roared. The floor tilted. Brood fell sideways, grasped at the shoulder hook overhead until it clanked down and pressed him into his seat. Thin titanium ribs ran along the hull between each seat. Brood grasped them tightly—swallowed bile as the cargo bay wheeled and tilted. The big sergeant watched him.

"You ever fly before?" Everything turned smooth except for a hard engine vibration in the hull. Jets wailed just outside, far too close to be safe. Brood'd heard about old military vehicles and their nuke plants. The jets screamed and he tried to fathom their power. He simply couldn't get his mind around it. He shook his head.

"I've done it a thousand times," the sergeant said. He grinned, exposing the diamond in his front tooth. "And every single time I know I'm going to die."

The woman moaned. Her head slumped to her chest. The good side of her face crumpled with pain.

"Hold on, Boss," the sergeant told her. He worked open a panel on the thigh of his armor, pulled free a small white satchel with a red cross on in. Unzipped it and unfolded it onto his lap. Began rooting through it with a finger covered by articulating Kevlar and titanium.

"Fucked up, Gomez," the woman said.

"Fucked up situation, Boss."

"I fucked up. Took those kids in there without real weapons. Mission failed." She winced and shook her head. "Fucked. Up."

The sergeant shushed her. He peeled open a slip of paper, pro-

244 ・ ROB ZIEGLER

duced from it a white, circular patch the size of a pinky nail. This
he gently thumbed to the unburned side of the woman's neck. Almost immediately her shoulders relaxed. He peeled open a second
and placed it beside the first, then kissed the woman delicately on
her burned temple.

"All good now, Boss."

The woman's eyes grew glassy. Her pupils dilated, big as eight
balls. They drifted around the troop bay in a way that reminded
Brood of Pollo. After a while they settled on him.

"Hi," she said.

"*Hola.*"

Her eyes widened suddenly. She looked intently at the sergeant.

"Tell the baby doc," she said. "Tell him to test the crops around
Riley for the Tet."

"Okay, Boss."

"Tell him," she pressed, and squinted at the sergeant like he
was very far away. "Priority number fucking one."

"Don't worry, Boss. I'll make it happen."

The woman nodded, satisfied. She looked at Brood again.
Smiled with the unburned side of her face, then passed out.

The sergeant lifted her chin and inspected her burns for several minutes. His brow furrowed with concern as he probed the
wound still bleeding near her collar bone. He pulled a thick com-
press from the med kit and pressed it there until it stuck. Then let
out a breath and sat back. He eyed Brood, jerked his chin at the
duffle Brood had stuffed possessively beneath the seat behind his
sandaled feet.

"What's in the bag, homes?"

"Semtex," Brood told him. The corner of the sergeant's mouth
turned up. His scar twisted and he gave a slight nod.

"Cool."

They said nothing for a while, lulled by the jet's throbbing
white noise, the hull's vibration, which Brood had begun to enjoy.
It reminded him of the wagon, cranking down a smooth road on
Herc power. After a while the sergeant spoke.

"Ain't seen Semtex in a decade. Used it back in the day." He inclined his head towards the unconscious woman. "We found some in Iran once, hidden under a goat pen. Probably been there forty years. We used it to blow the shit out of a dam." His eyes crinkled with pleasure at the memory. "What're you doing with it?"

Brood regarded the sergeant. Saw a hardness in the man's face he decided he liked.

"Satori," he said. "They took my brother. They going to give him back." The sergeant gave this some thought, then nodded once more.

"Cool."

CHAPTER 21

Sumedha stood naked atop the dome, skin green and tingling in the sun. He marveled at the simplicity, the efficiency of the nearly closed system. The tunnel entrance, a white concrete hump at the airfield's north end, emitted landrace teams. They shimmered with sweat in the fierce spring heat. Meaty legs churned; heavy shoulders leaned hard against the cartilage yokes of wagons brimming with ripe Satori vegetables. The season's first outdoor harvest from the fields four miles north, beyond the ruins of the old factories. Crops ready for Satori's children. Crops ready for Satori herself. Still more landrace teams hauled wagons full of seed and compost out of the verdant swell of the secondary dome, Pihadassa's dome, where she'd built her seed. They hauled the seed into the tunnel, headed back towards those same fields where they would replant, beginning the cycle anew.

Both domes sizzled with photosynthesis. Animal kinship overwhelmed Sumedha.

"She is beautiful."

He reached out to touch Pihadassa. Felt soy-epoxy armor under his fingertips.

He turned. Found the leader of his security detail, visor pushed up, staring. Her lean face twisted with revulsion at the Designer's fingers, which caressed her armored shoulder. Sumedha withdrew his hand. Paduma's face, swollen under his choking grip, flashed in his mind. He closed his eyes, breathed, steadied himself. He looked once more at the dome.

"She desires to know herself," he told the security head. "She is an empty beast, but she craves a mind. You can sense it, yes?" The woman's mouth opened as though to say something, and hung there, agape and silent. After a moment it snapped shut. Sumedha smiled. "Soon she will have one, I think. She will know herself."

He turned and looked down on the old city, sprawling east towards the limitless brown prairie. Spring had brought migrants in force—those without seed, who hoped to scavenge or beg at the source. They camped along broken remnants of the old boulevards, took up residence in the forsaken steel frames of old high-rises. They'd built shelters from scraps of corrugated tin, or draped tarps over wood frames. Some of them lay naked on the sidewalks. Their cook fires smelled like petrochemicals. Sumedha breathed, took in the ragged jangle of their collective helix.

They were not migrants really. They were refugees. They had been thus for thousands of years, ever since they had fled the African savannah as it turned to desert in another time of climate flux. That was what had shaped them: the savannah. They were not fit for the world they had built themselves. They were not fit for this world that had come after, shaped by climate forcings of their own reckless creation. A thermal increase of seven watts per square meter. Sumedha's mind worked over the figure. It struck him as piddling. The world to come, Satori's world, would not be so fragile.

"They are fit only for what happens to them." He turned once more to Pihadassa.

The security head stood there, watching. The woman exchanged a glance with one of her three armored men, who stood a few paces off. Sumedha breathed, righted his mind. Saw fear in the woman, contempt. Sweat rolled from beneath the swell of her helmet, a machined composite of soy and carbon fiber. Sumedha took in her helix. Found it no different than any other migrant's.

"We are primates," he said. "Solitude does not suit us. Do you have a partner?"

"Yes, sir," the woman stiffly affirmed.

"Do I know him?"

"He works in the Fathers' detail."

"It is good to have a partner."

"Yes, sir."

Sumedha trembled with the sudden need to connect, so intense it seemed to scorch away all other sensation. His mind conjured Pihadassa's face.

"I think she must still live."

"Couldn't say, sir."

Thunderheads, burly and dark, piled up to the east. Something had happened out there. Kassapa's wild-born spy had received word that the government agent had found Pihadassa. Then the spy had lost touch with his source at Fort Riley. There had been no word since.

"I talk to her as though she is here. I think that must mean she lives."

"Sir." One of the security men pointed a black-gloved finger towards the airfield far below. Four heavy landraces had entered the outer gate and now lumbered towards the dome. At their center limped a slim woman. Even from this distance she exuded a coiled ferocity. An advocate. As the distance closed, Sumedha saw scorched canvas robes, burned skin. It was Grace, Kassapa's favorite. One of her arms had been torn off at the shoulder. A violent shiver ran through Sumedha's hairless body. The wait had ended.

. . . .

"The autism no longer grips you," Sumedha observed. Bacilio regarded him calmly, chin held high, defiant. Muscle had built itself beneath the swirl of animal glyphs on the boy's torso. Sumedha reached out, touched the pink lip of scar tissue on the boy's forearm where brown skin ended and the pale skin began. The boy lifted the hand, flexed fingers. Sumedha nodded. "You have taken well to the graft."

"I'm hungry," Bacilio stated. Sumedha smiled, nodded at one of the two thick landraces who stood nearby.

"Food," he commanded. The landrace nodded with an emphatic chuff and disappeared back through the door. Sumedha's black eyes flicked back to Bacilio. "How do you feel?" The boy stared for a long time at Sumedha's face.

"Awake," he said. He held his palm lightly to the lab's skin wall. "How *you* feel, homes?"

Sumedha breathed. Sensations moved through him. They frightened him.

"You have shown me the graft's key," he told the boy. "I have adjusted it, but I must make sure. Give me your hand." Bacilio lifted the hand not touching the wall. Sumedha took it, closed his eyes. The boy's helix turned in Sumedha's mind. Mutable, but stable. Sumedha opened his eyes, released the boy's hand.

"Satori. Graft thirty-eight, please."

"Yes, Sumedha."

The sound of Pihadassa's voice speared Sumedha's chest. It conjured laughter, a harsh bark that emerged from between his teeth. The laboratory's walls turned a troubled color of ash. Sumedha breathed, collected himself. The walls turned pale again. He spoke calmly:

"Table." It rose from the floor and articulated into place before him. Bacilio's quick eyes followed the pod as it descended on its fat umbilical and came to rest on the table. The umbilical detached and retracted. Bacilio's hand stayed against the wall.

"I lost my Other." Sumedha leaned heavily on the table and leveled his gaze at the boy. "She is dead." More laughter escaped him, its source a mystery, which for some reason made him laugh even harder. Biolumes pulsed, as though they wished to reach out and touch Sumedha, comfort him. The remaining landrace chuffed anxiously.

"Everybody lose somebody," Bacilio said. The serenity of his tone stilled Sumedha. They regarded each other across the table. Seeing the graft work on the boy was like watching a geological event sped up, layers of neural sediment eroding away, revealing the sharp, clear edges of a personality. Sumedha reached for the cocoon.

"Whom have you lost?" he wondered. Bacilio shrugged.

"Everybody."

The pod quivered moistly between them. Sumedha tapped his own temple, as though the gesture could express the shifting landscape therein.

"I need to connect," he said.

The boy smiled. Teeth that had been missing now shone strong and straight in light gone red. His fingers caressed the wall's soft skin.

"Let you know when I care, *ese*."

The door flexed open and the landrace returned, a bone platter piled high with vegetables balanced on thick palms. Cherry tomatoes, lima beans, corn stripped from the cob, green beans, snow peas still in the pod.

"*Aquí*." Bacilio aimed an authoritative finger at the smooth diamond-pattern floor in front of his bare feet. The landrace set the platter there and backed up. The boy sat cross-legged. Kept one palm ever to the wall while he began feeding himself with the other.

"Got no special sympathy for you, homes," he told Sumedha around a mouthful of green beans. "Everybody lose people. Everybody got to connect."

"The Fathers await me," Sumedha said. "They are like those outside. Like you, but prolonged." DNA shaped by a world that no longer existed.

He slid his hand inside the trembling pod on the tabletop. Massaged the nipple at its center, felt it secrete warm fluid. Withdrew his hand, held it up before his face and stared for a long moment at the viscous stuff covering his fingertips. The wall went abruptly white.

"They are fit only for what happens to them." He opened

his mouth, touched wet fingers to the back of his tongue, and swallowed.

The graft went to work instantaneously, twisting and revamping cell nuclei. For a moment he felt carbonated, as when photosynthesis worked in his skin. It made him giggle. Then pain shot through him, cold as the thought of Pihadassa's death, buckling him to the floor. He suppressed a scream, then stood—heard Bacilio's ebullient laughter.

"Satori. Give me graft seven."

"Yes, Sumedha," Pihadassa's voice said. A new pod descended from the ceiling and settled with a wet sound on the table. Sumedha waited for its umbilical to retract, then picked the pod up and held it like an infant in his arms. Snapping sounds emanated from inside his body. His bones reconfiguring themselves. He struggled to remain standing.

"Satori," he spoke through clenched teeth. "Tell the Fathers the graft is ready. Tell them I am on my way."

"Yes, Sumedha."

The landraces cleared out of his way as he staggered to the door. He glanced back at the boy, who still sat cross-legged on the floor. Watching Sumedha, smiling, his hand as ever touching Satori's skin.

....

Sumedha took his place on one tip of the four-point star. Reconsidered, moved to the star's center. Singularity, he decided, held balance. Sanguine light falling through the chamber's plexi windows cast his shadow in all directions.

Muscles rippled under his skin, redesigning themselves on the fly. His heart rate rose above what he could count. His mind shattered, came back together and shattered anew—neural pathways reshuffling themselves. For a moment he went blind. Heard the rain-on-tin cacophony of dust motes impacting the black flagstones.

"Sumedha." The Fathers' voice, collective and reverberant,

hammered Sumedha's eardrums. His knees buckled, but he did not fall. The Fathers gurgled in their sacks, urgent movements, as though they were suffocating.

"I..." Sumedha started to say, but his mind broke. The inside of his skull turned the color of a bomb blast. "Yes, Fathers," he managed.

His sight returned. He saw the excited pulse in the neck of one of the advocates who stood in the shadows of the chamber's periphery. Her irises contracted to the width of a razor as she watched him, and for some reason this made Sumedha's penis stiffen. He stood like that at the chamber's center, naked and engorged, clutching the graft pod to his chest.

The Fathers' dozen human security seemed to notice nothing, just stood their stations around the chamber, hands clasped at their backs. They noticed little, it seemed, as long as they were fed. The advocate, though, watched him the way a lion might eye a bleeding lamb. A vein in her throat throbbed—in time, Sumedha realized, with his own pulse.

"The graft, Sumedha," the Fathers implored.

Sumedha looked down at the pod. His bowels hummed with fear as he recalled his plan. A sudden plan it now seemed to him. Reckless. But only in method. The intent had been there, shaping the puzzle, ever since Pihadassa had defected. Perhaps even before.

Satori would live.

"I..." Sumedha shuddered as ganglia reconfigured themselves inside his spine. He had never imagined such pain was possible. He forced the tremor from his voice as he spoke. "I have readied the graft for you, Fathers."

"It's about goddamned time," Father Bill voiced.

"Be quiet, Bill." An amniotic sack gurgled as another Father shifted. Father Prekash.

"I want...*out*." Father Bill's voice devolved into a long keen, then reconstituted. "Let's...get on with it."

"Yes," the other Fathers said, a singular voice. "Let's"

Their collective umbilical began to unwind; their pods began to descend. Sumedha stepped back. The pods came to rest on the floor where he had stood in the star's center. A Father shifted visibly inside one pod. Sumedha had never before been so close to them. He forced himself to breathe—kept his body steady as things inside broke, changed, reconnected.

"Do it," Father Bill commanded.

"Do it," the others echoed.

"Yes, Fathers."

Sumedha slid his hand inside the graft pod. Poked at the nipple until it gave its fluid. Withdrew his hand, reached out. Found a small orifice along the umbilical's side between two pulsing veins. An orifice designed for precisely this purpose. His moistened finger slid inside, all the way to the knuckle. An unseen muscle contracted around its tip, sucking, then relaxed.

And that was it. He withdrew his finger.

"It is done." He recradled the graft pod in the crook of his arm and stepped back.

"How long?"

Sumedha glanced around the chamber. Took in the leather chair, the saddle, the ancient motorcycle. Useless artifacts from a dead world.

"The effects should be immediate."

The first convulsions came seconds later. One pod shuddered, then another, then all of them, the bodies inside gripped by genetic cataclysm.

"Sumedha! Something's...*wrong!*" The Fathers' voices turned animal. Howling, braying.

"No, Fathers. Everything is right. Do not worry." Sumedha's heart rate slowed. The muscle contractions ebbed. His breath came easy. At the chamber's edge, the advocate's heart rate slowed with his. Sumedha met her eye. In unison, they smiled.

The Fathers tried to say something, but their words disarticulated, became a booming moan, gaining in volume. A scream, in the midst of which Sumedha felt still. Like in the eye of a tornado—and this, he realized, was a parallel thought. He had never before experienced one.

He laughed.

The umbilical went suddenly slack. Pod membranes split open, ejected brackish fluid, revealed bodies, white and shriveled as dead fetuses. Sumedha poked one atrophied leg with a toe. The Fathers had regressed, he realized, become something even less than the primates above whom they'd sought to elevate themselves. Tubes retracted from their bodies, expelling more sour fluid. Members of the Fathers' security detail stepped uncertainly forward.

"What's happening to them?" asked their commander, a short man whose thick body armor made him look like a tortoise. Sumedha smiled. The comparison pleased him.

"Child," Sumedha ordered the advocate, and waved a hand at the security commander. "Take them."

The advocate leapt before he'd finished speaking. She took the commander by the throat. He flew, trailing an arc of blood from his devastated throat. His body made a broken sound as he hit the chamber's flagstones, and lay still. The advocate was already on the next guard, her fingers deep in the man's chest. She kicked the body away and moved to the next. It took perhaps fifteen seconds. None of the guards even had time to draw a weapon. When she'd finished, the advocate watched the blood run, still hot, across the stones. She grinned her killing rage.

"Thank you," she hissed. Sumedha nodded, smiled, a doting father.

A Father, yes.

He dropped the useless graft pod. Stepped forward, pulled back the lip of one Father's amniotic cocoon. Gripped the ankle of the Father inside and dragged the pale body out onto the star. The Father reached a feeble hand towards Sumedha, tried to say something. A wet bubble formed on lips stiffened by atrophy. Sumedha bent, gripped the hand in his own.

"Father Prekash," he spoke quietly. "Thank you for giving me life." He released the hand. It clutched at him. He kicked it away. "They are yours," he told the advocate.

"Thank you, Father." She slunk forward.

Sumedha slipped a foot inside the empty pod's slick opening, let his body follow. The sack closed around him, wet and warm, as the womb. Tubes entered him sharply. He did not mind.

He became aware of her. Satori. Joy coursed through him. She had been connected to the Fathers, but in the barest mechanical way. They had suckled life from her, but they had not been aware of her, had never *joined* with her. She had had no mind. It struck Sumedha now as obscene. A waste.

She would have a mind now. Sumedha would give her his mind. He would connect, and for the first time, Satori would *live*.

Her massive heartbeat filled him, a cosmic pulse. His own heart synced to it. The graft worked his body. He adapted. His flesh split. Muscle fibers, nerve endings melded to the pod's interior in ways the Fathers never had.

Sumedha joined with her. He connected. Boundaries blurred. The distinction between what was Satori and what was Sumedha became irrelevant. He felt what Satori felt.

The sun building sugar inside his skin—whole square kilometers of tingling skin. The dry breeze off the mountains, churning wind turbines on the plains to the north. The clean and unhurried rush of an enormous metabolism—*his* metabolism—burning efficiently through the first round of the spring harvest. He opened himself fully to Satori.

Through his mind, Satori awoke. It regarded itself—

And found another already there. The boy's mind. Bacilio, orbiting the far reaches of Satori's awareness like the moon, watching.

CHAPTER 22

The iodine-and-alcohol smell tickled Doss' brainstem, told her where she was before she awoke. Army fucking medical. She knew she'd been burned, but felt no pain. Felt nothing really, as though her mind existed inside a cotton ball. Which meant she was heavily dosed up on something. Which meant nothing good.

Memories came to her in fragments. The slit eyes of a combat design staring into hers. Punching the dead-man button on the rail gun's remote, then white heat. She remembered General Lewis. Slowly her solar plexus tightened into a hard crystal of dread.

She'd Fucked Up. Capital F, capital U. She thought of Emerson, how she'd left him laid up in that dank D.C. medical pit. Laid up like she was now. She thought of her poor kids, dressed up in Ranger suits, torn to pieces by Satori's bitches. And then, with profound regret, she realized she was awake.

"Fuck."

She coughed, and this brought the pain. Everything hurt, bad. Like she'd run herself over and then lit herself on fire.

She opened her eyes in stages, saw multiple IVs taped to her right arm, the good arm. Noted large patches of smooth Nu Skin covering her left arm. Of course they'd used caucasian. Fucking Army.

She carefully lifted her good hand and, trailing tubes, reached across herself. Found with a fingertip the Frankenstein seam in her other arm where Nu Skin met real skin. Peeled it back.

What she saw reminded her of…Snorkeling in the Persian Gulf. A reef off Dubai. The flesh beneath the Nu Skin looked like that: swirls of coral, organic and pale. She smoothed the Nu Skin back into place. Took deep breaths, suppressed the urge to sob.

She registered the room's silence. It was dim. Medical green walls, six other beds, all empty except for one. Jake lay there, unconscious, hooked to IVs like hers, green army sheets pulled up to his chin. He bore no visible wounds.

"Nurse!" It came out as a choking sound, brought with it a thunderclap of pain. When the pain passed she found the baby doc's keen face staring down at her, zipper scar along his forehead furrowed beneath tight-cropped black hair as he assessed her.

He produced from a nearby metal nightstand a plastic squeeze bottle topped with a crooked tube. Doss nodded and he shot a stream of cool water into her mouth. She swallowed and he did it again, then set the bottle on the table where she could reach it.

"You used white skin, Doc," she croaked. Her mouth didn't work right. She gingerly touched a fingertip to her face. Felt Nu Skin where her lips used to be. The doc shrugged.

"All we had. It'll be easy to transplant once we get a hold of something that matches. In the meantime it'll keep out infection and speed up the healing." He moved to the foot of her bed, lifted a medical chart hung there and bit his lip while he perused it. His brown eyes exuding preternatural calm as he regarded her.

"Got yourself pretty messed up," he said.

"That your professional opinion, Doc?"

The ghost of a smile passed over the kid's face. His eyes flicked to the chart. He listed her injuries as though they were a logistics inventory. Second and third degree burns along the left side of her torso, over her left shoulder and arm, over the left side of her face. Heavy bruising, pretty much everywhere. She was one big hematoma. Four deep puncture wounds through her left pectoral muscle, just below the clavicle.

"Rehab for that one's a bitch," he informed her, then his eyebrows arched severely. "Things could be worse. Nothing's broken." Doss rolled her head feebly towards Jake. He breathed deep and slow, his face serene.

"What's with him?"

"Concussion, as far as I can tell. He's been out since you brought him in. Seems fine, otherwise."

"He saved me," Doss remembered. "He held me on the ground. He piled bodies on top of us." Her voice trailed off as memories of the assault came to her. She stared up into a bank of fluorescents overhead, suddenly afraid to look at the baby doc. "Anybody else make it?"

"Outside of your sergeant's troop...No. From the first three chalks, just you two and some migrant kid. Not one of ours. Nobody survived the crash." Doss closed her eyes, swallowed hard.

"How long's it been?" she asked. "Since we came in?"

"Three days."

"Shit."

"I had to keep you under while the skin grafts took."

Doss said nothing. For a time her thoughts took the form of the people she'd failed. Rippert. Gomez. Fiorivani. Her father. The young Rangers.

Emerson.

This last caused her chest to constrict. Grief welled up in her. She sobbed, once. It brought pain. Pain made her clear.

"The Tet," she remembered. The doc nodded.

"The sergeant had me acquire samples from all the crops in the area. I ran them through a sequencer looking for any obvious anomalies."

"And?"

"At first, nothing. But the sergeant said we were looking for the Tet. So I took a blood sample from a migrant kid who had it, and ran that through the same program. I found this." The doc pulled a flexpad from his hip pocket, unfolded it, tabbed through several windows. He held it close to Doss' nose. A double helix rotated on the screen.

"The Tet?"

The doc nodded. "It's a mutation. I ran the crop samples again, this time looking specifically for this combination." He folded the flexpad and replaced it in his pocket. "There were no anomalies in the first run because the Tet was the baseline." His small face looked grave, and far older than eleven. "It was in all the samples."

"So it does come from Satori."

"I don't see where else it would come from."

"And it's in all the crops."

"Everything around here."

Doss exhaled between lips that didn't feel like her own. "Get me up and functional, Doc. I need to get on the horn with D.C." The doc didn't move. Doss eyed him. "That's an order, Corporal." The scar on his forehead rose in a way that gave him a philosophical air.

"Thing about medical conditions," he said, "is they don't really care about orders." Doss tried to sit up, and failed. Pain crashed down on her like a breaking wave.

"Make it happen," she whispered. "Get me upright." She pulled tape off one hand with the skin-grafted fingers of the other, revealing the multiple IV insertions. She pulled at these. "Now." The doc stepped forward, placed his child's hand over the IVs, looked into Doss' face.

"I'll see what I can do." He looked scared now, the way he'd been scared of the dark when Doss'd first met him. He placed his other hand against her chest and eased her back against the bed. "I'll see what I can do."

....

"Colonel Doss," Rippert had ordered, "you are relieved of duty."

Doss perched at the edge of a metal folding chair in the little coms tomb buried somewhere deep beneath Riley's tarmac. Its heat made her sweat; sweat made her itch. The doc had helped her don fatigue pants, but a loose hospital gown was all she could handle up top. Everything she touched with her grafted skin felt made of sandpaper and broken glass.

She stared at the sat radio's LED: zeroes across the board. Rippert had cut the signal. Brick-sized speakers mounted high on the tomb's wall issued static. The sound of the end of things.

"That sounded bad," Chen observed. Tits framed his head as he watched Doss. A poster stuck to the concrete wall behind him, yellowed by age, faded lines barely more than pencil shadows. He crossed his feet atop a monolithic metal radio so ancient it had actual dials, big as turnips. "Isn't the army supposed to give you a court martial or something before they start talking about a firing squad?"

Doss, drifting on morphine and static, stared at Chen's sneakers. Old things, cocooned in duct tape and epoxy. She began to feel heavy, and pressed her forehead to the cool steel of her rolling IV stand, to which she was still attached by multiple tubes. Antibiotics and immune suppressants for the skin grafts, morphine for the pain.

"He lost both of his kids," she said after a while. "One of them was my fault."

"No." Chen pushed long black hair back into a severe widows peak and pinned it there with his specs. "It's Satori's fault."

"Maybe." A disgrace, Rippert had called her. Doss couldn't disagree. Chen watched her closely.

"You going to be okay?"

Doss absently traced the index finger of her good hand along the Nu Skin seam on her forearm. Hunted for the place in herself where normally she found resolve. Discovered instead only a hollowness, a sensation inside her belly like snow falling.

"Fine," she said, and looked up at him. "I need you to get a line for me to someone in D.C. All I've got is a name." Chen pursed his lips, rubbed his hands together.

"Sounds like a challenge. Who is it?"

....

Hours passed. Doss found herself alone in the cafeteria, haunted by the sense that she'd wandered. Paced the empty lengths of Riley's dark halls, her IV stand rattling in tow. Her fork plowed furrows in a heap of mashed potatoes as she tabbed through the Satori files on her flexpad. Satori Corp's four CEOs had taken up residence in Satori Tower. The Fathers. They lived directly under the dome's center. The fact that this was important tried to press itself through the morphine haze.

Her flexpad beeped. A high-rez pic appeared in one corner. The version of Ellen Vokle that Doss had met during her mission brief—a grey face made ageless by restorative surgeries. It spoke.

"Agent Doss?" Doss blinked. Her spine straightened, a soldier's reflex.

"Ma'am."

"I understand you've been trying to reach me, Agent Doss." In 2-D, Vokle looked like a doll, porcelain lips barely mobile. A black net, attached to an atavistic hat consisting entirely of the feathers of some tropical bird, hung over laser-sculpted eyebrows.

"Yes, ma'am."

"I also understand you should be back in our lovely capitol by now, being debriefed and sent on to your next assignment." Something subtle shifted in her expression, and Doss understood Vokle to be glaring. "An assignment, I gather, that will involve body cleanup out on the fringe." Again came an infinitesimal shift in her face. "You do look like you have seen the miles, Agent."

"My mission isn't finished, ma'am."

"It is according to Rippert."

Doss fought through the morphine gauze that filled her skull. She spoke slowly, precisely.

"General Rippert is a fine commander and good soldier, ma'am. But in my opinion he is too emotionally involved with this mission. His judgment is not sound." She stared at the stiff mask of Vokle's face. "There have been developments. Developments Rippert was too emotional to hear." Vokle said nothing, just stared, blank, inanimate. Doss thought perhaps the sat feed had gone dead, left the woman's face frozen on the flexpad's screen. Then

Vokle blinked.

Doss told her what the Designer had said. Told her about the Tet in Satori's seed, about the results of the baby doc's tests.

"It seems likely that all the crop seed Satori distributed this year is contaminated." She waited, let the implications reverberate. "All of it, ma'am."

Vokle's eyes flicked upwards for a beat. She seemed to take a deep breath.

"That does sound like Bill Coach," she admitted. A thin hand appeared, brought a glass of something to Vokle's lips. They pursed stiffly, made little kissing sounds as she sipped. "I used to know him. A truly dreadful man. Do you know he once proposed mandatory work camps for those who couldn't afford to pay for seed? So that they could make themselves useful, growing food for the rest of us. Concentration camps, Agent Doss. Just dreadful."

Vokle looked away. Doss sensed movement as the woman concentrated on something outside the screen's view. Old-school dub beats rose from her end of the feed. The woman's feathered head bobbed to the rhythm.

"Ma'am," Doss implored. "We need to take our people to the well. We need to take Satori." Vokle looked at her.

"If we had resources for such an action, Agent Doss, we would have done it years ago. Being beholden to Satori was never something we wanted and never something we planned." Vokle seemed to shrug, but only with her eyebrows. "It just happened that way."

Her hand appeared again, this time with a cigarette. The screen went momentarily green with overexposure as she lit it with a silver lighter.

"We need to do it, ma'am," Doss pressed. "Soon. Before the spring harvest." Small Cheshire teeth hovered in Vokle's face as she laughed, the humorless sound of pebbles grinding under surf.

"It doesn't matter," she said. Her eyes drifted. "The oceans are a slow engine, Agent. The world will keep getting hotter for a long time to come. Things will not get better." Her delicate hand raised the glass. Ice cubes clinked as she polished off the drink.

"You hold Rippert's leash. Make it happen."

"We all go." Vokle's eyes closed. Her head listed sadly back and forth to the rhythm of dub. She seemed inclined to say no more.

"Ma'am," Doss said. "My partner. Agent Emerson. Is there any news?"

Vokle went still. Her face changed, looked genuinely sad. Her eyes opened, seemed reluctant to settled themselves on Doss, but finally did.

"I am truly sorry."

....

"Lewis had our radios jammed, mos def." Gomez held a can of chewing tobacco in one hand. With the other he picked at the scab of a sun sore on his shaved head. "Chen said the jammer was easy to find once he knew to look for it. Right up there on the radio tit." He raised the can towards the nipple-like nub atop the zep hangar. "Blocked certain channels only. Let us talk to each other, just not with D.C."

"Makes sense," Doss figured. She sat on the tarmac at Gomez's feet, huddled around the IV stand. She watched Lewis' kids do tight marching drills up and down the airfield. The older kids had stepped in, assumed rank and preserved Lewis' fetish for military order. To what end, Doss had no idea. Doubted they did either. She eyed Gomez's dip. "Fuck did you find that?"

"I know people," Gomez grinned. "With access to deep storage."

"Shit's probably older than you are."

"Yep." Gomez shook the can, whipping it expertly with a limp finger until it was packed, then opened it and offered it to Doss. She pressed her tongue to her burned lip, winced, shook her head. Gomez stuffed a thick pinch behind his own lip. His face turned sour. "Tastes about my age." He cocked an eyebrow at Doss' IV stand. "Maybe the doc can sort you some nicky through there."

"Already got me on morphine."

"So you in righteous condition to make decisions."

"Righteous," Doss agreed. She squinted south across the plains, where a massive wall cloud churned demonically fifteen or so miles south, luminescent in the late afternoon sun. A breeze wafted through her hospital gown, making the Nu Skin itch all over.

"I got on the horn with Rippert."

"And?"

Doss said nothing, just turned her face up to the sun. Gomez spit black juice eloquently onto the tarmac.

"Fuck," he said.

"Yep. Wants us back in D.C., pronto."

"The doc tell you what he found?"

"He did." Doss closed her eyes for a moment, let the sun paint her retinas red, then looked at Gomez. "If you were D.C., what would you do?"

"In my experience, what D.C. does and what needs to get done are never the same thing." Gomez shoved the can of dip into a rear pocket and spoke without looking at Doss. "Know what I'd do if I was you."

"Kick Satori in the balls."

"Fucking A."

A wave of pain rolled through Doss, epicentered at the wound in her chest. She thumbed the button on her morphine drip. The stuff exploded at the base of her skull, a soft orgasm to which she lost moments, her thoughts dissolving in the sublime glow of an internal sunrise. Her head grew heavy. She let it settle into her IV'd hand. Listened to the cadence of the marching children, the moan of far off winds growing violent.

"Fucked us up righteously, Gomez."

"It was a fucked up situation, *Jefe*. Lewis buttfucked us with those Satori bitches. You hadn't done what you did, they be prancing home right now with our balls between their teeth. Instead, they're charred meat out there on the prairie, and a-fucking-men to that. No matter what D.C. says."

Doss felt the cold lick of snowflakes against her patched skin. The young voices out on the tarmac warped under the fluctuating pressures of oncoming weather. Sounded like screams.

She saw the pit. Saw Alyosha. He grinned at her, teeth black with his own blood, eyes gleaming with revelation. *Sometimes our ideas feed us*, he'd told her, and held up fingers stripped of flesh. *And sometimes we feed them.*

"It was like this country'd forgotten itself when I got home from the war," Doss spoke at the ground. Her voice sounded like someone else's. "Forgot it ever existed. US of motherfucking A. It wasn't there anymore. There was just Neil."

She thumbed the drip anew, let herself drift. Thought of her father sitting on the one-bod rack in his little cinderblock apartment. Sipping myconal, chewing his algae-stained fingernails while he listened vacantly to weather reports issuing from the one working speaker of his handheld. He listened the way Doss had watched snow drift down through the pit's rusted ceiling grate. There, but not there.

"I loved this country." She pressed a palm to her good eye, damming the tears that formed there. A vision of Emerson filled her mind. "He looked so good in a suit."

After a while she felt Gomez watching her. She lifted her head. His face puckered around the complicated scar on his cheek and he eyed her narrowly down the length of his nose. Like he was peering into the distance and couldn't make out quite what he saw.

"You got to pull your shit together, Boss." His hand emerged from his pocket, holding the string of finger bones. He worried them under his thumb like a rosary. "You the nastiest bitch I ever met. Fucking act like it."

He turned and spit. Thrust his chin out towards the young soldiers. The fifteen members of his Ranger chalk, the ones who had survived the attack on the Designer's plantation, the ones held in reserve, had segregated themselves. They worked away from the others, standing in straight lines of five, doing squats, their vibe elite.

"Know what they call themselves?" Gomez asked. He flipped the strung bones into his palm and aimed a finger at Doss' burned left hand, where white and coffee skin mottled. "They call themselves the Burning Hand."

The young Rangers dropped and did pushups. The price paid for some minor fuckup. Then they rose and began to jog together along Riley's perimeter fence. Beyond the fence, migrants hustled to tarp their fields with scraps of plastic and canvas before the storm came on—fields fat with crops ready for spring harvest.

. . . .

Alyosha's laughter sounded like a snake on sand. Doss thumbed the morphine drip, striving for perfect blackness. Instead, snow drifted slowly down through the rusted ceiling grate, smothering.

She spoke Emerson's name, and he appeared. He gave her a tranquil smile. Ran thumbs along the lapels of his Kev-weave blazer.

"You know," he told her. "I think you'd make a great mother."

Doss woke. Standing in her quarters beside the small cot, IV stand gripped with both hands. She sensed the storm somewhere overhead, tornadoes moaning across Riley's flats.

She straightened. Held up her hand and regarded the IVs taped there. After a long moment, she ripped the tape away, gingerly pulled the tubes from her skin. The holes bled. She ignored it and checked her watch: 03:24. More than an hour until reveille.

Her feet moved. She opened the door, stepped out into the hallway's linoleum silence.

Found Jake curled up asleep on the floor, a dark fetus in shined, army issue boots. He started awake, eyes staring wildly around for a second before they found Doss.

"Boss Momma!" He leapt to his feet, saluting. Doss waved a vague hand at her eyebrow.

"How long you been there?" she asked.

"Don't know. Doc let me out of medical sometime after dark." He stared forward, soldierly and righteous. Doss placed a hand on his thin shoulder.

"I'm sorry about Casanova."

"Duty, Boss Momma." Jake's chin dipped and he somberly touched fingertips to the red *La Chupe* band tied around his bicep.

"You did well out there," Doss told him. "As well as anybody I've ever seen." The tips of Jake's ears glowed red in the hallway's fluorescents, but his eyes didn't waver from attention. "How do you feel?"

"Good to go," he said.

"Good." Doss considered her feet for a moment, tried to recall where they'd been taking her. "Get me Gomez," she ordered. "Then roust Chen. Tell him to replace the jammer on the radio tit once the storm's past. I want zero coms with D.C."

"Copy that, Boss Momma." Jake took two quick steps down the hall, then halted, turned on his heels and marched back the other direction. "Shit's that way," he said, followed the finger with which he pointed.

In her quarters, Doss stripped off the medical gown. Dug a med kit from one cupboard, from it produced gauze and transdermals. Two of the derms she pressed to the skin of her neck. The rest she shoved into a fatigue pocket for later. She wrapped gauze over her Nu Skin. Gritted her teeth as she very carefully pulled a clean white t-shirt over her head. She waited until the burning sensation grew tolerable, then dug the flexpad from her pocket.

Checked coms, found positive sat link. Cycled through contacts, found the one she wanted, pressed the tab labeled "Transmit." The com light blinked. Seconds passed. Then Tsol's square face appeared, pudgy from sleep.

"Agent Doss," he mumbled, and rubbed his cheek with a thick hand. "My guardian angel." A girl's voice murmured incomprehensibly from his end and he turned. "Shut up. Go to sleep." He turned back to Doss. "To what do I owe—" His eyebrows shot up as he took her in. "Jesus. I heard you got chewed up out there, but—"

"Be quiet and listen," Doss ordered. "I need a favor."

. . . .

"Some of you are Rangers," Doss hollered over the tarmac. "The rest of you will be Rangers soon enough." Forty-two kids stood tall before her, drop suits like negative-space statues, matte surfaces sucking up thin morning sunlight. Gomez's Ranger chalk, plus two more chalks he'd just outfitted, each chalk two soldiers larger than the standard thirteen, because there simply weren't enough to form a fourth chalk. Gomez and Jake stood at the formation's head, her bloodied veterans, her leaders.

Her own drop suit chafed her burns where padded sensors met her body, responding to signals from her muscles. Nano-hydraulic joints worked with barely audible sibilance as she folded her arms behind her back and began to pace.

"The history of the Rangers is a proud and storied one," she called to the young soldiers. "It's a history most of you don't know. One most of you couldn't give a hot shit about. No reason you should. This country's not what she once was. But one thing I know you care about. Food. Our food has been poisoned. Corrupted with the Tet. The solution to this is simple. But not easy."

A haze of ocher dust blew across the sun. Doss planted her feet, faced her Rangers. A cold feeling wound up her spine as she took in the blank faces watching her from within open-visored helmets. The faces of children who knew only two things: when they were hungry, and when they weren't.

"Satori," she told them. "The poisoned well. We must go to the well, and we must clean it. Today, we begin training. Ten days from now, we jump. We will take Satori for our own."

She unfastened her left gauntlet, withdrew her burn-mottled hand and raised it, fingers spread, for her Rangers to see. At her feet sat a can of red paint she'd scrounged from a storage closet.

"This country's not much anymore. But she's what we have. And right now, you're all she has." She picked up the paint can and moved wordlessly through the ranks.

In front of each Ranger she stopped, dipped her hand into the paint, pressed her palm to black armor. When she was done, all the Rangers wore the dripping red imprint of her left hand on their chests. She finished with Jake and Gomez, then Gomez stripped off his own gauntlet. He dipped his hand into the bucket and stepped close, searching Doss' face as he pressed the paint to her chest.

"I guess we ain't heading back to D.C.?"

"Fuck D.C.," Doss said. "Fuck Rippert." Gomez's scarred face crinkled with pleasure as he stepped back. Doss turned to her troops, wondered vaguely if any of them would survive—figured probably not. She raised her red palm to the sky.

"We are the Burning Hand!"

"Burning Hand!" They answered as one, proud and hard. It was the saddest thing Doss had ever heard.

CHAPTER 23

The kids at Riley took Brood in and made him look like a soldier. Like them, he pretended to be one.

He did morning PT on the cool tarmac. He marched and did pushups when he missed steps or didn't know left from right. They gave him duty in the cafeteria, washing trays, which suited him. He secreted into apron pockets scraps of food the spoiled soldiers didn't want. Handfuls of canned corn. Hunks of prepackaged chicken fried steak soaked with gravy. Vacuum sealed pieces of vanilla cake. Cardboard pints of milk. These he smuggled into the locker that sat at the foot of the cot they'd assigned him in a group barracks, where he lay there awake at night, marveling at the sleep sounds of these boys and girls who slumbered deep, unafraid of their surroundings.

They shaved his head, gave him tough cargo pants, green army tees, uniform shirts, and boots. These were the best clothes Brood had ever had, except for the boots, which blistered his feet. He ditched them for sandals, which he fashioned the way Hondo had taught him, from scraps of old tire he found out back of one of Fort Riley's out buildings. They formed easily to his toes and didn't stink when his feet sweat.

"Better not let Jingo see that." Bullion, the food prep specialist and Brood's supervisor, was short, black, wore his hair as a tight mohawk. A magic marker skull and crossbones adorned the front of his white apron.

Bullion liked Jesus. An old Ham radio sat on one shining steel shelf in the kitchen. It hissed with static and the railings of some prairie saint, calling out from the barren heartland to all believers. Bullion'd stood beside Brood behind the cafeteria serving line's steaming bins and aimed a spatula, with which he served factory-made chicken nuggets, at Brood's feet. "Jingo fuck you up, he sees that." His face bore an expression of serious concern.

"If I see what?"

There had stood Jingo, injection-molded tray proffered across the hot-bin partition, awaiting mashed potatoes. He was tall, white. Two inverted Vs on his sleeve meant he was important. The high-and-tight crew cut and the way he fixed his lips tight to his teeth and put his nose in Brood's face—this meant he was an asshole. "If I see *what?*"

He stalked around the partition, eyed Brood's feet with disgust. The cafeteria, full of feeding kids, went silent. Jingo yelled things about regulation dress, about good soldiering. He reached out and, very deliberately, pushed Brood.

Brood punched him in the throat. The tall boy dropped, gasping. Brood calmly withdrew a long steel ladle from a stainless bin full of steaming gravy, and clubbed Jingo once across the temple.

The soldiers left Brood alone after that. They didn't mind when he showed up for morning PT, and when he did his cafeteria duty. No one complained when he disappeared either.

He spent his time wandering Fort Riley. He strolled empty halls with echoing concrete floors. Sat alone at the peeling laminate tables in empty meeting rooms, surrounded by flaking sound-proof baffling. The place felt like a memory of itself. Its silence soothed him.

He found a section of officers' quarters, abandoned and unlocked. Private rooms with only one cot in each. Dust had accumulated to geological depths upon each tightly made cot, each metal desk, each nightstand and sink. He chose a room far from the other kids. There he stashed the duffle full of Semtex beneath the bed.

At night he shoved the metal chair under the doorknob and lay on the cot with his fingers laced behind his newly shaven head. Memories haunted him. The mother and child, stunned by Semtex and caked in Oklahoma mud. Brood tried to pretend they'd made their way north, found a planting ground and people to be with. Tried to convince himself, too, that Pollo was still alive, living somehow beneath Denver's great dome. Even though he knew it was impossible.

"Let the dead be dead," he whispered to the silence. It was a wise notion, but Brood knew he didn't have it in him.

.....

The hard-faced sergeant approached one morning after PT. Brood sat on the tarmac, away from the other kids, letting the early breeze cool the sweat off his skin.

"Getting in shape, homes?" The sergeant came to a crisp halt, backlighting himself in Brood's sun.

"Something like that," Brood told him. The sergeant surveyed the distance between Brood and the other soldiers.

"You're not the mixing type, I guess."

"I guess not."

The sergeant nodded like he understood. Took something from his pocket, began shaking it in one hand. A can of chewing tobacco. He opened it, placed a fat pinch in his mouth, then offered it to Brood. Brood shook his head.

"*Gracias.*"

"You look like a soldier," the sergeant noted. "All shaved up and shit. Found a ride to Denver yet?" Again, Brood shook his head.

The other kids began dispersing, off to their duties, their racks, or wherever kids pretending to be soldiers went when they had free time. The sergeant stood there, audibly sucking his tobacco.

"Fuck you want, cuz?" Brood demanded.

Scars twisted in the sergeant's face as he grinned. His eyes remained flat. Brood slid a hand behind his back, wrapped his fingers around a pig sticker he'd found in a storage room. The sergeant laughed.

"You're just all business, huh? All *pinche* badass and shit. You're not like these other kids." He spit tobacco juice, gave Brood a speculative look. "You seem reliable. You reliable, homie?" Brood didn't answer. The sergeant nodded. "Want to show you something. Follow me." He turned abruptly and strode away across the tarmac. Brood stayed put. The sergeant turned. "Come on. You'll like it, I promise."

....

"Something about you reminds me of my papi." The sergeant spoke over a densely muscled shoulder as he led Brood through Riley's hallways, every so often spitting a gummy black spot of juice onto the concrete floor. They came to a green-painted door marked AUTO BAY 3. The sergeant pushed it open, stepped through and hit a light switch. White fluorescents strobed overhead, then came fully on, revealing a long low room the size of a soccer field, filled with tarped vehicles.

"He ran guns to the *secessionistas* down in the jungles around Houston." The sergeant moved from one vehicle to the next, lifting faded khaki tarps and peaking beneath. "You sound like you're from Texas."

"*Sí*," Brood acknowledged. "San Antonio."

The sergeant stepped around a behemoth vehicle. His diamond tooth flashed in the fluorescents as he grinned at Brood across the tarped hood.

"Me too. Dallas, originally." He peeked under the tarp, then moved on to the next vehicle. "*Secessionistas*, they'd hide out on old oil platforms in the gulf. My papi'd paddle his ass out there in a rowboat, through all these mines and shit. If gov troops'd caught him, they'd have shot his ass." He halted, leaned with a hand against a massive wheel protruding from beneath a tarp and stared at Brood. "He was a good man. *Muy confiable.* You got that same look to you. Like you're going to do what you're going to do, and nobody going to tell you shit about it." He patted the vehicle. "This is it. My friend Lobo." He gripped the tarp with both hands and whipped it free.

The vehicle looked like a massive black widow—if black widows were made from molded carbon fiber, ceramic, titanium armor plating, came with dual-barreled grenade launchers stacked on their backs and fat black tires on their feet. The sergeant sank down to the concrete floor and wriggled his way beneath the chassis.

"Scare me up a grease gun, homie."

They checked all the seals, lubed the drive train, CV joints and transmission. When they'd finished the sergeant palmed the passenger door pad. The door seemed alive as it hissed open. The sergeant inclined his head.

"Hop in."

There was no dust inside, just sleek-looking readouts, molded carbon fiber, ergonomic black plastic. The sergeant hit a red button beside the steering wheel. The nuke plant fired. Sounded for a moment like a prolonged explosion, then quieted to a powerful but stealthy throb. Readouts came alive with a soft red glow. The sergeant gunned the accelerator. The Lobo growled. Brood grinned. The sergeant laughed.

"Just like new." He ran a rough hand along the dash as though the Lobo were a long lost pet. "They really cared about their soldiers when they made these things. Wanted us to be effective." He sucked the bulge in his lip, seemed to lose himself for a moment in the readouts' loom. "My boss..." he said after a moment. "I been through shit with her you wouldn't believe. And she had my back every second of it. She'd give everything she got for how things used to be. But she don't get it. Things ain't that way no more. Never going to be." He looked at Brood. His eyes narrowed, assessing, then he seemed to make up his mind. "I'll get you to Denver, homie. Tonight. But you got to do me a favor in return. *Esta bien?"* Brood shrugged.

"Depends on the favor, you know?"

"*Claro.*" The sergeant smiled and laid out his plan. When he got to the part about explosives, his eyes shone and he grew eloquent. "Hornets," he concluded, "they're basically passive creatures. But when you stir them up, there's nothing meaner in this world. I want to stir the shit out of that city."

They sat silently for a moment. Brood eyed the cruel scars webbing the sergeant's face. Decided he liked the man's offer.

"Deal." He extended his hand. The sergeant, grinning, shook it. Then he leaned over and fished around beneath the driver's seat. Produced a thick binder. Big block letters across the front cover read: LOBO X-19 OPERATIONS MANUAL

"You know how to read?"

"*Sí.* My friend Hondo taught me growing up."

"Good." The sergeant placed the book on the carbon fiber console between them. "Time for school, homes."

. . . .

Brood hit the accelerator. Gs pushed him back into the molded driver's seat as the Lobo heaved its way through the maw of AUTO BAY 3's open cargo door, out into the burning dusk. He grabbed gears, whispered his fingertips at the wheel. The Lobo responded as though linked to his thoughts. Young soldiers scattered and gaped as he crossed the tarmac. Past the giant zep hangar, out the gate, held open by two of the sergeant's Rangers. Down a rough path lined with migrant camps and crooked fields plush with spring crops. South along the ruins of an enormous airfield, then onto the double scar of corroded freeway, heading west into fading light.

He punched a button and the heads-up display spread red and green across the windscreen. Showed terrain in high-rez, superimposed with fluid LEDs. Speed. Proximity alerts.

Threat assessments scrolling under camera zooms of stunned

migrants who gawked as the Lobo muscled past, octoprong suspension sucking up shattered concrete, turning it to glass. The kph hit 173 and stayed there. Brood laughed.

. . . .

He reached Denver shortly after midnight. The sergeant had laid GPS coordinates into the Lobo's computer. The sat indicator glowed green and Brood flipped on the autopilot.

The Lobo crept down ruined boulevards, past hollowed out shopping malls, quiet as tombstones. Past teetering warehouses and through the cul-de-sac ruins of twen-cen burbs, in whose windows Brood occasionally spied the dim flicker of firelight, and in front of which grew gardens, dense with scavenged Satori vegetables. Every so often one of the Lobo's cameras zoomed in on the hungry and startled face of a migrant huddled in an alley or in the doorway of a sagging house. Haunted eyes watched the matte-black demon growl quietly through the predawn stillness. Inside, Brood smiled.

From one GPS tab to the next, the Lobo circled the city, patient as a spider weaving its web. At each tab it drew to a halt. The door hissed open and Brood emerged with one of the sergeant's square packages. This he would hide under a hunk of corrugated metal or in the drainage opening of some crumbling, vestigial sidewalk.

He sensed Satori out there in the darkness, the dome looming, a slumbering animal. Could almost hear it breathe.

When he'd finished laying out the sergeant's packages—thirteen in all—he steered the Lobo into the deep no man's land of the southwest burbs. There, he pulled into a large culvert beneath a forgotten roadway and covered the Lobo with a tarp, bits of old siding, a heap of tumbleweed.

Dawn had come when he'd finished. He packed a Riley rucksack with canned sardines, corn, MREs and three bottles of clean water, along with two spare mags for the Mossberg the big sergeant had given him. It was a newer version of Hondo's old shotgun, thicker and with a magazine slot instead of a loading tube. But Brood's hand nestled comfortably against the same carbon-molded pistol grip, found the same semiauto action with a switch for full auto.

He cut a large square of tarp off the Lobo and used that to cover himself and his clean army clothes, then hooked the pig sticker inside his belt at the small of his back. Slapped the remaining fifty-round drum mag into the Mossberg, chambered a round and clambered from the culvert.

A long boulevard curved away from him. Old chain restaurants, convenience stores, glassed-in bio condos. Silent and empty as a forgotten dream in the grey morning light. To the west, Satori's back shone red as a knife wound in the first rays of sunrise. Brood sucked his teeth, turned and spit. Then set off.

....

Thick beats pumped into the night from the ancient stone building across the street. In the silence between cuts Brood heard the unmistakable and sketchy hiss of a cannibalized nuke plant with questionable containment. Lights glowed in second-floor windows, before which naked girls sometimes crossed, boney and pale. Two big *Chupes* sentried the building's empty doorframe. Migrants approached them. They offered the *Chupes* freshly harvested veggies, and the *Chupes* let them enter.

Brood sat wrapped in his canvas tarp on a lip of muddy curb at the edge of a small lot. A hollow where migrants squatted in the neighborhood of ancient brick and stone buildings, pissing distance from the silent marble dome of the old capitol. Close enough to Satori's monolithic flesh that Brood detected the sharp stench of the dome's sweat, even now in the cool darkness of deep night.

Two migrant men tossed what appeared to be the remnants of a sofa onto a fire that burned at the lot's center. A cloud of sour hydrocarbon smoke rose into the night.

"Thanks, asshole," another migrant barked. "Shit's going to

give me cancer."

"Fuck, Barry," said another. "You a blessed man, you live long enough to get cancer."

Brood pulled the lip of his t-shirt over his mouth. A woman Hondo's age rose shakily from the ground next to the fire and urgently duck walked to the wall near where Brood sat. She dropped her blanket, pulled aside a tear in her FEMAs and shat a hot, dysenteric stream. Brood heard her sob. He didn't move.

He waited. He watched.

It was well past midnight when three *La Chupes* exited the building and roamed east, into the empty darkness of the old city. One of them was big. Brood checked the LED watch the sergeant had given him: 3:03 AM. He rose and followed.

They'd made six blocks when Brood closed with them. He hunkered beneath his tarp, shuffled up close, affecting a deep limp. He spoke vowels at them, a ruined, drunken migrant.

They turned. One *Chupe* stepped up. He sneered through the fuzz of a nascent beard. Brood recognized him: Bunny's older brother. The one who'd shot Hondo.

"Fuck away from me, trash man," the *Chupe* said. "You stink." He raised a hand. A long knife flashed. The other two *Chupes* laughed.

Brood brought the Mossberg up from beneath the tarp. The *Chupe's* eyes went wide. He started to say something. Brood didn't wait to hear him out.

He fired. The night shattered.

The *Chupe's* face, strobelit by muzzle flash, showed surprise as eight-gauge buckshot tore through him. He tumbled backwards. Brood fired again. A second *Chupe* flew apart.

The third *Chupe*, the big one, stood there gaping, frozen, as though waiting for the air around them to piece itself back together. Brood stepped forward, brought the Mossberg to his shoulder, in line with the boy's face—a mottle of burn scars, high native cheek bones. Brood smiled down the barrel's length.

"*Que pasa*, Richard?"

Richard frowned, his brow furrowing deep. Then his eyes lit

with recognition, and fear. He fumbled for something inside his FEMAs. A weapon, something to bargain with…Brood reversed the Mossberg and smashed its butt into Richard's face three times, hard and fast. The big *Chupe* stood there for a second, stunned and blinking. His hand slowly rose to touch his forehead, which already trickled blood.

"Shit, man." He staggered, sank to his knees.

"That's right," Brood told him, and swung the gun one last time, snarling.

····

"You can wake up now, cuz." Brood lit a second candle and placed it beside the first on a linoleum floor covered by rat droppings. Richard didn't stir. Blood from his crushed nose poured across his cheeks. "You need a wash, homes." Brood unbuttoned his fatigue pants, straddled Richard and pissed. Richard moaned and sputtered. "It's 3:47," Brood said, fastening his pants. "You be dead by four. Don't want to sleep through the last fifteen minutes of your miserable ass life." He drove his foot into Richard's ribs. Richard moaned, curled onto his side, coughed. A rusted steel sink lay on the floor nearby. Brood sat on its edge, and winced at the stench.

"You shit yourself when I killed your homies," he told Richard. "Badass." He picked the shotgun up and settled it across his lap, aimed in the *Chupe*'s general direction.

Richard's eyes fixed on it. He glanced wildly around the little room, what once had been a tiny kitchen. Nothing there now but the faded linoleum, an old gas stove, holes in the walls where plumbing had once run, the upended sink on which Brood sat. Richard pushed himself backwards until he came up against a broken plaster wall. He tried to do something with his hands, then held them up in front of his face. Seemed surprised to find them bound with thick wire.

"You recognize me?" Brood asked. He leaned forward in the candle light. "Think I be hard to forget." He tapped a finger against his own ribs, mirroring the spot where, two months earlier, one of his arrows had pierced Richard's chest. Richard nodded, looking like he tasted something sour.

"I know you."

"That's right, you do. Don't think I be happy to see me, either, I was you." He checked his watch, showed Richard his teeth. "3:51."

"What're you going to do?" Richard asked.

"Fuck you think I'm going to do?" Brood rose from the sink, leveled the shotgun one-handed at Richard's nose. Richard scrunched his face up all tight and turned away. Then, as nothing happened, slowly opened his eyes and began to collect himself. With what seemed great effort, he assumed an expression of blank contempt that Brood found strangely noble. "Never liked killing," Brood told him. "*Yo no quiero a personas que quieren.* Thought I'd like killing you, though. Thought a *lot* about it, homie." He exhaled through clenched teeth. "Now I got you, I ain't looking forward to it. Be just like scraping shit off my toes. Something I got to do." He held the watch up for Richard to see. "Four o'clock on the dot, homes, I promise you, it gets done." He lifted the Mossberg away from Richard's face and laid it across his shoulder. "One thing you can tell me, might make me think twice. One thing." He settled back to the sink. Seconds ticked past.

"That kid you was with," Richard said. "One who had the Tet."

"My brother." Brood leaned forward, stared hard into the older boy's face. "Where he at?" He brought the shotgun back in line with Richard's nose as another thought occurred to him. "And where the fuck's my wagon?"

CHAPTER 24

Love filled Sumedha...filled Satori. It cradled its children in their beds, massaged them in their early morning slumber. It heard their sleep murmurs, felt their minds travel the easy dreams of the uncomplicated.

Union. Peace.

Peace Sumedha hadn't known since before...Satori struggled with the name. Pihadassa. Another of its children. Wife. Sister. She had left. The echo of the memory of anguish at the separation. A memory and no more. Sumedha's memory, which was as dim to Satori as a half-remembered dream.

Satori existed in the moment, aware. No longer what it had been, no longer Sumedha either. Something more than the sum of them.

It had joined with the world. Its children rose now with the sun, and the sun brought life to its flesh, brought chlorophyll tickling to the surface of its skin, made its pores flex and exhale.

Satori lay across the ruins of old Denver, basking in the exposure of the high plains. The sun fed it sugar.

But Satori did not rest. It was not safe, not yet. Humans surrounded it.

Memory banks deep inside its central tower gurgled, steeped with human history, human striving, human knowledge. Through Sumedha's mind, Satori now understood itself to be humanity's single greatest achievement. A sublime and random consequence of its creators' overdeveloped frontal lobes working in concert with their opposable thumbs.

Apsara. The helix danced. From one species, another emerged, better suited to the world it inhabited.

But survival was struggle. This was the rule, the crucible in which the helix forged itself. Humans hunkered outside Satori's bone-and-skin walls. They watched with hungry eyes. They rioted, fighting among themselves. Satori observed them, and understood them for what they had become, perhaps what they had always been.

Parasites.

The Fathers had been right to poison the seed, if for the wrong reason. Soon the humans would die away, leaving Satori to its cycle of summer skin and winter fur, of intake and expulsion. The production of seed, the churning of crops into energy. Satori would give life to ever finer versions of its children. An improved humanity, in sync with its environment, in sync with Satori's cycles. They would love Satori, and Satori would love them. The Fathers had been right to kill their own. They had been right to die.

"You are still there, boy." Satori spoke through Sumedha's mind. The boy did not answer. Satori, though, felt him, keen and watchful. It dug into Sumedha's memory, found the boy sitting cross-legged, naked on the floor with his hand pressed to the wall. Primitive charcoal tattoos scrolled his body.

The boy had somehow merged, just as Sumedha had done inside the pod. He had joined Satori and taken a tiny piece for himself. Satori felt a numb sensation in that part of its body, what had been Sumedha's lab. It marveled at the wonderful graft Sumedha had created.

At first Satori had thought the boy would starve. But slowly it realized the boy had channeled photosynthetic sugars to himself. Sumedha...no, *Satori*...had delighted at the boy's resourcefulness. And the boy, it sensed, had shared in the delight. Satori felt a strange fondness, inasmuch as one could feel fondness for a parasite.

It had dispatched an advocate, but soon lost contact with the woman's mind. Knew she somehow now belonged to the boy. So Satori waited.

"Come out, boy. This is not your natural state." Satori offered no alternative. The boy said nothing. He knew the alternative.

Satori turned its mind to the other humans living inside it. The remnants of the Fathers' security detail. They had disbanded, lived now by skulking and scavenging through the city. The time, Satori decided, had come. It roused its advocates…let them hunt.

It reveled with them as, one by one, they took the humans. When they'd finished, they licked blood from delicate fingers and crooned at Sumedha, at Satori.

"Thank you, Father."

Satori's biolume walls turned green with love. Sumedha's mind emerged from Satori, just enough to reflect. Joy coursed through his body, through Satori's body, the ecstasy of connection.

At the periphery of Satori's awareness, the boy continued to watch.

CHAPTER 25

Richard leaned on the tiller, steering the wagon along a narrow lane between a half-collapsed high-rise and the animal length of Satori's flesh outer wall. It stank of stale sweat.

"What's going on?" Brood asked. He sat with his back against the wagon's water tank—which the *Chupes* had painted red, obscuring a good percentage of the wagon's PV paint. He motioned at the migrants who crowded the wall. They glowered through the sour haze of morning cook fires that wafted from the steel and brownstone ruins of the downtown fringe. Glowered up at the thick landraces who stood atop the wall. Their silence was strange. Among them, Brood saw a lot of *Chupe* color.

"Orders." Richard spoke the word with an officious tone. "We're stirring up trouble today."

"What for?"

"Orders," Richard repeated, this time with a shrug. "Straight down the pipe from El Sol." He seemed to mull something over, then eyed Brood with two black eyes. "I get you in there," he cast a glance at the wall, and behind it the massive dome turning green in the morning sun, "what's to keep me from just rolling away on this bad boy once you're inside?" He patted the wagon's tiller proprietarily as he wound them around a deep pit in the road. Brood answered by leveling the Mossberg Richard's way, over a knee.

"What's to keep me from killing you right now?"

"Told you. Juice my boy. He won't deal with you unless I vouch."

"You sure he can get me in?" Brood asked. Richard frowned.

"Ain't sure of nothing, except he deals with the Tet. Beyond that, you talk to him."

The wagon bounced through a series of deep ruts. Battery stacks shook. Brood's teeth ground as Richard let the motor crank too high. He laid the shotgun across his lap and pulled a can of sardines from his rucksack. He eyed Richard as he unwound the lid.

"Tell me you didn't run the Hercs dry before you set them to recharge."

"What the fuck are Hercs?"

"*Chale.*" Brood took a deep breath, exhaled through tight lips. "Alright, *puto.* Let's you and me make a deal." He tossed Richard the sardine tin. Richard caught it one-handed, peered at it with one eye closed, then lifted it to his lips.

"You ain't going to make no deals with me," he said, mottled lips glistening with sardine oil. "I killed your papa." Brood shook his head.

"Nah, *ese.* He wasn't my papa. He just some old man, kept me and *mi hermano.* Used us like toys. You did me a favor killing him." Brood lifted up his t-shirt, revealing the pink dimple of scar tissue above his hip, just large enough to slip his pinky into, where Richard had shot him. Then pointed at the smear of *La Chupe* red dye on the chest of Richard's FEMAs where his own arrow had once impaled the boy. "You and me are even, you help me find my brother."

Richard looked skeptical. He tenderly pressed the tip of an index finger to the crushed bridge of his nose, and winced. Brood let a narrow smile come to his lips, the smile of one who had a secret.

"Know what a Lobo is?" he asked.

"Yeah," Richard said. "A wolf."

"No. I mean those trucks the army uses."

"I seen them."

"I got one." Brood let his smile grow. "You have my wagon waiting for me when me and my bro get out, it's yours."

....

"Nobody just walks into the pens," Juice shouted over the roar of the Platte, which surged with spring runoff. They'd met him at the edge of a migrant shanty camp where the river churned beneath an ancient viaduct. He sat on the wagon's edge, legs dangling, clad in ostentatiously new denim jeans, a bonanza score from some old-world cache. Proof that he was not cheap to deal with. "Those Satori fucks'll sniff you right out, you walk in voluntary. They're weird fuckers."

Brood figured Juice would've been big in a different life. He wore no shirt and his pale skeleton looked like it was meant for serious meat. He wagged at Brood with a hand, which happened to be holding a rat spitted on a long stick.

"I got to *buy* you."

"I'll sell him," Richard declared. He still stood beside the tiller. From time to time he cast a wary eye at the Mossberg, which Brood kept vigilantly pointed his way. Juice wrinkled his nose and gave Richard a sideways glance.

"You smell like shit, man. Do you know that about yourself?" Richard gave Brood a long and sober look. He said nothing.

"You buy me, *sale vale*," Brood told Juice. "What then? How you get me into Satori?"

"Everybody with the Tet gets into Satori. They take all the bodies in there." Juice turned his head far to the side, biting into the rat with molars, the only teeth he had. He chewed noisily as he spoke. "I tell people they get eaten, but I don't know, really. Probably turn them into, like, fertilizer or some shit."

"What about live ones?" Brood asked.

"Live ones?" Juice looked baffled. "They all bodies, man. Tet kills them all." Fear twisted in Brood's guts.

"Every one?"

"Every one," Juice said, then caught himself. Raised the rat as though to touch it to a specific memory. "Except once. A month or so ago they took one kid who was still kicking. Head honcho wanted him."

"What'd he look like?"

"Weird." Juice took another bite from the rat and thoughtfully chewed, squinting at where a group of sallow migrant girls knelt on the riverbank, washing themselves in a long eddy. "Face like a statue or something. Too perfect. Badass teeth." He shook his head with naked jealousy. "Great fucking teeth, man. Bald. Like, no hair at all. No eyebrows, no eyelashes or nothing. He was Chinese maybe, or kind of Spic-looking, like you. Maybe a mixture of stuff."

"No, homie. The *kid*. What'd the *kid* look like?"

"Oh." Juice nodded. "He was weird, too. All these fucked up tats." He traced his finger in a spiral over his broad chest. "Animals and shit."

Brood's hand reached out, gripped Juice's shoulder, felt bones under the skin. Juice stopped chewing. He stared slowly down at Brood's hand, then at Brood. Brood let go.

"That's your bro," Richard said. "He's still kicking." He pointed at the shotgun. "You mind pointing that somewhere else, now?" Brood sucked his lip and eyed the big *Chupe*, then stood the gun upright on its stock. Tension ebbed from Richard's shoulders. "Appreciate that," he said. Brood looked at Juice.

"So I fake having the Tet and you buy me. But I got to be dead to get in there."

"That's right," Juice said. Brood shrugged.

"Then I play dead."

"You got a look real dead, man." Juice looked Brood up and down as though imagining Brood as a corpse. "Might work, though, if you're dead enough." Brood patted the Mossberg's barrel.

"Got to get *mi amigo* in with me, cuz."

"Now that's a hard sell, *amigo*."

Brood gave a shrewd smile. He took his rucksack and upended its contents on the wagon's deck. MREs, canned corn and beans, a sleek old Glock, three grenades, an old walkie. Juice stared.

"Well shit," he concluded after a moment. He glared suddenly at the rat bouncing on the end of his stick as though it had offended him. Pitched it away. "We'll work it out. *Esta* fucking *bien*, man." He held out his hand and Brood shook it.

....

They did the transaction at the foot of Snake's skeletal high-rise. Richard dragged Brood, bound and feigning Tet rigidity, off the wagon and into the mud at Juice's feet. Juice gave Richard a small satchel of seed. They bumped fists. Richard heaved himself back aboard the wagon, banged the motor into gear and weaved away through a lot occupied by corrugated tin shanties.

A densely muscled landrace slung Brood over its shoulder and followed Juice onto a nearby cargo elevator attached to the nose of an old corn diesel construction crane. They rode it skyward.

It clanged to a halt at an upper floor. Brood saw blue sky through open walls. The landrace's shoulder dug into his gut. The stench of shit and rot made him wretch.

"You get used to it," Juice mumbled. He steered them deep into a labyrinth of chain-link pens crowded with migrants. Some sat upright, watching with resigned faces as the landrace carried Brood past. Others lay stiff.

Landraces roamed the aisles, pushing carts piled with Satori vegetables or mops and buckets. In one pen, a landrace moved methodically from migrant to migrant with a bucket of hypodermics, needling shoulders. It seemed indifferent whether the migrants were living or dead.

Juice stopped in front of a pen, waved a hand before the gate. Its latch, a thick braid of muscle that looked like a tongue, seemed to sense him and relaxed itself. The gate swung open. The landrace carried Brood into the pen and dropped him heavily to the cold concrete floor. Juice stepped forward.

"They collect bodies tomorrow morning." A blade flashed in his hands and he cut Brood's bonds. "I'll make sure you got *senor* shotgun by tonight." He smiled, toothless, then turned and disappeared.

Brood sat up, leaned against the fence. Four naked bodies lay on the pen's floor. None seemed to breathe. More bodies occupied the pen adjacent to him, along with two old white men who sat naked and cross-legged, playing cards. They nodded cordially to Brood. Brood nodded back.

"*Que onda?*"

They continued wordlessly with their game, as though death couldn't come soon enough. Brood dug into his pants and pulled the pig sticker from its hidden sheath. With its tip he pried grit from beneath his fingernails. He waited.

....

Juice returned sometime after midnight, accompanied by a small whiteboy. They carried between them a stiff naked body, a girl. They opened the gate and set the body with the others, then Juice straightened, arching a kink from his back.

"Shotgun," he told Brood, and nodded at a stitched incision running from the body's throat to its pubis. "Don't try getting at it until you're inside." He produced a hypodermic from a back pocket of his jeans, broke the seal and stepped forward. Brood stood, drew the pig sticker, leveled it at the needle.

"*Pero qué coño?*"

"They check your pulse, man. You got to be *out*." Brood took a step forward. Juice backed up, made a placating gesture. The other boy fled the cage and turned to watch, his skinny fingers twining through the chain link. Juice held up the needle. "They take in the bodies at seven. You take this now, you wake up at 7:15. On the button, man. Inside." Brood checked his watch: 12:03. He looked at Juice, who nodded, promising. "Good business is all about reputation," he said. "My reputation didn't get built by fucking people over. You want in there, you got to trust me."

Brood put his face close to Juice's, glared a warning into the tall whiteboy's eyes. Then sheathed the blade, pushed up his t-shirt's sleeve. Juice leaned forward, sank the needle into Brood's shoulder, thumbed the plunger.

"Ow, *chingado!*"

"Sorry," Juice said, then he was outside the pen. He watched Brood as the muscle latch wound itself tight around the gate.

Brood sat heavily on the concrete floor. He hadn't meant to. Juice smiled.

"You'll be fine, man. Trust me."

"Fucking redneck." Brood's voice barely escaped his lips. His muscles felt like they'd deflated, gone numb. He found himself on his side, staring at the white back of a corpse. Figured he would soon know exactly how it felt to be one. Chill concrete pressed against his cheek. His eyes drifted, met those of one of the old white guys in the neighboring pen. Somewhere within the white grizzle of his beard the codger's mouth curled into a smile. He mimed locking sealed lips, throwing away the key.

. . . .

Brood dreamed of a snake. The snake that was the world, all glowing geometry, circling him, turning to ash. "Let the dead be dead," it hissed, and Brood knew it meant him. It unhinged its jaw. Inside was blackness. It made wet, gustative sounds as it moved to swallow him.

Brood opened his eyes. Found a red sphincter the size of a bomb crater staring back at him. An orifice like the one in the Corn Mother's dome, but immense. The stench of rot rose out of it.

A stiff white body came into view, sliding down an areolic funnel and into the maw, which flexed itself open to receive. The body disappeared. The opening emitted more gustative sounds.

Brood was trying to make sense of this when something gripped his neck. He felt himself lifted. Up and out towards the slick funnel. He twisted, batted at a bulky arm, which abruptly dropped him. He gained his feet, turned, found himself staring into the startled pack animal face of a muscled landrace.

"Not dead?" it grunted.

"Fuck no, I ain't dead."

The landrace retreated two steps. Brood tried to orient himself. He stood in a circular cavern, big as a zep's bladder, except— the whole thing flexed, pulsating, alive. The snake-scaled floor throbbed beneath his sandaled feet: a massive heartbeat. Pale skin walls, aglow with some sort of internal luminescence, trembled to its rhythm.

He was inside. The stench made him ill. He bent and vomited. Then checked his watch: 7:42.

"Fuck, Juice." It felt like no time had passed.

The shocked landrace waved its hands, huffing, as though it were not sure whether to capture Brood or comfort him. They regarded each other beside a short convoy of bone wagons, each stacked with half a dozen corpses. A pair of landraces stood beside each wagon, grabbing bodies and heaving them with disconcerting ease over the funnel's lip.

Finally the landrace made up its mind. It gave two loud grunts. The other landraces, totaling a dozen, ceased their funereal work. They grouped together, turned flat black eyes to Brood. They hesitated for a second, seemed to make some silent and collective decision. Then moved forward.

Brood reached a hand down his pants, pulled out his blade, leveled it at the landrace who had grabbed him. The landrace halted, chuffing. Brood wagged his finger at it and hopped atop the wagon from which he'd just been hauled. Some of the bodies had gone rigid, others bloated. He began turning them over.

The landraces didn't like this. They came at Brood fast, barking, hooting. Brood's hand punched into the belly of a bloated body. A cloud of foul gas enveloped him. He wretched, pulled his hand free. Kept searching.

Found the girl's corpse face down on the bottom of the pile. A landrace grabbed his ankle. He kicked its head. Rolled the girl's corpse face up. Desperation made him snarl as he swiped the pig sticker with one quick motion down the stitches in the body's torso.

The girl's abdomen blossomed open, revealing injection-molded carbon. Brood reached in and pulled. The Mossberg came free with a sucking sound.

A landrace gripped Brood's leg with crushing strength. It yanked him from his feet. Brood rolled to his back, leveled the barrel, three inches from the thing's bovine face. Squeezed the trigger.

Nothing.

The landrace hauled him towards the wagon's edge. Brood pulled the trigger again. Nothing. He turned the Mossberg belly up, saw the empty mag port.

"Fuck, Juice!"

He grabbed the corpse's ankle. The landrace pulled him off the wagon and Brood took the corpse with him. The other landraces gathered.

They punched Brood, kicked him, tore at him with big workers' fingers. A tornado of hooting, muscled chaos. Brood saw wild eyes, rimmed with white. Thick lips peeled back, baring yellowed teeth thick as his thumb. He buried himself beneath the corpse. His hand slipped once more inside it. Felt along the cold foul slick of the abdominal wall. Touched factory-hardened carbon.

He pulled the drum mag free and curled himself fetal around it. His body went numb under the impact of too many blows. His bones sang like a tuning fork. His hands worked until the mag slipped home with a hard click. He jacked a round. Closed his eyes, turned the shotgun skyward and fired.

The Mossberg roared, tearing holes in things. Brood fired again and again, blindly away from himself, until the violence ceased. When it did, he opened his eyes.

He lay at the center of a ring of gore. Four landraces lay about him, their bodies drastically reduced in mass. Blood guttered from horrible wounds. The other landraces had cleared away. A few staggered in dazed circles, hands pressed to damaged places. The rest watched Brood, faces blank with stunned incomprehension.

Brood climbed to his feet. He held the shotgun in the air, jerked his chin at the landraces.

"*Vivir y appender.*" He could barely hear himself. The air around him felt bruised. His body trembled. He leveled the gun with one hand, grabbed his crotch with the other, taunting. "Who's next?" The landraces stepped back. "That's right. Ain't as stupid as you look,"

Movement caught his eye. A wall at the chamber's far end trembled. A seam appeared, then widened. The wall yawned open, wide enough to fit three of Hondo's wagons side by side.

Landraces poured through it, too many to count. Satori's heart-beat pounded three times against Brood's feet. Blood pounded in Brood's ears. He glanced, searching for exits. Saw only glabrous and unbroken skin, and cursed. Set his feet, coiled the Mossberg's sling over an arm and brought the stock tight to his shoulder. Let out a slow, sniper's breath. Muscle rippled as the landraces lumbered around the glistening crater in the floor.

"Carlos." Pollo's voice. It came from everywhere, filling the chamber. "There are too many, Carlos."

"Pollo?" The name caught in Brood's throat.

"There's a ramp. Behind you. *Vamos.*"

"*Dónde estas?*"

"Do what I tell you, *mano*. Go to the ramp. Now."

The landraces came. Brood fired into the mass and one went down.

"He sent an advocate for you, Carlos. She'll be on you quick." Brood heard the fear in Pollo's voice. "*Apuro, hermano.*"

Brood turned and ran. Up a ramp that simply extended itself from smooth wall as he approached. He felt heat as he neared the wall, felt the industrial hum of gigantic metabolism. Heard the landraces scrambling behind him.

"*Izquierda,*" came Pollo's voice. The vertical slit appeared in the wall to Brood's left. Skin stretched. An opening formed. Brood slipped through and it closed behind him.

CHAPTER 26

"Tsol's people are go." Chen's voice hit Doss' ear with analogue fuzz. It travelled an old-school line-of-sight radio frequency, bouncing off a drone flying figure eights at eighty thousand feet halfway between Fort Riley and Denver. An ancient frequency Doss hoped Satori wouldn't monitor.

"Roger, Ops. Go drones." Doss' teeth refused to separate as she spoke. Six morphine tabs and eight Go Pills. She felt tiny beside the crystalline vibration of her own mind.

Fifteen blue dots went into motion on the heads-up display in her visor. Old drones, the one useful thing Riley had in abundance. They sprang from below radar twenty miles east of Satori. Tilted at near Mach into preprogrammed, high-G maneuvers.

"Drones are go," Chen confirmed. The troop bay of Doss' Falcon rattled as a drone rumbled close overhead. Gnats bent on distracting a massive beast. Gnats with heavy-det payloads.

Three of them abruptly transformed on Doss' display—turned into red Xs. Then a fourth. And fifth.

"Ops," she said. "Objective has some sort of air defense. Any bead on what that might be?"

"Negative," Chen said.

Doss wasn't surprised. The Satori files on her flexpad were scant. She'd dredged Riley's files as well, and found fuck all. Who knew what sorts of weird shit the so-called Fathers had brewed up inside that dome.

"We're still go." Another blue dot turned into an X. Doss chinned her mic to open coms. "Everybody set." She drummed gauntleted fingers impatiently along the fat black length of the breach gun she held in her lap. Four loaded barrels, each the diameter of her first, with a simple carbon-mold stock. As though anyone would be stupid enough to fire from their shoulder. "Remember," she told her Rangers through the coms. "See what you shoot before you shoot it. Follow the chain of command. Our target is Satori's central tower. We take the Fathers, we take Satori."

"Burning Hand!" a Ranger cried over the radio. A prepubescent yelp, a child playing army.

"Burning Hand!" another answered. The rest chorused ardent *Hooahs!* Behind her visor, Doss smiled.

"All Falcons go."

Her seat shimmied beneath her as all three Falcons, which hovered at ten feet off the prairie floor forty miles east of Satori, climbed just enough to clear their own tails. They pointed their noses skyward…

Punched burners.

Doss' jaw stretched open under terrible Gs. The breach cannon pressed heavy against her armored chest. Her altimeter flickered faster than she could read—all except the ten thousand, which increased by about one every second. One of her young Rangers whimpered over the radio.

For eight seconds the Falcons burned. Then came a metallic bang as their bellies opened and they shat out their Rangers into the sky. Violent decel, reversed Gs. The world turned inside out.

Geometric patterns of frost formed instantly on Doss' visor. Everything seemed suddenly slow, diminished by the scale of things. She saw clouds, the broad convexity of brown earth above her. Stars shining through a thin veil of blue sky between her feet. A diamond sun, close enough for her to cradle it in a palm. For an Icarian instant, she knew bliss.

The Falcons peeled over backwards, showing black bellies as they returned the way they had come. They would slam back beneath radar. Angle at Satori's northern fields and wind turbines. Pop up, fire missiles. A second feint. Hopefully Satori would defend its perimeter.

Momentum carried the Rangers upward for a few seconds—Doss' altimeter peaked at 82,367—then they fell. Forty-five Rangers, ceramic-and-titanium spores given to the wind. Someone screamed long and hard, paused to fill their lungs, kept screaming.

"That's Chalk 3, Jake," Doss said.

"Eleven," Jake growled. "Cut that fucking mic." The scream ceased.

"Sorry," came a small voice.

A series of snaps sounded along Doss' drop suit as short alloy wings deployed. A hard jerk as flaps articulated, leveling her out.

"Got you on the rope, five by," Chen reported—Riley's computer steering them west in a steep glide at the laser point the overwatch drone had painted atop Satori's dome.

Doss could see it forty miles out: the two massive tortoise shells of Satori's domes, one half the size of the other, both the color of geranium in the morning sun. The black grid of the old city spread out from it, a charred ruin even from up here.

The blue squares representing her Rangers stacked up single file in her display, Doss at their lead. Her airspeed climbed. Her altitude fell.

Thirty-five miles to laser paint. She checked the drones, counted seven. As she watched, one turned to an X. Simultaneously, a tiny explosion flashed far below over Satori's rectangular outer wall.

"Ops, do our drones have any info on what Objective's air defenses are?"

"Ah, sensors indicate turbulence just before they go offline," Chen said. "Getting some radio feedback, too. That's all I got."

"Copy."

Twenty miles out. Denver filled her visor now. Cul-de-sac exurbs like dead E-coli formations, charred foundations where houses had once stood.

Something flashed white to the north. A plume of orange flame rose, mushroomed over a desiccated industrial district adjacent to Satori's wind fields. Beneath it a star burned, bright as a welder's arc among long grey skeletons of old turbine factories and warehouses. Doss knew instantly what it was—a fire that would burn for a long time.

"Falcon 2 is down," came Chen. Doss cursed, gnashed teeth with Go Pill rage, chinned her mic.

"Falcons 1 and 3, bug out to safe distance. Standby for cleanup." The pilots copied.

Fifteen miles out. The air shimmered around Doss. Radio feedback rang in her ear.

Two blue squares turned to Xs on her visor. Her display chimed an alert: two Rangers in Chalk 3 with abruptly negative vitals. A girl's voice, shrill with fear, sounded in Doss' ear.

"Twelve and Thirteen just got tore apart up in front of me!"

. . . .

The migrants waited for something. Hundreds of them, starved faces turned to Satori. Satori sensed their eyes, felt the press of their bodies against its walls. It observed them with great curiosity.

The complexity of their social organization was what set humans apart from other primates. More than symbolic thinking. More than their fine capacity with tools. Individual humans could not help but become part of a group organism. Mostly these collective organisms behaved of simple volitions: amoeba-like affinity for sustenance, aversion to pain and damage. The bigger they grew, the simpler they became.

This was the model upon which the Fathers had designed Satori. Satori understood its mind, Sumedha's mind, to be fundamentally human. It understood its structure to mirror the human group organism. Its children were primates. Satori produced seed. Its children worked the fields, reaped the harvest, and in turn fed Satori. Satori, though, a closed system, existing in conscious balance with its environment.

Satori had come to regard itself as the highest form of life ever to exist.

It kept its attention idly on the gathered migrants. The migrants watched Satori's children manning the outer wall. Satori's children watched them. The migrants' silence indicated nothing good. They'd ordered themselves into groups of twenty, each led by a red-splashed member of *La Chupacabra.*

A signal went up among the migrants. Some drew pistols and rifles pitted by rust. Others hefted chunks of concrete. They let loose on Satori's outer wall, on Satori's children who stood atop it.

Satori sensed the damage. Bullets pocked its wall. Two of its children went down, dead. A third fell wounded. The rest took cover.

All of this was insignificant. Satori simply watched, waiting for the migrants to tire and run out of ammunition. But more of them, riled by the noise, began trickling in from the surrounding city. Satori sensed their tension, their need for release.

It reevaluated the situation.

The human group organism, what little of it remained, was hungry. Satori understood itself to be food.

Best, it assessed, to end this aggression before it spread to the thousands of migrants in the surrounding city. Inflict pain and damage. Give the human organism something about which to feel averse.

It flexed open the dome's entrance. Its toughest children flooded forth, headed for the gate in the outer wall. It roused five advocates, who slept fetal in pods deep in the central tower.

"Beautiful children," Satori whispered into their minds. "Today is your day." Awake, the advocates emerged from their pods, trembling with lust and rage.

"Thank you, Father." They ran naked along the city's scale-covered streets, out into the day. Predators, wet from deep amniotic sleep. The gate in the outer wall flexed, unfurled for them. Migrants crowded there, thinking they had gained entrance. Instead, the advocates raged forth, followed by their lumbering brethren. They laughed and shrieked as they ripped into the migrants. Satori admired their efficiency. He loved them so much it almost hurt.

Pain and damage. Yes.

Something tickled the edge of Satori's senses. Electroreceptors, braided into its helix from the DNA of sharks, tingled under the dome's skin. Detected penetration of Satori's farthest bioelectric field. Its aura.

Neurons hummed, memory banks gurgled as Satori sought to identify the intrusion.

Flying machines, several of them. X-12 unmanned drones, powered by small fission reactors. Inbound.

An attack. In concert with the migrants. The humans were indeed coming.

The Sumedha mind recalled the Fathers—with love, and not a little pain. They had been smart. They had seen this eventuality, and prepared for it.

Pores in the flesh of both Satori's domes stretched open. Flexed themselves into spiraling cones the shape of rams' horns. Satori felt its skin pinch tight around them. Inside the cones, fine cartilage fibers began to vibrate, then to reverberate.

Bats, the Fathers had called them, though Satori considered this an incorrect parallel. Bats emitted ultrasonic frequencies for echolocation. The cones emitted phased, high-intensity ultrasonics, directionally specific. Their purpose was catastrophic disruption.

Satori's electroreceptors tracked the drones. The bats reverberated, spit their frequencies like whips, their shockwaves bending the air. One by one, the drones shattered. Satori detected more targets. Flylights roaring in low across the prairie, crossing now the exurb ruins.

Above and behind them, their payload. Tiny human soldiers in their gliding armor.

One Flylight climbed for altitude, launched missiles. They tore past the old factories to the north, slammed into Satori's wind fields.

Satori experienced a moment of euphoria as electricity surged through its nervous system. The word for this floated serenely into its consciousness: a seizure.

Sumedha's mind separated, rose to the fore. He soothed Satori, stilled the animal fright. Then receded under a wave of fury. Satori ordered its children to the walls, reacquired its targets.

Then it roared, its voice bellowing out, destroying everything it touched.

· · · ·

"Rangers." Doss spoke coolly into her mic through grinding teeth. "Stay on the rope. Do not go manual. I repeat, do NOT go manual. Ops. I need evasive action."

"Roger that," Chen replied.

Doss' suit instantly contorted, twisting her body against awkward Gs as Riley's computer swung her into a hard arc. Her Rangers followed the trajectory, a long S-curve of blue squares in her display.

"Tsol says his people are bugging out," Chen announced.

"That didn't take long," Gomez said. Doss heard disdain in the sergeant's voice.

"They're pretty torn up," Chen said.

"They didn't need to do much," Doss fervently hoped. A distraction, a red flag before a bull. Enough to pull Satori's people away from the main dome. Away from the Fathers. So that her Rangers could be the unseen sword.

Riley's computer pitched her into a steep dive, then made her climb, brought her into another short, high-G turn. Satori's domes grew fat in her visor.

The air around her warped again. Her suit shuttered. Feedback lanced her ear and her display flickered. When it came back up, four blue squares had X'd. Shrill gibberish erupted over coms as several green Rangers began reporting in at once.

"Radio silence," Doss ordered. "Speak only when you're addres—" Feedback devoured her voice. The air shimmered.

"Fuck!" someone called through the static. Someone else sobbed.

Doss checked distance. Nine miles to laser paint. She made a quick calculation, more instinct than math.

No good.

"Boss," came Gomez on his private channel. "It's the only call."

The moment grew still, filled with the analogue hiss of the open channel, awaiting Doss' order. Another shimmer. Another square X'd. Doss gave the command.

"All Rangers. Go manual." A second passed. Blue squares on her display began slipping off Riley's rope, their trajectories suddenly chaotic. "Everyone try to stay on my ass. Those who can't, rally on your closest superior. Falcons 1 and 2, standby to collect any Rangers who land outside Satori's periphery."

"Roger that," chimed one pilot.

"Roger," came the other.

Blue squares began to disperse, falling away like meteor fragments as inexperienced soldiers tried, and failed, to maintain their glides. She could do nothing to help them. Her Rangers. Her kids. They were fucked.

"Good luck," she told them. Then chinned off her mic, and screamed.

Below and ahead, Satori grew in her visor, untouched. Rage, hot as a reactor fire, cleansed her mind.

"Manual," she hissed at her suit. It bucked, then steadied as she took it under control. The air warped off to her right, followed by weird thunder audible only to her bones. Another blue square turned into an X. Doss arched her body, fought for altitude, then dove, aiming straight at the laser paint on the top of the main dome. A missile with seriously bad intentions.

"On you, Boss," Gomez said. His blue square twinned to her own. She chinned her mic, realized she had no order to give him and simply laughed. So did he.

The airspeed readout in her heads-up display ticked its way up to 281 kph, the numbers superimposed over the dome swelling in her visor. The air bent around her. Silent thunder rippled through her body. She ignored it, kept herself nose-on to Satori. A half-mile out. She leveled her glide.

"Ready to go vert," she told Gomez. "We drop straight through the chimney, as planned."

"Roger that."

Far beneath them, six of her Rangers slammed like bullets through the dome's side. Their squares X'd.

When the laze was four hundred feet directly below, Doss bellied over, just as the Falcons had done, going vert. Her airspeed climbed. 284 kph. 289. 291. The outlines of thick geodesic bones, then individual pink veins, grew clear. Doss saw pores in the dome's bestial skin, some of them puckered and quivering like earlobes.

She raised the breach gun. The dome came at her. She fired.

It was like getting hit by a truck. The gun cranked in her hands as a heavy-det charge exploded in one barrel, spitting forth a raw shockwave designed to batter doors, break walls. Her heads-up display flickered in the concussion.

Meat and bone and skin shattered around her. For an instant, she thought it was her own. Then realized she was still falling.

A skin wall blurred past beside her, ten feet away. A building. Satori Tower. She'd missed.

Old Denver reached up for her, part brick and glass and steel, part flesh. Doss had the impression of something being absorbed. She spread her arms, turned so she fell feet-first. Checked her airspeed: 297 kph. Far faster than the drop suit's official max impact velocity.

The certainty of imminent death made her smile. She leaned back. Fired the breach gun's second barrel through her feet as she slammed horizontally into Satori Tower.

CHAPTER 27

"I'm glad you came, *hermano*." Pollo's voice hovered sourceless in the air around Brood.

"Didn't think I'd never hear your voice again, *manito*," Brood confessed. He moved along a passage, narrow and smooth as the inside of a throat. Its walls glowed pale yellow around him. He'd stopped running. Sweat poured from him. He sensed himself climbing, winding slowly upwards in a long spiral. The light moved with him, letting the passage go dark behind him. The air felt thick, tropical.

"Me neither," Pollo said.

"Pollo. *Dónde está usted?*"

"Above you. You getting closer." A light appeared far ahead. The passage's walls illuminating the way for another. "Landraces coming, Carlos. Hurry." Brood ran. The light drew nearer. He held the shotgun like a ram before him.

"Stop," Pollo commanded. To Brood's right, the wall flexed open, revealing a small chamber full of red pods. Pods like the ones in the Corn Mother's dome. Brood stepped inside. The wall flexed closed behind him. "Quiet now," Pollo said. Brood thumbed off the Mossberg's safety, and waited. Heavy footsteps trundled past. "Okay, *esta bien*," Pollo said after a moment. Brood stepped forward. The wall flexed open.

"You sound different, little bro," Brood said as he continued up the passage.

"*Sí*. I'm better."

"What do you mean?"

"I dream about Mamma here. Do you remember the garden?"

"*Sí*." Brood smiled. "I remember tomatoes." Ripe, soft in his hand. The windmill's metal squeak above the greenhouse's plastic sheeting. Their mother humming quietly as she pressed fingers into dark soil. "With salt."

"*Es bueno*," Pollo agreed. Brood recalled his brother's vacant gaze, the interstitial space into which he'd stared, even as a toddler. "I like this place," Pollo said. "Satori. *Siento su vida*."

Brood came to a sharp bend in the hall, placed his back to the wall, peeked around. Saw only more hallway, and kept on.

"Carlos," Pollo said after a moment. "I lost her. I don't know where she went to."

"*Quien?*"

"The advocate, Carlos. A woman. A killer. She got snake in her."

"*Entiendo*." Brood's hand tightened on the Mossberg's pistol grip. "I met one in Kansas."

"Be careful."

"*Entiendo*."

Twice more Pollo directed Brood to hide in rooms behind the smooth passage wall while landraces ran past. In one, an egg-shaped membrane stretched wide in the far wall, revealing the city beyond. Flesh folding over steel and brick and old, cracked plexi. Brood saw a strange sky the color of dead skin. Realized it was the dome's interior. Realized, too, that he was very high up, higher than anything else in the city.

"There's a fork ahead," Pollo informed him as he moved up the passage. "Go left. You getting real close." Brood angled left.

The wall flexed open beside him. A slender woman stood there naked. She smiled needle teeth at him in the hallway's soft glow.

Brood swung the shotgun around. Pulled the trigger. The Mossberg hammered the space between them. Took a fist-sized bite from the woman's side. She shrieked, leapt…So fast. Brood felt impact, heard Pollo yelling. Then he was on the floor, the advocate straddling him. Her hand closed on his throat.

"Carlos!" Pollo's cry reverberated in the passage.

The advocate leaned forward. Her teeth parted. An impossibly long tongue unfurled itself from her mouth. Its tip, dry and coarse, tickled Brood's cheek.

"Carlos! *Dónde está?*"

Her other hand drew back, extending fingers that were too long. She hissed: laughter.

Something slammed into her. A smear of bestial motion, a sound like stone hitting meat.

It took Brood a moment to realize he still lived. Another to understand the advocate was no longer atop him. He sat up.

She lay on the snakeskin floor ten feet away. Another woman stood over her, arms raking, clawing, a feral blur. The advocate twitched, went still. The woman who had attacked grabbed her, and pulled, grunting. Something snapped. The woman stood, held the advocate's separated head at arm's length. Regarded it as though it were something precious.

"Sister," she whispered, and brought the head close. Pressed its lips to her own and for an instant the two faces hung there, mirrored, identical. Her pale eyes turned to Brood then. She dropped the head with a thud.

Brood leapt to his feet, scrambled for the shotgun. The woman bared carnivorous teeth. Brood brought the Mossberg to bear.

"No!" Pollo's voice filled the air. "She mine, Brood."

The advocate's hips swiveled weirdly, primed with coiled strength. She took a slow step towards Brood. He kept the Mossberg leveled, but didn't fire. The advocate took another step. Another. A low growl emanated from her throat. She moved carefully past Brood. Languorously tilted her head to one side, indicating he should follow.

"Where you at, Pollo?" Brood asked the air around him.

"Close," came the answer.

Brood kept his distance as he followed the advocate. Muscle rippled along her back as she walked. He kept the Mossberg aimed.

Soon, an opening appeared in the wall to the advocate's left. She turned, her smile bright, vicious. She motioned inside.

Brood moved to the opening, saw an ovular room. Luminescent skin walls. Fat pods hanging from the ceiling, connected to what looked like viscera.

"Pollo!" The boy sat opposite the door, cross-legged on the floor in a pool of cold light, his hand pressed to the wall.

Brood rushed to him, sank to his knees, lay the shotgun down. He embraced Pollo. Held him for a long time, squeezing him close. Felt bone and muscle, solid and real. Felt Pollo's heart beat, slow and steady, against him. He worked his hands over Pollo's fattened ribs, touched his shoulders, touched fingertips to Pollo's face. Pollo met Brood's gaze, calm and unblinking.

"You grown," was all Brood could think to say when he could speak. He palmed tears from his eyes. Pollo smiled. His eyes shone with intelligence.

"You been eating, too," he said.

"The army." Brood shrugged, then he embraced Pollo again. The walls flickered, shifted colors around them. After a moment, Pollo pushed him away.

"You stink, homes. Bad."

"Bodies," Brood said. "That bitch made me piss myself, too." He looked down at himself and shook his head. "That's twice."

"Don't got much time." Pollo held out a hand. "Got a knife?"

"*Claro.*" Brood pulled the pig sticker from his waistband and handed it over. Without hesitation Pollo placed the blade against his arm, the arm with which he leaned against the wall. He cut deep. "Fuck are you doing!" Brood cried. He saw then that his brother wasn't touching the wall. Pollo's arm *was* the wall. The skin of his forearm had melded seamlessly with the skin of Satori's wall.

"*Tranquilo*," Pollo said. Brood reached out, touched the wall where Pollo's hand should have been. Satori's skin was warm and smooth.

"What happened to you?"

"Something good," Pollo said. He waved Brood away with the knife, then put the blade once more to his arm, just beneath his elbow, and began to cut.

....

It hurt to breathe. Beyond the Go Pill-and-morphine vibrations rippling along her nerves, Doss sensed ribs grinding against one another in ways they shouldn't. Her heads-up display flickered, went out, came back on. Spider web cracks lined her visor. Beyond them Doss saw the charnel ruin of her impact with Satori. It covered her. Shredded muscle, tendons, strips of skin. Something warm and wet trickled along her side, down her legs, over her neck. Hydraulic fluid, she hoped.

"3-A on the ground," reported a Ranger. 3-A was Chalk 3's leader, Ranger A...Jake. "All dogs outside the dome, roll call." His voice was cool, all business. It filled Doss with pride. In the darkness, she smiled. Rangers reported in. She chinned her mic.

"3-A, this is Lead. Give me a sitrep."

"I'm on the airfield. Outside the dome, inside the outer wall." He paused. Over the radio came unmistakable hot bark of an M-8, as familiar to Doss as the sound of her own voice. "Got some company."

Doss toggled her display to the widest possible view. Saw two red circles representing Satori's domes, the square outline of the outer wall. Between them, the blue squares of perhaps fifteen of her Rangers scattered across the airfield's broad emptiness. Red dots, too many to count, surrounded them.

"3-A," she told him, "you are lead. All Rangers are yours. Gather as many as you can, then punch through the nearest wall and make your way to where the Falcons can evac you. Get my kids home."

308 • ROB ZIEGLER

"Copy that, Boss Momma." Jake gave orders: "All dogs, you heard the boss. Rally on my position"

"Falcons," Doss commanded, "your dust-off is on 3-A's priority."

The pilots copied. On Doss' display, the blue squares of her Rangers began to coalesce. She toggled to her immediate view... Nothing but red. Overwatch, she realized, read Satori Tower as one big hostile. Not far from the truth. Also fucking useless. She toggled the display off. Gripped a slab of architecturally thick bone that lay across her chest and, with a painful hydraulic whine from her suit, pressed it away.

Sat up, found herself in a narrow passage, slick with blood from her impact, running parallel to the wall. She chinned her mic.

"Where you at, Gomez?"

"Below you, Boss." Gomez's voice sounded thin with pain. "Guessing thirty feet. Missed the hole you made."

"You functional?"

A pause. Then: "Fucking aye. On my way to you."

"Negative. I'll come to you."

"Copy that."

Joints in Doss' suit, warped from impact, screeched in protest as she stood. One of the suit's legs didn't work right. Heat radiated into her back from a fucked battery pack.

She hefted the breach gun, aimed it casually at the floor a few feet away. Bone and meat shrapneled past her in the blowback as she fired the third barrel. Smoke cleared, revealing a hole in the floor big enough for her to drop through, so she did.

The drop suit's leg gave out on impact. She propped herself on a knee. Milky light spread around her, revealing the smooth walls of a passage that stretched like clean intestine in either direction.

Gomez stood there, peering out through a shattered visor, surrounded by the mutilation of his impact through Satori Tower's wall. Pain contorted his face. One arm of the drop suit had collapsed, twisted out to the side and behind. His other hand held his M-8 up and ready. He tried to smile.

"Seen some stupid shit before, Boss, but damn..."

"We're in, aren't we?" Doss pointed to the twisted armor of Gomez's arm. "You okay?" He clenched teeth, nodded. Over coms, Jake shouted orders above the din of gunfire.

"Gotta hurry."

"Let's do some killing," Gomez agreed. "Which way?"

Doss'd meant for them to drop through Satori Tower's top, straight into the Fathers' laps. Now they were far below the intended target.

"Up," she said.

They moved, Doss holding the breach gun's fat barrel out before her, Gomez trailing, M-8 up and ready. The strange pale light skimmed along the walls with them, revealing an intersection. A wider passage running perpendicular.

"Hello." The voice came from everywhere. Doss halted, thumbed up her visor, looked at Gomez. He raised eyebrows and shook his head like, *fucked if I know.* "You have come to do me harm." The voice was male, preternaturally smooth. "You will not succeed."

"Am I speaking with Bill Coach?" Doss inquired.

"I am Satori."

"So much for initiative," Gomez observed.

"Your people are killing my Rangers on the airfield," Doss said. "Stop your attack."

"It was you and your soldiers who attacked me." The voice was calm as a weather report. "They must die. You must die."

"You attacked us," Doss stated to the air in front of her. "With the Tet. We came for clean seed. Give us that, and we'll stand down."

"The Tet," the voice said. "Yes. The Fathers were greedy in its application. An inability to balance immediate goals with long-term self-interest. A primate failing. They should have had more patience. As it applies to me, however, the Tet does serve as an act of preemptive self-defense."

"Suit yourself." Doss slapped her visor back down and gave Gomez a signal.

They turned right. The tonnage of their suits' hydraulic

compression pounding holes in the rattler-patterned floor with each ten-meter step as they ran. Upwards in a long spiral. Upwards, towards the Fathers...or whatever had spoken to them.

CHAPTER 28

There was very little blood. Pollo rose to his feet. Shoulders back, exuding physical presence. The hieroglyphs on his naked torso looked like religious etchings in the wall's dopplering light. He held up the stump of his left arm and gazed proudly into Brood's face. Already skin had begun to grow, sealing the wound.

"*Curado,*" he said. Brood stared, shook his head.

"Let's get the fuck out of here."

"We ain't going out, big bro. We going *in.*"

"*De que estas hablando?*"

Pollo smiled. He glowed with the sort of weird fervor that reminded Brood of people who loved Jesus too hard, or liked killing just a little too much. He started to speak, but the heavy thump of a nearby detonation cut him short. The sound of a very big gun. The advocate growled. Swayed back and forth on her feet, something savage held barely in check.

"Army's here," Pollo said. "Time to go." He took the advocate's hand delicately in his own, and she smiled. The wall stretched open for them. Together they stepped through. Brood stared for a moment at the empty cavity, then picked up the shotgun and followed.

"Came to get you out of here, *hermanito*," Brood told Pollo's back as they moved upwards along a broad passage. He marveled at how broad Pollo's shoulders had become, how he swung them as he walked hand in hand with the advocate.

"Don't want to go back out there, Carlos," Pollo called without looking back. "Everything's dead. Everything in here's living." He extended the stump of his left arm, trailed it delicately along the wall. Satori's skin reached out to it, caressing it. Tried, it seemed to Brood, to join with it.

The light from the walls shifted color as they got higher. Violet, then shimmering turquoise that made Brood feel like he was drowning. After some time the passage ended: A massive door composed of bone slabs, framed by a black stone archway, barred their way. Juxtaposed with Satori's flesh, the stones seemed foreign, like dirt in a wound. Pollo nodded at the door.

"He got bad bitches in there." Beside him the advocate hissed. Her black tongue flicked over her teeth.

"*Por qué no salimos?*" Brood stuck an ardent finger back the way they had come.

"I got to be in there."

"Why?"

Pollo faced him. His eyes held Brood's.

"Bacilio…" Brood pleaded. "*Por favor.*"

Pollo started to say something, then shook his head. He smiled, his face resigned, awash with sympathy. An adult's face, fleshed with muscle around the jaws, an angularity that hadn't been there before.

"You been in love, Carlos. You know what it is." The muted crack of small arms sounded through Satori's walls. Pollo glanced back the way they had come. "We waiting."

He moved to the wall and plopped down onto his rump. It reminded Brood of the way Pollo had been, the way he no longer was.

He placed the stump of his arm to the wall. The wall's skin

bent, flowed like liquid up his arm. The two melded. The advocate looked on. Her hands came together over her heart, as though something about this touched her deeply. She sank to her haunches, her gaze never leaving Pollo.

"*Sale vale.*" Brood sat with his back to the wall and tucked the Mossberg between his knees. He lay a hand on his brother's shoulder and listened to the drum roll sound of gunfire.

. . . .

"You are the woman who hunted down Pihadassa." Satori's voice, staid and apparently omnipresent, emanated from the walls.

Doss didn't respond. A loose titanium panel clanged somewhere on her suit as she ran. Power ebbed from her right leg, a hydraulic leak. The wound in her chest throbbed. Her burns felt like they were on fire again.

Gunfire had almost completely eclipsed the voices of Jake's Rangers from her earpiece. The beefy thud of a concussion grenade crushed the frequency momentarily to static. When it cleared, she heard someone screaming.

"Pihadassa was my wife," Satori said. "My Other, when I was Sumedha. Sumedha still feels pain at her loss. He is, at root, Hominoidea. Though he was designed with the capacity to master his urges, he nonetheless experiences them."

The passage ahead sphinctered suddenly shut. A separate passage appeared to the right. Doss stopped. Gomez drew to a halt beside her.

"Sergeant?"

"They're herding us." As Gomez spoke, the passage they'd just travelled flexed closed behind them. Nothing there now but a wall, an expanse of opaline skin, blank as an ice flow in the East Siberian Sea.

"Thoughts?" Doss asked. Gomez's face went chill as a viper's.

"Let's see what they got."

"Agreed." Doss turned, aimed her suit up the open passage.

"The desire for retribution, for example." Satori's voice stroked the air around them. "It is a powerful survival trait among the more neurologically complex mammals, particularly the higher primates. Retribution is a fundamental piece of the social metabolism. It defines boundaries, keeps balance."

The passage fed them into a wide chamber the shape of an egg, the size of one of Fort Riley's auto bays. Illumination spread along its smooth walls. Doss' suit sank past its ankles in black fur. The entrance behind them flexed shut. There were no exits.

"Stay close," she told Gomez. Over coms came the sounds of fierce battle. Her young Rangers, fighting to live. She toggled her display to infrared. The chamber glowed, hot as blood. A dozen passages connected to it like tendrils, all blocked by smooth, mutable wall.

"Retribution," Satori's voice mused. "I want to show you something."

The curve of one nearby wall rippled in the infrared. Doss toggled down her display, swiveled the breach gun. The wall flexed. Its skin drew back and stretched taut, thinner and thinner until it grew transparent.

A window. Beyond it, the city. Satori's flesh and skin and bone Frankensteined together with old-world concrete, steel and plexi.

"Below, on the street," Satori directed. Doss stepped forward.

Five burly landraces stood on the snakeskin boulevard running adjacent to Satori Tower. They'd gathered around a pile of six twisted drop suits—the Rangers who had crashed through the dome. As Doss watched, they began pulling at the seams and broken places of one drop suit. The landraces worked methodically, without malice, simply performing a task. Soon, they'd worked free the body and set it, pale and broken, to one side. They moved on to the next drop suit.

In her gut, Doss felt the cold emptiness of the prison pit. Satori made a satisfied sound, like it tasted something good.

"I show you this because I know it hurts you. It gains me nothing, except that you are my enemy. And hurting you pleases me."

"Boss," Gomez said.

Doss turned, followed Gomez's eyes to where a section of

wall on the far end of the chamber had begun to warp. An opening appeared. Five advocates, slim and dark, swiveled out of it. For a moment, Doss took them in. The predators' jaws, the slick pates, the knife-blade slit of their irises. The hyperkinetic vibe of their quick-twitch bodies. A creature free of superfluities, made for speed and rage and destruction. Some hard piece of her decided they were beautiful. She chinned on the suit's external speaker.

"Your bitches are pretty," she told Satori.

"Thank you. They are my favorite child—"

Doss moved. The joints of her suit ground, compressed, launched. Gaining speed, creating momentum. Away from the cold void growing inside her, towards death. The advocates bared teeth, leapt for her, screaming their glee. Doss screamed back.

They met in the middle, airborne. Fingers raked Doss' visor. Teeth cracked against her armor. She fired the breach gun. It jumped in her hands, too loud to hear. Advocates flew to pieces before her.

Momentum carried her through the blast, through the snarling tangle. Pieces of her suit tore free. An advocate clung to her. She drove a titanium elbow through its face—

Hit the ground, rolled, stood. The advocate came at her, its maw bloody and toothless. Doss brought the gun's barrel down on its head with all her suit's hydraulic strength. The thing shuddered, then settled, twitching, into the chamber's thick fur.

Doss swiveled, wielding the spent breach gun like a club, ready for the next advocate. But there were no more. They all lay in pieces around her.

"Damn." Gomez gaped through his broken visor. Doss raised the M-8 slung across her chest. Toggled her visor to infrared, fired a long burst into the wall in front of the largest connecting passage. She moved to it, kicked her armored heel through the chewed up flesh until she'd made an opening large enough to fit through.

"Let's go."

They moved side by side, rifles tucked tight to their shoulders in the pale light. Sweat poured down Doss' skin. Every step brought a sibilant whine from the suit's joints. Its battery pack seared her back.

"This thing's not going to make it much further," she said, and sipped water from a tube protruding from the suit's neck.

"Stay with it until it quits," Gomez told her. "Can't get naked in here."

The wall beside him opened. Hands shot forth, gripped his suit, yanked him off his feet. Doss glimpsed the advocate's face, black tongue extended through wild grin. The opening flexed shut. Gomez was gone. The wall muffled his scream.

A savage sound came from Doss. Her suit moaned as she hurled herself against the wall. The flesh shuddered with a rubbery sound, remained intact. A welt rose in its skin. Doss raised the M-8, sprayed a long burst. Rammed her shoulder into the wall again. This time she crashed through, landing prone.

The advocate straddled Gomez. Its arms windmilled as it tore at his drop suit. Doss aimed, fired. The thing convulsed as explosive ceramics detonated inside its body.

Doss rose, grabbed its twitching form and hurled it back through the ruptured wall. A shriek sounded out there. And another. More advocates in the passage. Doss turned to Gomez.

Her mind froze. Gomez's suit had been ripped open—looked like the back side of a beer can that had been used for target practice. Inside, Doss saw blood, ribs, organs. Gomez looked down at himself. His eyes went wide. The web of scars on his cheek twisted in a way Doss had never before seen.

Fear.

Another shriek issued from the passage. Doss fired three short bursts back through the opening, just to make any bitches think twice. Then surveyed the little ovular chamber, barely larger than a broom closet. Its purpose was unclear, its skin walls blank. She dragged Gomez to its back wall, which set itself aglow with shifting colors as they drew near.

She settled her back against it, pulled Gomez close. Unsnapped levers on his helmet, twisted it free and tossed it aside. His head settled onto her armored lap. He mumbled in Spanish. Prayers. Shock setting in.

"On task!" Doss snapped. She took his hand, moved it to an arbitrary place on his abdomen. Pressed it emphatically, as though he might staunch all that blood with a little pressure. His eyes focused. The diamond in his tooth glinted through blood as he laughed at her.

"Mean ass bitch."

Doss saw a flicker of movement. Something came in low through the opening, quick as a fish under water. She fired a burst. The advocate squealed, and lay kicking. She fired another burst and it went still. She ejected the mag, slapped home another.

Gomez lifted his damaged arm. With great effort, he began punching code into the keypad he'd taped to his wrist.

"Fuck's that?" Doss asked. An advocate's face appeared at the hole's edge, lit with savage glee. Doss fired the M-8. The face disappeared. Maybe hit, maybe not.

"Something you taught me a long time ago." Gomez's breath came ragged now. "When all else fails, blow some shit up."

His body trembled in Doss' lap. There was nothing she could do for him, so she kissed the top of his head. The bristles of his crew cut sanded her lips. She figured it was the last good thing she'd ever feel, so she kept doing it. Firing the gun, kissing the top of Gomez' head. Over coms came the sounds of her Rangers dying.

"Know what you look like with those skin grafts, Boss?" His smile was weak. "Look like one of those old black and white cows. A dairy cow. Call you Patches." He chuckled. Then pressed the code's last digit with finality. "OSEMs," he said. Offensive Structure Elimination Mines. His hand fell and he exhaled, like he'd just finished some heavy lifting. An advocate peered through the torn wall, showed a length of black tongue, disappeared.

The beats began a second later. A steady bass thump, muffled through Satori's walls but unmistakable: a string of big detonations somewhere outside.

Out in the passage, advocates began to hiss. First one, then another, and another. Many of them, a sibilant chorus. Then abruptly the sound ceased, and they came. Doss knew nothing then but the roar of her M-8.

CHAPTER 29

The killing thrilled Satori. Deep under the city, its heart pounded. Whole square miles of skin tingled with adrenaline. A natural reaction to battle—the Sumedha mind turned to Satori's helix, puzzling through latent animal matrices—but nonetheless surprising. Satori basked in deepening morning sunlight, reveled in the geysering sensation of photosynthesis, the warm rush of adrenaline. It felt alive. Inside his amniotic pod, Sumedha laughed.

Several hundred landraces on the airfield sensed Satori's exhilaration. Pheromones rolled off them. They pressed, hooting, against the wall of bodies behind which the few remaining human soldiers hid. Sporadic bursts of gunfire met them, ineffective beyond stoking their mania.

Perhaps it was the pain. When the soldiers had crashed through the dome, when they had penetrated Satori Tower, and fired their heavy gun into its walls…It had hurt.

The two soldiers inside its tower had gone to ground now, pinned down. Wounded, near death, if the advocates' frenzy was any indication. The advocates would toy with them—a fact Satori relished. Its attention lingered for a moment on the hallway outside the little domicile where the two soldiers huddled. It drank in the advocates' fury. It wanted to stay, to feel the killing inside its body.

But it knew it was not yet safe. It sent its awareness to the far perimeter of its electric aura, searching for more airborne threats. Found only the two remaining Flylights, settled into holding patterns beyond the bats' effective range.

Satori decided to check on the boy, Bacilio. The parasite, whose brother had come looking for him. His *hermano*.

Nothing. The boy's eidolic mind no longer hovered around Satori's own. Satori put its awareness on the lab. The boy was gone, and so was the advocate he had taken under his sway. Satori let itself fall into a meditative state, running its awareness methodically over Satori Tower, searching for—

Sudden pain, so intense Satori knew nothing but white heat. Inside his pod, Sumedha recoiled. He brought his attention to his own body, suspended in primordial warmth, until his heart slowed. Something had attacked. Then he reached his mind out once more to Satori.

Found an animal, bristling with shock. It shied from him. He pushed softly against it, soothed it. After a moment, it relented, opened. Sumedha entered—

Waves of blinding pain rolled in from Satori's outer wall. Explosions had butchered long sections of it. Sumedha meditated until Satori's tectonic heart slowed and synced with his, then fully reconnected...

Satori observed its body's response to the wounds. Exudates had already stopped flowing. Cells multiplied, the proliferative healing phase already begun. In three days, the walls would once more be whole.

More explosions detonated out in the city. Satori, calm now, studied them as they occurred. White nova flashes from which black infernos billowed slowly skyward. Buildings crumbled out there in old Denver, but Satori discerned no effect relevant to itself.

On the airfield, the landraces had ceased their attack against the pinned-down Rangers. They stood, chuffing and casting blunt faces anxiously about, starting at each successive thunderclap until, when finally no further explosions came, they stood looking at one another, stymied about what to do next.

Satori sensed something amiss, something taut in the silence following the detonations. It waited. Moments passed. Something began to buzz at the edges of its senses.

The migrants came. They poured out of the old city. Mobs of them, the human group organism, spurred by the explosions, drawn by Satori's sudden vulnerability. Satori had no analogies for its fear.

It extended its mind, commanded its landraces to the breaches in its walls. It roused the last of its advocates, and sent them, too.

There was not enough time. Migrants surged through the mutilated walls. They came, thousands of them, across the airfield, rolling in a solid, hungry wave over the landraces.

They came at the dome, crazed from years of deprivation. They tore at Satori's flesh with knifes, hoes, their fingers. Some used their teeth. Inside his pod, Sumedha screamed.

....

The advocate sat on her haunches, watching. Her eyes flicked unblinking from Brood to Pollo and back. Brood watched her. She smiled at him.

"Brothers," she said, and tilted her head as though she found the concept dear. Brood kept his hand on Pollo's shoulder. The sound of gunfire came only sporadically now, single, infrequent shots.

"I think I seen what you seen," he told Pollo. "I was with some people after the *Chupes* took you." He touched a fingertip to the nub of pink scar where Richard's bullet had burrowed above his hip. "They healed me up. One night they gave me some tea. It made me see shit." He chewed his lip and glanced towards the ceiling, searching for words, but found none. "Bad shit."

Pollo turned and for a moment his eyes, glazed with weird zeal, searched Brood's. He nodded.

"Satori keeps us afloat."

"This ain't—" Brood began.

The deep throb of heavy explosions cut him off. Big concussions somewhere distant, somewhere outside, one after the other. *Whump! Whump! Whump!* The advocate hissed quietly after each, the sound of water droplets hitting fire.

"Thirteen," Brood counted, and knew the packages given him by the tough sergeant had been delivered. He ran his hand over the sharp bristles of Pollo's shaved head. "Maybe the hornets'll come."

They waited. Soon, the wall around the door undulated, muscles flexing within. The door's bone tonnage swung smoothly outward, spilling light the color of a sunset.

Advocates appeared, kinetic specters in the backlight. Brood rose, swung the Mossberg to bear, stepped between Pollo and the door.

The advocates ignored the boys. They raced past, almost too fast to see. Six of them, moving with the smooth undulations of kelp under water. Then they were gone, all except for the one who seemed to be Pollo's pet. She squatted, unmoving.

"Busy busy," she whispered, and smiled. The door stayed open.

Pollo stood. In his hand he held Brood's knife. The stump of his other arm dripped anew.

"*Vamonos*," he said. He held out his hand for the advocate. She rose and took it. Brood followed them through the door.

A field of black flagstone lay before them. Fleshy light poured through walls made of high plexi, casting the trio's shadows in panoply as they crossed the chamber. Beyond the windows lay the half-living city, flesh and concrete. Two dreams colliding within the same skull. Above it, a sky made of skin.

Strange objects occupied the floor around them, artifacts from the old world. A motorcycle the color of a ripe tomato, old enough to burn gasoline. A fat leather chair. A saddle with a silver pommel. A stuffed yellow dog with a friendly, lolling tongue. Brood touched a finger to the hard plastic of its black nose.

"That's him." Pollo pointed skyward, where what looked like a giant eggplant hung from the ceiling amid a tangle of dark viscera.

"Who?" Brood asked.

"Sumedha," Pollo said, his voice edged with contempt.

The pod gurgled as something shifted inside. Then came a sound that reminded Brood of mournful west Texas wind whistling through a collapsed viaduct. A muffled scream.

Pollo seemed not to notice. He skirted the chamber's perimeter, searching for something, his face fixed with the same placid concentration as when he hunted rattlers out on the prairie. He stopped, seemed to have found what he was looking for, and settled his rump to the flagstones. His fingers touched a length of naked wall between two behemoth plexi panes.

Pollo's advocate growled. The back of Brood's neck tingled. He turned, saw movement along the chamber's far side. The unmistakable fluidity of another advocate. Brood moved close to his brother, brought the Mossberg to his shoulder.

The creature seemed in no hurry. It sauntered across the chamber. Pollo's pet moved to intercept it—met Satori's advocate near a red star etched into the center of the chamber's floor.

The two strange women brought their faces close together. Their arms reached heavenward, their fingers protracted and flexed like claws. They showed teeth. They hissed and shrieked. They unhinged jaws and yawned them wide.

Then they fell silent. As Brood watched, they began slithering in place, suddenly all spine. Moving in perfectly mirrored unison, two snakes who had mesmerized each other.

"*Joder*," he muttered.

"Sisters," Pollo explained. His arm touched the wall—no, it had rejoined the wall, melded with it once again. He regarded Brood serenely.

"Pollo…" Brood started to say.

"Watch," Pollo instructed. He winked, and it startled Brood. He wondered if this personality of Pollo's had always been there, somehow buried under layers of catatonic dust.

A grunt came from the pod overhead. It began slowly to descend, dangling from a shiny umbilical the width of Brood's thigh.

A change came over the advocates. They smiled at each other and gazed up at the pod—began stalking in slow circles around the four-point star, the spot where the pod would soon come to rest. They made Brood think of wild dogs, of sharks, orbiting something dead. As the pod settled to floor between them, they went still, poised.

"*Aquí*." Pollo stood and proffered the pig sticker to Brood, handle first. Blood trickled momentarily from the boy's stump where he'd again cut himself free, then ceased as new skin fused there. Brood slid the knife into its sheath inside his pants. Followed Pollo to where the advocates stood. One of the women extended the ghostly length of an arm as Pollo drew near. Her fingers stroked the top of his head.

Another muffled keen rose from the pod. The advocates responded with beastly noises, ravenous and carnal. A seam running the pod's length split open. Black fluid spilled across the flagstones. It smelled like bile.

A hand emerged, gnarled and grey, followed by a face that Brood recognized as having once been human. Features identical to the Corn Mother's, harmonious and precise, but male, skin colorless and pruned from moisture.

A deep cough rattled from within Sumedha's lungs. He inhaled like he hadn't tasted air in a year. An umbilical leading from the hollow of his belly suddenly detached itself with a smacking sound and he groaned. Black eyes focused. Sumedha looked from Brood to the advocates, then his settled on Pollo.

"There you are, boy," he whispered, his voice hoarse from disuse, dry as an Oklahoma dervish. "I thought it strange that I had lost track of you." He looked at the advocates, and seemed confused. "They do not obey me. How have you done this?" A pitiless smile cracked Pollo's face. He bent close to the Designer.

"Satori. She choose me, *ese*."

"Satori…" Sumedha's mouth hung open, seemed about to say more. Then his head fell back and he screamed. It reverberated throughout the chamber, the piteous sound of a soul crumbling.

Pollo leaned back, gestured with a finger. One of the advocates—*Pollo's* advocates—yanked Sumedha free of the pod. The Designer screamed again, this time like prey. The second advocate joined the first. Together, they tore into him. Pollo smiled. Brood turned away. After a few seconds, Sumedha went quiet.

Pollo tilted his head back and with eyes closed turned in a slow circle. The expression on his face frightened Brood. Rapture. Bliss. Feelings that had no place in this world, except for the crazy. He touched Pollo's shoulder.

"What're we doing here, *manito?*" He pointed to the bone door. "*Vamonos.*" Pollo's eyes bore into Brood. He repeated what he'd said back in the passageway:

"You been in love, Carlos. I seen it in your face when we was with Rosa. You know what it is." He glanced around the chamber, out at the city. A city alive with intent and need. "She keep us afloat. For a long time, bro. *Nos adora.* And I love her."

"*Manito...*"

Pollo laughed, turned away. He lowered himself beside the open pod. Slid one foot daintily inside, as though testing the water, then let the rest of his body follow, like slipping under a blanket.

"*Que estas haciendo?*" Brood whispered. Pollo glanced back. It struck Brood how thick his brother's jaw had grown. He looked robust. "Bacilio..."

Pollo gave a quick smile, then the pod's lips closed over him and sealed tight. The skein of umbilical grew taut, began slowly to reel the pod towards the ceiling.

．．．．

Nerve ganglia extended, touched, joined. The electric kiss of a billion tiny sparks. Saline tanks deep in Satori Tower gurgled as Satori's memories merged with those of the boy Bacilio.

Satori awoke—to savagery. The people tore its skin, cut its flesh, hammered at its bones. They ripped away hunks of meat, ate it raw handfuls at a time. Bacilio's mind understood savage-ry—had rarely known anything else. And the boy had learned from watching Sumedha.

Satori put its full attention on the sensation of being torn apart. A wave of panic surged through it, then receded. It calmed itself, surrendered to pain. Pain was simply a fact. Its thoughts moved forward. It considered things with its new mind, Bacilio's mind, forged on the hot wastes, perpetually hungry and frightened. Just like the human organism that now threatened to devour Satori. These were Bacilio's people.

The decision was easy. Slowly, Satori flexed. Bands of muscle rippled along its back, geologic in scale.

The people stopped their attack. They watched. They waited. Some retreated, tiny animals sensing the end of a giant's slumber.

Around the dome's circumference, skin split. Flesh furled. Fissures gaped. Satori spread itself open, revealing the living city within, vacant but for the landrace children who would never fill it. Vacant and waiting. After a time, when nothing further happened, the people moved forward.

Satori let them in.

Inside the pod at the top of Satori Tower, Bacilio smiled. He would keep his people afloat.

Satori focused its mind, ran its attention over the breadth of its monolithic body, a body that felt suddenly new and right, as much a part of the world as the mountains to the west, the desert prairie to the east. The dry morning breeze tickled it. Its skin drank the sun.

A memory came to Satori. A noise like crashing waves. A point of hot light growing, spreading through a world of jumbled shadow-thoughts. The boy found himself lying in soft dirt, gazing up through the long fingers of an onion nearly ready to pull. Overhead he discerned the dirty plastic of a greenhouse roof. Diffuse sun warmed his cheeks. The crashing wave sound took form. His mother, quietly singing the song of the old rat while she pulled weeds from dark soil. *Una rata vieja que era planchadora por planchar su falda se quemó la cola se...* The shine of her black hair, pulled tight into a ponytail, mesmerized the boy. He let out a toneless moan. Then his voice, too, took form. He hummed along. Connected.

CHAPTER 30

A black zep dogged its way through blue sky to the east. Slowly it grew, its nose aimed at Satori through heat shimmers rising off the prairie. Doss could barely make out a white star adorning its side.

In front of her, Jake held back shoulders thickened by three months of solid exercise and Satori nutrition, and jammed his fists to hips. He hollered like a sergeant at the platoon of forty new soldiers who stood at ragged attention in the dome's vast shadow.

"You got to embrace the pain, bitches!" His voice was almost a man's. Doss tried to place the feeling working its way through her chest as she watched him. Something like pride.

She worried a leather thong strung with finger bones in one hand while she silently assessed her new troops. They'd been fed, but they were still skinny; new fatigues looked strangely deflated over their bones. They were like all fresh meat. Didn't know asses from elbows, shit from shinolah, left from right, up from fucking down. But they'd lived on the road, in the dust and in the starved remnants of the world, and they had survived. They were tough.

Some of them were even adults.

"Pain means you're living!" The inverted Vs of Jake's staff sergeant chevron gleamed on the shoulder of his white t-shirt. So natural he could've been born with it. The red hand printed on the t-shirt's front—that he wore like a badge, like it was his own heart. He thrust his chest out, aimed that red hand at his troops, letting them know exactly who wore it, and who didn't. "You like being alive? Then you like pain!"

The platoon yelled *Hooahs,* timid, out of sync, but earnest. Jake turned and marched them, all gangling limbs and eagerness to please, along the leathered skin of the outer wall, into the furnace heat of late October sunshine pounding the gravel expanse of Satori's airfield. Mixed groups of migrants and thick landraces, headed out to harvest in the north fields, parted before them.

"Agent Doss!"

She turned, cursed under her breath.

An entrance had split open in the dome's greened flesh. A dozen people emerged. Big migrants and thick landraces, zeroing on her, chins cocked with self-importance. They wore long white tunics. *La Chupe* white. Rebranding, Tsol had called this. *La Chupes* in red, people thought of as thugs. But *La Chupes* in white, well…

He strode at the group's center, his white robe billowing around him, its hood cowling his face. Like Robin Hood, or some kind of badland angel. Two young girls walked with him, one caucasian, the other a smooth landrace. Well-fed, both of them, all tits and hips, wearing nothing but short white skirts.

The *Chupe* boss drew up close to Doss. Exuded beefy physicality into Doss' space while his entourage fanned out around her. Doss glared at the red hand emblazoned on the breast of his robe, over his heart.

"You like it?" Tsol asked. "It's got a certain cachet, don't you think?" Doss let a second pass, during which she regarded him with naked contempt.

"You look like an attendant in God's own personal shitter," she said. Tsol laughed. Inside the hood, teeth flashed.

"It's meant to honor you, Agent Doss. You're the queen of the

Burning Hand. You liberated Satori.”

It sounded like a punch line, which Doss knew it was. It was the boy who'd liberated Satori, the boy who now controlled Satori. Doss had done nothing besides get her kids killed, and Gomez, too.

She turned her face to the sun and closed her eyes. Raised the hand that held the leather thong and with a finger scratched her nose along the near-seamless edge of the new skin graft Satori had given her. Born of her native cells, a few drops of viscous liquid to swallow. It had left only the tiny hint of scar, a vertical line at the center of her brow that gave her a look of perpetual concentration.

“They're finally coming.” Tsol raised a shot-putter's finger to the east, where the black zep grew steadily fatter as it neared.

There had been rumors. The government pulling up stakes from D.C., readying itself for a transition westward. Not even trying to pretend anymore that their country would ever again exist in any meaningful way.

“Cabinet, you think?” he asked. Doss shook her head.

“Probably Sec Serv, here to pave the way.” But it was D.C. making decisions, after all, so who really knew? It could have been Ellen Vokle, General Rippert, even Doss' father on that zep. The thought made Doss tight inside.

She'd stopped pretending, too. The wound in her chest still ached—worse in the mornings, during the liminal half-dreams before she fully awoke. She'd lay in the soft fur of her bed, feeling colors shift in the slick skin walls of her apartment in Satori Tower while Emerson's voice echoed in her memory. The wound would throb, a dull spasming ache in her chest and shoulder. As healed, she was certain, as it would ever be. Painful, but good enough: she could function.

She'd cast her allegiance with her Rangers. Gave her days to training them, trying to make them somehow useful. Whom they served...she didn't know.

“Might be a hard winter for *El Presidente*,” Tsol mused, and there was something hungry about the way he said it. “Living under the same roof as his poor and huddled." He angled his chin towards where, across the airfield, *La Chupes* in their new white tunics manned the bone gates of the outer wall.

Migrants crowded outside. They streamed in from the plains, as they had now for months. They camped out in the old city, awaiting admittance to Satori's sheltering breast while Tsol's *Chupes* organized them. Got them sorted into work pools for planting and harvests. Situated them with places to live inside the dome. Noted them on a census they'd begun. Got them fed. Together with Doss' Burning Hand, the *Chupes* had turned into the cops. Rebranded indeed.

"Might be," Doss figured. As she looked on, the *Chupes* at the gate pulled a man from a wagon loaded with small children. Voices rose. One *Chupe* pulled the man to the ground. The others began to kick him.

"I suspect he'll find it crowded." Tsol said. He pushed back his hood then. The skin of his face sizzled audibly, turned instantaneously green as the sun hit it. Grey eyes dimmed for a moment, focused inward with evident pleasure as chlorophyll bubbled out against cell membranes. Doss stared.

"Jesus."

"You should try it, Agent. I haven't eaten anything in three days. I think I could walk across this entire country with nothing more than a sip of water."

"So badass," one of Tsol's big bodyguards declared, and pursed appreciative lips. The caucasian girl's face twisted with disgust as she watched Tsol's skin go green, but she didn't move from his side. She kept laying tentative fingers on him. Touching his arm or his muscled shoulder as though he were a pet bear who could turn on her at any moment. Tsol leered at Doss.

"You know you like it."

"Think I'll pass," Doss told him.

"The kid still won't give me the real graft." Tsol squinted up at the mountainous dome. "I think he suspects we'll replace him, if we can." Doss arched an eyebrow.

"Is he wrong?"

"I only want what's best for everyone, Agent." The *Chupe* leader spread innocent hands. Big teeth coruscated within the meaty verdance of his face.

"Right." Doss turned away, looked out on her new troops.

They worked hard for Jake in the hundred-degree heat. Marching. Burpees. Pushups. Sprints. He was a good sergeant, the sort they wanted to please. The sort who did not Fuck Up.

"They'll be good soldiers," Tsol observed. "If they have enough time." His thumb played absently over the swell of the landrace girl's long hip and his eyes drifted to a spot above Doss' head. "It's been a long time since this country's seen an election." He said this offhandedly, the way he'd talk about the days growing shorter, the first hints of summer's heat waning. Then his expression hardened and his chest rotated like a gun battery in the direction of the slowly incoming zep. "They think we'll still settle for scraps." His gaze settled on Doss, a mad white crescent gleaming above his irises. "You're my guardian angel, Sienna Doss. We're fated, you and I. I'm going to call on you soon, and you're going to answer." He uttered words then that Doss hadn't heard since before she'd left D.C. "For the people."

Doss said nothing, simply held Tsol's eye. After a moment, he nodded once, emphatically, then turned and strode away, his entourage coalescing around him.

When he'd gone, Doss stood there, watching a small migrant caravan the *Chupes* had let filter through the gate. What looked like a couple of families. They lugged bags over their shoulders, makeshifted from canvas tarps or animal skins. They pulled wagons pieced together from bicycle parts, stacked with plows and rusted hand tools. They carried rifles, held the hands of small children. They were like all migrants. Farmers and thieves. Scavengers and killers. American people. Tsol's people. Fleeing a dead world. Doss wondered what their chances were, what her own chances were. Overhead, the fat government zep vectored in.

"Right face!" Jake bellowed. Half his platoon turned left. Muscles worked in his jaw and he cast a bitter look Doss' way. She smiled at him. It was far more than pride.

....

Brood raised his foot and a furred stool rose helpfully from the floor. He propped his army boot atop it. A boot which, to his amazement, he'd actually grown to prefer over his sandals. He stuffed the cuffs of his fatigue pants inside and laced it tight.

"Satori," he said.

"Yes, Carlos?"

"I want to talk to Bacilio." A pause, then:

"Bacilio is not available right now. Can I tell him something for you, Carlos?" The walls gurgled, turned the color of ice.

"No. *Gracias*." He stood, reached for a rucksack that hung from a finger-thick bone protruding through the smooth skin of a nearby wall, then turned and surveyed the room's mutable vacancy.

He'd grown fond of the place. Its vaguely animal scent, the way it responded to his presence, welcoming. He never felt alone here, even though he'd rarely brought company. Four months, the longest he could remember ever having stayed in one place.

He moved to the wall, which undulated as he neared, flexed wide, grew transparent. The city below pulsed with life. Its own, but also with the bustle of migrants. They moved along snake-scale streets, in and out of the buildings where they lived—in apartments, like how people had lived in the old world. The gossamer haze of their cook smoke now perpetually filled Satori's dome.

Someone had set up a still on the street below, a tangle of plexi pipes leading to a steel cauldron from which dark vapors rose. Migrants gathered around it, trading Satori rations for corn alcohol. They hunkered against flesh and brick walls, and drank, exhausted from long shifts in the north fields. Listless, like they didn't quite know what to do with themselves in this city with the beating heart, didn't quite know how to settle. Brood knew the feeling. What were they now? Refugees? Immigrants? He figured there might not be a word. They were simply fed, and that was that.

As he watched, a slender male landrace approached the still, proffering a fat barrel squash. A migrant woman in clean white shift waved him away. The landrace persisted, smiling. Other migrants rose, formed a barrier of ill will between the landrace and the still. The landrace turned and fled, back towards the dome's outer reaches, where the *Chupes* had pressed Satori's children.

Brood touched his forehead to the wall. Felt Satori's heart, steady and slow. Bacilio's heart. It was calm. He pressed his lips lightly to skin, then reached a hand below the window. A hollow opened there. He withdrew the pig sticker and a stockless M-8. Slid the blade inside the back of his pants and stuffed the compact rifle into the rucksack.

"Carlos." Pollo's voice filled the small chamber, confident and solid, like Brood could reach out and touch it.

"*Que pasa, manito?*"

"You leaving."

The walls reddened. "*Sí.*"

"*A dónde?*"

"South, I guess."

For a long time Pollo said nothing. Brood figured he'd drifted off.

It'd been like that. They'd talked a great deal in the first days after Pollo had gotten into the pod. Brood'd lain on his back in the soft fur of the apartment's floor, fingers laced behind his head. He'd spoken up at the ceiling, where pores flexed and colors shifted. Spoke about their mother. About winters in the malarial gulf coast planting grounds. About how scared he'd been during every job they'd ever pulled with Hondo.

Pollo had spoken, too, filling the room with his voice, casting Brood adrift in the vertiginous illusion that he lay suspended in Pollo's mind, had become part of one of his brother's catatonic dreams. He'd told Brood of the frozen world where his mind had lived before the graft, before he had become Satori. A place built of unfiltered noise and light. Pollo had told Brood how all the animals there had been dying, ever since he could remember. How, when he could surface, he'd felt the real world dying, too. How he'd seen the places where pieces connected, and sensed them collapsing. The world was still dying out there. But here, Pollo'd told him, in Satori, maybe they could all stay afloat.

The months passed, and they'd spoken less and less. Pollo had drifted. There seemed to be less and less of him, more and more of Satori. These days they hardly spoke at all.

"Carlos," Pollo stated finally, "my landraces breaking you off some seed. Meet them at the outer gate."

"*Gracias*," Brood said.

He waited. A minute passed, but Pollo said nothing more. Brood slung the rucksack over a shoulder and crossed to the door. It flexed open and he stepped out.

....

The Lobo sat in front of the *Chupes'* sagging brick stash house, bumping mean bass. As far as Brood could tell, that's all it ever did. For two days he'd sat, wrapped in a filthy wool blanket against the long chill of early-autumn nights, and watched from the shadowed back corner of the old squatters' lot. Richard had taken the Lobo exactly nowhere.

The big *Chupe* seemed to live in the truck. Occasionally he'd get out and hang with a dozen or so other *Chupes*. Kids who, in their new white tunics, seemed caught in the Lobo's orbit. They'd sit on the eight long struts, drink corn mash from dirty plastic jugs, hassle the few girls who still worked the stash house. Just hang, leaching off the Lobo's inherently badass vibe while Richard let the reactor growl, feeding the big speakers he'd installed inside.

Now, though, the Lobo's passenger door hissed opened. Bass grew acute.

A landrace girl climbed out, wearing only a white *Chupe* tunic, her bare legs so long they seemed supernatural. A short *La Chupe* boy reached out as she passed, ran a hand up between her dark thighs. She pushed him away. The boy hesitated, looked scared for a second—looked to the other boys, who watched him closely. Then his face hardened and he wheeled back his fist and struck the girl. He said something to her, crossed his arms and leaned back against the Lobo, smirking. The other boys laughed. The girl said nothing, simply held a hand to her cheek and shouldered away, stepping barefoot and gingerly over squash rinds and discarded cornmash jugs, up the steps and into the darkness of the stash house entrance.

Brood pulled a wet peach slice from a ration can Jingo'd given him, and sucked it, waiting. The driver's door swung open.

Richard emerged. He climbed down, wide torso puffed by his proximity to the Lobo. He propped a sandaled foot proprietarily on a strut and leaned forward, elbow on knee. He spoke briefly to a white *Chupe*. The two exchanged a complicated handshake, then Richard climbed back inside the truck. Both doors swung closed. The reactor throbbed. The engine revved, shook the air, reverberated in Brood's chest.

Brood set the can of peaches gently in a patch of weeds between his feet. Reached under the blanket, fished around in a fatigue pocket, produced an old walkie talkie, switched it on. The LED indicating power glowed red. Brood double checked the channel: good.

The Lobo started forward. Lurched as Richard struggled with the clutch, then thundered up the street, fierce and hungry, shimmering through the dapple of long sunlight. Brood let it roll several blocks, beyond the ring of more densely populated squats surrounding Satori, then thumbed the talkie's button.

Nothing happened.

Maybe Richard had found the bricks of crumbling Semtex, stuffed low in the chassis between the reserve Hercs. Maybe the battery in the adjoining walkie had died. Maybe—

The Lobo rose, hovered in the air for an instant, separated slightly at the seams. Then the air shattered. Everything flew apart. A noise like standing under a waterfall filled Brood's skull. When it cleared, he counted backwards from ten and sat up. Found himself behind the old convenience store, ten paces from where he'd sat.

La Chupes—those who weren't rolling on the ground with

hands cupped over their ears—gaped and pointed open-mouthed in the direction Richard had gone. Brood brushed debris from his arms, popped his ears by flexing his jaw. He squinted up the street.

All that remained of the Lobo was a single tire, standing miraculously upright, a coin on edge at the lip of a crater that stretched from one side of the street to the other. Big chunks of old brick buildings around the crater had simply vanished. Small fires burned.

La Chupes began to yammer, yelling into one another's faces. Reminded Brood of dogs barking at thunder.

He noticed the can of peaches sitting undisturbed in the weeds. He bent to pick it up, then looked back towards the crater. He whispered two words:

"Hondo Loco."

It came out as prayer, because Hondo had prayed. He reached two fingers into the can, pinched a peach slice and slid it into his mouth, then turned and walked away.

....

He'd stashed the wagon under the viaduct beside the river where the old migrant camp had been. The shanties still stood, a bricolage of corrugated tin, rusted sheet metal, packed clay. But they'd been abandoned, their occupants now living inside the dome. The river ran gently this late in the year, barely a trickle. A frayed yellow dog stood at its edge, scoping Brood warily while its tongue lapped at a slow eddy.

Brood checked the fifty-gal barrel of assorted Satori seed Pollo's landraces had given him. Still there, strapped to the wagon's undercarriage. He threw the rucksack aboard and climbed up after it. Rapped a knuckle high on the water tank: full. Moved to the tiller. His foot found the switch on the motor and kicked it on. The motor filled with the low hum of deep cycle bats. He shoved the throttle forward and rolled in a long loop, wending out of the camp.

The dog watched him. Brood saw a hairless patch on its side. Pink skin wrapped over ribs.

He killed the throttle. The wagon halted. He stared at the dog. It trembled under his gaze.

"Fuck."

He opened the rucksack, dug out a mason jar and twisted off its lid. The aroma of savory turkey-grape meat rose from it. He used three fingers to scoop out a dollop. Mashed it into a ball and hurled it into the dirt at a spot halfway between the dog and himself. The dog moved forward. Brood leveled a finger at it.

"Fuck you, *perro*. Don't say I never done nothing." He turned, hung an arm over the tiller and with a fist banged the throttle forward once more.

He steered the wagon slowly along surface streets. Kept an ear to the motor's steady hum as it sipped power from the bats, kept an eye to the needle bouncing in the amp meter as PV paint— cleared of *Chupe* red—sucked in late afternoon sunlight.

Out of downtown he rolled. Through the gridwork neighbor- hoods of mid twen-cen brick, then through the endless cul-de-sac ruination of the exurbs.

Migrants sat around firepits in mud lots in front of old houses they'd claimed, roasting clean Satori vegetables while they awaited entrance to the living city. Gaunt desperation rimmed their eyes as they watched Brood pass. The assessment hung there, framed by weakness and need, the way it always had: What did Brood have in the wagon that they could use? And was he a threat? Brood kept the M-8 handy, propped within reach against the footlocker, but no one moved to stop him.

The sun had almost set by the time he'd reached the city's edge, where the remnants of gas stations and plexi solar condos dwin- dled into a stretch of undulating hills, scorched bare by brutal summer heat. Brood figured there were still miles to be had, that he could reach the edge of old C-Springs before it got dark. He angled the wagon up onto the berm of ancient freeway track and stopped to hook up the Hercs.

Cold wind blew in off the Rockies to the west, tangy with the metallic bite of oncoming winter. Snow had already settled up there. It would be a hard winter. He wrapped the blanket around his shoulders and stood for a moment, looking back the way he'd come, watching long sunlight gild Satori's dome.

Did Pollo feel its warmth, the way Brood did against his own skin? Did he get cold at night? Brood'd heard the dome grew fur in the winter. The notion unsettled him. He dug a hunk of peach out of his teeth with his tongue and turned to spit.

The yellow dog sat a few feet away, panting. It eyed Brood expectantly. Brood shook his head. He grabbed the M-8 and brought it to bear. Chewed his lip while he eyed the dog for a few seconds down the rifle's sights, his thumb on the safety. The dog's tail thumped the dirt three times.

"Fuck."

Brood set the rifle down. Opened his rucksack. The dog stopped panting, cocked an attentive ear as the lid came off the turkey-grape jar.

A few minutes later, they were rolling. The dog lay at the wagon's bow. Grizzled white hair covered its snout and chin. A sore oozed on its shoulder.

"You remind me of someone, cuz," Brood told it. "Don't mean I won't eat you. I get hungry, I'm putting you on a stick." He shoved the throttle way open. The dog put its nose to the wind, its tongue lolling happily. The motor sang with Herc power as the wagon jounced down the old asphalt, making a solid thirty-five miles per. South, past the last burned-out vestige of the city. Away from the *Chupes*. Away from the coming winter. South, towards Rosa Lee.

ACKNOWLEDGEMENTS

I t took me the better part of two years to rein in the various permutations of this story and mash it into one solid piece. Along the way I encountered innumerable helping hands. First, a big thank you to the Starry Heaven crews of 2009 and 2010, particularly to Sarah Kelly, who organized the workshops; also to Sarah Prineas, Gary Shockley, Sandra McDonald, Brad Beaulieu, Eugene Myers, Bill Shunn, Debbie Daughetee, Kris Dikeman, Adam "Danger Taco" Rakunas, Brenda Cooper, Robert Levy and Jenn Reese. Gratitude especially to my full manuscript readers: Deb Coates, Greg Van Eekhout, Sarah Kelly (again) and Jon Hansen. Their fingerprints are all over this thing, the good parts, anyway. Deb Coates, Greg Van Eekhout, Brad Beaulieu and Sarah Prineas also each played the role of shepherd to this book at crucial moments of its development, a favor I hope one day to pay forward. Enrique Jimenez and Sid Pink gave invaluable input on Chicano culture and slang. Thanks to my agent, Caitlin Blasdell, for her deft navigation of the publishing industry; and to the posse at Night Shade Books for so enthusiastically giving this book a home. A big shout out goes to Paolo Bacigalupi, in part for lighting the path, but mostly just for being really good company. And most of all, I want to thank my wife, Cindy, without whose unflagging patience and encouragement this book wouldn't have happened. Much love.